This book is dedicated to –
All the wonderful people who have bought it.

Principal cast

Galactic Jump

Andy Cross .... Admiral Scott .... Orion Galactic Brigade

Clive Monkton .... Captain Login .... Orion Galactic Brigade

Georgina Best .... Captain Benjie .... Orion Galactic Brigade

Malcolm Bingham ...... Navigator .... Orion Galactic Brigade

John Pearce .... Promoter /director

William Easton .... Director / producer

Frank .... Marketing

Thomas Carmichael ... Sales assistant

Bob & Vera Stickles .... Super fans

Woodford Abbey

Aloysius D'Macey .... The Duke of Exford

Jules D'Macey .... Viscount of Exford

James .... Butler

Louise .... Housemaid

Colin .... Head of security

John Hammond .... Head keeper

Oliver & Henry Clarkson ... Safari staff

Mike .... Park warden

Wilf Trunnion .... Actor / Resident Ghost

George Shakespeare .... Actor / Resident Ghost

Alice Bennett .... Actress / Resident Ghost

Flint .... Resident Ghost

Melinda Goodall (Molly)..... Academic

Barbara Greenacre .... Tour guide

Mavis .... Housekeeper (London)

Finn .... Steamboat crew / resident ghost

Carl & Nick .... Estate Mechanics

Edith .... Train driver

Holeford Police

DI Eric Montgomery .... Lead investigator

Sergeant Ian Dexter .... Assistant to above

PC Singleton .... Assistant to above

Song Thrush Productions

Justine Song .... Owner / presenter

Peter Fellows .... Co-producer

AlexTulloch .... Sound engineer

Dylan Lee .... Camera

Chloe Nolan .... Production assistant

Fred Smith .... Night vision

Mystic Michael .... Paranormal investigator

Also starring

Eric .... The Grim Reaper

Claude Sheppard .... Highwayman

Jeff .... Landlord (Abbey Inn)

Jason .... Fellow art student

Charlie Clarke .... Manager (Price Less Supermarket)

Peter & Joan Goodall .... Melinda's parents

Professor Dominic Halford ..... Holeford Museum

Carolyn Bonfield .... Gypsy Carolyn

Brother Leopold .... Lay Brother

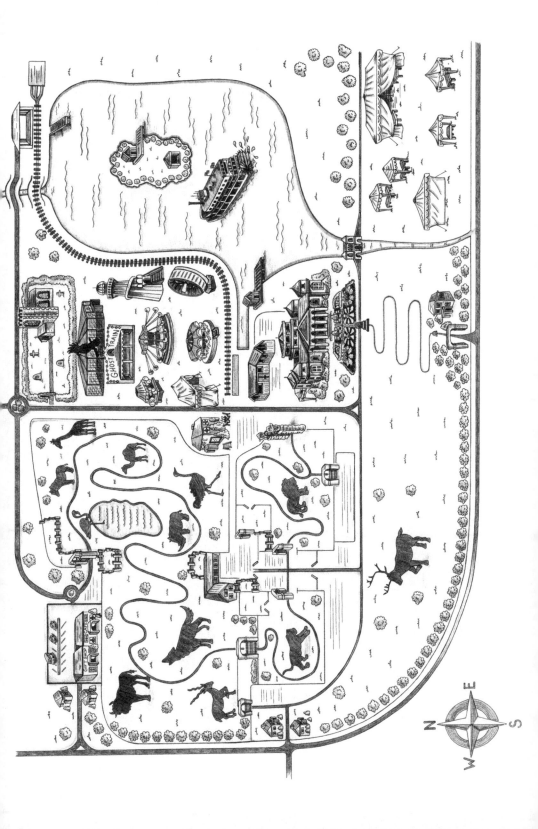

Contents

Prologue

George, Wilf and Alice were looking forward to this weekend. Months ago the posters went up around the park advertising the '*Galactic Jump*' Sci-Fi festival, with stars of the stage and screen making appearances and a special screening of the new series opener. For them, it would be extra special to see fellow actors and compare notes on modern techniques and the discipline of film acting. It would be so different from their own days treading the boards, performing with an orchestra in front of a live theatre audience. Their careers were brought to an abrupt end when they sadly died in a fire at the Holeford Opera House in 1955.

This all seemed a long time ago now. In recent years they had been given the opportunity to brush up their skills and perform again for a very different audience. Thanks to George's contacts at the golf club they were now in demand for variety shows, mostly at golf club dinners but now expanding to death day parties and the odd wedding anniversary. The chance to work in the film industry had eluded them in their mortal career, so it was with great anticipation that they awaited the start of the festival.

The Estate was a hive of activity, support vehicles arrived carrying stage equipment, scaffolding, temporary seating and a plethora of props from the film and TV series. The marketplace was set up in the stable yard and the Ballroom had been turned into a theatre where performers were doing sound checks while the cinema screen and exhibition of props were being set up. The air of excitement was palpable, not just for them but also for all the estate staff. This was a new venture for Woodford Park and if it proved successful could pave the way for more innovative events in the future.

1
Packing Up

Friday 2ⁿᵈ of August, 1985

Evening

Tom moved the last of the stock from the courtyard market into the hay loft of the stable complex for overnight storage. The stall selling memorabilia at the Sci-Fi festival had done remarkably well for the first day. Most of the more fervent fans (and therefore more likely to spend freely) would not arrive until the weekend, or 'Galactic Saturday' as it was advertised. This is when all the stars from 'Galactic Jump' would be in attendance, together with a further preview from the long-awaited new television series, followed by a party. For the fans that would be too good to miss.

He lugged the boxes up the worn timber stairs into the dusty, disused upper floor where it was dry and roomy, if not particularly clean. The odour of dry grass, molasses and horses still permeated the air despite its redundant appearance. He cautiously placed the last of the boxes on the wooden floor and checked the tubes of posters, arranging them in reference number order, for quick selection the next day. The light was rapidly fading through the small windows overlooking the large stable yard where the market stalls were laid out. The full moon rising through the skylight above him, cast an eerie glow. He shivered although it was still warm. He unexpectedly felt as if there was another presence in the loft. He pulled himself together. *'This was an old building with history going back hundreds of years, perhaps he was detecting the spirit of a ghost?'* At that thought he felt a cold shiver run down his spine and his imagination went into overdrive. From the shadows behind the stacked boxes in the far corner, he sensed a movement.

'*Oh No! Not rats,*' he thought, and shuddered again. He heard a slow footstep on the wooden floor. Not rats then.

Perhaps it might be one of his colleagues. "Hi, I'm nearly done. Boy, what a day. I'll be glad to get back to the hotel. It's gonna be busy as hell tomorrow."

There was no reply, but a shadow moved. He could now see the outline of a tall man wearing a long black coat and flat cap.

"Hi," repeated Tom, trying to figure out who was up here with him. "Are you security? I've just finished loading the last of the stock. Are you waiting to lock up? I won't be a tick."

"You know who I am. You've been expecting me," said a deep voice. "Just give me the goods and you can go off to your nice, cosy hotel."

"What goods? I'm sorry, but I don't know you or what you're talking about. Were you expecting someone else? Oh, God, you're not going to steal this stuff are you? I'll be in big trouble and it's not worth much except to die-hard fans."

"Let's not play games, son. Just give me the picture. I don't care about all this Sci-Fi crap," he said kicking the boxes carelessly. To Tom's complete surprise the stranger pulled a gun out of his pocket.

"Is that... have you got a gun?" Tom asked unbelievingly. He felt the pit of his stomach churn and beads of sweat began to form on his forehead. He could see the unmistakeable outline of the gun glinting in the moonlight that now streamed down on them both through the skylight.

"Don't play the innocent with me. You know who I am and what I've come for. Just give it to me and I'll be on my way. No harm done."

'This was ridiculous.' Tom thought. 'He was just a festival hand. This must be a joke. Perhaps it was one of the more extreme fans doing role play or something. That had to be it.' He managed a feeble laugh.

"Look, I don't know which character you're pretending to be... I'm not really into all that stuff, but you certainly had me going for a minute. That was very good. Where did you get the costume and prop gun?" The stranger took a laboured step towards him.

"Look, I'm not one of those sad idiots and this gun is not a fake. D'you want me to prove it to you?" He raised his arm pointing the gun directly at Tom. "Stop stalling. I prefer not to have any trouble and if you're thinking of keeping the picture for yourself you'll be in even bigger trouble. It won't be as easy to get rid of as you might think and believe me you won't be able to find anywhere safe enough to hide so just hand it over now and I'll forget all this, but hurry, I can't waste any more time with you."

Tom's brain was working overtime trying desperately to understand what was happening and who the gunman thought he was.

"What picture?" Tom repeated desperately. "All I know about are these boxes of posters and stuff and you're welcome to all of it. If there are pictures in there you like, take them with pleasure. I don't want any trouble believe me. Just put the gun down, please. I just hike this stuff around and sell it for the TV Company." He looked desperately at the man and hoped he had convinced him. The stranger clicked off the safety catch with a sickening mechanical clarity. Tom knew his next move would be to pull the trigger.

"I won't ask again. Hand it over. Now."

"Look mate, I really don't know what you're talking about. You've got the wrong person. I just sell memorabilia from the stall," Tom said frantically. Although this was the truth, he could tell the man wouldn't believe him, but he was trying to think what to do and stall for time. He would have to take action of some sort but what?

The stranger, still pointing the gun, moved towards Tom. His long coat caught on a tall display unit temporarily placed in the loft. Unaware, he continued advancing as the unit unbalanced and fell heavily against a roof truss. A cloud of dust fell from the timbers. He stopped, coughing and temporarily blinded. Automatically he reached with his right hand to clear the dust from his eyes. The left hand, gripping the gun, dropped to his side.

Tom acted quickly. This was his chance. The gunman would not be distracted for long. He ducked low, ran through the door to the stairs and pushed it shut behind him. Damn, there was no lock and he had no time to barricade it. With only a few seconds advantage he could think of nothing else but to run. He practically fell down the stairs and fled out of the barn and into the yard, the gravel crunching noisily under his feet. He was clear of the building now but having only arrived that morning he had little knowledge of the layout of the grounds. He turned left onto softer ground and with his hand touching the wall he snaked around the perimeter of the building, staying in the shadows. His footsteps were now silent on the grass.

However his assailant was not as quiet and could be heard, lumbering from the stables.

Tom came to a stone buttress projecting away from the wall and moved quickly behind it sinking, breathlessly, into its dark shadow. He couldn't hear any noise behind him now but pushed himself tightly against the cold stone and tried to control his rapid breathing. High above, a glow from an un-curtained window spilled out into the night. He prayed that whoever was in the room would look out. Slowly his heart rate began to drop and he was able to think a little clearer. There was no one at the window, no help was coming. He needed to get away from the estate to the relative safety of the nearby village. He had to move but was terrified he'd be detected and shot at. There was no doubt his pursuer wouldn't give him any more chances. He had never before experienced such a feeling of helplessness.

The gunman moved from the stable yard and turned right, scanning the terrain in the moonlight, listening for movement of any kind. He studied the bushes intently on the opposite side of the road. The leaves rustled and he moved across to investigate.

Tom, peeping cautiously around the buttress, now caught sight of him and stayed perfectly still, watching him cross the road away from his location. Thank God for whatever creature had inadvertently joined them in their chase and unwittingly lured the gunman away from his position. He was now some fifty yards away and continued heading in the wrong direction – it was time to move.

Tom could see the line of the road and a gap in the undergrowth on the opposite side. He had to run for cover and edge closer to the boundary of the estate towards the village, some two miles away. He glanced back and saw no sign of the gunman and broke cover, moving forward crouching low, all the time watching and listening intently.

He reached the undergrowth undetected until a twig snapped under his foot. To him it sounded like a clap of thunder, he froze.

The gunman stopped, turned and started walking back down the road in Tom's direction. Tom edged further into the undergrowth and came to a chain link fence, far too high to get over, running parallel to the bushes with a narrow path alongside.

It was darker here, but his eyesight had now adjusted to the moonlight enabling him to easily follow the fence. After about fifty yards it turned at right angles. He figured that this must be the road to the village and followed it, keeping low, sneaking a look around for any sign of his pursuer. Ahead of him was a pair of large gates, big enough for a bus to drive through. They were closed. As he approached them he could see a small personnel gate in the fence alongside. That looked more promising. He felt for the large steel bolt and to his relief it slid sideways. The metal creaked and groaned but it continued sliding. Thank God it hadn't been locked. 'Some security!' The gate wavered on its hinges, but the bolt was now free. Before he went through he listened carefully for any movement behind him.

Tom could hear the gunman walking along the path he had trod only seconds ago. Fearing that his position was known he threw caution to the wind. He pushed the gate open and slipped through, closing it behind him and quickly sliding the bolt back. He then followed along yet another fence line. There was no grass this time, just hard tarmac.

"Stop these games, boy. Just give me the goods and I'll let you go," shouted an angry voice from behind. Too close behind for comfort.

Tom had no option but to run for his life. In front of him was a large wooden shed. He guessed it was the ticket booth and quickly moved into its shadow. Behind him he heard the sliding of the gate's rusty bolt and hinges creaking loudly as it was carelessly thrown open. He felt nauseous and had a sudden urge to go to the toilet. There was no time. Keeping the shed between him and the gunman, he ran down the road, only to be confronted by another large pair of gates. The footsteps were close. There was no choice but to make a dash and pray there was some way to open them. He could see the words 'Woodford Abbey' emblazoned in gold lettering arching over the top of the gate. Breathlessly he leant against the cold iron of the gates and fumbled for a lock or bolt. His fingers found a heavy steel bar which appeared to be pushed into a socket set into the tarmac. To his relief he could feel the padlock hanging loose by its side.

"Stop right there, Sunshine, or you're a dead man."

Tom turned, quickly looking back down the road. He could clearly see the outline of the man pointing the gun towards him. Tom was non-sensically reminded of a scene from a Clint Eastwood film. Reaching behind him he gripped the arm of the long steel floor bolt. There was more undergrowth on the other side of the fence where he could take cover, if only he could just get through this barrier.

"Where is the painting?"

"I don't know what you're talking about. Leave me alone, why won't you believe me?"

A shot rang out and the bullet ricocheted off the tarmac. The time for reasoning had passed and Tom was now certain he was running for his life.

Hastily he pulled on the bolt and to his relief it lifted out of the ground. He pushed the gate open, slipped through the gap and ran.

'BANG' a bullet ripped through the sign over his head. He sprinted for cover, zigzagging to dodge any gunfire, like he'd seen in films. He dived into the undergrowth and cautiously looked back.

The gunman stopped at the gates gazing intently in his direction. Whether or not he could see him, Tom couldn't tell, but the stranger didn't follow. Instead, he pulled the gate shut sliding the bolt back into the pocket in the road, hooked the padlock around it and turned the key, securing it in place. Tom saw a flash of light as he struck a match and lit a cigarette. The exhaled smoke was quickly whipped away on the breeze.

'Maybe he was just going to wait it out. Well, I can't go back that way,' he thought.

To his surprise and relief, the man turned and walked back in the direction of the house. What was that about? He'd been sure he was going to follow him. He sighed with relief and now focused on getting to the safety of the village. He continued to study the gates from the shelter of the bushes, watching for any sign of movement, thinking this might be a bluff and the man may still be watching, ready to shoot. His mind was a swirl of confusion. Unsurprisingly, he had never had a real gun pointed at him before. The urge to go to the toilet was now unavoidable. All was calm, so he relieved himself behind a tree and then began to tremble uncontrollably. The adrenalin had subsided and revealed his true physical state. He felt sick, cold and disorientated as he stared into the distance. He could just make out the lights of the village across the valley which gave him comfort and focus.

He stayed still for another 10 minutes and having regained some strength and composure, he decided to move.

Cautiously he picked his way through the branches to a clearing, careful to keep the undergrowth as cover between himself and the gate. He walked quickly across the rough grass, alert for any obstacles that could trip him. He could easily see the trees and the line of the road over to his left. However, he couldn't shake off the feeling he was being watched. There was a rustle in the trees nearby and without warning an animal ran out of the undergrowth on the other side of the fence. His heart raced. Tom wasn't sure who was the more surprised as he watched the shape quickly turn away and run off into the dark. It had to be a deer, he'd noticed a large herd from the minibus when he arrived earlier in the day. It fled as if being pursued by a predator. Tom grinned, he knew what that felt like, however, he wouldn't feel totally safe until he reached the village. An owl hooted in the tree above him. At least birds don't carry guns, he thought, continuing to follow the road away from the estate towards the warm glow of nearing civilisation. *'They can stuff their job selling all that tat,'* he thought.

He hadn't realised what a circus these events were when he'd agreed to help out for bed, board and some pocket money. It all sounded so glamorous, with the added thrill of perhaps meeting the stars of the show. In fact, it had turned out to be a slog, lifting and shifting box after box of plastic models, T-shirts, posters and replica props being sold to obsessed fanatics whose only social lives revolved around a second-rate show. If the crowd that had shown up today were anything to go by then Saturday would be completely crazy. All ages, some dressed as their heroes. Yes, their heroes. That's a laugh. Most of the actors only turn up for the money. Just adding it to their already overflowing bank balances as they fleece their fans with signed photos, air-brushed to hide their true ages and imperfections.

If those loyal followers knew how they were thought of behind their backs they might re-assess their allegiances.

He suddenly heard a rustle and another creature ran out from behind him and dived for cover in the undergrowth. *'Another deer'* he thought.

Suddenly, he felt a heavy impact to his back and was immediately thrust forward, falling awkwardly on the rough ground, hitting his head on a boulder as he landed.

2
The Hiker

Tom came around feeling dazed and confused. *'What had that been about?'* He remembered falling heavily but curiously felt no pain from the impact. He put his hand to the back of his head but felt no bruise. He stood up easily and shook his head in bewilderment. He had no idea how long he had been unconscious. He listened carefully but couldn't detect the sound of anyone around. He quickly continued walking, his eyes focused on the lights of the village.

The grounds hereabout were clear of trees which were now replaced with low shrubs and hedging dotted around the edge of the path. Ahead was what appeared to be a low sprawling timber shed outlined by the moonlight. Tom stopped, he could see a figure sitting on the edge of the sloping roof humming to himself, his legs dangling down above a straw covered veranda. He assumed it was a hiker by the casual clothes, baseball cap and backpack resting by his side.

What was a backpacker doing sitting on a shed roof in woodland at night? Immediately he looked around for an easy escape route. After the events of this evening he certainly didn't want to encounter anymore strangers. He prepared yet again to flee for his life.

The figure noticed him and turned in his direction.

"Hi, you must be Tom," he called out, in a friendly manner.

Tom stared at him in bewilderment. *'How did he know his name? Was he from the village and had come looking for him. No, how would anyone there know about the events of the evening or his name. Could he be another of Frank's colleagues?'*

"It is Tom, isn't it?" the hiker enquired. Tom felt a peculiar familiarity with the stranger and moved closer to get a better look at him. He still couldn't make out his features but inexplicably felt it would be safe to climb up on the roof alongside him. He looked around and saw a stack of hay bales leant against the back wall of the shed. Cautiously he climbed up onto the roof and sat next to the stranger.

This was so weird, but then his whole evening so far had been bizarre and, curiously, he felt no fear in the backpacker's presence, quite the reverse actually.

The stranger pointed to a spot a short distance away. Tom followed his bony finger and saw a group of animals who appeared to be oblivious to their presence. Perhaps they were downwind of us, thought Tom abstractedly. He assumed they might be foxes, he'd never seen a fox in the wild but they were still too far away to be certain in the moonlight. Tom turned to the stranger, "Sorry, I feel that I should know you," he whispered. He didn't want to disturb the wildlife, nor could he shake off the instinct to keep a low presence.

"Hi, my name's Eric," the stranger said. Tom felt an absurd urge to giggle. Here they were sitting on a roof in a wood and behaving as if they had just been introduced at some mutual friend's dinner party.

"Luckily I was nearby," continued his new companion. "I just happened to be passing when I received the pager message. It's supposed to be my day off but in my line of business you have to be prepared to go anywhere at a moment's notice."

Tom looked him up and down, "I'm sorry, I'm still at a loss. You seem to know me, but I can't place you. Are you from the Sci-Fi market or the production company?" he asked. He realised how ridiculous it sounded but it appeared to be the only answer. He scrutinised the stranger who was dressed in a Barbour Jacket, jeans and baseball cap that obscured his features. Maybe he was undercover? He was struck by a sudden thought. "Are you security?" he asked excitedly.

The stranger said nothing. Tom looked at the backpack and noticed a long wooden handle alongside.

"What's that?" he asked, wondering what use it was for hiking, it was far too big for a walking stick. Maybe it was a weapon of some sort.

"Tool of the trade. Well, more a status symbol, I suppose. People I deal with seem to get upset if I don't have it with me. It's a bit of a nuisance really but it goes with the job, and I'm used to it now after all these millennia."

Tom looked closer, trying to fathom out exactly what it was. Then the penny dropped.

"It's a scythe!"

"Yup, tool of the trade!" Eric confirmed.

The clouds above them moved, allowing the bright moonlight to reveal the scene in more detail. Tom then noticed that his companion was not solid! He could make out the outline of the roof through his body. He recoiled in shock.

"Sorry Tom, I thought you'd worked it out," Eric apologised. "This might be difficult for you. You see when you were hit in the back and fell, you knocked yourself out. The brutal fact is, you're dead!"

"What... Who are you then?"

"Sorry to put it so bluntly but your mortal existence on this earth has just ended. Please, let me introduce myself further. I'm 'The Angel of Death' or if you prefer, 'The Grim Reaper' but my friends call me Eric."

"I'm sorry too but this is difficult to take in. If this is true, how did I die? The knock on my head?" he asked, reaching up to feel his head for a wound. He then thought back to the sudden shunt in his back, "Was I shot in the back?"

"No, you just took the wrong direction and he watched you walk into a death-trap. Better for him but very bad for you. Shooting you would have been awkward, it would have guaranteed a murder investigation. However, when you walked through that gate he realised that your disappearance would be much easier to explain. You, my friend, have just been eaten by a lion. As far as anyone else is concerned your death was an unfortunate accident, or possibly suicide!"

"Sorry, I'm totally confused. Did he put a lion in here with me?"

"No, it was here already, he just let you walk in. See the animals moving over there in the shadows?" Eric pointed across the field. Tom noticed now that his hand was skeletal. "If you study them carefully you will notice they are lions having a late supper."

"Don't be ridiculous, this is Exford not the Masa Mara. Lions don't inhabit the English countryside, they're kept in the enclosures on the park."

"Exactly, you're in the enclosure. True, it is the Exford countryside, but this is their home none the less. This is a Safari Park after all."

Tom looked towards the animals. He could now see that they were much larger and more cat-like than he had first assumed. Not foxes at all. He put his head in his hands. '*Oh God... that's why he didn't follow me through the gate. I thought this was the way out of the park,*' Tom groaned.

This day was turning into a nightmare. He had to get his head around all this. "Look, if I'm dead, why am I here speaking to you? You don't look like the Grim Reaper I've seen in films."

"No, you caught me out a bit there. I have the cloak in the backpack and obviously the scythe is to hand if you would prefer me to be in uniform."

"No, you're alright. I prefer you as you are." Tom's shoulders dropped. This was unbelievably depressing.

Eric floated down off of the roof, grabbed his backpack, slung the scythe over his shoulder and beckoned to Tom.

"Good, you are getting the idea. Now come on, I'll explain more on the way and introduce you to some friends. Sorry to rush you but I am on holiday after all."

Tom climbed down and followed. "You're telling me there's some explaining to do! I didn't feel anything. Shouldn't there be pain and suffering involved in death? Hang on, where are you going? … Wait up, I'm coming. This is all a bit of a shock you know… Wait." Tom needed time to think but it seemed he had no choice but to move on.

Eric waited by the road. Tom had to move quickly to keep up, not sure now whether he was walking or floating, but he made progress and caught up somehow. *'That's another question to ask sometime,'* he thought, trying to adjust to the situation. They walked together towards the gate he had passed through earlier.

"Hang on. How come I'm walking? Aren't ghosts supposed to float around?"

"Well, you can develop those skills later. Follow me."

"Wait, shouldn't I be going to heaven or whatever 'the other place' is?" He didn't want to say Hell and tempt fate.

"Again, that's up to you. Stop asking so many questions. Wait till you meet my friends, they'll explain all your options from their first-hand experience. I'm just the courier or your travel guide if you prefer."

"Options?" Tom was even more confused. "What friends?" They had now reached the gates, padlocked by the gunman. Eric continued walking, passing through the solid iron mesh as if it wasn't there.

"Oh… that's neat, but I can't do that."

"Yes, you can, just keep going." Eric encouraged him, beckoning him to join him on the other side.

Tom faced the gate and through habit tried to push it open. His hands passed through the mesh, a tingling feeling rushing up his arms.

"Ouch, I got an electric shock!" he quickly pulled them back.

"The sensation wears off after a while, now come on, you can do it."

Tom closed his eyes and walked straight ahead, his whole body prickled and then the sensation cleared. He opened his eyes and found himself now on the outside of the gate.

"Wow, that's cool! Something's changed but I don't feel any different. Am I really a ghost?"

"I can assure you, you are. Now let's go to the house, I'd like to make the most of what remains of my holiday and there are some residents there I'd like you to meet. I tell you what, come and stand by me, grab the other handle on this backpack and I'll transport us to save time."

3
Another World

Earlier on Friday

On the horizon, the blue undulating dunes of the planet's surface gave way to a range of black mountains topped by a grey cloud base. The wind was strong, blowing the grains of sand up into dust clouds, whipping off the top of the banks, threatening the vulnerable sensors mounted on tripods near the summit.

The heat from the two suns was almost unbearable and without the protective clothing the two men would have fried. They drove their vehicle back towards the landing craft a mile away, it's outline just visible through the orange fog. They navigated by carefully retracing the tyre tracks that they had created while surveying the dunes earlier. The open topped vehicle, which resembled a dune buggy covered in scientific instruments, stopped near a large crevasse. The tall figure of Captain Login climbed out, tested the ground with both feet and cautiously stepped away from the vehicle. He pressed the communicator switch mounted on his helmet.

"Stay here Olag, the ground seems firm enough. I'm just curious about the geology around this hole. It doesn't look natural, and I want to take a closer look." From the passenger seat, Olag signalled with a thumbs up. Login took some test equipment from the storage box mounted on the back of the rover and anchored the cable into the port on the side of the machine.

In this hostile environment, Olag was relieved to stay where he was, "OK by me," he radioed back. He would be much happier still when they were both safely off the planet surface and back at sky base.

Login approached the sheer face of the fissure and keeping a safe distance from the edge, fed the cable through his gloved hands and lowered a probe into the abyss. His whole body was primed ready to abandon the probe and return to the vehicle at the first sense of danger. Without warning the area shook violently and he fell to the ground. He let go of the cable, fearful it could tear his protective suit. Through the dust arising from the tremor, he could see the attached rover being pulled helplessly by the cable towards the edge with Olag desperately fighting to release his seat belt and escape the vehicle. Login watched helplessly as the craft tipped over the edge. Olag released the belt and leapt wildly from the vehicle as the rover, still attached to the probe, plunged into the abyss. Olag, not yet on firm ground, clambered frantically at the edge of the cliff grabbing at the loose surface for some kind of grip but it was too late and he plummeted after the vehicle into the unknown.

Login clawed frantically at the ground trying to find purchase and avoid the same fate. His right foot found a rock and he pushed hard against it until the tremors subsided. He then crawled to the edge of the fissure desperately hoping his companion was safe. The rover and Olag were nowhere to be seen in the bottomless black pit. He slowly stood up and staggered awkwardly towards the safety of the landing craft. He lifted his gloved hand and pressed the button on the side of his helmet. "Benjie… Benjie… come in Benjie…Olag has gone," he said, his voice breaking as he tried to control his emotions. "Something's very wrong, it felt like the rover was being pulled into the abyss. I'm upgrading this planet to hostile. Send out the spare rover to pick me up."

Unnervingly, there was no reply from Flight Captain Benjie in the Century Hawk lander. He watched the illuminated ramp under the craft for signs of movement, expecting to see the spare rover descending out onto the planet surface. His hope turned to shock as the ramp rose up into the underbelly of the craft and with its anti-gravity impulse drive engaged, the lander lifted silently off the planet's surface, up through the atmosphere and away. His only hope of rescue gone. The view zoomed back to the stranded astronaut. Behind, undetected by his limited vision, a tentacle the size of a telegraph pole rose out of the crevasse and started to paw the ground dragging itself towards him.

Still facing away and unaware of the danger behind him, the spaceman flipped back the orange tinted visor on his helmet revealing his harried and distraught face.

The image froze and the words. TO BE CONTINUED were overlaid on the screen.

The audience went wild, standing as one, clapping, cheering, and whooping their approval as the camera zoomed in on their hero's stricken face. Clive Monkton then entered the stage and stood in front of the cinema screen. This was too much for one member of the audience who fainted at the sight of him in the flesh. The duty first aider, poised at the end of the aisle, leapt forward and attended to the casualty while Clive continued waving to his adoring fans. He moved towards the right of the stage, pausing to milk the applause and then took his place behind a lectern. He was back and he loved it.

He lifted his hands high into the air appealing for quiet and slowly the audience responded. The applause subsided and they all sat back down, creating a crescendo of squeaks as the rubber feet of the loose chairs scraped on the wooden floor of the ballroom.

"Friends," he began. The sound level from the microphone was set too high and a squeal of feedback bounced around the room. He looked angrily at the poor wretch on the sound desk at the back of the hall, who hastily adjusted the control.

"Friends," he began again and paused to listen for feedback, this time the level was correct. He smiled and continued, his glance sweeping across the whole room. "Friends," he repeated. "It is a great pleasure for me to be here with you all today." The applause started again but was more subdued and shorter lived this time. "I hope you enjoyed this excerpt from the new series of Galactic Jump." Cheers confirmed that they had. "I can only thank you for your support and kind messages over the last two years. Through the fan club, I received many letters from you, which sustained me through those dark days. Despite the terrible injustice being handed out by certain gutter press, you kept me going. The evil lies being written, took me down a very dark road but you... yes, all of you," he again stopped to sweep the whole room with a glance, "saved me from the abyss." Cheers rang out again as the fans congratulated themselves on saving their hero. Some were aware of the irony when moments earlier on screen he was unable to save his friend from the abyss. Clive held his hand up to quell the adulation.

"I now stand in front of you cleared of all charges, ready once again, to fight the Gorog and bring lasting peace to the Orion Galaxy."

He briefly studied the audience, some were wearing uniforms from the Orion Brigade wardrobe and carried replica pan blasters. He also noted, in the front row, a group of Gorog guards sitting uncomfortably in their heavy rubber armour and masks. A cross between rhinos and red squirrels, they looked fearsome and yet rather pathetic at the same time. A wry smile appeared on his face as he looked out over the crowd, this couldn't have gone any better. Despite the recent court case they were in the palm of his hand.

"Gorog, Fleet commanders, Replicants and Orion guards, Ladies and Gentlemen let me introduce you to my crew," he announced with a flourish.

From the right-hand side of the stage entered four of the Orion Galactic mothership crew, in uniform, waving and enjoying the cheers of the audience. They lined up looking across at Clive and gave the traditional left-handed two finger salute. Malcolm Bingham held the salute a fraction longer than the others, looking across at Clive and smiling politely. This was a smile calculated to hide his thoughts, but Clive could read his true feelings towards him. But hey! This was show business and success always brought with it envy from other, less talented, actors.

The muted greeting was not lost on the fans, who were fully aware of the friction between the two lead actors but at least most of the crew were now back together. Hope of a long successful reunion was possible now that Clive had returned.

Malcolm moved to the centre of the stage and the crew surrounded him with the Orion Galactic Emblem projected on the screen behind them. Clive moved across to join them but kept a small, deliberate, distance between him and his subordinates.

"Wow, what a way to start the festival guys," Malcom said, with a bright cheerful voice. "I hope we'll have the chance to meet you all over the weekend. We also have many treats in store. We'll be signing books and memorabilia in the stable yard, so look out for the timing of our appearances on the notice board by the concession stand. Take a chance to see the display of new props and costumes along with some of your old favourites from the show before their move to London for the UK Film and Television Festival. Now, before we leave the stage, we'll pose for you to take pictures as we reveal the new Orion Galactic Insignia." The circular emblem pierced by a laser blast from an Impulse Lander was projected behind them and now morphed into a more simplistic colourful version of the same thing. It met with muted applause, appearing to the fans to be a somewhat low budget version of the original. Regardless the audience gathered round, cameras at the ready, to capture the moment for posterity. They felt honoured to be the first to see glimpses of the new series before it was broadcast on national television. Malcolm looked around the stage and glanced to the wings. One of the crew was missing.

"Have any of you seen Andy Cross?" he whispered to his colleagues. "He should be here, I spoke to him yesterday, he said he was coming." They all shook their heads.

At the back of the ballroom, Jules Exford watched the proceedings, mentally calculating the average spending per head. The opportunity to hold this event could prove very profitable for the estate and they needed every penny they could extract from the punters. He himself had never seen Galactic Jump, however, he was very aware of the show's popularity. He struggled to see the appeal himself, having just seen the trailer for the new series on the big screen. It looked banal, he could only imagine the dialogue would be clichéd and story lines unimaginative. Still, as long as the tills rang out, who was he to criticise? The promotion company had paid a good fee for the use of the house. The estate also took any entrance fees to the grounds and he had negotiated a 15% share of the profits from the trade stands. All in all, a good weekend's work without risk.

Meanwhile back on stage, Malcolm was getting further agitated at the 'no show' from the show's headline actor, Andy Cross, which was not missed by the diehard fans as the performers left the stage. It was also notable that Clive Monkton wandered off before the others, leaving the stage by the opposite side. The audience could detect some tension between them, but this was to be expected among such fine actors at the top of their profession, or so they chose to believe. They filed out of the ballroom into the gardens and headed to the market yard and Café. Where to go first? The next presentation in the ballroom would be Saturday afternoon followed by a disco in the evening.

The promoter John Pearce watched from the wings and was thrilled by the audience's response to the first preview. The show this afternoon was not much more than a dress rehearsal for the technical crew to set sound levels and check the projection equipment. But why not take money from the punters at the same time? '*win, win*' he thought and headed off to the stables. Tomorrow was going to be the big day when he hoped to impress new investors with a show to remember. Oh, and the fans of course, ultimately it was their money he wanted a share of.

Clive was first on the rota for book signing so made his way quickly to the security of the tack room which had been set up as a green room for the actors to relax away from the fans, have a drink and prepare for their appearances. He found these events tedious. The same stupid questions would be asked by the same tiresome fans, some of them dressed in low quality replica uniforms. But money flowed and why not have a cut of the action? He'd been out of circulation for two years because of the blasted court case and he counted himself lucky to be back on the gravy train again.

Outside it was a beautiful summer's day. The overflow car park was full to bursting. Dedicated fans, the mildly curious and visitors who had no idea the festival was even taking place, were finding amusement in the outlandish costumes worn by some of the fans. Ironically, they themselves had become part of the entertainment and were being photographed as much as the actors.

The market was now a hive of activity. The stalls were arranged in a circle with their attractive red and white stripped canvas tops. On display were books, costumes, models, full sized replica props of weapons & helmets. Numerous posters packaged in clearly numbered cardboard rolls referenced those displayed on the back wall. The list of items was endless but there was something to suit all sizes and pockets and all at an extortionate mark up by the production company.

The interior of an unused stable was hung with black drapes and decorated with several full-size cardboard cut outs of the stars in costume. A long table at the far side contained books and photos to be signed by the actor on duty. John Pearce now took up his place behind this merchandise desk with cash box ready. There was a buzz of anticipation from the queue now snaking around the perimeter of the yard. He could hear Clive in position behind the curtain talking forcibly in hushed tones to someone who then thumped angrily up the stairs into the hayloft. John made a mental note to find out what Clive was up to but now was not the time. Now was the time to extract money from the fans.

John asked the first people in the queue to approach the table and purchase books for signing. They had a choice of 'Galactic Jump', the scripts - series one to four or Clive's autobiography 'Jump for Joy'. Both priced at twenty pounds, only five pounds over the marked price.

The curtain twitched and Clive emerged in a flourish, to spontaneous applause. He waved at the queue, visible from the open door, their cheers ringing around the enclosed courtyard. He seemed rather preoccupied between signings, but as a true professional turned on the charm for each of his devoted fans as the till happily rang in the background. Everyone was satisfied.

4
The Surprise Visit...

Friday night in the attic

George was disappointed after having watched the preview in the Ballroom.

"Well, if that's the level of actor being trundled out by RADA these days, they should be ashamed." He shook his head in dismay.

Wilf, however, knew a little more detail. "Hold on, George. It's too early to judge, they're not all here yet. I eavesdropped this morning on the meeting with the producer, and he said the biggest star won't arrive till tomorrow because apparently, they don't want to pay him for two days, I don't think the other actors know that though."

"That's not the point. There they are swanning around, playing the big movie star but they couldn't act their way out of a paper bag. They may not all be top billing yet, but they have no pride in their craft. How are they going to become better actors if they don't care? All they're interested in is the money and fame."

Just as George finished his rant, a dense cloud of smoke gathered in the corner of the attic room. Alice stood up and stared at the manifestation.

"Looks like we have a visitor," she said interestedly.

The smoke cleared quickly, leaving a faint musty odour. They could now see a hiker holding a rucksack and scythe. Alongside him a very agitated young man was also gripping the rucksack whilst trying to swish away the smoke around him.

"Hi Eric," Alice called out cheerfully, as the three of them moved over to greet their visitor. "We weren't expecting you. Is everything alright? We're not due our annual appraisal yet, surely."

"Why can't you just float up the stairs and through the door like any normal ghost?" asked Wilf grumpily. "All these gimmicks are just showing off."

Eric turned towards him and rose into the air raising his arms dramatically.

"I am The Angel of DEATH," he announced in a deep booming voice. The atmosphere around him turned dark and foreboding, Tom backed away in fear. "The Grim Reaper... Gate keeper to Eternity... The Ferryman... etcetera. Oh boy that does go on a bit! I don't think I can keep this up for long," he said pleasantly, while floating back to floor level. "I have to admit.... its effective when rounding up the more cocky individuals who think they are the most frightening creatures ever to walk the earth. I do enjoy it when they sink to the floor and plead for mercy. Serves them right, besides Wilf, you're just jealous that you can't raise to my heights, literally."

"What's got into you?" asked Alice.

"Sorry, I've just been on a corporate training weekend on Dartmoor. I've been doing this for years, so for me it was a refresher, but some candidates were first timers, learning the seriousness of it all. We had all this stuff drummed into us. Some of the recruits were a lot younger than me and so sure of themselves. They think they know it all, but at best they've only read one textbook on the subject and attended a few seminars. There's no respect for experience these days. Still, they had a rude awakening, it was fun to see the realisation when their incompetence sunk in."

"How old are you then?" Alice had always wondered but had been too polite to ask.

"I lost count at seven hundred and twelve."

"When was that?"

"Two hundred and twelve years ago, in fact it will be two hundred and thirteen years in June."

"Then you do know!" Alice was a little confused. "Never mind, aren't you going to introduce us to your travelling companion, I thought you worked alone. Is he your new apprentice?"

"Sorry, very rude of me. It's my day off but my pager went and as I was close by, I popped in to collect Tom."

"Hello," Tom said, nervously waving at them.

Alice, George and Wilf looked him over quizzically. Tom was trying to process the scene in front of him. The moonlight beamed through two circular dormer windows into the attic. The room was large, full of boxes, tea chests, old furniture and odds and ends piled up in the corner.

Two wardrobes, the size of garden sheds, were so full of clothes that garments were poking out of the doors and drawers preventing them from closing properly. In the centre were two large well-worn leather sofas surrounding a low coffee table. All this sat on a moth-eaten floral carpet which must have been magnificent but now looked sad and neglected like the rest of the room. Dusty paintings and empty picture frames were stacked against the exposed brickwork of a chimney breast rising through the floor. One picture contained old, tired faces looking at him solemnly. One was of a wrinkled old lady, her hair pulled severely back from her face with a small dog resting on her lap. Was that a King Charles spaniel? He wasn't sure. The whole feeling was of abandoned grandeur. Some of the chests looked out of place, the stencilled writing on the side reading, 'Trolley Cart Opera Co.' indicating a theatrical history rather than that of a stately home. Tom wondered what exactly it all meant and what role he could possibly play here for eternity. He began to consider his life and concluded that it had been cut short before he could actually amount to anything. The only interesting bit so far was being eaten by a lion and he would have happily forgone that.

George looked sympathetically at The Grim Reaper, "Things are no better then Eric, still rushed off your feet, so to speak? What happened about additional staff to reduce your catchment area?" he asked.

"Not a hope. It's just getting worse with the government incentives for care homes and hospices to be developed in the southwest. Even more mortals are moving here to die, putting a bigger strain on our resources. The paperwork is getting worse too. There has been the promise of a new computer system to save time, but I have yet to see it. The ones we have in the office are pathetic. It takes ages to type in the information and then they spill out reams of paper that have to be archived in case the memory fails. It's a pity it can't all be stored in a cloud and floated off somewhere. No one will ever want to reference it!"

Alice caught his eye and pointed at Tom.

"Ah yes, sorry, let me introduce Tom. To put it bluntly, he's just been eaten by a lion."

They all stared at Tom in disbelief at his awful fate. Then they stared unbelievingly at Eric, who just shrugged his shoulders.

They continued to study him curiously.

Tom broke the silence. "Sorry, this is all very confusing. I was being chased by a man with a gun when I went the wrong way and ended up in the lion enclosure."

George interrupted, "Whoa! there... You were chased by a gunman? That's a hell of a way to start a story, let's hear that bit first."

"He chased me from the stables where I was packing up and shot at me several times," Tom replied indignantly. "That's the truth... honest. I was storing the stuff from the stall in the hay loft, and he came out of the dark, going on about handing over something. He drew a gun and started threatening me, fortunately he was distracted by dust falling from the rafters, so I ran off down the stairs to get away and then he followed me."

Alice went to his defence, "He has to be telling the truth. You wouldn't make that up. But how could you get in with the lions? The gates are locked at night."

"Well, they weren't tonight," he replied angrily. "I went through two of them following the road which looked like it was going off the estate to the village. He didn't follow me through the second gate. I know why now, he must have known. I ran towards the lights of the village but tripped and hit my head. When I came to, I met Eric who told me I was dead and here I am." He shrugged his shoulders again.

"He knocked himself out on a rock. Never felt a thing, as the lions went in for the kill and helped themselves to a late supper. Just as well he was unconscious really. He was doomed as soon as he entered the compound." Eric added stoically.

"I don't want to be a ghost! I'm just helping out on a market stall. I packed up for the evening and got caught up in some sort of robbery. Can't I just go back... please?" He pleaded to Eric, "This is so unfair. This can't be it. I must have more life to live... haven't I?" he finished pathetically.

Alice moved over to his side and tried to comfort him. "Please don't cry. I know this must be a shock. It was the same for us, but you get used to it. It's not bad... just different."

"I don't want to be different, I just want to go home," he mumbled through his tears.

"Sorry lad, no hope of that," Wilf rather bluntly informed him. "Now sit on the sofa and tell us in precise detail what happened from the beginning, this is so interesting," he added excitedly.

Tom glared at him but regaled them with the whole story from the setting up of the market, packing away the goods in the stables, his confrontation with the dark stranger and subsequent chase, leaving nothing to the imagination. George too was enthralled.

"This is like some cheap detective novel. Who would've thought this could happen for real… and in our own home!"

Wilf reached into one of the overstuffed wardrobes.

"I think we need to do some investigating ourselves." He pulled out a tartan cloak, deerstalker hat and placed a large curly pipe in his mouth. "It's time to do some sleuthing," he declared, clumsily shifting the large pipe around in his mouth.

"Pack it in Wilf, this is serious. You don't get gun slinging murderers at sci-fi festivals. We need to call the police, someone's been murdered… sort of." Alice said.

"And how do you suggest we do that? The spirit world has a poor reputation for communication with the mortal world at the best of times. I don't think a phone call is going to work. For one thing it would put all the clairvoyants out of business in one fell swoop!"

"We need to follow the actors and crew around and see what we can find out. I'm sure it's only a matter of time 'till Tom's body is found, or… what's left of it," George added rather insensitively. "The police will soon come then. In the meantime, we've a duty to dig around and see what we can find out… Wilf, please take that ridiculous garb off and get up to date."

Eric was getting impatient. "Look guys, if you don't mind, can I leave Tom in your care? You can explain the ropes to him. I'd like to get back to the rest of my day off. There's a busy time coming up. A bus crash is due on Tuesday, so I'm going to be extremely busy. I'll pop back in a few days with all the paperwork."

"Don't worry, we'll look after him," Alice said with a motherly tone in her voice and a little excitement too which she couldn't contain.

Despite all the confusion at his circumstances, Tom curiously felt safe in the company of the three actors. Life and Death were more similar than he had thought.

He couldn't believe that although he definitely was dead there was still bureaucracy to be dealt with. '*Red tape gets everywhere*' he thought.

Before they could change their minds, Eric started to spin faster and faster, he quickly waved a hand and morphed into a tornado of smoke. "See you soon," he echoed joyfully and vapourised into nothing.

"You know he's getting very good at those vanishing tricks!" Wilf said in admiration.

"Right," Alice said. "First things first, I'm giving you a guided tour." She grabbed Tom by the hand and before he knew what was happening, they were off down the stairs into the upper apartments of the stately home.

"This is going to be fun," George said rubbing his hands together. Wilf discarded the deerstalker, tartan cape and pipe, ruffled his hair and reached into the wardrobe pulling out a dishevelled old buff coloured raincoat and a box of cigars.

5
Galactic Saturday

Saturday 3rd August. Morning

By ten o'clock the marketplace was extremely busy and there was a buzz of anticipation about the appearance of the actors and the second showing of the preview, along with the singalong to 'Revenge of the Gorog.' But behind the scenes there was concern that Andy Cross still hadn't arrived. Although renowned for his poor timekeeping he was the lead actor and main draw, despite what Clive thought.

The promotor, John Pearce, was getting rather agitated with Clive Monkton and Malcolm.

"Come on Clive, you must know where he is. You were with him on set last week," chipped in Malcolm.

"I'm not his bloody keeper, he's a waste of space, you should never have invited him. He's always letting us down!"

"Well, that's big coming from you, you've been banged up for six months. We had to delay the filming because of your stupid behaviour."

Clive looked daggers at his co-star, "Oh Malcolm, I'm so sorry, I forgot this is your only job and I've let you down," he said sarcastically.

"Leave it out you two, if he's not here we'll manage without him. The upside is we'll share his cut of the takings," John said with resignation.

The market place was frenetic. Most popular were the posters showing the stars on board the spaceship or fighting with the Gorog. Replica props were slower to move but at a hundred and fifty pounds for a blaster and two hundred for the communicator, as seen in series two, it was no surprise they were beyond most pockets. The replica space suit, as seen in series three episode 4, where Captain Login, single handed, fought off the Hestine monster, was an astronomical eight hundred pounds. It even had the scorch marks and a tear from the Scrany knife held by the Hestine. These were specialised collectables and only for the keenest of fans.

Tom's absence created more work for the exasperated stall helpers. Speculation, however, was rife regarding his whereabouts. On Friday night the stall manager, Frank, had left him to tidy up, lock away the goods and join them in the pub. The rest of the market staff had returned to the Abbey Inn in the village on the shuttle bus. Tom would have some serious questions to answer when he did finally turn up.

Earlier Frank had found the stable door unlocked and the loft in a mess. Posters in their cardboard tubes were strewn all over the floor. Nothing appeared to be missing, as far as he could see. It was as though Tom had been beamed up. He could only speculate that he had spent the night with one of the girls from the production team. While away from home, the temporary staff had a reputation for getting up to all sorts of mischief. He would have to question him later.

In the house, The Duke of Exford was in the library (which doubled as his office). He sat behind a large, shabby mahogany desk. The top was a mass of books, papers and faded photographs mounted in silver frames. The leather inlay of the desk could be seen curling up between the telephone and a pile of books as it tried to escape its bond. The room had once been the most magnificent display of wealth, with gold leaf accentuating the elaborate plasterwork on the ceiling. Exotic hardwood panelling and tall shelving full of leather-bound books covered the walls. Oil paintings and wall hangings, along with maps of the estate, displayed the wealth and status possessed by the owners. A precarious looking mahogany stair mounted on wheels, for access to the high-level shelves, stood in the corner. Time however, had not been kind to the building or its contents. The dwindling wealth of the family did not allow for the continuous specialised work required to maintain this once opulent stately pile.

The tapestry hangings were faded and moth eaten. The varnish had lost its shine and the huge elaborate stone fireplace was dark with years of smoke stains. In front of it lay a floral carpet bordered by two long, red, cracked leather sofas, the stuffing trying to make its escape through thread bare seams.

The Duke himself was a human manifestation of the house. He was tall and thin with a long face worn by worry. His nose was pronounced, a feature carried by all the males of the family. He was once known as a veritable catch, wealthy, attractive and of a pleasant demeanour.

These attributes were still true, but no one could consider him young anymore. He was physically and mentally exhausted from the relentless effort of trying to maintain his inherited burden and worried that his family's prosperity could end whilst under his tenure. It would break his heart to have to sell the home that had been in his family for some five hundred years.

The enormous mahogany door at the opposite end of the room creaked open and a man in his thirties entered, his crumpled Pierre Cardin suit slightly at odds with his training shoes and shoulder length hair. He had a jaunty walk as he approached the desk, hands in pockets. He nodded to the Duke who looked up over his glasses.

"Hello father, what's up?"

The younger man had inherited his father's gift for style. With no effort he managed to look good, no matter what clothes he chose to throw on. He was also seemingly easy going and carefree. The Duke wished he would, sometimes, be a little more aware of the responsibility the family had for the continuing welfare of the estate, its tenants and workforce. Not forgetting to adhere to the traditions and respectability of the family name.

"I'll tell you what's up, this place is turning into a circus. I hand you the responsibility of overseeing the estate because you have the energy to take on the task. But I look out of the window and see the stable yard has turned into a market full of film junk, the ballroom looks like a cross between a film set and a cinema and have you seen the lawn? It's been ruined by the huge vehicles bringing in all their staging. Your mother would be turning in her grave if we could afford one for her." He glanced over at the urn sat on the mantelpiece next to a faded picture of a 1930's wedding where his younger self looked out with an optimistic, beaming smile whilst holding the hand of a beautiful young woman in a flowing wedding dress and flowers in her hair. The Duke paused for a second remembering the loss of his one true love.

"But father, this is what people want. Have you seen the car park? It's full to overflowing. Have you any idea what this weekend will net us? I'll tell you now, it will be in the tens of thousands and by God we need every penny to keep this place going. Even the safari park will turn a profit with the extra footfall, and we can't say that very often."

The Duke's shoulders sagged. "It's so depressing that we have to sell our soul to the highest bidder just to survive. It's no way to live Jules, look what it's done to me. I'm exhausted and riddled with health problems brought on by the years of stress trying to keeping this place solvent. There has to be a better way for us to live. I don't wish this for you."

"We have to fight father, this can work., Jules said earnestly. "You've grafted tirelessly to keep this place going, Grandad tried his way, but his investments nearly ruined us. The safari park is a money pit, but it just about breaks even. At least he had one good idea, it put us on the map and still does... it's our greatest asset. Look, we need to use that to attract new money with other ventures to prop up the expenses of the estate."

"I admire your enthusiasm son, but this weekend is not enough, it won't make a lot of difference... we need more."

"I can do more father, but I need capital to expand my ideas."

The Duke rose out of his chair. "Capital is one thing we don't have."

The temperature dropped suddenly, and they both looked around for a cause. Alice and Tom had entered the room through a secret passage behind the bookshelves. The hidden door had been sealed years ago but this was no obstacle to them.

Tom blinked in the sunlight beaming through the large window at the far end of the room. They watched as the two men, who appeared to be in deep conversation suddenly stopped talking and looked towards them. Tom stood perfectly still. "I think they've seen us," he whispered.

The men just turned away and carried on their conversation.

"No, not them, they just felt the temperature drop. That's perfectly normal when we're around. You have to be careful though, there are some mortals who can see us, but that's rare. We made some lovely friends at our old residence in Holeford. They helped us stop the redevelopment of a supermarket, thus saving our home in the hidden basement of the burnt-out theatre where we died in a fire."

"So, you didn't die here?" Tom asked with surprise.

"No, we got a transfer to this place... its complicated, I'll explain that later, but let's go down to the market now. By the way, this is the grand library. The Duke uses it as his office and dayroom. The public aren't allowed in here, so it's a bit more homely than the public rooms."

"So, who are those men?" Tom asked, pointing to the mortals.

"The old one is the Duke of Exford and the other is his son, the Viscount Jules Exford. He's taken on the control of the estate while his dad just looks after the running of the house."

"It could do with some renovation," Tom observed, looking around at the shabby furniture and peeling paper. He then looked wistfully out of the window at the busy marketplace. "I should be down there selling the 'Galactic Jump' stuff, it looks really busy."

"George saw the show in the Ballroom yesterday. He said the acting is very poor, they're all in it for the money with little talent. It sounds disgusting. We worked so hard for low wages, but we did it for the joy of performing. Now, come on, I'll show you the public rooms."

They moved through the tall, polished oak doors and arrived on the landing. They looked down admiringly at the imperial staircase covered in Axminster carpet, woven with the family crest, as it swept down to the lavishly tiled entrance hall. The upper landing was highlighted by Corinthian columns linked by gothic arches salvaged from the ruins of the abbey that once stood on the site of the house. The walls were adorned with family portraits staring vacantly out into the vast hall.

"Inigo Jones," Alice said knowingly.

"Inigo who?"

"Inigo Jones. He had a hand in the design of this place. I don't know exactly what he did but the guidebook goes on a lot about him. The Duke gets groups of historians here from time to time who drool over the architecture. You have to admit it's special though, don't you? Now come on, we can get to the yard down there through that side door."

Back in the library the two men were oblivious to the ghosts' departure and continued their conversation. Jules was not to be bowed.

"I will have some capital from this event which I intend to invest in more profit-making exercises." He noticed that his father was looking over his shoulder at the photos on the mantel piece. "It's no good using the 'Mother wouldn't have approved,' ploy. She ran off with the seal keeper of all things."

The Duke sat down distraught. "Don't remind me. I'm trying to wipe that from my mind and remember the good times... but the pungent smell of dead fish just won't leave me. Her clothes stank of it.

I knew something was wrong between us but why him? What did he have that I couldn't provide?"

"Fish suppers, presumably," Jules replied sarcastically, "anyway, you're in no position, you were messing about with the girl from the ice-cream parlour, so you're not so innocent."

"True, I didn't hide that very well, but I couldn't resist those neat little biscuit cones... and her Tutti-Frutti was something to behold... Now while I have your attention... I haven't told you what happened at the club in London. I met up with my old Eton chum Iroko Pine. You remember, I've told you about him. Fancied himself as a bit of an actor but he was too wooden. He ended up as a producer, spending most of his legacy on West End musicals, which as it happened, netted him a tidy profit. He's also a trustee at the Victoria and Albert Museum and I happened to mention the idea of updating our guidebook."

"What idea?"

"Well, it came to me on the spur of the moment. Our guidebook is ten years old and it's about time we revamped it."

"We can't afford it for goodness' sake. The budget for the house maintenance has just been blown by you on the restoration of the paintings in the gallery and you know we can only spend where it's guaranteed a profit."

"That's the point Jules. He mentioned a scholar doing their PhD who needs some field experience. It's a no brainer. They get experience, we get a new guide and just for the cost of bed & board for a couple of weeks. What do you say?"

"I'm not happy about it, there are still the printing costs to contend with. Well, you can deal with it, but I want to approve the final proof and we need to watch the budget carefully. Don't forget the new attractions we need to include in this new guide, not just the stately home."

"Deal."

Jules was surprised at this sudden twist in the conversation. They did need to improve the guidebook, but had he been duped again by his cunning father?

Suddenly static chatter came from a two-way radio disrupting their conversation.

"VJ…VJ… are you receiving, over?"

Jules unclipped the radio from his belt and held it to his mouth while pressing the button on the side, "VJ receiving, over."

"Can you please report to the ballroom?… Over."

"Roger, will be there in ten, out." He turned his attention back to his father, "Sorry, I need to go and check on the festival, there are people waiting for me. Find out the printing costs before you go too far. We can budget the expense between the house and the other departments but only if we can afford it, and I mean, if!" He nodded at his father and hurriedly left the room, thoughts of the new guidebook drifting into his subconscious.

The Duke again looked towards the wedding photo and urn on the mantelpiece shaking his head in resignation. "Well, at least you came back to me in the end," he said wistfully. He then stood up and exited the room through the door in the bookcase.

6
The Meeting

Saturday 3rd August. Morning

Under the tree opposite the entrance to the stable yard an Orion Galactic trooper sat on a park bench. The stable clock struck eleven as excited children approached the trooper for pictures, eagerly encouraged by their parents poised ready with cameras. To make their day even more complete, he was now joined by a member of the Gorog high command. The arch enemies greeted each other. The Gorog was in full combat uniform, his rhino head poking out of an oversized spacesuit while his long, red squirrel-like tail sprung up against his back. He was carrying a six-foot lance equipped with laser generator at its tip. It was a strange mix of imagination by the writers but seemed to fit the surreal storylines and the outlandish, imagined planet of their birth. He waddled towards the trooper, stopping for pictures with children and geeks who were old enough to know better than pose with rubber suited imposters. But such was the draw of the programme that it didn't seem to matter. Security eventually appeared and ushered the public away to give the characters a break under the shade of the tree near the cafe. The Gorog reversed towards the seat but had difficulty sitting.

"Pull the tail up between your legs." He followed the instruction from the trooper and sat with the tail now sticking up between his thighs. He hastily adjusted it and closed his legs together, which did little to improve the situation.

"This latex mask stinks!"

"You should try this full-face helmet, I can't see a thing and it smells like it's been stored near the urinals. It's not healthy," the spaceman grumbled.

"Quite frankly, I don't care. Using this weekend as a smokescreen for the exchange was foolish. I want the money. You've got the goods, I have an agreement with your boss."

"We don't have the goods!" The spaceman protested. "It's been lost in transit. I went to pick it up from the drop last night, but it wasn't there.

Your stooge didn't play the game and ran off."

"I don't have a stooge. We had an agreement. There were to be no intermediaries. I stuck to my end of the bargain."

"Well, either someone was in the wrong place at the wrong time or you're lying."

"Who did you see?"

"Young lad in the loft saw me in the shadows. I had to deal with him. No witnesses that was the deal. He fled along my alternative escape route. I locked the gate and went back to the stables but the goods were nowhere to be found."

The Gorog became more animated. "I didn't have anyone there... what do you mean, dealt with him?"

"Well, whoever he was, he won't be bothering us again," the Trooper assured him casually.

"Was your cover blown?"

"It would have been if I hadn't acted. Anyway you can still claim the insurance."

"Don't be ridiculous." He turned violently towards the Trooper. The squirrel tail sprang back up between his legs and hit the horn on his mask. He hastily pushed it back down. "If this is uncovered there will be an investigation by the insurance company and we'll all be in serious trouble! This is turning into an Ealing Comedy. Tell your boss the deal is off. I want no more to do with this amateurish affair. I regret ever getting involved."

The Trooper considered the Gorog's words carefully. "My mother's from Ealing and she's not a comedian. You had better watch your step. The Boss wants the goods or someone else might get hurt."

"You oaf! Ealing comedies were films made at Ealing studios in the forties and fifties. Don't you know anything? It's not a personal slight on your mother, whom I'm sure is a lovely person."

"Wouldn't know, she abandoned us when I was five... never seen her since."

"This just gets worse." The Gorog attempted to put his head in his hands, but the horn caught on his sleeve. "Tell your boss you missed the drop and the deal is off," he said angrily.

"No can-do rubber features, think on."

"No, it's up to you. You sort it out. I should never have trusted your Governor, he's been getting into hot water ever since prep school. I want the money, or the goods returned." He stood up and the tail sprang back but now with a distinct kink where he'd been sitting on it. He didn't care, he had to get the hot, sweaty mask off, it smelt even worse following exposure to the sun. He waddled off towards the kitchen garden. Immediately after, the Trooper stood up and headed towards the marketplace. On the way, both of them were accosted by fans for pictures, which they reluctantly posed for.

7
Into the Lion's Den

Saturday 3rd August. Morning

At eleven thirty, the Safari Park was full of activity despite the distraction of the festival at the house. A good percentage of visitors had chosen to take in the estates' attractions before ending with the sci-fi events in the courtyard.

Brothers, Oliver and Henry Clarkson, were first employed by the estate four years ago to empty bins and keep the public areas tidy. Their willingness for hard work didn't go unnoticed by the head keeper and before long they were co-opted into pets' corner where they learnt to care for the small, friendly animals. Goats, rabbits, hamsters and chickens wandered free in an enclosure near the stables. It was a favourite meeting point for families, with ice creams and a restaurant close by to satisfy their hunger and extract money from their pockets. After two years of small animal husbandry, they were promoted to the safari park enclosures. Now, they were part of the team responsible for helping with the care of the larger animals under close supervision of the gamekeepers.

It was feeding time for the big cats. Dressed in their khaki overalls and pith helmet outfits, the brothers loaded joints of meat into the back of the black and white zebra striped Land Rover. Henry climbed in the back where Oliver then secured him in the yellow tubular protective cage enabling him to safely distribute the food. Oliver climbed into the driver's seat and drove from the compound to the entrance of the lion enclosure, passing the vacant pens used to house the lions in inclement weather and carry out veterinary duties. Jan was at the gate to meet them and unlock the outer gateway, letting them into the holding area. Once she had relocked the gate, she pressed a button and the inner gate slid silently open accessing the four acre enclosure. Oliver drove forward as it glided back stopping with a loud clang as it hit the stop and the magnetic lock secured it.

Henry felt safe in the steel cage, however, he always had butterflies in his stomach at this moment. After all, they were in the lion's domain with a cargo of raw meat. Not your everyday job. This was a long way from feeding the rabbits in Pets corner.

They could see the public road snaking its way around the enclosure. Visitor's cars moved slowly, their expectant passengers gazing out, wide eyed, noses pushed against the glass trying to glimpse the King of the Jungle. The presence of the Land Rover only added to the anticipation. Feeding time hopefully meant more activity from the lazy cats snoozing in the shade of the trees. Oliver drove to a clearing and stopped while Henry eased the first joint of meat out of the hatch at the back of the cage, checking first to ensure they were not being stalked. There had been incidents in the past where keepers had been caught unawares. Although behind bars, the power of the animal lashing out at the delivery hatch had caused injuries. The leg of beef dropped to the ground with a thud. From the shelter the alpha male lion, Goliath, lethargically watched the activity taking place 100 yards away. Oliver drove across the clearing to an area near the pride of females sunning themselves by the fence. Henry repeated the dropping of meat, this time only 50 yards away. Again, they were treated with indifference.

Oliver slid open the small window behind the seats, Henry knelt down and holding the cage, looked into the cab. "Lazy lot of buggers today, there's usually one who shows some interest before they all come over. Must be the warm weather making them dopey," Oliver said.

"Well, I'm not wasting meat, we're not here to feed the crows," he slid the window shut, noticing the birds circling down from their high roost ready to pounce on a free meal as soon as he drove away.

He restarted the engine and followed a track through the undergrowth near a rocky outcrop away from the gaze of the public road.

Henry banged the roof of the cab. Oliver slid open the window again.

"Somethings not right," Henry shouted over the noise of the engine. "Pull over to the right behind those rocks, I think I saw something." Oliver did as requested.

"Oh God! No… it can't be!"

Oliver looked across to where Henry was pointing. He could see some rags and red staining to the back of the rocks. He could hear his brother heaving in the cage behind him. Now, directly in front, he could see what appeared to be a carcase with sinews being pulled at by greedy crows. He grabbed the radio.

"Oliver to base, over. Oliver to base, are you receiving, over?" There was a crackle of static.

"Base here, what's up, over?"

"We have a Code One… repeat Code One… Clear the enclosure now… We are in sector seven, south side of the VIP gate, over."

"Roger that. Code One procedure will start now, hold your position, a team is on its way, out."

The scenario taking place was practiced monthly as part of the regular emergency training. Never did they think they'd actually be doing it for real. Oliver was now beginning to feel faint as the enormity of the situation sank in.

"Oliver, are you receiving… come in?"

"Receiving, over" he replied faintly.

"Ok, the cars are slowly being cleared without raising alarm and none are now entering. Head keeper is on his way, and we are preparing the paddock to receive all the lions. Round up will take place in about ten minutes… are you both safe, over?"

"I'm fine… Henry's been sick and looks awful, but we are ok, over."

"Roger that, the team is leaving now, out."

Oliver reversed back from the scene and reached to the shelf under the dash, grabbed a bottle of water and passed it through the hatch behind him to Henry. "No wonder they weren't hungry!" he said trying to lighten the air. "I've radioed base, they're on the way."

"Did you tell them it's a Code One?"

"Yeah… How are you feeling?"

"Horrible… I think I'm going to be sick again… I can't believe it. Who do you think it is or was?"

8
Galactic Market

Saturday 3ʳᵈ August. Morning

At eleven forty-five, Jules walked out the front door of the house and around the side to the ballroom, taking time to soak up the atmosphere in the stable yard. The market was thronging with visitors, some wearing outrageous costumes, he had no idea who they were meant to be. The fanaticism around the television series had gone completely over his head. He had little time for science fiction, preferring historical drama and documentaries, and that was only when he could find time to sit and watch television. He made a mental note to investigate the sci-fi genre further, he could be missing something, and it may be in his interest to understand the appeal of cult TV for future ventures.

He moved behind the stall where Frank was working frantically, serving the enthusiastic fans. A father and son were buying a poster. They had chosen the iconic image of the crew stood at the base of the Century Hawk landing craft, blasters drawn, facing out to protect the access ramp.

"Wow dad, this is heavy," the boy exclaimed, holding the tube containing the poster."

"And so it ought to be, charging these prices for a printed piece of paper!" His father was not amused at the cost of £10.00 for what he perceived as worthless tat. "Now, go careful with it, we need to wrap it up nicely for your brother's birthday."

"Can I have one too, what about one of Captain Benjie?"

The poster of Georgina Best, 'Flight Captain Benjie,' was by far the most popular among the teenage boys. Her body-hugging outfit accentuating her voluptuous figure, with blaster held in a provocative manner, was irresistible to the pubescent fans.

"I don't think so, son!" his father said, not wishing to shell out another ten pounds but even he could see the appeal. The vision stirred long forgotten memories of his teenage years and the poster of Marilyn Monroe on his bedroom wall.

"Hi Frank, I can see you're busy, are you having a good day?" Jules asked.

"It's crazy," Frank replied as he stuffed cash from a purchaser into the money belt around his waist. He then turned to face Jules, "One of the lads didn't turn up this morning so it's been a bit frantic. It'll calm down soon, when the show starts in the ballroom. Hopefully I'll have time then to tidy the stall and re-stock ready for the next wave. You can stay and help if you like?" he appealed but knew the answer.

"That's very nice of you to ask but I can assure you I'd be no help, I'll leave it in your expert hands. I want to go to the ballroom and see first-hand what all the fuss is about."

"Have you heard any news about Andy Cross, I hear he hasn't arrived yet?" Frank asked, continuing the conversation while taking money from the eager punters.

Jules looked back as he was turning to leave. "I don't know. What does he do?"

"You really don't know your Galactic Jump history do you? Perhaps it's best if you stick to observing!" Frank laughed.

"No, sorry... I think I have some catching up to do. I'll ask John Pearce if he knows anything when I get to the Ballroom."

"He should be with the other actors ready for the midday show. That's one reason why there are so many people here. He rarely makes public appearances, and the rumour mill has been alive with anticipation of a visit today."

Just the very mention of his name was having an effect on the crowd around the stall listening to the conversation. Jules could sense the increased anticipation and hear the whispered confidences. It had to be true. Their hero was going to be there.

Jules was now getting intrigued by the expectation. "I have to go, I'm not going to miss this, see you later." He moved quickly to the private kitchen garden where he could enter the stage area by the back door, to avoid the crowds. As he entered the building the two-way radio crackled into life.

"VJ, are you receiving over? Come in VJ, over."

Jules grabbed at the radio and unclipped it from his belt. "COME IN VJ," it screamed at him again. He hastily pressed the 'talk' button, "VJ receiving... over,"

"VJ, base here… please contact the Keepers Office by a land line urgently…over."

Jules paused, his mind went into a spin. *'There must be a serious problem if he had to phone the keeper directly.'* He could feel it in the pit of his stomach, *'One of the animals must be sick… has someone been hurt? Has something been damaged?'*

"VJ did you receive… over?" The voice was louder and more urgent.

He squeezed the radio again "Roger… received… will call… standby… over and out."

He was pleased that his response sounded professional and ran across the kitchen garden entering the Orangery. He fumbled for his key as he approached the office at the far end of the glass house. He unlocked the door marked private, entered and grabbed the phone on his desk. The keeper's number was keyed in, so he pressed the illuminated button labelled 'K'. There was the slightest of ring at the other end and he could detect the urgency of the receiver being grabbed.

"VJ here, what's happening?"

"Code One sir, in the lion enclosure. Looks like a feeder. The protocol has been followed, public removed, and the lions are being moved out of the drive-through enclosure into their paddock."

"My God! That's just terrible, I prayed this would never happen again,. Who discovered it?"

"The Clarkson brothers, they were out on the regular feeding run, but the lions weren't hungry. Then they found out why."

"Poor boys, they must be in a real state… where are they now?"

"They're with the nurse in the first-aid room. Still in shock but distracted by going through the incident forms."

"Good, she'll monitor them. As soon as she thinks they're ready, take them home to get some rest. Send a car down to pick me up, I'd like to see them before they go, we need to assess the incident before calling the police."

Jules hung up the phone and sat at his desk. Burying his head in his hands, he breathed heavily. *'Why do people do such stupid things?'* He felt sorry for the victim, they must have been in a terrible place mentally to consider such a thing. It had happened once before back in the sixties and cast a shadow over the park for many years. The practice drill was instigated following the enquiry, in case it should ever happen again. Jules mind was in a whirl. Horror, sadness and fear for the future of the park, hit him in equal measure. Perhaps they were wrong, perhaps it wasn't a feeder, (the rather flippant nickname given to a suicide victim). He had to see for himself.

He left the office and went through the house to the front door where a safari Jeep arrived and whisked him away.

The keeper's office was part of a long log cabin in a compound over-looking a large gravel yard surrounded by pens of various sizes to accommodate animals when sheltering, feeding or receiving veterinary services. Radiating away from these pens was access to the large, fenced enclosures of the safari park.

Head keeper, John Hammond, was waiting on the veranda for Jules's arrival. He greeted him solemnly. "Thanks for coming so quickly, I know you're busy."

"That's irrelevant John, how are the boys?"

"Follow me." John led the way to the first-aid room where Oliver and Henry sat with the nurse. On seeing Jules, they automatically stood up. "Hello sir, sorry about this," Henry said, while Oliver looked more sub-dued.

"Don't be ridiculous, it's not your fault, you followed the training to the letter, well done. How are you feeling, it must have been shocking?"

"The lions just weren't hungry, we guessed something was up with them but... God it was horrible." Henry started to break down. The nurse held his arm and beckoned him to sit down again. The thought of what they had seen was too much for anyone to imagine.

"You've had a terrible experience. Don't worry about anything, take some time off. The nurse will visit every day to see how you are. You remember from the training, it's important for you to talk about this and relax. You're currently in shock but it will subside. You're not to return to work until you and the nurse consider you are ready. Don't worry about your wages, they'll not be affected."

"Thank you, sir. Why do people do this? I can't imagine what they are thinking."

"Neither can I, it's very sad. Nurse will take you home after the police have had a chance to talk to you. I don't want you driving till the shock has abated, it's too dangerous. You can come and pick up your car in a couple of days if you feel up to it."

"Thank you, sir," Oliver said.

"I have to go now, but if you need anything or just want to talk, my door is always open to you." Jules turned to John. "Can we go to the site now please?"

"Yes sir, I've just had the 'all clear', the cats are now secured in the paddock. Jump into my car and I'll take you to the scene. Two keepers have gone ahead to check the area."

They drove past the lion house where the food is prepared and they can be isolated for health checks, treatments and simply to provide shelter from inclement weather. The outer gate of the 'airlock' into the enclosure was open, indicating the lions were secure. They could be seen patrolling up and down along the fence producing terrifying roars, leaving the staff in no doubt about their annoyance at being brought back into the smaller paddock. The Land Rover went through the inner gate which was opened by one of the staff and closed immediately behind them. This was done to protect any wildlife from getting in rather than a cat getting out, after all they were safely locked away.

They moved into a large, wooded area and then emerged into the open, undulating grass land interspersed with shrubs. The now empty single track public road could be seen weaving around inside the enclosure. They headed across the grass and joined the road nearer the VIP gates. They could see two other black and white stripped vehicles off the road to their right, with keepers standing around uncomfortably. Jules and John joined them and stepped out of the car.

Although screened by the trees, they could hear music and the bustle of the crowds coming from the house and stables. It was a distant world of joy just the other side of the fence, the polar opposite of the horrific environment they found themselves in.

"What have we got Mike?" John asked the nearest and more senior man.

"See for yourself," Mike replied, and then noticing Jules, touched his cap in a vague salute. "Sir," he added in recognition, bowing his head slightly. He beckoned them over behind the shrubs, to the site of a dark bloodstained rock, behind which were the remains of a body. Unmistakably a human body, its clothes torn to shreds, dismembered bones stripped of flesh strewn over a wide area. Flies were buzzing around in a frenzy, disturbed by the bravest of the crows that couldn't resist the chance of a free meal despite the men's presence.

"OK," Jules said trying to separate his feelings and maintain a professional detached demeanour. "Don't touch anything. I'll call the police. You all go back to the lodge, you can do nothing here. We continue the Code One protocol. Talk amongst yourselves but don't share this with the outside world until we have investigated the incident."

Relieved, they quickly mounted their vehicles and headed back across the field to the courtyard.

"Right John, take me through the VIP gates, I'll phone from my office."

They drove along the road away from the scene to the gates, a guard let them into a long airlock with a security lodge halfway along. The guard noted Jules in the passenger seat and saluted. As the gate closed, Jules caught sight of damage to the 'Woodford Abbey' lettering mounted over the gate.

"What's happened to the letter 'F', we only replaced the sign a couple of months ago for the royal visit?" he asked.

"I have no idea sir, looks like it's been hit by something, that's a nasty dent. I'll get it looked at straight away."

"No, leave it for now, nothing must be disturbed. We only use it as an entrance for special guests, so it can be sorted out when all this is over. Do the guards know what's going on?"

"Not exactly sir, they know there's a Code One, so I'm sure they've worked it out."

"OK, tell them, but keep it brief, ask them to stay on duty till the police get here, we'll be guided by them. Then I want you to do a full check of the perimeter fence for any breach and report back to me. It should be fine, but you never know. I can't understand how the victim gained access."

They then passed through the outer gate and across the road to the house. Jules got out and weaved quickly through the families, aliens and spacemen enjoying the festival in the glorious sunshine, happily oblivious to the horror only a short distance away behind the fences. He walked through the yard past a queue of autograph hunters holding books and souvenirs, waiting for a chance to meet their heroes in the stables. Once through the private wooden gate in the far corner, Jules broke into a trot along the kitchen garden path, through the orangery and into his office. He lifted the receiver and dialled Holeford Police station on their direct number.

After a short conversation with the duty officer, he replaced the receiver and went to the filing cabinet. He retrieved the folder marked Code One on the spine, where someone had also written 'Feeder File' in red ink. This didn't seem funny now, this was no time for jesting. He retrieved a black marker pen from his top drawer and obliterated the writing. He opened the thick file on his desk and scanned the first page which contained a list of critical actions for a Code One incident in the form of short bullet points. All appeared to have been done correctly, the keepers had followed the protocol to the letter. Relieved that the regular training had prepared his team well, he sat down and jotted notes on the incident into an A4 notebook, he would write this up fully in his diary later when he had time and a clear head. The diary was part of the Health and Safety procedures. It had to contain an accurate summary of all the day's events. It was not the place for emotional outpourings, which, in the future, may not read correctly. He was aware that the diary was a legal document, the official record of everything that happened in the park in the unlikely need of reference in the future. He placed the file in the cabinet, then headed across the kitchen garden, through the back door of the house and up the servant stair to the library. Pushing the hidden door into the library open, he strode in, finding his father sitting behind his desk staring vacantly down the extensive room. His face was flushed red with recent exertion, his hair was damp and clung to his scalp.

Jules approached. "What happened to you, you're all wet?"

"I was feeling uncomfortable, the heat in here was getting unbearable so I went for a swim to freshen up. Is there a law against that?"

"Not at all father, but it's just not like you, are you feeling alright?"

"Never felt better, don't count on me curling up my toes for a long while yet. Anyway, what's up with you? You could do with a cool down running in here like a scolded cat."

"I've just called the police, there's a Code One in the lion enclosure." He waited for the penny to drop.

"No, not another feeder, that's all we need." The Duke buried his head in his hands. He was fully aware of the consequences after the incident in the sixties that nearly closed the park for good. "What happened?"

"The keepers have followed the protocol to the letter. I visited the site, there's definitely a body, or what remains of one."

"We need to handle this carefully Jules. The place is crawling with press and visitors. If this news gets out now without a proper investigation there'll be panic and untold damage to our reputation."

"I'm aware of that father. I'm going to meet the police at the front of the house and take them straight to the compound. We should be able to contain their investigation out of sight of the public, at least for a while."

"Good lad. Why couldn't they jump off a bridge? What on earth possesses someone to jump out in front of a hungry lion, they must have a screw loose. I'll call our legal advisers." The Duke fumbled with the telephone and dialled the number of the family lawyers. Jules left the room, closing the door behind him and headed across the landing, pausing to look at the paintings of his ancestors, wondering what they would be thinking if they were alive today. He then ran down the stairs to the entrance hall where James, the butler, was poised to open the door. '*How does he do that? He must have a sixth sense, always in the right place at the right time*', he thought.

"Thank you, James."

"Very good, Sir," he replied using his best 'Jeeves' accent. "Will there be anything else, sir?"

"No thank you."

Jules stood on the steps as the large heavy oak door closed behind him. He smiled to himself, he still found it surreal that James should act like all the butlers he had ever seen on television. In this day and age, he found it comforting that some traditions continued, aware that his life was a privilege reserved for the few. He felt a pang of guilt that he held his position on the back of great men who had shaped the history of the country, while he played at sideshow attractions to support the estate and provide employment for his tenants. He looked over to the immaculately clipped Knot Garden, its colourful aromatic flowers popping their heads up over the box hedge frames, giving the impression of an Indian silk carpet laid out in front of the house. It was framed by the drive, which started a mile away at the main gate just visible from the house, the tarmac road zigzagging across the immense undulating field of the deer park eventually changing to gravel as it encircled the garden, looping past the lichen patterned stone steps below the main entrance doors. He sighed, he had no time to admire the work of the gardeners, he could hear the distant sound of a siren heading towards the estate. He radioed ahead to the keeper's office for assistance and then tensed, rehearsing his greeting in preparation for this unwelcome and distressful undertaking.

9

Portland Bill

Saturday 3rd August. Morning

Wilf and George moved to the ballroom to see what all the excitement was about. The area on the lawn to the side of the building, was a hive of activity, with articulated lorries being offloaded into the auditorium. Large black reinforced boxes on wheels rattled down the metal ramps and across to the loading bay at the side of the stage. Several men were struggling to negotiate long sections of cumbersome lighting gantry from the vehicle and through the doors. Raised voices could be heard and colourful language pierced the normally tranquil setting.

Alice decided to take Tom on the remainder of his house tour. George was always drumming into her the risks of moving around near the public, as they may cause a psychic incident. There was always the chance of being seen and triggering unnecessary upset. Alice, however, was in a rebellious mood today.

"It's OK for them to go swanning off to the ballroom, so stuff it, let's go to the market," she said to Tom, as they wandered across the landing and floated down the ornate stairs. "We'll go through the long gallery, you haven't seen that yet, it's pretty special." They turned right in the entrance hall, through large ornate hardwood doors and entered a long room running the whole length of the house. "Historically the gentry would promenade up and down here, all dressed in their finery showing off their wealth," Alice explained.

Tom was in awe of the room, with its high ceiling decorated in the rococo style, reflecting the opulence of the house. The walls were dotted with hundreds of paintings gathered during the family's grand tours of Europe. Chippendale furniture placed against the walls, sat upon silk carpets from the Far East. Several red velvet upholstered chairs were placed down the centre facing the walls, for visitors to sit and admire the artwork. They wandered slowly along, Tom admiring the paintings. "These are amazing, Alice. They must be worth a fortune."

"I suppose so, I think they're a bit dull. I like more modern paintings myself. There's one down here that I do quite like." She pointed to a canvas opposite the large fireplace, whose coal black cast iron fireback, featured knights on horseback, hemmed in by the grate, unable to escape.

"This is a good one." She was pointing at a geometric painting of a single-story house. A single palm tree arched over in the background with a swimming pool in the foreground, the sunlight appearing to dance over the surface of the water.

"That looks like a Hockney! The splash or little splash… something like that. Anyway, it looks original."

"You seem to know a lot about painting," Alice said, surprised at his reaction to what she saw as just a nice picture.

"I'm studying art at University, I was only here to help out at the market and earn a few quid." His face contorted with anger. "It's not fair, I had my whole life ahead of me and now…"

"That's terribly sad Tom, but these things happen, you just need to make the best of it."

"That's easy for you to say. I don't know what's going to happen to me. Do I stay here or go somewhere else? Do I just fade away? It's so horrid. I have so many questions."

"Eric will be back soon. He'll go through the paperwork with you and give you some options, I'm sure. In the meantime, let's try to have a bit of fun."

Tom didn't look convinced. "Fun! That's pushing it a bit, I haven't even seen anyone looking for me, it's like no one missed me and no one cares."

"I'm sure they do. I know, let's go out to the market and see if anyone's asking about you."

As they moved down the gallery heading towards the doors leading to the stable yard, Tom spotted another painting. "That's a Rembrandt."

"I have no idea. It looks very dark. I don't like it much, he should've put the light on when he painted it."

"I didn't know this was on show here."

"Why would you?"

"No reason, just look at it though, it's beautiful. Look at the way the light plays with the velvet on the costume."

"It's too dark."

"It's not. Stand here." Tom pointed to a spot on the floor a few feet away from the picture. "Look at the dark background… study it, do you see anything?"

"Yes, now you mention it, I can see something…there's a table… and a vase of flowers. I've never seen them before. Hey! That's pretty cool."

"I'll take cool for now, that's a good start. You see, you have to look closely into the paintings. They all have a story to tell, with knowledge you can decipher the images. Anyway, enough of an art lesson, can we go and see if anyone is missing me?" The paintings had momentarily distracted Tom. His mind now returned to the activity outside and his disappearance. He moved ahead towards the door.

"Hang on, I'm coming," Alice said catching him up. "You know a lot about art, I'm impressed."

"Yeah, well I suppose it's my thing. Or rather was to be my thing."

They passed through the doors together towards the marketplace, and soon found their way to the poster stall where Frank was busy trying to keep up with demand. Tom closely studied the cardboard tubes containing all the posters. All were neatly arranged in their display boxes. He moved behind the stall, "Sorry Frank. I wish I could help you, but I have a strange situation here."

Frank was cursing under his breath, unaware of Tom's spirit being next to him.

"Bloody students, they always let me down. When I get hold of Tom, he's going to have both barrels, he can pay me back for the lodgings and walk home. Bloody loser."

"Well, at least he misses me. That's something I suppose." Tom shrugged his shoulders.

"Can you see the man who tried to shoot you?" asked Alice, insensitively.

"I don't know what he looked like. It was gloomy and he was wearing dark clothes. He did have a slight limp now I come to think of it, so that's worth looking out for, and of course he had a gun."

"What about them?" Alice pointed to three Orion Guards walking around the stalls with blasters hanging from their belts.

"Don't be stupid, they're just toys."

"They look like guns to me."

"It's just fancy dress, plastic replicas from the show."

"These people are rather sad, don't they have better hobbies?" A portly Orion Guard passed them, his stomach pushing the skin-tight combat shirt to bursting point. His trousers were held together by a silver belt as the zip was unable to pull right up. His helmet sat on top of his head above the ears in a delicate balancing act. Rather like a sea lion performing tricks with a football. "Look at him, he must be fifty and he's far too fat for that uniform, he looks ridiculous," Alice said giggling.

"That may be, but their enthusiasm for this show is making a lot of people rich and who are we to say what's good or bad, they love it."

"I guess so," Alice said shrugging her shoulders. "Never mind that now though, we need to see if we can track down your killer. Let's have a good look for a man with a limp, then go and see how George and Wilf are getting on. They'll be in the Ballroom watching the stage preparations."

As they moved from the stable yard, Tom looked back to the stall. '*Sorry Frank, it's not my fault,*' he thought wistfully. Alice led the way as Jules ran past brushing through them towards the walled garden.

"What's up with him?" Tom asked.

"That's Jules. Something must be up for him to be running around, he's usually quite a cool customer." They continued the search for anyone with a limp.

They finally gave up and headed to the ballroom, entering at the side of the stage to be greeted with the clang of metal and thump of hammers as the set was being assembled for the evening show. The dance floor, which formed the auditorium, was full of chairs in neat rows. At the back of the room portable, terraced seating had already been erected to improve the view for the audience and maximise the capacity of the room. To the sides, were scaffold platforms containing cameras and lighting. Sound technicians were frantically connecting cables to the mixing deck and barking instructions to their colleagues on the stage. In the front seats, half a dozen people were watching the stage crew fill the area with boxes and scenery from the transport outside.

The ballroom was built during the time of the fifth Duke. He adored the theatre and was a major sponsor of the Royal Opera House in London.

In return for his patronage, they brought productions to the estate. To enable this, he had a stage built by extending the old Georgian ballroom and installing a stage to West End specification.

He was then able to invite his wealthy contemporaries and entertain them while showing off his wealth and power, thus improving his status in London society.

It was this facility that made Woodford Abbey so desirable to the makers of *Galactic Jump* for the launch of their new series. The festival was a golden opportunity to draw in backers by demonstrating the demand for new shows and promote future merchandising opportunities. *Galactic Jump* had last aired five years ago, and despite its cult following was destined never to return to the screen. There had been production issues with the last series due to the television companies reduced budget, coupled with actors' controversial activities, not least Clive Monkton's brush with the law. This issue alone had caused problems with the stakeholders, but such was the continued demand for the show, contracts were renegotiated to bring back the cash cow that is, '*Galactic Jump*.'

Tom looked in awe at the sumptuous ballroom. Gold embossed plasterwork and classical works of art painted directly on to the high ceiling. The chandeliers' crystal glass refracted rainbow colours from the sun light striking them through the tall sash windows overlooking the lawns and lake.

"There they are." Alice spotted Wilf and George high up on the terraced seating. She moved with Tom to the front of the stage, carefully avoiding the stage crew, busy bolting together the complex steel structure.

"Cooee", cried Alice.

"Give us a song," Wilf shouted back, seeing the two of them appear. Tom looked totally bemused.

Alice however, obliged by singing the first two verses of '*Oh Wandering One*' from '*The Pirates of Penzance.*' This was the production they were all appearing in at the Holeford Opera House when they were killed in the devastating fire.

Tom listened in admiration at the short performance. "Wow, you've got a lovely voice. Alice, that was wonderful."

"Thank you, I've still got it," she smiled and curtsied low. Wilf and George stood up, applauded and beckoned them over.

They floated down off the stage. Tom went too far, and his legs disappeared into the floor, but he soon corrected himself.

Alice laughed, "You'll soon get the hang of it."

Tom repositioned so his feet were at ground level, and they headed to the back of the room. They passed several men sat in the stalls looking at clipboards, while shouting orders to the stagehands and engineers.

"They must be the directors with their support staff," Tom suggested. "Rumour has it that tonight's show is going to be extra special. There's been a lot of speculation about who's going to be here, but the producer has given nothing away."

They joined Wilf and George watching the antics on the stage. The stagehands stood on tower scaffolding, clanking and banging the prefabricated metal sections together as they were lifted into place by a forklift. At the back another team were attaching weathered metallic painted backdrops to another section ready to be lifted into place.

"Can you work out what they're building?" Alice asked, perplexed by the whole thing.

George watched, fascinated by the mechanical ballet being performed in front of them. "No idea, but it looks like it's going to be something special, what with the fancy staging and the media area being set up. This is very elaborate for a second-rate television series. Have you seen who's here? Look over there, BBC News and ITN are setting up cameras. This is going to be a national event," he said excitedly.

"By the way," Alice said, just noticing what Wilf was wearing, "Where on earth did you get that scruffy trench coat and what have you done to your hair, you look like a tramp?"

"He's releasing his inner Columbo in the hope of detecting who killed Tom," George said sarcastically.

"And is that helping?" Alice asked, somewhat sceptical that dressing as a fictional detective would improve his powers of deduction.

Wilf grinned, "Well, at least I am trying rather than swanning round like an ethereal tour guide," he said, looking directly at Alice and Tom.

"That's a bit unnecessary Wilf. I'll have you know we've been out into the market looking for clues, but Tom didn't recognise anyone from last night. Or rather, we didn't see anyone limping, which is about all we have to go on."

"I can't help that it was dark, and I was too busy running and hiding to take down his particulars," Tom said indignantly.

"Well, I am currently observing my prime suspect," Wilf announced proudly, pointing to the group of men in the front row. "You see that man on the left with the notepad barking out orders? I think he's the producer, well, he has a distinct limp and a black coat hanging over the seat."

Alice put her hands on her hips and squared up to Wilf. "Is that it?" she asked scathingly. "How closely have you been watching him?"

"I noticed him as soon as we came into the ballroom actually. All I need now are motive, opportunity and evidence."

"Then you probably don't care that his left leg is lying on the seat next to him. It's a wooden leg, you muppet! He can certainly limp but running down rickety stairs will be a bit beyond him and he doesn't look like a smoker. I noticed his leg when we came off the stage to join you two."

"How do you know he's a non-smoker?" Wilf asked challengingly.

"I can tell, call it a woman's intuition, he doesn't look like one. Also, if he was going to keep popping out for a cigarette he would keep his leg on."

"Hmm, good point", Wilf conceded.

"Anyway, Tom would have noticed someone with a wooden leg chasing him."

"Alright, smarty pants." Wilf turned to face Tom, "Do you agree with me or Alice, does he look like your pursuer?"

"Well, I don't think so. He was a well-built man and much taller."

"Hello, who's this?" Wilf said. Suddenly, from the side door a heavily built man entered the room wearing a long black leather coat, scarf and fedora hat. "Doesn't he know it's thirty degrees outside, he must be boiling." The men in the front of the auditorium stood up and waved him over.

"Wow, that's William Easton… you know…the film director," Tom said.

"Never heard of him. But he looks the right size and shape to be your murderer," Wilf said.

Tom was scathing at the idea. "Nah, he's worth millions. He directed *'Galactic Jump: The mines of Poodoor.'* You must have heard of it, it launched the whole series and kick-started the cult following. That's why so many fans are here today. Also, he hasn't got a limp."

William joined the men on the front row, they shook hands, and all took their seats. The director raised a megaphone to his mouth. "All clear the stage. OK Tech, are you ready to go?"

"Good to go sir," a voice yelled from behind the terraced seating. The stage crew climbed down off the platform and stood well back in the ballroom.

The megaphone rose again. "Ready, on my mark, three, two, one… action."

They could then hear the whine of electric motors and slowly the skeletal steel framework shuddered. The front section laying on the stage rose like a huge jaw, gently and assuredly, it continued on its path, slowing to a crawl as it softly touched against the upper frame.

"And down, on my mark, three, two, one… action," the director bellowed.

The frame came to life again, the motors now acting as a brake to control the descent and the steel structure came to rest on the stage again with a gentle thud.

The team in the room applauded, relieved that the test had gone well. "Right, double check the mountings and get the panels fixed on. We have until five, then its full rehearsal and curtains closed, ready for tonight's performance. Well done everyone, now let's get going." William Easton shook hands and walked towards the door deep in conversation with the director.

"Hardly worth him coming to see that," George commented.

Loud music and sound effects reverberated around the now near empty room as the engineers tested the sound levels.

"I think it's time for us to leave, this is unbearable," George shouted over the din. "Tom, you'll have to give us a briefing on '*Galactic Jump*,' before we return tonight. I'm looking forward to seeing what they're going to do, knowing more of the story might help."

As they moved away past the temporary bar being positioned in the long gallery, they heard a siren.

They stopped and listened carefully, "It's getting closer, I think it's coming down the drive, let's go and have a look," Alice said excitedly.

They detoured through the wall out onto the grass verge by the road not far from the point where Tom had hidden from his pursuer. He could see the buttress he had concealed himself behind and the bushes opposite, shielding the high fencing of the lion enclosure. In the daytime it all looked so normal, a far cry from the dark foreboding forest he had imagined himself in on that fateful night.

A white panda car was heading down the drive towards the house, it's blue lights flashing and siren screaming unnecessarily on the empty road. It eventually rattled over the cattle grid and pulled up behind a black and white striped Jeep, the blue light stopped flashing and the siren was hushed. Jules and the Head keeper approached the car as two police officers got out. They shook hands and started talking. The Head Keeper pointed at his jeep and across to the lion enclosure. The ghosts were too far away to hear the conversation, they moved closer, but before they could get in range, the officers got back in the panda car. Jules and the keeper jumped in the Jeep and, leading the way, they all headed off up the service road into the safari park.

"My guess is they've found your body Tom," Wilf deduced as he removed the stubby cigar from his mouth in a self-assured manner.

Alice looked at him disgustedly, "Since when did you start smoking? That's disgusting. Do you know how bad that is for you?"

"Firstly, my dear Alice, it's only a prop. Secondly, it's a bit late to worry about the effect of smoking on my body."

"Well, it stinks!"

Wilf took a drag on the cigar and blew out nothing. "See it's a prop one, perfectly safe for all. I think you can smell the one that William Easton is smoking." He pointed to the director walking slowly through the formal garden with the producer, his head in a swirling cloud of blue tobacco smoke from a very real cigar.

"Never mind that, I think we need to follow the police. Tom, can you take us to the spot where you were killed so we can see what's happening? You never know, old Kojak here might be able to deduce something," George said sarcastically.

"Columbo," Wilf corrected him, not getting the joke. "You go with Tom, and I'll follow William."

Tom was understandably nervous about re-living the night's events. "Portland Bill," he said.

"What are you talking about? That's a bit random," Wilf said.

"That's what they call him. There's a town on the Isle of Portland called Easton. He shot some scenes for a war film in a quarry there a few years ago and the nickname stuck. He hates it."

Alice could understand Tom's reluctance to return to the scene of his demise, "Don't worry, come on Tom, nothing can hurt you now and maybe you'll remember something important."

"Meet you in the attic at six, we need to be in the ballroom by six thirty, I'm not going to miss this show for anything," Wilf said urgently, as he headed across the lawn to catch up with William Easton.

Alice, George and Tom crossed the road towards the Lion enclosure, Tom accepting that he couldn't keep putting off this moment.

10

Crows

Saturday 3rd August.

In his office, Head keeper John Hammond, along with Jules, briefed Sergeant Dexter and Constable Singleton on the incident area and outlined the security measures they had put in place. The Code One procedure had been developed in conjunction with Holeford Police and John was pleased to report that it was still being followed correctly after many years without an incident.

"We believe it to be a suicide, Sergeant. There are all the hallmarks of the incident in the sixties. The body was discovered during routine feeding at one pm. The two keepers who found it are with the nurse if you wish to see them, I'd then like to send them home, they are still in shock."

"Very good sir, we'll have a quick word with them before we go to the scene." They entered the empty canteen as the nurse came out of her room, closing the door gently behind her.

"Good morning officers, I assume you'd like to speak to Oliver and Henry? I've put them in the treatment room where you can talk privately. When you're finished, I'll take them home, if that's OK?"

"Certainly, we won't keep them too long, they've had a terrible experience," Sergeant Dexter said.

"I'll bring you in a cup of tea," she stood aside and opened the door.

After half an hour the brothers were allowed home and the Police car followed the Jeep containing John and Jules into the enclosure. They drove along the tarmac roads to respect the Ford Escort's suspension. The two policemen had conflicting emotions. The thrill of a significant incident at odds with the reality of what they may find at the scene. They didn't have long to worry.

They soon arrived at an area surrounded by several safari vehicles all emblazoned with black and white zebra stripes and the 'Woodford Abbey' crest on the doors. They were led to the remains of the body by Colin from the estate security team. Dexter took one look, turned away and threw up into the hedge. PC Singleton was more resilient but was none the less sickened by the scene. The remains of the body were now drying in the sun. Flies formed a cloud over the carcase as nature began her natural process of decay. Crows were not deterred by the police activity, flying in to grab at sinews while others circled above, crying out and warding off a buzzard that had also flown in to investigate. Dexter regained his composure, drinking water from a bottle given to him by a member of the estate staff. He moved back to the car and radioed the station for support and returned to Colin.

"Right sir, the area is to be treated as a crime scene until further notice. Please move your vehicles back to the compound, we'll remain here and wait for the arrival of a senior officer." He then spoke to Jules directly, "An inspector is on the way, sir. We'll take it from here but please keep your team on standby until further notice."

"Very good Sergeant. If you need anything I'll be at the house. John Hammond and Colin will be in the keepers' lodge awaiting your instructions. Please let me know when the senior officer arrives."

The estate staff climbed into their vehicles and drove back to the compound.

Dexter grabbed a roll of incident tape from the boot of the car and averting his eyes from the remains, wrapped it around the trees and bushes to delineate the area of the incident. He then sat in the car with PC Singleton while they quietly waited for the officer.

George, Alice and Tom moved to the roof of the lion's shelter to watch the police investigation commence.

"This is where I met Eric," Tom explained.

"Now you're here can you remember anything else about that night?" Alice asked.

"Just that I was able to open that gate over there and run down the road. I dived into the bushes for cover, but to my relief the gunman didn't follow."

"Why would they leave the gate to the lions unlocked?" George asked, scratching his head.

"No idea, I just thought it was the road to the village. I could see the street lights. I thought if I could get there, I'd be safe and could call the police… then I tripped and banged my head. Well, you know the rest."

Alice had an idea, "I know what we can do. Tonight, we'll go the village after the show and join the market traders in the pub. They might be talking about you. We may even discover your killer," she added eagerly.

At the house, the sci-fi festival carried on oblivious to the true-life drama unfolding only a short distance away. From the main gate another car could be seen entering the estate at speed. It too had a siren wailing and a flashing light magnetically stuck on the roof just above the driver's door. It drove past the front of the house at some speed, pulling up sharply alongside the ballroom entrance, close to a group of fans. They watched with interest as the brakes squealed fiercely and the car shuddered to a halt. The blue light slid from the roof, bounced off the door mirror and smashed on the road while remaining attached by a cable hanging from the driver's door. The siren then squealed and stuttered to a halt with a sound like someone strangling a chicken.

Clive Monkton had just finished a book signing in the stables and was heading to the ballroom followed by a herd of admirers. He was flanked by two burly security men to ensure his safe passage. The copper brown Ford Consul however caught his attention. It brought back a memory of his days as a child actor in gritty dramas set in the back streets of London.

Inside the car the plain clothes officer looked in disbelief at the curious crowd now gathering around the car. He was surrounded by aliens and spacemen who mixed with what appeared to be ordinary looking families. Some were pointing at the car, recognising the model, trying to work out its role in the weekend's science fiction attractions.

D I Montgomery could see the attention his vehicle was attracting and attempted to get out and enjoy the moment. It took all his might to open the door, it creaked and groaned at the force being applied. Finally with a metallic squeal it obliged, and immediately the window slid down like the blade of a guillotine and thudded into the bottom of the door cavity. He climbed out awkwardly to be greeted by Clive.

"Looks like the one in the Sweeney," Clive said, unaware that he was addressing an officer of the law.

"It is," Montgomery said, smugly standing to attention. "This is the actual one from the 1975 series."

"That's amazing, I thought it ended up at the bottom of the Thames during a car chase," added Clive, now fully aware of the car's provenance.

"It did!" Montgomery said proudly. The crowd of fans, overhearing these facts raised their cameras to get a picture, trying to get an angle where Clive was also included. However, he was somewhat obscured by the attentive bodyguards determined to shield him from the unwanted attention.

"Wait a minute. You're Colin Monkford, aren't you?" Montgomery asked.

"Close, it's Clive Monkton actually."

The officer held out his hand, "Detective Inspector Montgomery." Clive winced at this unexpected introduction but shook his hand regardless, reasoning that the inspector had no idea of his recent brush with the law.

Montgomery was in awe. "You played a schoolboy running an East End protection racket in series two, episode four. It's an honour to meet you. But why are you here? Are you filming?"

"Didn't you notice the posters? I'm here for the *Galactic Jump* festival, it's on all the signs."

"I didn't notice. I can't stand Sci-fi, load of nonsense. Why aren't you still acting in hard hitting crime shows? There must be plenty of roles for you."

"Sadly not, I'm type cast now. No one wants me for police drama, the casting directors won't take me seriously anymore." Clive succumbed to the fans attention and was now using the car as a photo opportunity, much to the thrill of his devoted followers. Montgomery pulled a notebook from his back pocket and held it out for an autograph.

"Sorry, I don't do autographs." Montgomery looked disappointed. "If I do one for you, they'll all want one," Clive explained, gesturing towards the crowd while maintaining his fixed smile. "However, if you go to the marketplace, I do have signed copies of my book for sale. I guess you're not here for the festival then?"

"No, I'm here on official business," Montgomery replied, dejectedly replacing his notebook in his pocket. The radio in his car suddenly crackled into life. "Sir...Sir are you on site yet?" came a broken voice from a speaker set in the dashboard.

"Excuse me, duty calls," he said, lowering himself back into the stained velour upholstery of the driver's seat. He reached out for the handset hanging over the rear view mirror on a spiralled cable and pressed the switch.

"Receiving, over," he said, watching Clive and his entourage move away towards the house.

"Please confirm your position, over."

"I'm by the side of the house, over."

"Very good sir, stay there and someone will come and lead you into the incident area, over and out."

Montgomery got out of the car again, retrieved the broken flashing light from the road, inspected the magnetic base and threw it on the back seat.

Soon a Safari Jeep arrived, and the driver beckoned him to follow. Montgomery pulled the door shut. It creaked and groaned but finally complied. He twisted the ignition key and the engine turned over several times, eventually firing. There was a bang as a bazooka flame fired out of the exhaust followed by a cloud of black smoke. The crowd that had been following Clive stopped and turned to see what new attraction was taking place.

He engaged drive and lurched after the Jeep as his exhaust haze drifted away on the breeze.

Clive reached the ballroom lobby where security let him pass and prevented the fans from following. John Pearce greeted him. They shook hands.

"What a load of freaks out there. They're unbelievable and did you see that car, what a rust bucket, it was driven by a Detective. What do you think he's up to?" Clive said.

"More importantly what have you been doing? If I hear you've been up to your old tricks, that's it, you're out. I'm not having you mess this up again. Tonight, if this works, we're on the road to another film contract and we'll be made for life, so don't you go messing it up," John, still holding his hand, squeezed it so hard Clive winced. "Do you understand?"

"OK boss, I've got it. Now tell me about Andy Cross, where's your golden boy then?" Clive asked sarcastically.

"Never you mind about him, there's plenty of time for him to turn up. Now get in there and act like the star you are meant to be."

Clive, rubbing his sore hand, moved obediently into the ballroom towards the stage.

Montgomery followed the Jeep to the compound where it was a hive of police activity. Several more panda cars had arrived along with an ambulance. As he pulled up, Dexter moved towards his car. "Hello Sir, 'uniform' are replacing the estate security at the gates. Forensic are on their way."

"Good, let's go to the incident room, you can brief me there."

"We've commandeered the canteen, sir. I can't believe you're still driving that scrapheap, why don't you have a pool car until they can supply you with a new Rover?"

"That, my dear Dexter, is a classic. If it was good enough for Regan, it's good enough for me."

"But they dragged it out of the Thames, it's got more rust than the Titanic." Montgomery gave him a hard stare. They had known each other for a long time, both joining the force the same year, but Montgomery was more ambitious. Eight years ago, he moved from Holeford Police to secondment with the Metropolitan Force to further his training and move up the ranks, only returning to Holeford six months ago to replace the retiring Detective Inspector. Dexter shrugged, now was not the time for banter. They moved to the canteen for the briefing and emerged half an hour later. Dexter then drove them to the scene.

"Look, that's Sergeant Montgomery, we know him Tom! He investigated the burglary at our supermarket ten years ago. He's the one who tried to track down a fancy dress vigilante group not knowing it was us. Wow, this is exciting!" Alice said. Tom looked totally confused.

"It's a long story." George said, "we'll tell you another day. I suggest you both stay here, it might be too traumatic for you. I'll go over and see what's going on."

Montgomery stalked the area, studying the scene. Dexter followed. "You don't seem shocked, sir. It's not a pretty sight."

"Dexter, I've just served eight years with the Metropolitan Police. Nothing can shock me now. You have no idea how depraved criminals can be in big cities. Right, I want the whole area sealed off. No one is to enter."

"Sir, this is a lion enclosure, they don't come much more secure."

"Good, well done, so what do we know about this character?" he said pointing to the remains on the ground.

"Nothing yet, sir."

"What about pockets, have you looked?"

"The clothes are torn to rags and soaked in blood."

"Fingertip search then."

"We haven't found a hand yet, let alone a finger, sir."

"No, you idiot, not the victims' fingers. Have you scoured the area with your fingertips?" Montgomery glowered.

"No sir not yet, we were waiting for your arrival." Dexter said uncomfortably.

A Land Rover arrived driven by the Head Keeper, Jules got out of the passenger side. They both walked over to Montgomery and Dexter, ignoring the incident tape.

"Oi you! Stop right there. No one is to enter. Now go back to your vehicle," Montgomery shouted and headed menacingly towards the unwelcome onlookers.

Dexter ran to catch him up and got between them. "May I introduce you to Viscount Jules Exford, Sir. He owns the estate."

Montgomery stalled for a second and nodded his head, "My apologies your highness, but you must leave the crime scene until I have completed my investigations."

"I'm terribly sorry, I didn't mean to interfere. Please call me Jules, I'm not a highness just a meagre viscount. I don't move in those higher circles."

"Very good sir, my name is Detective Inspector Montgomery, I'll be taking the lead for the criminal investigation."

"Is it a crime scene then? I thought this was a suicide?"

"Thinking is a dangerous game, sir. We in the police don't encourage it. We have to investigate all possibilities at this stage." He shivered suddenly as a cold breeze hit him despite the warm weather. George had joined them, surprised to note that Montgomery appeared to be just as inept as he had been all those years ago in Holeford.

Jules obediently moved back behind the tape. "I just wanted to extend all our services to you while you're based here, if you need anything please just ask one of the keepers. This is rather callous, but will you need to close the whole park? Only we have a festival on and it would be sad to disappoint the visitors." He was conflicted. His heart went out to the poor wretch who had died in such a tragic way but the business side of him was concerned that the cancellation of the festival could do untold damage to the finances of the estate. The penalty clauses in the contract with the film company would be crippling.

Montgomery pondered. He now understood the bizarre sight of people in fancy dress that had greeted him and his encounter with Clive. "Not at this stage sir. You carry on, I don't see any harm. Dexter, I want four men in plain clothes to mix in with the fans. I need them to watch out for anything out of the ordinary, if there is foul play here it's better that we monitor the situation without raising alarm."

Dexter looked confused, "That could be difficult sir, have you seen the crowd? Everyone is out of the ordinary!"

Ignoring the Sergeant, Montgomery turned to Jules, "Sir, my men will need access to all areas, can you arrange that?"

"Of course, I'll get onto it right away."

"I'll send the officer to your security office in one hour to collect the passes, now if you don't mind, I would ask you to leave the enclosure until I contact you."

"Very good detective, don't forget, if I can be of any assistance let me know. John, take me back through the exit gate by the house, it'll be quicker."

Jules and the keeper got back into the car and drove off. John stopped at the gates and blew the horn. The gatekeeper came out of the lodge, slid up the heavy bolt and pushed the tall gate open to let them pass. Seeing Jules, he saluted.

"What's going on John? Is it really a Code One?" the guard asked.

"It looks that way but it's in the hands of the police. So you know the drill, keep it to yourself until we know the facts. The police are going to relieve you soon so come to the keepers' lodge for further instruction."

Jules stayed in the passenger seat looking intently at the damaged Woodford sign he had noticed earlier, while the gate keeper closed and locked the internal gate and then opened the outer gate opposite the house. He saluted again as they drove off.

From the verge a police officer approached him. They had a short conversation and together they closed the gate and locked it.

George re-joined Alice and Tom on the roof of the shelter. "Well, you're not going to believe this, but Montgomery is now Detective Inspector and Dexter is a Sergeant."

Alice laughed, "Are you serious? He couldn't detect his way out of a paper bag."

"That may be so, but Her Majesty's Constabulary thinks otherwise. This is going to get very interesting."

Tom looked depressed. "I get a bad feeling about this. If he's as incompetent as you say, we're never going to find out who did it."

"Then it's up to us," Alice said defiantly, paused, considered and looked at George for help. "What are we going to do now?"

"There's not much we can do here so let's go back to the attic and hope Wilf has found out something helpful."

Tom was relieved to hear that. Sitting watching the police investigate his death was depressing. He just wanted to get away from the enclosure as soon as possible.

The work commenced in the incident room with officers gathering a portfolio of missing persons. They cross referenced any possible link to the estate or science fiction festival. It was now late afternoon, and the light was beginning to fade, challenging further investigation in the enclosure. Dexter instructed the team to lock down the site and cover the exposed remains with sheeting till it could be carefully removed by the forensic team in the morning. Montgomery had already left the scene to report his initial findings to The Duke of Exford.

George, Alice and Tom returned to the attic, avoiding the crowds as much as possible. Tom was fascinated to find out that psychic people do actually exist and could really detect spirits. He thought that was all a load of old baloney. Just a cheap form of entertainment crafty tricksters use to extract money from the curious and gullible.

In the attic room they sat round on the old sofas debating what would be in the show that evening, while waiting for Wilf to return from his investigation of William Easton. Time was moving on, they had to be ready to go to the Ballroom by six thirty. It was already six o'clock and there was no sign of Wilf, he was cutting it fine.

Without warning he rose up through the floor. "Sorry I'm a bit late, I got held up on the way back… literally." He shrugged his shoulders in resignation.

"Back from where?" George asked impatiently.

Wilf moved into the centre of the room in order to tell his story. "I followed Bill across the garden where he had a car waiting. No ordinary car, this was a Rolls Royce with chauffeur. He got in the front, so I got in the back, the air conditioning was on, so they didn't detect any change in temperature which was useful. It was a lovely car, soft leather seats with loads of legroom. It had little polished wooden tables that lowered out of the back of the seats with a special hole to place your glass and get this… It had a drinks cabinet concealed in the armrest."

"Ooh! Lovely, I'm pleased for you," George said sarcastically. "But what did you find out?"

"Never mind that for a minute, I've saved the best till last…" Wilf paused for dramatic effect. "The car had a telephone. A real one. Not a two-way radio. A proper phone with big receiver and a push button dial."

George was not impressed, "Well, did he phone anyone?"

"Yes, he did," Wilf said excitedly. "He phoned his office. Unfortunately, he didn't say anything about *Galactic Jump* or murdering Tom. Just something about a problem at the studio, but it worked just like an ordinary phone. Isn't that brilliant?"

"Brilliant but useless, we need information about Tom," Alice said.

Wilf continued undeterred by their reaction. "We ended up at the Kings Head in Holeford. He's staying there. You won't believe what they've done to the place. The ceiling in the bar has been lowered and filled with exposed beams. It looks like a barn conversion with old plates and vases displayed on high shelves, tacky or what! You can't see any of the Georgian detailing apart from the fireplace which they've painted black. The restaurant looks nicer though and they've turned the front lounge into a tearoom, so it's not all bad. That's where he went for a coffee while the chauffeur sat in the bar with a cup of tea and a sandwich. Cheese and pickle, I think."

"What does it matter what he had in his sandwich?" George said growing more impatient.

Wilf ignored him, "I had a chat with the Grey Lady, after all, it is her gaff to haunt. She hates the changes. She said the old coach house where she would go for a bit of peace has been turned into themed bedrooms and the stables is now a late-night bar with loud music and live bands, it heaves with young people at the weekends. She's thinking of applying for a transfer."

"This is all very well, but did you find out anything?" Alice asked, also getting impatient.

"No, not really, so I went up to the Collington Club to see if any of our ghostly friends had heard anything on the grapevine. It was nice to catch up with them but not surprisingly, they knew nothing about Tom. Lionel said he's looking forward to the golf tournament and sends his regards to Alice." Alice nodded in appreciation. "Other than that, it was completely pointless. By the time I got back to the Kings Head the Rolls had gone, I think he's here having dinner with the Duke. He did mention something about it when he was on the phone."

"Considering you're dressed as one of the most successful detectives on television you're useless, I should have gone myself," George chided.

"Oh! I nearly forgot, he did say in the car that he couldn't wait to get back to the studio. He thinks this is going to be a waste of time. *Galactic Jump* is a dead duck, but he's hoping he might persuade the Duke to invest in one of his other films."

"Well, that's one small nugget of info I suppose," conceded George. "Sorry, nearly forgot that bit." Wilf looked down at his feet embarrassed.

"Cheeky bugger, William Easton's just using this event as a way to tap the Duke for money. That's business I suppose," George shrugged.

"Well, I don't like it, it's underhand, abusing the trust of the production company to wine and dine him while he taps the Duke for support on a different project." Alice was disgusted.

"He's very wealthy already, so I don't think he needs the money,"

George said, "and anyway, you haven't told us how you got back here if you missed your lift."

"That was a bit of luck. As you know, the Kings Head was originally a coaching inn and by sheer good fortune the ghostly mail coach and its four horses still pass by every day at five on their way to Salisbury, so I got a lift. We were making good time until we got to the middle of Exford Forest. A man on horseback wearing a black tunic and a tricorn hat rode out onto the path in front of the coach, lifted his musket, fired it in the air and shouted, "*Stand and Deliver*," just like in the films. The coachman pulled up and told him to get out of the way. But he wouldn't move and aimed the musket directly at him. "*Hand over your money, jewellery and post sacks or I'll fire.*"

"Just stop this and go away, Dick," the coachman admonished, "you know this doesn't work anymore, that's why they hung you in 1730."

"*I won't ask you again*," the highwayman said. It all turned into a bit of pantomime after that. The coachman cracked his whip and the horses moved forward. The horseman stood his ground and so this went on for a few minutes until he eventually rode off shouting back obscenities. I couldn't make out what he said exactly, probably just as well."

"Was it really Dick Turpin?" Alice asked excitedly.

"No, that's what I asked the Coachman, when we finally got underway again. He said his real name was Claude Sheppard, but he got the nickname Dick because he was a bit of an idiot."

"How rude," Alice said.

"Sorry Alice, but that's what they call him. So anyway, that's what delayed me, I just got dropped off at the main gate and here I am. None the wiser but I had a good day out. How did you get on?"

George sat up on the sofa, "You're not going to believe who's leading the investigation."

Wilf shrugged his shoulders. "How would I know?"

"It's only Montgomery from Holeford police."

"What, our Sergeant Montgomery? I thought he went to London. He was useless. He thought we were a group of vigilantes in fancy dress after the supermarket robbery where the burglar confessed about seeing us."

"Well, it's him alright, but he's now Detective Inspector and his sidekick is now Sergeant Dexter."

"Saints preserve us, what hope has he got of finding Tom's murderer?" Wilf was finding it hard to believe the police force would promote someone so incompetent. "Does he still act like he's in the Sweeney?"

"One better, he's now driving round in one of Regan's old cars." Alice giggled.

"Who knows, perhaps his policing skills have improved," Wilf joked.

"I doubt it," George said.

"Never mind that now, did you learn anything?" Wilf asked.

"We sat on the lion shelter all afternoon but... nothing! It was all very boring, they taped off around the body and fumbled round in the grass for hours looking for clues. Jules turned up but he was sent away. The whole enclosure's now under police guard so we came back up here to wait for you."

"Alice jumped to her feet. "I had an idea earlier. After the show Tom and I are going to the pub where the crew are staying to see if they mention anything. They might drop something into their conversation, especially if they've had a few pints."

"No harm in trying," Tom said pleased to be actively involved at last. After all it was his death! "But first we'd better get to the ballroom, the show's due to start in ten minutes."

11
Let the Show Begin

Saturday 3rd August. Evening

The Ballroom was ready. The velvet curtains were drawn across the stage and the cinema screen lowered in front. Television South News had earlier interviewed Georgina Best about the new series. Much to the annoyance of the presenter, Georgina was more interested in promoting her new range of beauty products, manipulating the conversation at every opportunity.

The market in the courtyard was now closed for the day, with most of the traders catching the shuttle bus back to the Abbey Inn, leaving only three of them to work on a small stall at the evening event. Most of the stock was returned to the stables, while popular items were moved to tables set up in the lobby. This position between the bar in the gallery and the entrance to the ballroom attracted a lot of interest. Tee-shirts, posters, books and videos were displayed alongside full size cardboard figures of the main characters, played by Andy Cross, Georgina and Clive, along with a Gorog costume and other expensive replica props. The space was limited, but in the confined area of the lobby it had impact, appealing to fans whose wallets were now loosened by alcohol and anticipation.

The ghosts headed from the attic to the Ballroom, taking the direct route down through the floor and past the bedrooms. Going through the state dining room and into the Gallery, they passed through the wall into the void under the terrace seating and took a position high up by the TV camera. The camera operator shivered and put his coat back on.

"Look there's Portland Bill," Alice said, excitedly pointing to William Easton who had arrived deep in conversation with the Duke, followed by Jules, his secretary, John Pearce, and two other men who they assumed worked for the production company. The group moved to the roped off seating at the front of the terrace affording them the best view. The security guard let them in, re-clipping the thick red rope across the end of the aisle.

The entourage had come from the state dining room where a lavish reception had been paid for by John Pearce to woo the potential investors.

He hoped the fine dining and flowing champagne would help his cause.

The audience's excitement was palpable, increased by the presence of the cameras now panning around, filming the gathering crowd. As they entered the ballroom a TV presenter even found time to interview a couple of fans dressed in authentic costumes. The arrival of the police in the afternoon and the closing of the lion enclosure were hot topics of speculation, but it was assumed to be additional security due to the size of the event. It was just another element adding to the heady mix of anticipation. The audience were most interested in whether Andy Cross would appear, while the police, now aware of his non-attendance, were speculating if it was his remains they had found. The plain clothes officers were blending in. One was working on the souvenir stall, two were mingling with the crowd, while an unfortunate junior officer had been given a Gorog costume. He was not happy. The rubber suit was unbearably hot and awkward to move in, especially indoors. His squirrel tail was constantly being pulled by children, while the rhino horn mask kept hitting people on the head. The danger and fear provoked by the aliens in the films was certainly not reflected in real life.

The volume of the audience rose as they continued to file into the auditorium. For those that had attended the Friday show, the room looked familiar except for the addition of TV cameras. The portable metal terrace creaked under the movement of the audience finding their places. Plastic seats banged repeatedly as people sat then rose again and sat again as everyone found their places. The lighting was now more theatrical, pencil thin spotlights of blue, green and red scanned the tops of their heads. In the background was the sound of low bass synthesizer music embellished with eerie sound effects lifted from the show's soundtrack. The curtain rose a couple of inches, allowing a light mist of back-lit dry ice to drift from the stage, and tumble to the floor, like a technicolour waterfall. By seven, the room was packed and noisy. The fans dressed up as Gorogs were instructed to stand at the side of the room as the seats couldn't accommodate their voluminous costumes and particularly their bushy tails. The music slowly increased in volume and chatter became louder to compensate. Without warning, there was an almighty metallic, echoing clunk as if a spaceship door had closed and all the lights went out. Immediately there was silence from the awed audience and a single white spot picked out the left-hand side of the stage. The promoter, John Pearce entered, and the audience spontaneously applauded, many not knowing who he was, but that didn't matter, the show was beginning. That was good enough.

When John was finally able to speak into his hand-held microphone, he welcomed everyone and thanked The Duke of Exford for the use of the estate. Following the pleasantries the scripted element began.

"Ladies and gentlemen, tonight is the highlight of our weekends' events. Shortly, we will show you the preview from the new series of *Galactic Jump*. But before that, please let me introduce you to the stars of the show, Mr Clive Monkton!"

Clive entered the stage from the right to huge applause. He waved and stood under the 'Orion Brigade' insignia now projected onto the cinema screen above his head.

"Miss Georgina Best!" Georgina entered down the centre aisle waving at her adoring fans, her skin-tight outfit accentuating her curves. The fans expected nothing less and responded with wolf whistles and tumultuous applause. She climbed the steps and joined Clive on stage.

"Still got it then, love," he whispered sarcastically to her. She ignored him, while continuing to smile and wave to the fans.

"Mr Malcolm Bingham!" He joined them from the right side of the stage to more muted applause, after all he had only started speaking in the last episode of series two. He responded with a more placid wave. He knew he still had to earn his place with the diehard fans.

There was a tangible unrest in the auditorium, where was Andy Cross? Were the rumours unfounded about his surprise appearance? The plain clothes officers, however, were thinking, '*is he the one that's been eaten?*'

Clive took the microphone from John and stepped forward. "Hello Jumpers," he screamed into the mike. The crowd responded with cries, whistles and applause. "Thank you all… It's with great joy that we join you for this very special event. It is of course the launch party for series three, but also, we're pleased to have with us tonight the esteemed film director William Easton. Please stand-up William."

William reluctantly stood up, looking daggers at Clive and turned to the room, raising his right hand in a grudging wave. The room erupted with a spontaneous standing ovation. William hated the fame that inevitably came with his success, but these things must be endured. After all, '*it's these people who provide his wealth, allowing him to fulfil his artistic desire.'* If he had ever doubted whether or not he should support a new *Galactic Jump* film, it was obvious now that there was a lucrative market for it.

John smiled from the wings. He knew the magic was working. By the end of the evening, he will have hooked his backer and the film would be in the bag.

William sat down and the audience settled once again. Clive lifted the mike and continued. "Tonight is a special evening and we are pleased to welcome the TV companies who will share this event with Jump fans all over the world. We will shortly be showing the preview followed by a few surprises. Later this evening, we will be having the disco here in the ballroom with special guests, so get your dancing shoes on, also the bar will stay open until late." A cheer came from the audience. "Now let's settle down and enjoy the preview." As he left the stage, a countdown was projected onto the wide screen and the fans shouted out the numbers. "Three... Two... One..." The show began.

The preview film shown on Friday, once again delighted the audience. As it finished and while the audience were still applauding, the room remained dark, the screen rose into the ceiling and a monotone bass sound began quietly building up as dry ice again poured from under the slowly rising curtain. Spotlights fanned out through the gap cutting through the mist. The sound became louder and louder, drums began to pound the room, dust fell from the chandeliers and the windows began to rattle. The audience could feel the reverberation in their chests. The drumbeat began to morph into a familiar sound. The audience could make out the melody of '*Into the Void*' by Black Sabbath emerging in the cacophony. They rose as one, clenching their left fists, holding them to their left temples in an Orion Brigade salute. This was the anthem they'd first heard in *Galactic Jump, The Mines of Poonor*, the iconic episode securing the shows' place in science fiction history. Then slowly the curtain began to raise further, red spotlights danced around the room as the dry ice mist now fell like a waterfall from high above the proscenium arch.

Through the descending fog they could make out the unmistakable under carriage of a 'Century Hawk landing craft.' The atmosphere was electric now.

The TV cameras panned the room trying to capture every moment of the jaw-dropping spectacle unveiling before their eyes. The smoke began to clear and reveal the underside of the spaceship, in all its glory. The music still pounded as Ozzy Osborne's voice sang out. The stage was still, the metallic ramp to the spaceship remained firmly closed. The audience looked to the wings, expecting the crew to emerge and walk to the centre of the stage, but no. There was a hiss of compressed air and the ramp eased open, lights shone out from within the ship and jets of steam sprayed out from the hydraulic rams. Then began a metallic cranking sound as the ramp slowly lowered to the stage, landing with an audible thump. The audience watched open mouthed. They could now see the interior of the loading bay. It was beyond their wildest dreams. The lights went out again and from the depths of the ship, a single spotlight burst out, temporarily blinding the crowd. As they adjusted their vision, they could make out movement. The silhouette of an Orion Brigade space suit could now be seen. The spaceman moved slowly to the end of the ramp and stepped onto the stage. The pounding music began to fade back to the dull monotone bass. Some of the fans recognised the uniform and the insignia, but couldn't quite believe it. The spaceman reached up and released the catches at the base of his helmet with a hiss of air. He loosened it and lifted it slowly, deliberately milking every second.

"Good evening, have you missed me?"

The room exploded with screams, cheering and applause. He was here. Andy Cross. The elusive star of *Galactic Jump* was in the room. Two girls near the front fainted, causing a ripple of concern to the members of the audience standing nearby. The first aid team were prepared. They moved quickly through the compliant crowd and brought the casualties to the side of the room with minimal fuss. The cameras had stopped panning and now focused on the actor, capturing the event for the evening news.

From the back of the landing craft, the other actors entered through the smoke and joined him at the front of the stage. Again, the applause rose, then the ominous music that signalled the presence of the Gorog struck up and the atmosphere in the room changed. From inside the craft more movement could be detected and then the Gorog High Commander emerged wearing his tight-fitting black uniform trimmed with gold, his horn, tipped with a golden cone, glinted in the spotlight. His highly coiffured tail was standing proud above his head. In his right hand, he was holding his long, black, intricately carved ceremonial staff of office topped with a golden Gorog head. Holding it aloft he headed to the front of the stage. The actors moved to allow him centre stage where he stood silently and slowly surveyed the audience, menacingly. The audience were hushed, as if their lives were actually under threat from a man in a rubber costume. He raised the staff high over his head and held his clenched left fist to his chest. The fans in their Gorog costumes around the aisles stood to attention as the music faded away.

"*Goo nee forsun dectrya impago*," The High Commander said, sternly.

"What on earth is he saying… is he having a stroke?" Wilf asked.

"That's Gorog for 'good evening earthlings,' I think," Tom said.

Alice just burst out laughing. "Is this for real?" she spluttered. George just looked on, bemused.

"*Rogor toonee shapclot forgato*," the Gorog, continued.

"*Forgato tolloney cragrock*," the audience replied in unison.

"Well, I've seen it all now," Wilf said scathingly.

"No, you haven't," Tom quickly added. "Not yet."

With that, the theme tune to the West End musical 'Revenge of the Gorog' began. The actors started swaying in time with the rhythm and then dancing girls appeared from the spacecraft wearing what looked like metallic swimsuits with squirrel tails looped up from their bottoms up over their heads. They danced a highly choreographed routine while the actors and the Gorog High Commander sang the opening song. The audience went wild. They rose in unison, singing at the top of their voices, jigging around, raising their clenched fists and beating the air, in time with the melody.

"Told you, you hadn't seen it all," Tom said smugly.

Wilf, George and Alice just watched open mouthed. This bore no resemblance to the theatre of their time.

John watched from the terrace and clapped his hands together, he had done it. This could not have gone any better. The extortionate cost of staging this production had paid off. He looked along the row to William who was talking to his PA, as she frantically took notes. John could name his price.

The plain clothes police officer moved to the lobby, found a quiet corner and contacted the incident room on the radio concealed under his collar.

"Vector one, come in, over."

Through the earpiece hidden under the long hair of his wig came the reply, "Receiving Vector one, go ahead, over."

The policeman whispered into his transmitter. "Suspect one has shown up at the Ballroom, repeat, suspect one is alive and well."

"Received... over and out."

In the incident room the WPC walked over to the blackboard and with a tooth-grating squeal from the hard chalk on the painted surface, drew a line through Andy Cross's name. The body was to remain anonymous for a little longer.

After two encores, the musical section of the evening came to an end and the fans settled into their seats. Andy Cross, centre stage again and surrounded by his crew and the dance troupe, raised his hands to calm the enthusiastic audience.

"Ladies and Gentlemen, Oh, and Gorog's of course," he added to acknowledge the fans in costume. The audience laughed while the costumed devotees waved to the best of their ability inside their restrictive suits. "Thank you all for coming to our launch event. I, or rather, we, have many people to thank, too many to mention in person and I apologise now if I miss anyone out. I must thank His Grace, the Duke of Exford and the staff of Woodford Abbey for hosting the weekend... The amazing team from the Amaldy Theatre for staging this spectacular production...The sound and lighting team...The local constabulary for their additional help in policing the event, due to the unprecedented numbers attending our festival." He had no idea of the real reason for the police attendance.

Between each name check, the audience politely applauded. He continued, "John Pearce, for his belief in the show." Loud applause. John stood, waved and sat down again. "But mostly, we thank all of you." He spread his arms wide as if to embrace the whole room. The actors and dancers raised their hands and applauded the audience. The fans responded with cheers and more clapping. "Without you, there would be no *Galactic Jump*."

"And you'd be out of work," Clive whispered loud enough for Andy to hear. He ignored the remark and continued to milk the adulation from the room.

"Now we're going to have a short break while the chairs are cleared and the disco is set up. So please, go and get a drink, have a look at the merchandise in the lobby and we'll see you back here for the after-show party. We'll be taking it in turns to meet as many of you as we can in the lobby during the evening and sign your books and posters." The background music volume increased and the performers filed off the stage. The VIP's were escorted from their seats to the state dining room for a drinks reception as the room began to clear.

The fans were buzzing with delight. The music still ringing in their ears, they gradually filed out of the ballroom, swamping the stall for more souvenirs, while even more headed to the bar in the long gallery.

"Well, that was something you don't see every day," George announced.

Alice was still grinning. "These fans are completely bonkers, the production quality was amazing, but the content was unbelievably poor."

Backstage, Andy was removing his gloves and unzipping the top of his space suit to get some cool air to his sweating body. He was soon joined by Clive, Malcolm and Georgina.

"Where the hell have you been, Cross?" Clive fumed.

"Don't you start on me, sunshine," Andy taunted. "I've been in hiding if you must know. John paid me to stay out of circulation for two weeks to build up the suspense and mystery. I came here in disguise today ready for the surprise appearance tonight. You must admit it worked, it's been all over the papers and even on the Evening News."

"He paid you?" Malcolm asked scornfully, "To stay away? Well, that takes the biscuit."

Georgina was more understanding, "I can see the point, the fans were overjoyed to see you here. John will get even more column inches in the papers now. Did you see the reaction of Bill Easton, he was lapping it up. That can only be a good thing for all of us," she added.

Andy looked at Clive, "How was the prison food?" he mockingly asked.

Clive stepped forward, facing up to him aggressively. "Shame you ever came out of hiding, why don't you crawl back to whatever stone you were hiding under."

Andy grabbed his arm, holding his face only inches from Clive's. "You need me. I don't much like working with conmen but for the moment

I'm willing to try, just for the good of the show. How about you?"

Malcolm stepped in trying to diffuse the situation. "Come on boys, leave it. We've got a long, lucrative road ahead of us if all goes well, let's just try and get on. Anyone fancy a drink?"

The two stars backed off and silently nodded like two admonished schoolboys. Both knew there was big money to be made if they played their cards right.

"Yeah, come on you two, let's get out of these costumes. We've got a lot of hands to shake and I want to get close to Bill Easton, I need to work my charms on him," Georgina added.

"Well, I guess the shows over," Alice said. "It's time for us to visit the pub and see what we can find out, the shuttle-bus is waiting outside for the crew so we can get a lift. Come on Tom."

"You two go on, we'll stay here and keep an eye on the others," Wilf said.

George pulled a face, "Do we have to? Judging by the size of the speakers, the disco's going to be awfully loud," he said, sticking his fingers in his ears.

12
Time for a Pint

Saturday 3rd August. Late evening

The minibus was waiting outside the Ballroom to take staff and crew back to their lodgings at the Abbey Inn. Alice and Tom made themselves comfortable as market traders, stage crew and helpers trickled out of the building and settled in their seats for the short journey. They were full of praise for the show and thrilled that Andy Cross had actually turned up. However, the revised logo was not proving popular. It didn't seem to stop the fans reaching deep into their pockets for the overpriced products.

"Come on driver, let's go, I need a pint," cried one of the lads at the back.

"That's Chris," Tom said. "He's got a loud mouth. He makes a lot of noise, but manages to be out of the way when work needs doing. I don't recognise all of these people, but the stalls were quite spread out and some of these guys were just marshalling the queues for the signings."

The driver ignored the impatient request and waited another five minutes. Two more crew ran up and jumped in just before the door closed with a hiss of compressed air. The driver then slowly drove off keeping an eye in the mirrors for any stragglers. He steered the bus up the main drive and through the gates onto the main road. The security guard then closed the barrier and went back to his gatehouse from where he monitored the grounds with the CCTV screens mounted in the control room. The driver was under strict instructions to use the main drive, avoiding the quicker route through the service roads across the safari park. Although shorter, the road passed the compound, and DI Montgomery was concerned that the passengers may be curious about the level of police activity and start asking awkward questions. He was determined to keep a low profile for now, and monitor the last day of the show, after all, something may come up to help the investigation.

Just one more day and the lid could come off the incident and he could make a public appeal for information. The Duke would have to deal with the repercussions from that event and any negative publicity. But that was not the police's problem. They had to be sure there had been no criminal activity connected with the death.

The bus entered the village, over a small humpback bridge and after a short distance turned off into the car park to the rear of the Abbey Inn. The Inn itself was over three hundred years old, brick built with stone mullion windows. The front elevation facing the road was shrouded in Russian vine now turning vivid colours of red and yellow. The thatched roof was punctuated by two tall twisting brick chimneys. The pub sign depicting the abbey swung gently in its frame, mounted on a timber post by the entrance.

In the car park, the door of the bus opened with a hiss and the passengers spilled out into the cool night air. Two of the younger men ran to the door of the public bar to beat the rush. Alice and Tom waited for the bus to empty and then floated over towards the beer garden, stopping to look at the stream which meandered through a deep, brick lined culvert. This was crossed by a paved bridge with iron rails, leading to the outdoor dining area, dotted with heavy wooden picnic tables topped with colourful '*Holeford Ales*' umbrellas.

There was no rush, their investigation could begin when the crew had settled down with their first drink. After a few minutes, they entered the public bar. The room was long and narrow with space for one row of tables either side of the door with the solid wooden bar opposite. To the right was an open fire, its grate laid ready with logs. The blackened oak mantelpiece was embellished with horse brasses. Sepia photographs of the village in days gone-by hung on the wall.

To the left, the room opened out into a dining area with tables surrounding a central open fire, a large iron grate sat on a brick built plinth with copper chimney over. By the doors leading to the beer garden, long, low oak plank coffee tables sat alongside heavy green sofas waiting for unwary customers to sit and be swallowed up by the time softened leather. This is where the crew had now congregated and separated into individual groups of friends and colleagues. There was a convivial buzz as they chatted.

In the public bar, now that the wave of new arrivals had settled, the regular customers could resume their evening chatter and interrupted game of darts. Tom and Alice moved towards the lounge.

"Bloody Nora! Jeff, there's a cold draft in here. Soon have to light that fire," one of the regulars yelled to the barman. He had no idea that he was surrounded by ghosts. The door latch rattled, and a younger man entered, poorly dressed, in torn stained jeans and faded tee shirts advertising the local brewery. He gave the impression he had just finished mucking out the cow stalls with (what the landlord hoped) were only muddy shoes now leaving residue on the flagstone floor.

"About time you got here, Steve," observed one of the dart players standing near the fireplace. "Were you out shooting rabbits last night?"

"No, why?"

"I could hear shots over by the estate, I assumed it was you. I expect Jeff needs some meat for his pies." He laughed and looked across at the landlord.

Tom's ears pricked up, "Did you hear that? They heard the gunshots. We've got a witness, that's a good start."

"You don't know that they weren't shooting rabbits, it does go on round here. I think they call it country life. Poor little bunnies," Alice said sympathetically.

"You have to admit it's a coincidence," Tom said.

"If it weren't rabbits, what were it?" the dart player continued.

"Could be Zebra," the scruffy lad said as he approached the bar where the landlord had already set up his pint. "What about it Jeff, you could do a good line in exotic pies. How about, 'lion burgers,' the burger with bite!' There, you can have that slogan for nothing."

"That's not even funny. If the Duke hears things like that, he'll be sending the estate manger down here to check me out."

"We know you get your pies from the freezer cabinet at Price Low," the lad replied with a knowing grin, he knew the landlord would bite.

"I do not! Bloody cheek! They're made on the premises with the best cuts from the estate farm. I've won prizes for them at the county show, so watch your mouth Steve, it's going to get you into a lot of trouble one day." Steve just laughed and sat with the dart players, gulping down his pint of Exford Best. "I had one of his 'rhino pies' once, but the crust was too tough," he whispered to the other lads who laughed obligingly.

"I can still hear you," Jeff said, leaning over the bar pointing his finger, while maintaining a grip on his bar towel and scowling at his regulars.

Tom and Alice positioned themselves in the centre of the lounge to overhear all the conversations, hoping for a few titbits. The crew were full of chatter about the festival and even more interested in debating the fractured relationship between Clive and Andy.

"That Georgina's a bit of all right," one of the lads said. "I wouldn't mind going into space with her."

Tom pointed to the chap talking, "That's Jason, I was supposed to be working with him on the poster stall. We are, or rather were at Art College together. He's a bit of a twit and fancies himself with the ladies."

"Well, he needs to grow up," Alice said with disgust. "He'll never catch their eye with such childish comments."

At eleven, the minibus returned with more staff from the evening event. They joined the others in the lounge bar with stories of the after-show party that was still in full swing. They had returned promptly from the ballroom, as they needed to be well rested for the early start in the morning.

"This looks more promising," Alice said optimistically.

"Let's face it, they don't care about me. Most of them didn't even know me," Tom said dejectedly.

"Let me try something." Alice went over to Jason, stood behind him and lowered herself down so that her head was directly behind his. Jason shivered and looked to see if the door was open. It wasn't.

She began to whisper in his ear. "Where's Tom? Have you seen Tom? He was there yesterday but I haven't seen him today, where can he be?"

Jason rubbed the back of his neck. "Bloody draughty in here... Hey, has anyone seen Tom today? He was supposed to be helping me."

Alice stood up with a big grin, "Tah Dah, you have to admit you've either got it or you haven't."

"Rumour has it he went off with one of the girls from the production crew last night," said a tall lad in a '*Galactic Jump*' tee shirt.

"He looked the type," one of the girls piped up.

"What do they mean? I look the type. How dare they!" Tom snapped.

"I know who you mean, smartly dressed and very good looking. He stayed to put away the merchandise. Didn't see him come back though, he was a bit of a dish," Julie from the marketing team added.

"That's great, first they don't miss me, now I find out one of them fancies me. Bit late now."

Jason took a quick swig of his pint and put the glass down carefully on a beermat, "He's got a habit of going AWOL, he's done it a couple of times at college. Just disappeared for a few days then comes back all sweetness and light. He drove the tutors mad. He's a good artist though, he runs rings around the rest of us," he said.

"Well, at least they've acknowledged your existence," Alice said, "that's something."

"I've heard enough, the bus is still outside, let's catch it back," Tom said. "This has been a waste of time but thanks for trying."

They both left the pub and slumped down in the back of the bus and took the short journey back to the house.

The bus finally got them back at eleven thirty and as they arrived the fans were pouring out of the ballroom, heading for the car park. The remainder of the crew were waiting for the shuttle. Alice and Tom could see the disco equipment being loaded into the back of a transit van.

Wilf and George were already in the attic room flaked out on the sofas when they got there.

"Blimey, you two look knackered," Alice commented.

"So would you be, it was hell in the disco. Well, at least I assume it was like hell, I'd rather not find out. The noise was unbelievable and the music... well you can't call it music it was just a constant thump, thump, thump with no discernible melody," Wilf whinged.

"You're just showing your age," Alice laughed.

"The so-called dancing was a disgrace, all those sweaty bodies just jigging around, absolutely no coordination."

"Except when they all sat on the floor and pretended to row a boat, what was that all about?" George added.

"Who was the guest star they mentioned?" Tom enquired.

"Hardly a star," Wilf said disappointingly, "It was a DJ called Terry Prance apparently, he's on Radio Benelux. I think his 'raison d'être' is to play music so loud in Brussels you can hear it in Luxembourg without the need of a radio!"

"But did you find out anything?" Alice asked impatiently.

"Yes, we did...never go to a disco again!" George said rubbing his head. "My ears are still ringing. I think I've done them permanent damage."

"What else, apart from that, which I'm sure you'll soon get over," Alice said unsympathetically.

"We spent some time in the lobby and the bar, but they were both heaving with fans trying to get a beer or a glimpse of their idols. It was hopeless."

"What about you two?" Wilf asked from the comfort of the sofa.

"Well, Jason, that's one of Tom's friends from college, said Tom's got a habit of disappearing from lessons, so in a way he wasn't surprised when he didn't turn up."

"Oh great, well done, an unreliable reputation is not going to help with our investigation, you idiot!" George exclaimed in frustration, looking at Tom.

"Sorry, I didn't know I was going to die, or I would have been more punctual," Tom said sarcastically.

Alice put her hands on her hips and turned to face Tom, "Look, we're only trying to help you."

"I played truant once," Wilf recalled. "When I was at school, three of us managed to get matinee tickets for King Lear. When I got home my father was incandescent with rage, I got such a hiding. I never did it again."

"Who was in it?" George asked.

"It was no one famous. The production was very poor. The reviews were so bad it closed the following week... Anyway, that's not the point, there's no discipline these days. A good education is a collaboration between teacher and pupil, not something to be taken for granted. It has to be worked at," Wilf looked with distain at Tom. He had gone down in his estimation.

Alice continued. "I also found out that Tom's a gifted artist who gets right up the nose of his teachers with his shenanigans."

"Is that right, Tom?" Wilf asked, as he put the fake cigar in his mouth, pulled a little black note pad out of his raincoat pocket and wrote a memo.

"Well, I suppose I could have behaved better but I get bored sometimes. Some of the exercises they ask us to do are stupid. For instance, one day we had to do a life drawing. The model was an old man holding a stuffed cat."

"Was he naked?" Alice grinned.

"Yes, it was a life drawing,"

"Who was, the old man or the cat?" Wilf asked. Tom glared at Wilf and ignored him.

"Yuck," Alice said trying to erase the image from her mind.

"We had to study the model for two minutes then sketch him while blindfolded."

"Why, was your drawing going to be so bad even you couldn't bear to look at it?" George joked.

Tom was now losing his patience. "No! While we were blindfolded it was carnage. We knocked into easels and tables. The paint went everywhere. Jason fell over his chair and bruised his leg…Ridiculous." They all laughed at the absurdity of the situation.

"Were getting off the subject," Wilf looked annoyed. "Did you find anything out about the murder?" he said, pencil poised to make notes in his book.

"Two villagers who were playing darts said they heard gunshots last night and accused one of the other drinkers of being out shooting rabbits, which he denied."

Wilf scribbled in his book. "Did they say what time?" he asked eagerly.

"Sorry, Sherlock, I forgot to ask," Alice replied sarcastically.

George decided to call a halt to the evening, "I think we're all tired, it's been a long day. Let's get some rest and make a fresh start in the morning. We've got one more day of the festival to snoop around and we need our wits about us. I have a feeling the culprit may still be amongst us."

13
The Morning After the Night Before

Sunday 4th August. Morning

The evening had been a huge success, way beyond the dreams of John Pearce. The atmosphere in the ballroom, along with the theatrical presentation, had impressed and inspired all in attendance. The evening news had shown extracts of the show along with pre-recorded interviews. That sort of advertising, money couldn't buy. He was also approached by Southwest Television about recording a special feature, which could be broadcast during their Christmas scheduling.

Best of all, William Easton's office contacted him that morning requesting that he attend a meeting at Pinelodge Studios on Wednesday. John could not be happier, he had hooked the big fish, his future was assured, fortune and success were sure to follow.

The fans were enjoying the final hours of the weekend. Despite it being the final day, record numbers had turned up. Some just out of curiosity after seeing the evening news or reading the morning paper. But the majority were die-hard fans, many in costume, simply enjoying the shared experience of dressing up, exchanging stories and importantly, not being laughed at by those who *'didn't understand.'* For the stars it meant more public appearances, one last running of the preview film followed by yet another Q&A session going over the same old dull questions, which they politely answered with feigned delight and light banter between them. Sitting behind a table on the stage, now draped with the new Orion Galaxy emblem, they were secretly willing the event to end. Their wrists ached from book signings, and they were mentally exhausted from keeping up the pretence of being pleased to be there. However, they couldn't ignore the fact that it had been a rewarding weekend.

Additional stock arrived for this morning's signing sessions as tills again rang constantly. A nice little earner for everyone involved.

The market opened slightly later than planned, while an exhausted and dishevelled Frank waited for additional stock to arrive. He was shocked to find that the hayloft had been disturbed for a second time. Posters strewn over the floor like a grand game of pick-up sticks. Tee shirts, new books, magazines thrown carelessly around, and empty storage boxes piled up against the wall. Someone or something had had a high old time up here overnight. This time he couldn't blame Tom, he'd put it all away himself and ensured the door was securely locked. He hadn't ruled out paranormal activity, he'd seen programmes about such things on late night TV. After all it seemed to fit the evidence. The door was still secure when he arrived and after checking against the stock list, he was certain nothing had actually been stolen.

The police were more visible this morning, he assumed as a reaction to the TV coverage. Their attendance seemed to add to the gravitas of the event without revealing the real reason for their presence. The estate, by some miracle, had managed to keep the investigation under wraps avoiding unnecessary alarm despite the close proximity to the press and thousands of visitors.

While Frank was setting up the market, John Pearce took time to inspect the high value replica props for sale and noted some disturbing scratch marks on them. He instructed Frank to box them back up immediately and put them in the van. He entered the Ballroom, the stage set was being dismantled and loaded into the vehicles. The dance floor was being swept clean ready for the chairs to be laid out for the final preview screening that afternoon. He tracked down Clive getting ready for his book signing. John stormed into the dressing room, "Clive, I want to remind you of something."

Clive looked up in surprise as he zipped up his uniform, "Good morning to you too John! What's the matter with you this morning, been attacked by a Gorog?" he asked sarcastically.

"I'll attack you by the Gorogs if I find out you've been up to your old tricks." John pulled out a Pan Blaster and held it up in front of him. "Look at this," he said, pointing to a flattened area under the grip. "This is where the studio prop number has been scrubbed out. This is not a replica it's one of our actual blasters. If I find you're behind this.... and may I remind you, you do have a track record for flogging studio property, you'll be out. No one is bigger than the show, I can have you written out just like that," John clicked his fingers.

"Come on John, do you think I would be that stupid. I learnt my lesson. I swore on the bible in front of the judge and promised I wouldn't do it again."

"I wish I believed you. Have you seen the police presence, they're not here just for crowd control, somethings going down. I'm sure one of the Gorog at last night's show was an undercover copper."

"Don't be ridiculous. Why would they want to do that?" Clive asked nervously.

"I'm not joking, Rhino/squirrel hybrids don't wear highly polished black shoes. I reckon there was another one, wearing a wig as well, he was behaving very peculiarly. He was the only one looking round the room when the show was on, and he kept pressing his hair against his ear. I think he was wired up."

"You're getting paranoid, John."

"No, I'm not, but you're getting the sack if I see anything else out of the ordinary, mark my words," John threatened.

"I don't know what you mean, but if I see anything suspicious, I'll make sure it's stopped at once," Clive said obligingly.

"Good, as long as we understand each other. I'll be checking the accounts very carefully next week. If I find any discrepancies, you're out!" With that he left the room by the side door, as the last of the seating was being wheeled back in.

For the police officers confined in the lion enclosure, time was dragging. They could hear the buzz of the fans only yards away beyond the undergrowth, trees and fences. Children screaming at the sight of a Gorog, mothers and fathers trying to calm their offspring while attempting to attract the attention of the actors and costumed performers, for pictures. A murmur of anticipation emanated from the queue forming outside the ballroom for the last showing of the film.

Dexter was not familiar with this type of investigation. His normal contact with the criminal element was restricted to burglary and traffic offences. Holeford was not renowned for armed robbery, riots or murder.

He spent most of his time on crime prevention with Neighbourhood Watch groups and school visits. "This is so slow Gov," he said to D I Montgomery as they watched the row of twenty officers in overalls crawling along on all fours in a line, feeling their way through the grass and undergrowth in search of evidence. So far, they'd bagged lollipop sticks, three crisp bags and a toy soldier that had obviously escaped from a passing motor car. One can only imagine the conversation in the car as the parent discovered the open window and Johnny pretending to shoot the lions with his *Action Man*.

"This isn't TV, Dexter. It's not all action, these things take time. No stone must be left unturned."

"But it's obviously a suicide, Sir. It's happened before, in 1968 if I remember correctly, the file's in the incident room for reference."

"I know, I read the report, but it's got no bearing on this incident. I smell a rat, call it instinct, but something isn't right."

A man in light blue disposable overalls and rubber gloves walked towards them, removing his face mask and discarding it along with the gloves, into a bag being held by his assistant following alongside.

"What can you tell us Kev?" Montgomery enquired.

"Sorry Gov, not much at the moment. It was a male, aged between twenty and forty. Your only hope of finding foul play is from any surrounding evidence. I can tell you this though, he's definitely been eaten by a lion. Any evidence of prior foul play can't be determined from the remains. It's all chewed up."

"And that's it?" Montgomery looked disappointed.

"Best I can do at present. We'll get it all back to the lab and complete the tests but don't expect anything enlightening."

"Ok thanks. Let me know as soon as you've concluded the post-mortem. Come on Dexter, we'll go back to the incident room." As they travelled back in the panda car Montgomery was unusually quiet. Dexter knew from his years of working with him not to disturb him when he was deep in thought. Montgomery was turning over the scene in his head, comparing it with the sixties report. '*Perhaps it was suicide, but why? Who was this man? Someone must be missing him. The remains of clothing indicated a well-dressed individual not a tramp. How did he get there? You can't just walk in. He had to get out of a car to gain access. Where's the car? No one saw him in here yesterday. The wardens are on patrol all the time. No one can stray from the road or even open a window without being spotted and reprimanded immediately.*'

He suddenly looked up grinning. "Right Dexter, we're looking in the wrong place," he announced, rubbing his hands together.

"I think you're enjoying this sir," Dexter observed.

"I'm going back to the station. Meanwhile I want you to get the perimeter and all entrances checked for forced entry, especially the gates. Get someone on the CCTV footage. Watch it, then watch it again for anything suspicious. The victim had to get in here on foot, there's no other explanation."

In the compound, Jules was just getting out of his Land Rover as the two officers arrived. "Ahh, perfect timing," he said. "Have you made any progress?"

"Sorry Sir, we're not at liberty to discuss the case at this stage, suffice to say our investigation is ongoing," Montgomery said in an official tone.

"But do you know who the person is yet?"

"Not at this stage, but I would ask for your help by reporting to us any person or persons you deem to be missing or absent from your teams," Montgomery said, hurriedly getting into his Ford Consul, not wishing to engage in deeper conversation with the viscount. He put the key in the ignition and turned it. The starter motor whined and engaged, turning over the six-cylinder engine. It spluttered into life blowing a cloud of unhealthy black smoke out of the exhaust. Then abruptly the engine died. Montgomery turned the key again, the starter motor obliged a second time but with less gusto. It whined in protest and slowly ran out of enthusiasm, grinding to a halt.

Jules opened the passenger door, the unexpected smell of the interior hitting his senses. "Wow, it smells like a stagnant pond in here."

"You get used to it after a while," Montgomery replied, slightly embarrassed that his planned dramatic departure had failed to materialise.

"Why don't you leave it here? I'll get our mechanic to take it into the workshop and give it the once over. Nick is a brilliant engineer and a classic car enthusiast, I'm sure he can work his magic on it."

"That's very kind sir, she's very precious to me."

"Please call me Jules. It'll be my pleasure to help."

Montgomery forced the reluctant door open by pushing it with his foot and moved to the panda car.

"I'll leave the keys in the ignition, thank you... Jules," he stuttered, finding it awkward to address a member of the aristocracy casually by their first name. "Dexter, I'm taking your car, I'm sure you can get a lift. I'll leave it in the compound and requisition a pool car for the time being."

Dexter handed him the keys with a wry smile, "Very good Gov," he said.

The narrow-gauge steam railway was a big attraction at Woodford Abbey. It ran on a loop through the woods and around the lake, however, for this weekend it was acting as a shuttle from the overflow car park to the house and gardens. Lakeside Station, at the top end of the lake had been renamed Space Station for the weekend and was emblazoned with Galactic Jump emblems. It was normally a request stop for visitors walking the grounds, however, while the extra car park was in use it had proved a life line for those who didn't want to walk the one and a half miles along the lakeside path. It also provided welcome revenue for the maintenance of the rolling stock and the ongoing upkeep of the line. Locomotive 'Silver Jubilee' had been imported from South Africa in 1973, after it became redundant when the mine using it changed its gauge from two feet to three feet six. After a major restoration in North Wales, it came into service at the park in 1977 and had proved steadfast at hauling the Victorian carriages. It delighted visitors during the summer and provided an added attraction at the end of the main season with Halloween Fright Fest trips, then during the Christmas season as Santa specials.

The shuttle train had arrived at the main station positioned between the stable yard and Pets Paradise with a full load of visitors. The excited families, which included several enthusiastic fans dressed in their Galactic Jump costumes, made their way from the platform towards the market, guided by two Gorog Guards who silently pointed the way with their ceremonial staffs.

The engine driver Edith, a rotund lady in her early fifties, squeezed herself from the footplate onto the platform and waddled up to the guard. "That's it. If VJ thinks I'm going to wear this bloody space suit again today, he can stuff his job. I wore it for the whole of yesterday's shift and that's enough. I can't move in it, it's hot and quite frankly, unhygienic." David, the railway guard, watched as she unclipped the helmet and lifted it off her head. He was amazed that she had agreed to wear it in the first place, and astounded that, wearing it, she was able to get onto the footplate of the locomotive at all, let alone operate it. She looked over his shoulder to a lone passenger hanging around on the platform.

"Oi you! Get off the platform or get on the train, this is not bleeding *Brief Encounter.*"

The tall muscular man dressed in a black suit with white shirt, black tie and dark sunglasses slowly turned and looked back at her. He reached inside his jacket. David tensed. The man looked (for all intents and purposes) like a CIA agent going for the gun in his shoulder holster. David gallantly stood in front of Edith to act as a human shield, but it was rather like trying to protect a beach ball with a snooker cue. The man withdrew his hand, held his ticket up in the air then slowly walked off through the station building without a word. David breathed out. The increased police presence had made many of the staff nervous.

"Stupid man, how rude," Edith said, "I'm going to the staff room to change into my proper overalls and if they don't like it, they can drive the flipping train themselves."

One of the Gorog guards hanging around outside the platform entrance followed the stranger across the grounds towards the Café. A second Gorog guard shadowed their movements staying a safe distance away. The first Gorog and the black suited man sat on the circular seat under the tree by the cafe, out of view from the public as much as possible. The other, surreptitiously watched them both whilst posing with children for pictures. PC Singleton had volunteered for this undercover work as a distraction from the ongoing investigation in the enclosure. However, he hadn't foreseen being given the cumbersome rubber costume to wear. It was heavy, hot and uncomfortable. His only view of the outside world was through narrow black gauze in the neck of the creature. His vision was very limited, as was his access to fresh air. The smell of the latex was almost overwhelming. No wonder Dexter had leapt at his request. Next time, before he volunteered, he would think more carefully. He sincerely wished he was back on traffic duty.

As he observed the two behind the tree, he could see their conversation had become heated. There was much waving of arms and finger pointing. He dare not get any closer for fear of blowing his cover, so could only imagine what was being said. He reported his surveillance to the incident room via the two-way radio clipped to the inside of the suit, which operated by voice command. The meeting was obviously over as the Gorog waddled away purposefully, moving towards the garden at the side of the ballroom. Singleton followed, again keeping a safe distance and as he turned the corner into the garden, he was shocked to see at least twelve other Gorog milling around. But which was his target? Totally confused now, he walked on and joined the others blending in perfectly, trying to discern which he should follow. From the side door of the Ballroom, the Gorog High Commander appeared dressed in all his finery of black space suit trimmed with gold edging, the gold cap on his horn glinting in the sun. Seeing him appear the platoon of guards lined up on the gravel path, as if waiting for orders. Singleton played along, trying to scan the others through his little window for any clue. It reminded him of his time in cadet training learning to march on the barrack square.

The High Commander lifted his staff and crunched it down on the gravel path. "*Doo rog pan dakee,*" he shouted.

"*Dakee ron hoog ragoff,*" the platoon replied in unison, standing to attention.

Singleton didn't know whether to laugh or cry. He was obviously now in some sort of re-enactment. He radioed the incident room, "Gorog one, come in," he whispered, trying not to raise suspicion.

"Go ahead Gorog one, over," Dexter replied as he settled into his comfy chair with a fresh cup of coffee in one hand and a custard cream in the other.

"Sarg, I seem to be in a re-enactment with more of these monsters, what do I do?"

Dexter was laughing, imagining his predicament and nearly spilt his coffee in the process. "Have you got an eyeball on the target?"

"Negative, I've got an eyeball on twelve targets," Singleton replied, now in some distress.

"Carry on your mission and try to re-engage," Dexter ordered unsympathetically.

"Roger," Singleton responded wearily.

With that, an order was issued by the High Commander, "*Goo hagnog.*" The Gorog platoon turned to the right awaiting the next instruction. "*Boo Lee Trag Mooch.*"

In unison the line of guards started to march towards the gate of the kitchen garden, which was quickly opened by a security guard.

In the orangery, Andy Cross was entertaining members of the fan club who had booked for a private drinks party, where they would meet their idol in exchange for fifty pounds. They watched in amusement as the platoon of Gorog with their unwieldly gait waddled through the kitchen garden towards the far exit. Andy saw an opportunity, he signalled to the security guard to stop them.

The High Commander's path was blocked by the burly guard, who told them to wait.

"*Dakee ron hoog*," he instructed, and the platoon stood to attention. There was some mumbling from the latex masks as they saw none other than Andy Cross walking towards them followed by a group of excitable fans.

He stopped by the High Commander, who in his best Gorog said, "*Noo Geer grog hoon dof.*"

"You can cut that out," Andy said under his breath, "just shut up and stand there for a couple of minutes."

Inside his costume, Bob Stickles was taken aback by the abruptness of his hero. "OK," he said timidly.

"Who wants a photo?" Andy said to his entourage taking full opportunity of the unscheduled sideshow. After a couple of minutes with pictures taken, they all moved back to the orangery.

"Thanks a million. You all look great. Enjoy the rest of your day," Andy said insincerely, waving off the platoon. The security guard moved away and opened the gate to the stable yard.

"*Doo rog pan dakee,*" the leader shouted.

"*Dakee ron hoog ragoff,*" the platoon replied in unison, and they marched on with renewed vigour after their brief meeting with the star of the show.

"Sarg...Sarg... I think we're going on a route march," the tail end Gorog whispered into his radio, wishing this farce could end now.

"Roger that... have a nice time," Dexter replied unhelpfully.

They did indeed do a route march. The Gorog platoon, resplendent in their uniforms waddled out of the stable yard joining the path alongside the lake. Visitors, walking from the car park were highly amused by the spectacle and stopped them on several occasions for pictures. The sun was now at its strongest, beating down on the latex masks and thick heavy costumes. By the time they had negotiated the mile and a half walk to the 'Space station' and overflow car park, all of them were overheating and sweating profusely. Bob however, dressed as the high commander, was enjoying the feeling of power that the uniform gave him. It was a far cry from his day job in the accounts department of Holeford Council.

Bob's wife Vera was at the station to greet them. "Hello everyone, now if you all follow me, the station master has given us access to the area behind the waiting room where I can give you all a little treat." There were some vulgar comments from the platoon. Vera grinned, "Now there's no need for that, follow me." She opened the gate marked '*staff only*' and they arrived in a small yard shielded from the public by hedges and railway buildings. They helped each other off with their masks and gulped in lungful's of fresh, cool air. Vera opened a cool box filled to the brim with drinks which they leapt on like wild animals.

"The drinks are just past their sell by date, but they should be fine," she warned, in case they tasted a bit strange. She had acquired the out-of-date stock from the vending machines at the Holeford Council offices where she worked in Supplies. "Well, it was a shame to pour them down the drain," she'd reasoned. She needn't have worried.

The Platoon didn't care. They rolled the ice-cold cans on their foreheads to cool themselves, the condensation on the tins mixing with the sweat running down their faces. They then gulped down the cool refreshing liquid. None of them took any notice of PC Singleton, assuming he was a new member of the Gorog re-enactment club.

Vera then went to her bag and pulled out a large jar of Vaseline, holding it aloft for all to see. "Now who needs relief from the chafing of their suits?" she said with relish.

They all looked at the ointment and considered the offer seriously. All of them were feeling the aftereffects of the long march on their bodies from the unforgiving costumes.

Bob stepped in. "You can get your hands off my Gorogs, Vera, I know your little game… you're incorrigible."

"Only joking darling," she replied insincerely, whilst winking at one of the creatures out of Bob's eye line.

Bob knew his wife too well. It was time to move on before she got any other lewd ideas. "There's a train due to leave in ten minutes, why don't we go on the platform and wave the passengers off then head back along the path to the ballroom. I want to see if we can get a copy of the photograph of us all with Andy Cross. Wasn't that brilliant?" Bob said.

"He didn't think much of your Gorog language," one of the platoon added.

"No, that wasn't like him. He must have been on edge with all his fans wanting pictures," Bob said trying to excuse his hero.

They finished off the remaining drinks, replaced their Rhino Head gear and marched out of the yard onto the station platform, where they were greeted with screams and applause from the amazed passengers eager to get pictures with the evil aliens. After waving the train off, they waddled back to the house, the sweat again pouring out of them, stinging their eyes with no means of wiping their faces. Struggling for fresh air and with the costume still rubbing parts of their body that they didn't know existed, they had no option but to brave it out.

PC Singleton radioed the incident room, "Sarg, I think I'm going to die, please help me," he pleaded.

Dexter took pity on the constable and arranged a golf cart to collect him when he finally returned to the stables. He had to stand on the back, his tail making it impossible to sit. As he stepped off the cart in the compound, he stripped off down to his underwear without a care who was looking. The relief was bliss. Cool fresh air and an ice-cold drink handed to him by Sergeant Dexter revived him in minutes. "Well done, Singleton. Did you enjoy your first taste of undercover work?"

"It was a living hell sir... I lost him when he joined the others, they all look the bloody same."

"After you radioed in, we checked out the ballroom where we found a discarded costume in the changing room. I guess he dumped it and disappeared into the crowd."

"You mean that route march was a complete waste of my time?" Singleton was not amused.

"No, it's never a waste of time, some might call it character building," Dexter laughed. "Anyway, you never know what else you might have discovered," he added, trying to pacify the distraught, half naked constable, now attracting loud wolf whistles from the officers watching from the incident room.

14
The Arrival

Monday 12th of August. Morning

It was eleven o'clock when the red Renault 5 stopped at the main gate.

"Good morning, can I help you, Miss?" asked Justin, the tall, uniformed security guard. She handed him a copy of a letter which he quickly scanned.

"Very good, Miss. Please follow the road down to the house where you will be met at the front door." He lifted the barrier and she drove through the Gothic style stone gateway, its crenulated top some eight metres above, dwarfing her car. Two huge carved rampant lions stood guard on the apex, seemingly assessing the visitor. This was, by all standards, a grandiose statement of power and she couldn't fail to be impressed. After the gate, she passed a large Victorian house standing in modest grounds flanked by colourful planting. A gravel car park to the front was bordered by low wooden posts with black chains strung between. Amongst a small number of saloon cars, she noted two dark green Range Rovers with gold coloured estate crests on the doors and a Zebra striped Jeep. To the front, more surprisingly, was a police car. The entrance to the car park was indicated by a neatly painted sign which read '*ESTATE OFFICE*.' She drove on through a wooded section with wide manicured grass verges. The kerb was dotted with more low timber posts, preventing vehicles from being driven onto the grass, '*Subtle but effective*,' she thought. Sadly, she couldn't see beyond the woods on either side, as she drove slowly, trying to take in the landscape. The more she looked past the trees into the depth of the woods, the darker it got. The view in front finally opened out, revealing the vista. The valley before her looked like a huge green salad bowl. The road snaked away from her, zig zagging down across open pasture with specimen trees dotted across the estate, their trunks wrapped in timber cages to protect them from deer.

Her tyres made a metallic thrumming sound as the car passed over a cattle grid and the fields now became more pastoral. She could clearly see the cream and brown sheep munching away contentedly on the lush grass. Just one sentinel sheep looked up impassively and watched her slow progress along the road. In the bottom of the shallow bowl sat the magnificent country seat of the Duke of Exford.

The house stood on the site of Woodford Abbey, a Cistercian monastery which had been surrendered to Henry the eighth's Commissioner during the dissolution of the monasteries in the sixteenth century. Following the acquisition, its destruction was rapid, taking only seven years and by 1545 the abbey lay in ruins. The estate was then granted to William D'Macey, the First Duke of Exford. This was an accolade and evidence of his high position at court. William then began to transform the former abbey. Traces of the old buildings were found at lower levels and incorporated into the fine new house. In 1635 the second Duke remodelled the south wing and modernised the façade in the Palladian style with identical wings centred with a portico of five Corinthian columns supporting the stone gable, framing the D'Macey crest. Within, he created a new complex of staterooms. However, in 1648, the building was ravaged by fire and Inigo Jones, along with local architect Sir David Headings, redesigned the interiors of the state rooms and the central stairs.

She continued, driving slowly to take in the view. To the right of the house was a huge lake. Water cascaded from a weir down a series of steps under a Palladian style bridge. On the lake she saw a colourful Mississippi steamboat. It's bright red stern wheel ploughing the craft through the water, past a heavily wooded island. To the left she could make out the vast enclosures of the safari park. They appeared, from this distance, to be a random patchwork of fields surrounded by high metal fencing, softened with trees and bushes. She stopped the car momentarily to look at the animals but from this distance, other than the giraffe and zebra, it was difficult to make out exactly what they were. She drove on, the little car thrumming across another cattle grid, to arrive at the level area approaching the house. The road looped around the knot gardens, their low box hedges neatly clipped to a perfect square framing the colourful planting within.

The tarmac gave way to gravel which swept up to the front of the house. Parking the car to the right of the stone balustrade stair leading to the imposing front door, she got out and retrieved her handbag from the rear seat. She was dressed in a well cut black suit which accentuated her slim figure, white blouse, and grey stockings. On her feet, she wore black, low-heeled shoes. Her long auburn hair was swept back and gathered into a ponytail. Pausing briefly to look up and admire the craftsmanship of the old masons, she walked up the steps.

As she approached the door, it was opened by the butler.

"Good morning, Miss Melinda, the Duke is expecting you, please follow me."

She entered the building. "Thank you, this is a magnificent house."

"Please call me James, Miss," he replied greeting her with a handshake.

"Thank you, James," she said, trying to smother a grin. It was like entering another world, the sort of world you only imagine exists in historical dramas. They headed up the stairs of the Gothic entrance hall which was encircled by a cloistered landing rising three floors, topped by a stained glass cupola. She assumed the oil paintings of the historical figures who watched her ascend the red carpeted stairs, were all related to the D'Macey family.

"This way Miss." James removed a red velvet covered rope barrier from its brass post and beckoned her into a long corridor. This was a thrill. She had visited many stately homes before and had always wondered what was beyond the 'private no entry' signs and now, here she was, being escorted there by a butler. It was all a bit overwhelming. James stopped at a pair of ornately carved mahogany panelled doors and waited for his charge to catch up. As she joined him, he opened both doors together, aware that this action added to the spectacle of entering the voluminous library. As they moved into the book lined room, she could see the Duke D'Macey sitting at the far end behind a paper strewn desk. "Miss Melinda, sir," James solemnly announced.

The Duke was wearing a pale green check jacket over dark corduroy trousers and had a pipe clenched between his teeth. He looked slightly dishevelled but relaxed. As they approached, he removed the pipe from his mouth and stood to greet her.

He was tall, with lightly greying hair. He looked down kindly at her. "Ah! Miss Melinda, this is indeed a pleasure." The Duke was pleasantly surprised to see the historian from the Victoria and Albert Museum was so attractive. He was expecting a dusty old archivist devoid of personality.

"Please, call me Molly. No one calls me Melinda other than my mother, when I've done something wrong."

"Very good, Molly it is. I can't light it, you know," he said, waving the pipe. "Apparently, it's a fire hazard and also the smoke ruins the décor, anyway nurse has forbidden me from smoking on health grounds." He pulled a sorrowful face. "Still like to suck on it though, it's probably some Freudian thing." He shrugged his shoulders, gave a warm welcoming smile and held out his hand. She relaxed in his company, any anxieties about meeting the Duke dissipated like the phantom smoke from his briar.

"I love your sheep," she said randomly, whilst shaking his hand.

"Thank you, they're part of a Herdwick national breeding programme, they're a bit stupid but their meat is sweet and tender. The lions like them as well." He paused for a reaction. Molly looked confused. "Sorry, my little joke… that's in bad taste. They're more partial to beef actually." He looked at the butler, "Thank you James."

"Very good sir," James walked to the doors and closed them carefully behind him.

"Where are my manners? Please take a seat," he said, pointing with his pipe to the soft leather chair on the opposite side of his desk. He fumbled around on the desktop and replaced the pipe in a rack hidden under some official looking papers. "We used to grow tobacco in Africa, but the market is beginning to falter, probably just as well, times have moved on. Now we know the health issues, it's not something we want to be associated with. We've changed production to ethical chocolate which has made us very popular on the stock market. Took a while to establish but now it's paying dividends."

"Pardon me, I don't know how you wish me to address you," Molly said.

"Sir, is fine."

"You have a beautiful place here, sir. It's going to be a pleasure writing your new historical guide."

"Not before time Molly, the existing one is so out of date."

"Yes, I can see it's going to be a bit of a challenge. I took the liberty of obtaining a copy and studying it before I agreed to take on the task. It's going to form part of the portfolio for my PhD, so I wanted to be sure it was of value."

"That's very enterprising of you. You are of course welcome to work here for as long as you need."

"I've written a paper on the demise of stately homes and loss of inherited wealth. It'll be fascinating to see it from an inside perspective."

"Hopefully, we're not heading for the poorhouse yet," the Duke said, surprised at the bluntness of her comment.

"Sorry, that may have come out wrong. I'm sure you have a solid foundation here, but I've discovered other estates during my research that are not as well blessed as Woodford. I promise the new book will be an accurate, and historically correct document and I hope, will portray the personality of the current titleholders. I didn't mean to imply…"

"No, you're right," the Duke, interrupted. "We are incredibly lucky that our ancestors had restraint and didn't gamble everything away or make catastrophic investments. It's a fine balancing act for us though. We strive to be self-sufficient, all of our enterprises have to stand on their own or it could all tumble down like a house of cards. You'll learn more as you delve into our archive. Fortunately for me, my son Jules is now taking the reins of the estate. Places like this need young blood with energy and drive, I'm getting too old to manage it effectively now. However, his ideas take a bit of swallowing sometimes. Take last weekend for instance. We had a science fiction festival. He turned the place into a bloody theme park."

"Yes, I saw it on the television and in the papers. There must have been thousands of people here."

"I've never seen anything like it. The lawns will take months to recover."

"It was terribly sad to read about the suicide though. It was the headline on the Evening Standard. The miners' strike and Margaret Thatcher's actions were demoted to the inside pages."

"It's terribly sad for everyone. Jules has been in a meeting with the police investigator this morning. As far I'm aware they haven't officially confirmed the cause of death yet. The empty lion enclosure is still guarded by the police, we're not allowed back in yet. I hope they'll be able to open it soon, the lions are getting stir crazy in their paddock. Sadly, some of the financial gains from the festival will be used to cover the reduced revenue due to the bad press, also they want to see the lions, that's what we are famous for and at the moment they're out of bounds. It happened once before in the sixties and since then we've been primed for a repeat, but nothing truly prepares you for the reality of the incident.

The keepers are in shock, it'll take years for some of them to get over it... if ever, it leaves a mental scar, terribly sad."

Suddenly the doors from the corridor flew open and a dishevelled young man quickly entered, his face red and nostrils flaring. "Do you know whose car that is parked out the front?" he demanded of his father. The Duke looked on impassively, he was used to his son's manner.

"Ah, Jules, let me introduce you to Melinda Goodall, this is the lady from London who's going to write our new book."

"Charmed, I'm sure," Jules said, barely looking in her direction.

"There's a cheap little red car parked on the front drive by the steps, its making the place look like a council house. Visitors may already have included it in their photos. What will they think?"

"It's mine," Molly confessed. "I'm terribly sorry, I didn't mean my little car to be a nuisance."

"Didn't the security guard tell you to park in the staff car park?" Jules asked, eying up the offender.

"No, sorry!"

"Right, I'm having words, they're getting sloppy."

"Don't be too hard on him, he was really sweet," she said as the Duke watched on, amused that Jules histrionics appeared to have no effect on the young lady.

"He's a security guard, he's not supposed to be sweet." He turned tail and started to walk away, "I'll come back and tell you about the meeting later, father. You're not going to believe what they've found," he said, walking out of the door. As he did so, James entered, walked up to Molly and held out a small silver platter. "If you wish to pass me your keys, I'll move your vehicle to the car park for you," he offered the platter.

"Oh... I... well, if you don't mind, that's awfully kind. Thank you, James." She retrieved the keys from her handbag and placed them on the tray, he nodded and exited the room with barely a sound.

She couldn't help smiling, and turned back to the Duke, "That's so kind of him," she said.

The Duke smiled back, "Sorry about the drama, my son's a bit highly strung. I guess the meeting with the police hasn't gone well this morning. Right, now, where were we... have you sorted out your accommodation?"

"I've booked a room at the Abbey Inn for now. My mum and dad live in Holeford, so when I've gathered enough information to start writing I can work from there."

"Let me make a phone call." He picked up the receiver and dialled. "Hello, is that Jeff… The Duke here… no it is, I'm not taking the mickey… now listen. You've got a Miss Goodall booked in from tonight…" She could hear the landlord mumbling on the other end of the line. "Good, at least your diary's working, now transfer her to the Dukes Room and put it on my tab. She's working for me, and I want her to be comfortable… very good, thank you." He hung up. "I think you'll like that room, it's light and airy with a good desk and a comfy sofa.

"That's very kind, but I don't want to put you to any trouble and expense."

"It's no trouble, I own the pub, in fact I own the whole village, but you'll learn more about that when you start work." Molly already had a good knowledge of the estate and family from her research, but she played along. '*No one likes a smart Alec,*' she thought.

The Duke rose and walked to the other end of the library, approaching a large desk nestled in the corner. He picked up a pile of papers and pushed some loose books into a drawer, clearing the top. "I hope you'll use this area for your research, all the documents are to hand," he said gesticulating around the room. "It's all here somewhere, and the indexing is actually very good. Don't judge the archive by the state of my desk, that's just the way I work, in a bit of a muddle. It does get filed eventually, with a bit of help from James." Molly was not convinced about the filing, but it did make good sense to base herself here, initially anyway.

"Now, I suggest we have a cup of tea and then James can give you a tour of the house." He returned to his desk and pressed a small ceramic button set in a brass surround alongside the telephone. As if by magic a section of the bookshelves swung open, and James appeared carrying a tray of tea and cakes, which he placed on the coffee table, sensibly positioned between large, well-worn sofas in front of the fireplace. He was followed by a young maid neatly dressed in black with a white apron, again, directly out of a period drama. She proceeded to lay out the bone China service and tiered cake stand displaying a delicious looking selection. The Duke indicated to Molly to take a seat. He sat himself opposite as the tea was poured and sugar bowl offered to the guest. "That will be all Louise, thank you." The maid did a little curtsey, picked up the tray and left the room followed by James.

Over tea, Molly told of her upbringing in Holeford. How her parents were both now retired, her father from the dairy and her mother from management of a supermarket. How she had volunteered at the museum in the last year of her schooling, where the curator, Professor Halford, helped her get a scholarship to Oxford. The Duke was impressed by her achievements especially having come from such a modest background. It turned out the Duke was a good friend of Professor Halford and had joined him on several expeditions. Hung on a wall of the library was a sepia photograph of the Egyptian expedition, which she recognised as a copy of the picture hanging in the Professor's office at the museum.

"I'm a trustee of the museum, I really must get in touch with Dominic, its ages since we saw each other." The fact they had a common link, filled the Duke with confidence that this enterprise was going to be very successful. Molly's initial unease at meeting an aristocrat was also fading, she felt comfortable in his company. He was just a normal person who happened to live in a strange, alternative world of privilege. She didn't envy him, it had already begun to dawn on her the extent of the responsibility that came with that position. They finished their tea, the Duke pulled a cord by the fireplace and Louise returned to clear the crockery.

"Now, I think it's time for your tour." Yet again the ubiquitous James appeared on cue. "James will take you round, then I'm sure you'll want to go to the village and see your room. Jeff does a good rabbit pie but watch out for the lead shot." He grinned. "I'll expect you in the morning at ten and then we can discuss how you want to proceed. I'll also arrange for the head keeper to take you on a tour of the estate tomorrow, you'll need to see everywhere to appreciate what you will be writing about."

"Thank you for your hospitality, I'm looking forward to my time here, I just hope I can do you justice."

"I'm sure you will, my dear."

"This way miss," James indicated. They left through the hidden door in the bookcase and headed down the back staircase. This was the staff access and was devoid of the splendour of the main entrance but would still be perfectly acceptable in most ordinary houses. The walls were painted eggshell blue and tall, narrow, leaded windows gave glimpses over the well-stocked kitchen garden towards the orangery. The stone steps and metal balustrade with hardwood handrail, were immaculately finished. They descended to the lobby, it's floor of large, timeworn stone slabs leading directly into the garden.

James paused, "Sorry to take you down the staff stairs but it's much quicker. I've parked your car in the staff car park, just through that door and turn right, you can't miss it," he said, handing back the keys. "Let's go this way. We'll start in the long gallery. Give it a few days and you'll be able to find your way around easily, it's quite a modest pile compared with some stately homes."

They headed to a simple painted panel door. He turned the large brass knob and they entered the long gallery. The austere stone and bare walls of the lobby gave way to exotic wood panelled walls, tapestries and artwork. The ceiling was a textbook example of Dutch plasterwork with painted sections that would not shame the finest palaces in Europe. James started to give her a potted history of the room. Molly could hear him talking but she was distracted, her eyes trying to take in all the details.

Suddenly, Alice and Tom walked through the door at the far end of the gallery.

Alice couldn't believe her eyes and stopped abruptly. "Molly... Molly!" she cried out, and ran down the corridor. Tom watched in wonder as Alice ran up to a young lady being guided by the butler. Molly was also surprised and thrilled to see her old spirit friend from Holeford.

It had been a long time since they had been together, with Molly going off to Oxford and then London while the three ghosts, who had resided at the Price Low supermarket in Holeford since their death, had moved to this new location. James, unaware of the encounter, continued his well-rehearsed narration. Molly turned away from him to smile and wink to her ghostly friend, without detection. Tom watched the interaction with interest, he now understood that it was possible to communicate with mortals and this could be useful to him in finding his assailant.

"I'm sorry James, this is all fascinating but is there a powder room I could use?"

"Certainly, I should have offered earlier, forgive me. Through the door at the far end is the lobby, with public toilets. Follow me."

Molly secretly signalled to Alice, and they all headed to the ballroom lobby, which had seen so much action during the recent Sci-Fi festival. As they entered, Tour guide Barbara Greenacre appeared from the ball-room with a group of visitors.

"Good morning, James," she declared, giving the impression to her charges that she was on first name terms with the senior staff.

"Good afternoon," James answered stiffly, rather deflating Barbara who nervously checked her watch to find it was now twelve thirty.

"This way ladies and gentlemen, into the Long Gallery," she instructed, avoiding further eye contact with the Duke's butler while whisking her charges quickly away. Molly and Alice headed into the 'ladies' while Tom and James remained in the lobby.

"Well, James, how long have you been working here then?" Tom asked.

Meanwhile James had moved to a vase of flowers on the sideboard and adjusted the blooms whilst checking the area for dust. He felt the lobby was unusually cold today, so he moved to the doors and checked for draughts.

"Are you going to watch the football tonight? I'm a United fan myself, what about you?" Tom continued undeterred.

In the ladies, Alice was beside herself with excitement. "Molly, you look amazing! What are you doing here? This is so exciting. I can't wait to tell the others you're here. I've got so much to ask you."

"You look good too, this place obviously suits you. Who's your boy-friend?" Molly asked.

"Tom's not my boyfriend. He's just been eaten by a lion, Eric dropped him off for us to look after, until he can get back to sort out all the paper-work."

"Is he the suicide I've read about in the papers?"

"Ahh! That's just it. It wasn't suicide, he was chased in there by a gun-man. Oh! Molly, it's ever so exciting! Wilf is leading our investigation and Detective Inspector Montgomery is doing the same for the Holeford Police."

"Don't you mean Sergeant Montgomery?" Molly queried.

"No, he's a detective now. Can you believe it?"

"What hope has Tom got of finding his killer?"

"A lot more now you're here, this is wonderful."

"I need to go back to the lobby, James will be waiting. We'll talk later," Molly said, flushing one of the toilets for effect.

"Can you meet us by the big oak tree at three o'clock?" Alice said, impatiently. "It's by the Café, you can't miss it. Please, George and Wilf will be so pleased to see you!"

"I'll do my best," Molly washed her hands, activated the noisy hand dryer and re-joined James in the lobby. "Thank you. Where next?"

Alice followed her out, waved and disappeared through the wall into the gallery, closely followed by Tom, still studying Molly curiously over his shoulder.

"Bye, James. See you tonight then, I'll get the beers in," he called out jovially.

James continued the tour, visiting the ballroom before going out into the gardens via the staff car park to show Molly where he had parked her car and then back into the house through the French doors of the state dining room. Also known as the Italian room, it contained a fine collection of paintings, furniture and artefacts gathered by the Duke's father and grandfather during their lengthy grand tours of Europe. "We've recently had this room licensed for weddings," James said. "It's proving very popular, especially with our formal gardens for photographs and the ballroom for the evening party." He showed her some of the more exceptional items and explained their significance. Molly was beginning to glaze over, it was only possible to take in so many facts, her mind was in a whirl, especially after the revelation about Tom. She was desperate to know more. James astutely detected that Molly was reaching information overload. "Let's go up the main stairs to complete the tour for today, it's a lot to take in, in one go. At least you know roughly how to find your way around the house. I understand the Duke has arranged for someone to give you a guided tour of the park and grounds tomorrow."

"Yes, the Duke said the head keeper is going to show me around the park. Thank you so much for the introduction today, it was so interesting."

They returned to the library. The Duke looked up from his paperwork, "How did you get on?"

"Marvellous, thank you, it was a lot to take in though. If you don't mind, I'd like to have a little walk around the gardens, then go to the Inn, get settled and have dinner."

"That's very sensible, I'll see you in the morning. Then we can discuss the new book and send you on the estate tour. That'll take most of the day I'm afraid, but I think you'll enjoy it, there's a lot to see."

"That will be lovely sir, I think I'm going to enjoy working here and I promise you will have a book to be proud of." She picked up her handbag. "May I use the back stair?"

"Be my guest."

Molly grinned, there was a childish joy in going through a secret door, but it also made for a short cut to the car park. She checked her watch. It was two thirty, just time to pop back to the car, go to the Café for a drink and then be at the tree for three. "See you in the morning," she said, practically skipping towards the dummy bookcase.

In the Café, Molly found a table overlooking the stables and house. Just to the left was an ancient oak tree with wooden seating curving around the trunk. This must be where her meeting with Alice was to take place shortly. With not a cloud in the sky, she could see the visitors milling around the stable yard looking at the display of horse- drawn coaches, their spotless paintwork sparkling in the sun. Families were trekking back and forth, to and from pet's paradise and the aviary. Some stopped for refreshment at the Zambelli ice cream parlour. She could hear the toot of the train whistle as it departed from the station, the steam organ playing '*Puppet on a String*' in the fairground and the clang of the bell from the Mississippi steamboat on the lake, all adding to the atmosphere.

She studied the advertising flyer for the safari park that she had picked up from the information stand. It showed glossy pictures of the animals and other attractions along with a colourfully illustrated map. It contained just enough information to entice prospective visitors, but it lacked the detail most would value when they commenced their visits. They would need to buy the guidebook for more in-depth information.

In the Café there was a constant burble of conversation punctuated by the clinking of china and the whoosh of steam from the coffee machines. While reading the flyer, she also considered the fate of Tom, there were so many questions. She noticed a policeman standing by the gate to the lion enclosure, deducing that the investigation was underway. The public wandered round the attractions oblivious to the activity shielded by the hedges and fencing.

The clock in the tower on the coach house struck on the hour and as if by magic, Alice, Wilf, George and Tom arrived at the tree. Looking through the café window she was thrilled to see them just as she remembered them at the Price Low supermarket in Holeford. Alice, wearing her fine Victorian dress with Wilf and George dressed as pirate and policeman respectively. The young man she assumed was Tom, looked out of place wearing tee-shirt, jeans and trainers.

She quickly finished her coffee, stuffed the leaflet into her handbag and headed outside. The quartet were full of smiles and rushed over to greet her.

"Hello you three, Oh! and you must be Tom, how wonderful."

A passer-by looked across at her as if she had lost her marbles. Molly became self-conscious, "Can we go somewhere more private?" she whispered.

"Follow us," George said. They headed past the station to a lawn overlooking the lake, screened from the visitors by the fencing of the steam driven fairground. The sound of the pipe organ also helped to cover the sound of Molly's conversation.

"It's so lovely to see you all, it must be two years since you moved here, how's it going?"

"We love it," Alice said. "Not that we didn't like it in our old home, but there's so much space here and always so much going on. We have a huge attic room, and we don't need to hide during the day. It's part of the job description to move freely around the house."

Molly looked surprised, *'They had job descriptions?'*

"It's an important element of ancient monuments and historic houses to have resident ghosts, it all adds to the atmosphere," Wilf explained, "and it's not everyone that can carry it off."

"Our predecessors got the sack," George whispered confidentially, "They were three tin miners from Cornwall, killed in a mining accident who wanted to better themselves. Trouble was they just stayed in the crypt of the chapel."

"Wouldn't come out, they didn't like the sunlight and refused to move around during the day," Alice sniggered, "It took Eric ages to move them on, employment rights and all that, but he finally found a deserted railway tunnel to haunt, and they happily moved. So this Woodford Abbey position became vacant again, and we decided to take it. We were ready for a change this time, especially after you left for university. It just wasn't the same. But enough about us, how about you?"

"Well, after getting my history degree I was offered a contract at the British Museum. The university suggested I continue studying towards my PhD so I've been flitting back and forth between London and the university to do my studies. My mentor then suggested moving me around other museums in London to gain more knowledge. It's been a massive learning experience. I'm currently on a six-month secondment to the Victoria and Albert Museum, then this assignment came up which will help with my PhD submission, earn me a bit of pocket money and place me near home for a couple of weeks. The icing on the cake is seeing you all again, you're going to be a huge help with the new book. It'll be just like old times when you helped with my homework."

"Are you staying at the Abbey Inn?" Wilf asked.

"Well deduced Wilf, that's where I'm going next, I need to check in. His Grace has arranged for me to have the 'Duke's room,' do you know it?"

"Yes, that's lovely. It's just been refurbished," George said.

Molly watched Tom who was looking confused about this relationship with a mortal. "Now, what about you Tom? Alice tells me you were eaten by a lion. The papers say it was suicide, what really happened?"

Tom told Molly the full story and the fact he's waiting for Eric to return with the paperwork.

Alice then enthusiastically took over, "We've been trying to find the gunman and look for clues. Wilf has even tried dressing as Columbo, but I don't think that actually helped." Wilf looked a little upset at this dig at his detecting skills. She then told Molly about the '*Galactic Jump*' weekend and their investigative trip to the Inn. As they talked, the Mississippi paddle steamer gently sailed by, its white paintwork glinting in the sunlight. The two tall black chimney stacks puffed smoke as the engine turned the pistons, just visible through elaborately painted fretwork covers on the side of the boat. The huge red stern wheel rotated slowly, pushing the vessel through the water at a steady four knots. On the top deck, Molly could see the captain dressed in period costume with gold braded black cap, standing in the pilot house. It was a beautiful sight from a bygone era.

A young man dressed like a character from a Mark Twain novel was stood by the deck rail waving his cap frantically at them. Alice waved back just as enthusiastically, "That's Finn," she informed Molly, "Wave to him." They all waved, and Finn waved back even more vigorously. "He came over here with the boat," Alice explained. "The Duke's father rescued it from a ship yard in New Orleans and shipped it back here. He paid for a full restoration, with new steam engines and everything, isn't she gorgeous?"

"She's beautiful. I love the fancy detailing around the canopy, it must have cost a fortune to renovate."

"I expect so. Finn had smuggled on board when it was working on the Mississippi, but was killed when the boiler suddenly exploded. Apparently that happened a lot in America, but he decided to stay on the boat when he heard it was going to be restored. He's a lovely chap but he's got a really funny accent. He always takes his cap off when he sees a girl… very polite."

"He looks very friendly," Molly observed, as she waved. Finn looked a little confused when he realised a mortal was able to see him and raised his arms, shrugging his shoulders questioningly.

Alice cupped her hands to her mouth and shouted to him, "I'll explain later." He did a thumbs up, as the boat turned away to circle the island in the middle of the lake.

"Wow, that was unexpected," Molly said. "Now where were we… so, Tom, have the police got any closer to the truth about your murder?"

"I don't think they've even worked out that it's Tom. You know what the Holeford police are like, nothing's going to happen fast especially with Montgomery involved, judging by his past record," Wilf said, scathingly.

"I saw a policeman guarding the gate, so they must still be investigating." Molly commented.

"That's a good point," George said, "if you'll excuse me, I think I'd better go and have a snoop round the enclosure and see how they're getting on." They all nodded in agreement as he moved off towards the gates.

"I love the parrot Wilf, it finishes off your pirate outfit beautifully." Molly observed.

"He's lovely, just flew into the attic about a year ago. He's very friendly, we think he came from the aviary," Wilf said, stroking the large blue and red macaw, happily sitting on his shoulder.

"He must have fallen off his perch," Alice joked.

"Don't be cruel," Wilf said, affectionately stroking the parrot's beak. "We don't see him for weeks, then he reappears for a while, then off again… don't know where he goes, he never talks about it."

Molly was thrilled to meet her friends again but there would be plenty of time to chat over the coming days. "It so lovely to see you all but if you don't mind, I'm going to go to the Inn now. I'll catch up with you tomorrow. I'll be back at ten, but the Duke is arranging a tour of the park so I don't know where or when I'll be able to join you. I'll start asking some discreet questions. Don't worry Tom, we'll sort this out," Molly reassured him. She slung her bag over her shoulder and wandered back to the staff car park. Alice, Wilf and Tom waved her off and then went to find George.

In the library the Duke sat at his desk, studying *The Racing Post*. He looked at the ormolu clock on the mantelpiece, it was nearly three thirty. He put the paper down, moved to the sofa and found the remote control for the television, under a magazine on the table. He then settled down on the sofa and pressed the power button. The light on the corner of the television went green and after a few seconds the screen lit up, accompanied by a fanfare, the racing from Kempton Park was on and the Grampton Ales steeplechase was about to start.

He was interested to watch the progress of *Nedrum*, a horse part owned by Sir Nicholas Saint, his friend and fellow member of the Grantchester Club in London. The cameras zoomed in on the stalls. The last horse was being reluctantly ushered into place by the stable hands. Once all safely loaded, the gates sprung open and the spectacle of the galloping horses with their multi-coloured silken jockeys began. He looked closely to pick out the pale blue and maroon striped silks of *Nedrum's* jockey. Having spotted him, he pointed at the screen, "There he is, come on boy!" he shouted to the empty room.

The door opened, "Who are you talking to, father?"

"Shut up and sit down. This is Nick's horse, he's in third place."

Jules sat obediently. Inside he was still seething from his meeting with the police, he needed to share it or he was going to burst.

The race neared its climax, *Nedrum* was in second place. The Duke was on the edge of the sofa slapping the cushion next to him, urging *Nedrum* on. Two horses were competing neck and neck towards the finish line, "Come on… Come on… no… no!"

It was a photo finish. The commentator couldn't determine the winner, it would be down to the stewards. "Can you believe that? He had it in the bag… let's hope he's done enough." The Duke sank back into the cushions to wait for the decision. "Now, what's bugging you? You were awfully rude to that poor girl earlier, she's here to help us and you didn't have the decency to be polite. I'm disappointed in you, I thought you had good manners but that was plain rudeness."

"Sorry, father. I was in a foul temper after the meeting. I needed to tell you the news at once."

"Well, perhaps you'll be less distracted now and calmer." The Duke was again distracted by the television. "Yes! Yes! He's done it! What a horse. Nick's going to be thrilled. Look… Look there he is in the winner's enclosure," the Duke added, again pointing at the screen while sitting on the edge of the sofa. "I need to call him tonight."

"What were you saying about being distracted?" Jules chided.

"Sorry… where were we?" The Duke flushed. He turned off the set and sat back in the chair, giving his son his full attention.

"That Detective Montgomery chap and his Sergeant were there with the head warden, chief of security and myself. They've found ricochet marks from a small calibre gun. That dent in the new sign was actually caused by a bullet. I was only joking when I saw it originally. They've got witness reports from the village of gunfire being heard on Friday night. They're not ruling out its possible link to the disturbance of the market stock in the stable loft. To top it all, one of the student helpers from the market is missing. This is now a possible murder investigation, can you believe it?"

The Duke was ashen faced. "You're joking… it can't be." His shoulders dropped, and he sunk even lower into the sofa. This latest development appeared to shock him deeply.

"They're serious, father. This could ruin us… I don't know how to handle it, if the press get hold of it they'll have field day."

The Duke sat up slowly, quietly considering what to do. "It won't take the papers long, they're already all over the suicide story. We need to brief the staff without delay, one false word in the wrong ear and it'll get out of hand. We need to take a 'no comment' response to any questions and carry on as if nothing has happened."

"OK, I'll go and draft a memo then arrange a series of staff meetings in the morning. I'll start with the warden and keepers. They're the ones closest to the incident."

"What are the police doing now?" The Duke asked.

"Montgomery said they're following up leads from the Sci-Fi festival and trying to track down the missing student. He's going to keep us informed."

"Good, that buys us time, now get going Jules... I need to make some calls."

15
The New Recruit

Tuesday 13th August. Morning

Work in the safari park starts early, the keepers arrive at five thirty, congregating in the mess room for a short meeting before heading off to their allotted sections for feeding, mucking out and routine health checks. John Hammond, the Head Keeper, gave them a basic update on the police activities and asked them to be in the Ballroom for a nine o'clock briefing from Jules. They could then return to their duties with the park opening being delayed until ten thirty to allow time for the completion of their routine tasks.

At nine Jules finished his telephone conversation with DI Montgomery and went to the Ballroom via the stage door. He was pleased to see the safari staff were already there, tucking into the biscuits and coffee prepared by housekeeping. This was to be the first of four morning briefings, with different departments being called in separately to minimise the impact on the operations of the estate.

Jules relayed in detail, the recent developments in the police investigation. There was a stunned silence when he revealed that the incident was now being treated as a murder investigation. The staff were like a large family, many of them had worked there since leaving full time education. Several of them were second and even third generation families, who had devoted their working life to caring for the animals. Jules respected their professional integrity as well as their loyalty and treated them as his extended family. In turn, he knew they would respect the sensitivity of the information. He made them aware that there would inevitably be increased press interest and if they were approached, were to make no comment, and report the incident to their line manager or directly to himself. He then read a statement from DI Montgomery, reiterating the confidentiality of the investigation and asking them to report any unusual activity they could remember during the Sci-Fi weekend, no matter how trivial they thought it may be.

"The whole weekend was unusual, sir," John Hammond said wryly. The staff didn't respond. The enormity of the news weighed heavy on their minds.

Jules told them that the lion enclosure would be cleared for opening soon, he was just waiting for confirmation from the police. This lifted their spirits a little. Getting back to a normal routine was what they all wanted. He thanked them for their time and sent them on their way. As he finished, he drew John to one side.

"Can you go and see the Duke please? He has a little task for you this morning."

"Very good sir," John made his way through the gallery to the main stairs. Housekeeping cleared the mugs and replenished the stocks ready for the next meeting, while Jules returned to his office to check the morning post before he returned for the next presentation, this time to housekeeping and the garden staff.

At ten o'clock, Molly pulled down on the cast iron lever by the front door and heard the bell ring in the entrance hall. James welcomed her and presented her with an 'access all areas' pass hanging on a colourful Woodford Abbey lanyard. She put it proudly over her head, now feeling like part of the team. She was now able to go up to the library without escort, where the Duke was waiting for her alongside a man wearing walking boots, khaki trousers and a 'Woodford Abbey' fleece.

"Ah good, knew you'd be on time Melinda," the Duke said. "This is our head keeper, John Hammond. He's going to take you on a tour of the animal park this morning and after lunch you'll be going on a tour of the estate and gardens."

Molly moved forward and shook John's hand, "Thank you, please call me Molly, everyone does."

"Sorry, forgot that", the Duke said. "Oh, I've got these for you," the Duke then handed her two clear polythene parcels. She opened the first one and unfolded a dark green fleece identical to John's, in the other was a showerproof jacket in the same colour, embroidered with the estate logo.

"That's very kind of you," she said, taken aback by this generosity.

"It's nothing. If you're going to be with us for a while you need to look the part. It'll save a few odd looks from the staff as well. I hope they're the right size, James picked them out, he's got a good eye for these things. Any problem and he'll change them for you."

"Right miss, shall we go? The Jeep's out by the Ballroom entrance," John said.

"Yes, that would be lovely," Molly slipped on the jacket which fitted perfectly, her hands instinctively stroking the soft new fleece.

"Should be back about one," John informed the Duke.

They went down to the Jeep, Molly got in the passenger side and tossed the jacket, still in its polythene wrapping, onto the backseat. She was surprised to see Alice sat there.

"Hi, where are we going today?" she enquired excitedly.

"The animal park, I can't talk now," Molly whispered. Alice understood and pretended to zip up her mouth as John climbed into the driver's seat.

"It's cold in here, you'll need to keep your fleece on," John said, adjusting the heating.

"It's a lovely day, I'm sure it'll soon warm up," Molly said.

"Have you visited the park before?"

"Not for a while, I came with mum and dad a few years ago, I think it was when you opened the tiger enclosure."

"Good grief! That was ten years ago, you'll see a lot of changes since then. The savannah enclosure has been opened out and we've built new animal houses to provide cover in the winter... Well, we had to, the numbers have increased due to our successful breeding programmes. We work with other parks to mix up blood stock and with overseas organisations to reintroduce animals back into their habitat, where it's safe to do so. Sadly, poaching is still threatening some species, places like this may be their only hope of survival."

"That's so sad. What you do is so important. Why would anyone want to harm these wonderful creatures?" Molly said.

"We also opened the new aviary last year. That's been a huge success, we'll pop in there before returning to the house."

"How long have you worked here?"

"I've been here thirty years, my father worked here before me.

I grew up with the park as my playground, so it was just a natural progression to follow in his footsteps. I can't imagine being anywhere else. My brother's based in the deer park, he looks after the zebras. My sister's the manager of the shop and coffee house near the entrance. We'll probably meet them on our way round."

"I met the Viscount Jules Exford yesterday, he seems a bit grumpy," Molly said.

"The staff call him VJ. He's normally very nice, a bit too laid back some say, but he's got a lot on his plate, I don't envy him. You must have caught him at a bad moment."

"I think he'd been in a meeting with the police. How are you all coping with the suicide, it must be awful?" Alice leant forward and listened very carefully to his response.

John was conflicted after the morning briefing, "I'm not sure if I can discuss it." He thought for a few seconds. "Well, I don't see why not, you're officially a member of staff, but you must promise not to breathe a word outside the park. All the staff are being briefed by VJ on the recent developments, so you're going to hear us all talking about it. Anyway, the latest is, that it's not a suicide, the police are treating it as a murder investigation."

"Hooray, they're getting somewhere at last, good old Montgomery!" Alice cried out.

Molly ignored her, "But that's awful," she said to John.

He turned the vehicle right along the gravel road signed posted '*staff only beyond this point*'. They passed through a gate into a wide grass area interspersed with bushes. High fences lined both sides in what Molly assumed was the big cat enclosures beyond.

"Is that the lion enclosure, where it all happened?" Molly asked.

"Yes, lions to the right of us, tigers to the left," John confirmed as he pulled up in the keeper's compound. "This is the centre of operations, all the wardens are based here. Over there is the vehicle workshop and in front, the offices, mess room and kitchens where we prepare the majority of the animal feed. Over to the left is the housing for the lions and behind us is for the tigers. There's another set up like this near the public entrance to the park that supports the savannah wildlife, we'll go there later. If we time it right, you can help with the feeding of the giraffes. But first let me introduce you to some of the team."

They stepped out onto the gravel yard closing the car doors. Alice followed.

"There are a lot of police cars here," Molly noted.

"Yes, the canteen has been requisitioned as their incident room. They've made themselves at home in there while they gather the evidence. VJ seems to think they'll be moving out soon and we can re-open the drive-through enclosure."

"I'm going to the canteen, see you later," Alice called out excitedly and wandered off to see what other information she could glean. Molly did a discreet wave, and Alice was gone.

Sergeant Dexter emerged from the canteen and recognised Molly. "Hello, it's Miss Goodall, isn't it? Unless I'm very much mistaken," he said holding out his hand.

"You have a good memory for faces. It must be ten years. I thought I'd grown up a bit since then," she said, smiling and shook his hand. "I see you're a Sergeant now, congratulations."

John was amazed, "You two know each other?"

"It's a long story," Molly said.

"I met Miss Goodall during the arrest of a pair of burglars in Holeford ten years ago, sir," he informed John.

"Not precisely true, my mum worked at the shop where it happened, I was just a bystander," Molly corrected him.

"But you still recognised her. She must have been a school child then," John observed.

"I guess it's the police training, sir. I bet you know all your animals individually, while to my eyes, they all look the same. You just attune to these things," Dexter said smugly, "Now, if you will excuse me."

"Certainly officer. Right Molly, let's go and grab a coffee, meet the crew and then I'll show you the rest of the animal park. They're all squeezed in the food prep room while the police are here so it's a bit cosy."

After meeting the staff they looked around the compound and the big cat houses with their large pens, visible from the car park. "These are the holding enclosures or paddocks," John explained, pointing at a fenced area beyond the building. "We can isolate the cats here, they still have room to roam but they prefer the space of the drive-through enclosure. They're just going to have to be patient till the police have finished their investigation. The vets are monitoring them in case there's a reaction to the unusual flesh they've eaten. It's purely a precaution. However, the police have asked us to gather all their poo so they can check it for clues. Rather them than me!"

"What a strange thing to do," Molly said.

They jumped back into the Jeep and John drove out of the compound along the track reserved for the park's vehicles. They passed through a pair of gates and emerged at the highest point of the drive, overlooking the savannah enclosures. The vast green space was divided into sections with strategically placed trees and undergrowth disguising the seemingly random lines of fencing. The public road weaved around and through the various areas by crossing cattle grids and passing through manned gates. In the middle of the valley sparkling ripples glinted off the surface of a lake, it was smaller than the one by the house but no less impressive. On the far side of the water flamingos gathered together, prancing like ballerinas on stilts. A narrow river supplied the water and acted as another barrier between compounds.

Molly could see a herd of zebra grazing and close to a pair of elephants frolicking in the mud at the edge of the lake. In the distance were unmistakable, ungainly but elegant, tall brown and yellow giraffes slowly meandering towards their house. Along the roads fenced parking areas were interspersed with picnic tables, serviced by refreshment huts disguised as log cabins and even a colonial style tea-room with souvenir shop. The visitors were not going to be thirsty or hungry on their slow drive through this area. John gave her an insight into the daily routines carried out by the keepers to maintain the animal's health and wellbeing. They drove over the grass, away from the public, stopping to talk to wardens sat in their vehicles observing the visitors at a discreet distance. They arrived at the giraffe house in time to greet the animals returning for their regular feed. Molly joined the keepers in the huge aircraft hangar of a building and with their supervision was able to help. Long prehensile tongues reached through the bars to take the carrots from her hand. Having had their quota, they politely and gracefully wandered out through the massive doorway into the open.

Molly was then able to join the flamingo feeding and still had time to visit the zebra house, before heading back through the park via the tiger enclosure. Wardens monitored the visitor's cars closely as they drove slowly along the tarmac road creating a more sombre atmosphere.

"They're making sure all the car windows are kept closed and the tigers don't get too excited. We've had incidents where they've ripped the bumpers and even a bonnet off a visitor's car," John explained.

"I see the wardens have rifles. That's a bit scary," Molly said.

"The keepers in the big cat enclosures are all trained marksmen. They've never had to shoot to kill, I'm pleased to say, but it's necessary for our insurance to protect the people driving through. They do work for the vets too, darting the animals when we need to sedate them for treatment. But both the cats and public are well behaved overall."

"It's a shame the keepers weren't there when Tom got attacked," Molly said.

"Tom? How do you know that name?" John asked with surprise. Molly's blood drained from her face. She had spoken out of turn, even the police hadn't confirmed the identity yet.

"I saw it on the board in the incident room," she said trying to quickly recover the situation.

"Oh yes, they must be closing in on the identity, but you must keep to yourself what you see."

"Don't worry, I will. Have we got time to see the aviary?" she asked, quickly changing the subject.

"Yes, I think so, I just need to pop into the office. I won't be a minute so please wait in the car," John said, as they returned to the compound.

While Molly waited, Alice emerged through the wall of the incident room and got in the Jeep. "You're not going to believe what they're doing... they're collecting the lion poo and pulling it apart with their hands. They've got gloves and masks on, but yuck! I bet when they joined the police they didn't have that on their job description. But you'll never guess... while I was there, they found a watch. It was still buckled like it had been round a wrist. They washed it off and... now this is the amazing bit. It was still working! and when you push a button the face lights up. When we get back we need to check if it was Tom's. This could be the breakthrough they need to identify him."

"Well done, Alice," Molly said then held her finger to her mouth.

John returned, started the engine and drove back along the road towards the house. "We've only got half an hour, so it'll have to be a whistle stop tour of the bird house, but you can go in there anytime you like by just showing your pass." He parked outside the entrance of the huge domed, aviary similar in shape to the glass house at 'Kew Gardens.' They walked through the two sets of doors to be greeted by a cacophony of bird song in a jungle of plants and trees, with meandering paths around a central water feature. John introduced the aviary manager Charlotte, who gave a quick introduction to some of the exotic birds, who were happy to perch on her arm for the reward of a tit-bit, it was then time to return to the house.

In the library the Duke was waiting for them. "Ah, welcome back, how did you get on?"

"It's been fascinating, I can't thank you enough John. But I'm feeling guilty that I haven't started any work on the new book yet," Molly admitted.

"You'll have plenty of time to do that, I think you'll find it invaluable to have a good understanding of the estate and its layout before you start. Now, go and get some lunch and be back here at two for the tour of the estate. Thanks for your time, John, I've arranged another guide for the afternoon tour."

"Very good, sir, Come with me Molly, They do a mean pie and chips at the café and it's complimentary for staff, I'll show you how it works," he explained, as they walked to the restaurant opposite the house and stables.

"Good, you're here. I have an interesting job for you this afternoon," the Duke said, as he watched Jules enter the library over the rim of his reading glasses.

"Come on father, you can't just drop a job on me at a moment's notice. I've got the police roaming the grounds, the car festival to sort out with the Holeford car club this afternoon and a million and one other things to do."

"Then you need a break. Look at yourself, you're stressed out. You need to stop rushing around. We can't afford for you to be ill."

Inside, Jules knew he was right. He was frazzled. The incident in the lion enclosure hung heavy on him and was affecting his concentration.

"Alright, what's so important?" he asked peevishly.

"You remember Melinda… or rather Molly, as she prefers to be called… the lady you were very short with yesterday?"

"Yes, what of it?" Jules frowned.

"Well, you're taking her on a tour of the estate this afternoon. Farms, grounds and gardens. John took her around the animal park this morning. She needs a good insight into the size and complexity of the whole estate before she starts writing the new book. It'll do you good as well. You need to remind yourself what the estate looks like through new eyes, it may help to remind you of the beauty and wonder of it all. It'll also give you a chance to show her you're not the grouch she thinks you are. Remember, she's going to write the story that will promote this place for years to come and we need to look good."

"But we've got…" There was a knock at the door which stopped him in mid-sentence.

"No buts Jules, turn on your charm, here she is."

Molly entered the room, surprised to see Jules and wary of how he may react.

"Good afternoon," she said politely.

"Perfect timing, Molly," the Duke said, "Jules has offered to take you on this afternoon's trip."

Jules reluctantly gave a polite smile. "Hello Molly." They shook hands, Molly, still on her guard. Her first impression of him was still firmly lodged in her mind.

Jules summoned up his charm as requested. "Before we start, I must apologise for my behaviour yesterday. I'd just had a stressful meeting with the police. You caught me at a low ebb. Can we start again?" He paused and studied the young woman before him, "Your face is familiar."

"I don't know why," Molly said, taken off guard.

"We'll see if we can work it out on our trip this afternoon. I see you already have the security clearance."

Molly looked confused. Jules pointed to the badge. "Oh, I see what you mean. Yes, I had a very instructive tour of the animal park this morning, it's fascinating to see behind the scenes."

"OK, Father, I'll deal with those issues we discussed tomorrow," he said, still scrutinising Molly, "Come on, let's get going, we've got a lot to see."

They went down the back stairs and out through the kitchen garden to the staff car park. He blipped his key ring and the lights on his dark green Range Rover flashed and the car bleeped in response. Molly couldn't help beaming as she climbed up and sank into the plush passenger seat. She was cocooned in buff leather and surrounded by walnut veneer. This was a different world to that of her more austere Renault. She couldn't resist caressing the hide seating as she looked down the long bonnet, so high off the ground. An action that was not missed by Jules as he tried to work out the connection between him and the attractive young lady sat next to him. He smiled. "I think we'll go round to the farms first. We won't have time to visit them all but it'll give you a good idea of the extent of the estate and you can always go back another day. We own the village too," he added.

"Yes, so the Duke was telling me. I'm staying in the Abbey Inn… in the 'Dukes' room."

"I bet father arranged that for you, he always puts special guests in that room. Is it OK?"

"It's lovely, thank you," Molly began to relax, Jules seemed more companionable this afternoon. *Maybe she had misjudged him?*

They drove off, the car seeming to float over the surface of the road as they headed up the drive to the South gate. The cattle grids didn't even register, as the metal rails were absorbed by the compliant suspension.

"What do you think of the car?" Jules asked.

"It's beautiful, and so smooth."

"It was only delivered yesterday, it's part of the sponsorship deal with the Polo Club. I only have it for six months and then it'll be back to my old Defender. Pretty cool though, isn't it? Now let's talk about you. Your surname, Goodall, are you one of the Hereford Goodall's?"

Molly laughed, "No, I'm one of the Holeford Goodall's. My dad was a milkman and mum has just retired from Price Low."

"But you went to Oxford," he stated with bewilderment.

"Yes, I was very lucky. I volunteered at the museum when the 'Holeford Hoard' was uncovered in the supermarket car park. Professor Halford became my mentor. I studied hard and achieved the A level passes I needed. Then with the Prof's contacts, I was able to get a scholarship to Magdalen College to study history. Now I'm based at the Victoria and Albert Museum while I work towards my PhD."

"I remember the discovery, it was all over the papers. I went to the opening of the exhibition with father, he's a trustee of the museum. I remember the Professor talking about his child prodigy, which must be you. That's where I must have come across you. Father used you as an example of how I should study hard and go to university."

"Sorry about that," Molly said sheepishly, surprised that she should be a role model for a viscount. "I've seen a picture of the Duke and the professor on a dig in Egypt, they must be old friends."

"They go back a long way. I haven't seen Uncle Dominic for ages. He's not my real uncle you understand, but that's what I always call him."

"I hope to visit him at the museum while I'm working here."

"Give him my regards when you see him," Jules smiled, his resistance to this afternoon's distraction fading fast.

They drove up to the South Gate where the guard saluted and lifted the barrier. "I wish they wouldn't salute," Jules said embarrassed, "Right, let's go to Home Farm first." He turned left on the main road away from the village. Molly relaxed and looked forward to an interesting afternoon.

Before their first farm visit Jules stopped at Colebarrow Hill located next to an ancient burial mound and a dilapidated stone folly built by the second Duke. From their position Molly could see for miles, out across the lush green rolling down land divided by a patchwork quilt of fields and woodland that had evolved over the centuries. On the horizon, the ground rose into purple topped hills with a distant glimpse of the sea just peeping through a valley. Jules pointed out the extent of the estate and the various farms. The house and safari park could also be clearly seen.

From there, they visited three farms, meeting the managers and surveying their operations, arriving just in time to witness the milking in the new parlour at the Abbey dairy. Jules was proud to show off of the new installation, the state-of-the-art carousel system had only recently been installed. Molly watched the cows walk from the yard into individual stalls, while the whole parlour rotated around the dairyman like a giant roundabout. The operation was mesmerising. The cows seemed very much at home with the technology.

The afternoon flew by, it was now five o'clock and they'd hardly scratched the surface of the planned itinerary when the time came to return to the house.

Jules was apologetic, "I'm sorry, I didn't have time to show you the park and gardens, I hope it gave you a bit of an insight into our operation."

"It's been fascinating, thank you for finding the time. You must be really busy, especially with the police investigation."

"It's been my pleasure. In fact, it did me good to get out and clear my head. Tell you what, why don't we grab some time in the next couple of days and complete the tour."

"I'd like that. I'll be based in the library for the rest of the week while I start work on the outline for the new manuscript. There's a lot to do. Without wishing to be rude, the old one is a shambles, historically it's all over the place so I'm going to start again. I may need your help to fill in some of the blanks."

"Good, we can sort out a time tomorrow. Thanks for your company, Molly."

She climbed down out of the Range Rover and went back to her little Renault for the drive back to the village. She was surprised how small and metallic her car felt after the luxury of the green monolith, but it was hers, it had never let her down and she still loved it to bits.

16

Just for the Record

Wednesday 14th August. Morning

At ten o'clock Molly arrived in the library. The Duke welcomed her as she took up her position at the desk by the door. She opened her brief-case, took out an A4 lined pad, pens, dictionary and thesaurus then laid open a copy of the original 'history of the estate.' She had already confirmed with the printers that they held copies of the maps, photographs and other images to use again in the new publication. This would save the Duke time and money, as he was already tasked with gathering more up to date pictures. She had arranged a photographer to spend time on the estate recording the current attractions and personnel. The Duke busied himself looking through photo albums and files. Part of her wished he would leave her to work alone in the library, his presence was distracting.

"What about this one?" he said holding up a group photo of the staff at the Christmas party, three years previously.

"That's lovely, if you make a note of when it was taken along with the names of the people, we'll put it with the others. I'll sift through them and decide what may be useful." '*This is going to be long winded,*' she thought. She studied the existing book to reaffirm her new chapter headings. Aware of its contents, which she had now read three times, she had copious ideas written on 'post it' notes stuck between the pages for further consideration.

At eleven there was a tap on the door and James entered with Detective Inspector Montgomery.

Montgomery turned to greet Molly. "Hello Miss Goodall," he said warmly, holding out his hand. She rose and shook it, somewhat surprised that he remembered her. "Dexter told me you are working here. I would say you haven't changed but you're all grown up," he said, trying not to sound patronising.

"Hello sir, you've gone up in the world, Detective Inspector, very impressive."

The Duke watched the meeting with some interest. "You two know each other?"

"Good morning, your lordship," Montgomery said.

"It's Duke," he said correcting him.

"My apologies," Montgomery said, horrified at his faux pas, "Good morning, your Duke-ness."

"Just call me Sir," the Duke replied in amusement.

Molly stepped in to help Montgomery who looked a bit embarrassed. "Yes Sir, we met about ten years ago, after a robbery at the supermarket in Holeford where my mother worked. It's a long story, you could write a book about it. Suffice to say, the burglars were caught. Did you ever find the fancy dress vigilantes who scuppered the robbery?"

"No, we didn't, they just disappeared into thin air, but they never bothered us again, they knew we were on to them." Wilf and George looked over from the sofa where they were watching with amusement and waved cheekily.

"Here we are," Wilf called out. After all they were two thirds of the so-called vigilante group.

"It's nice to be remembered," George said with a chuckle. Molly looked sternly at them. They mischievously grinned back at her.

"I'm here to update you on the investigation, Sir," Montgomery continued, getting the conversation back on track.

"Good, about time. Come with me, we'll go into the boardroom and leave Miss Goodall to her work, I expect she'll be glad of the peace and quiet." Molly smiled politely '*thank goodness for that*' she thought and sat back at her desk as they left the room, closely followed by James.

"Where did you two come from?" Molly whispered to Wilf and George.

"We just popped in to see how you're getting on. Alice and Tom have gone to the incident room to eaves drop. So, we're at your service."

"That's lovely, but you must behave yourselves, any hint of someone coming in and you must promise to sit quiet."

"Very good, M'lady. What do you want us to do?" Wilf asked.

"Never mind that, I'm going to the boardroom to see what I can learn," George said, "I'll be back to help later." He then walked up to the panelled wall and passed through into the next room.

In the boardroom the Duke asked James to bring tea and biscuits. They moved to the long mahogany meeting table whose centre was inlayed with intricate marquetry displaying the family crest. The table was surrounded by twelve high backed chairs with padded leather seats. At the far end was a large carver embellished with carvings of animals and the family crest embossed in the padded leather back. The Duke gripped the lions' heads carved into the arms and lowered himself onto the seat. He indicated one of the smaller chairs for the detective.

Montgomery sat and removed a notebook from his inside pocket. "As you know, we have upgraded the incident to a murder investigation. The circumstances give us reason to believe that the victim was forced into the enclosure. The evidence revealed that a gun had been fired. We have fresh ricochet marks on the road and the sign on the gate has also been damaged by a small calibre bullet. We have witnesses in the village that heard two gun shots at the time in question. Are you aware of any of this?"

"No, I am not!" The Duke said sharply.

Montgomery ignored the abrupt response and continued. "We have reason to suspect that the gates were left unlocked or had been unlocked deliberately. We've spoken to your wardens, and it appears that their security procedures are exemplary. Therefore, we deduce the gate must have been unlocked deliberately. As you are aware, the keys are held and controlled by the head keeper, who records their issue in a register. We understand you have a duplicate set kept here in the house, can you confirm this?"

"Yes, of course we do," the Duke spat out, his face now red with rage, "Come with me." He stormed out of the room with the detective hot on his heels, back into the library where Molly was busy at her desk, examining old leather-bound volumes and making notes. She looked up in surprise as they both hastily entered the room.

George followed behind pulling faces at Molly and Wilf, "This is getting good, I've got lots to tell you."

The Duke went to a large picture, hanging on the wall behind his desk and pushed the frame on the right-hand side. It clicked and swung open, revealing a wall safe with a large dial.

He twiddled the dial clockwise and anti-clockwise several times, pulled the lever and the heavy door swung open. He reached in and retrieved a shabby old '*Cadburys*' biscuit tin. "Here you are," he banged the tin down on the desk and prised the top open.

"That will do sir. I'll take it from here, I need to check the contents against the keys at the lodge." Montgomery leant forward, pushed the top back on and picked up the box. The Duke was now visibly shaking, trying hard to control his temper. Montgomery, aware of Molly's presence wanted to continue the conversation in private.

"Now, perhaps we should resume the briefing next door?"

"Briefing? Briefing? This is more like an interrogation," the Duke spat out. "Come on then." He led the detective back, with George in tow, grinning from ear to ear, he hadn't had so much fun since playing the detective in '*The Mousetrap*' many years ago at the '*Ambassadors Theatre*' in London.

Molly and Wilf looked on perplexed by the whole incident.

The two men returned to the boardroom and sat at the table where the tea things had been laid out along with a platter containing Hobnob and Bourbon biscuits.

"Now, what exactly is this Montgomery? Come out with it man, you think I'm hiding something."

"I'm sorry if you think that Sir, I'm just trying to get all the facts together. It's my boss you see, he wants to know everything, it's nothing personal, it's just for my report," he replied soothingly.

The Duke took a deep breath and his red complexion receded to pink. "Good, as long as we understand each other," he said.

"We believe that the body is that of one Thomas Carmichael, an art student who was assisting at the market over the festival weekend. We had little identifiable remains to go on, that is why it has taken so long but a watch recently turned up in the lion excrement and has been identified as the make and model he was wearing. It was still working and so unfortunately was not able to confirm the exact time of death. The watch is a '*Timex Expedition*' the face lights up when you push the winder… and yes, in case you're curious, this backlight was still working. After replacing the stock in the stable loft, he didn't return to the Abbey Inn on Friday evening and cannot be traced. He has, in effect, disappeared."

"He's in the incident room with Alice," George chipped in helpfully.

"We are trying to figure out the motive, opportunity and evidence. The opportunity obviously occurred, but was it premeditated? That is the big question, we have evidence of the gunshots and witnesses to the sound of the gun, but motive is still eluding us. I hope you don't mind me sharing this with you. If you have any ideas, please feel free to share them with me."

The Duke slowly poured a cup of tea and sat back in the chair but said nothing. His irritation subsiding as the inspector now confided in him. George watched on as the scene unfolded.

"We believe the incident is linked to a criminal organisation in London. During the last day of the festival, we planted officers among the staff and visitors, which resulted in the following of a suspect back to the city. He is known to Scotland Yard and is now under surveillance. Can you think why he would possibly be here?"

"No, I can't, why on earth are you wasting time on this line of enquiry? You've been watching too many cop shows. This has to be a bloody suicide," the Duke insisted.

Montgomery ignored the comment. "We'll be moving the incident room back to Holeford Police Station on Friday and you'll be free to re-open the lion enclosure on Saturday, if you wish."

"Am I a suspect, Inspector?" the Duke asked bluntly.

"Would I be sharing this information with you if I thought you were?"

"What about Jules? He should be here to share this."

"Sergeant Dexter is speaking with him now." Montgomery rose, shook hands with the Duke and headed for the door. "It was nice to meet Molly Goodall again, she was a bit of a celebrity in Holeford, the first person from the Modern School to get a place at Oxford, quite an achievement. Thank you for your time, sir." He went through the door to the hall and began to close it. The Duke relaxed back into his chair as the door swung open again.

"There was just one more thing, just for the record you understand, where were you on Friday evening?"

"What on earth! You do think I'm involved, don't you?" The Duke asked indignantly, shifting uncomfortably in his chair.

"It's just for my report sir." George clapped his hands. This was a classic Columbo trick, confront the suspect while they are off guard and catch them out. He was impressed, '*The others are going to love this.*'

"Right, I'll show you where I was 'just for the record.'" The Duke angrily stood up and went to a small door in the corner of the room. "I was in here," he opened the door to reveal a room positioned within a corner turret of the house. The walls were lined with shelves containing thousands of records positioned between tall thin leaded windows to three sides. Adjacent to the door, on a sideboard sat a Bang and Olufsen turntable with a very impressive looking amplifier. Arrays of speakers were distributed around the room, large ones on the floor and little ones high on the shelves, all facing towards the centre. Opposite, was a single red leather chair and nearby a small side table on which lay a large pair of headphones with its cable plugged into the amp. In the far corner a grand piano stood, it's black gloss finish softened with age. Montgomery could only wonder how it had been possible to get the instrument through the narrow door. Other musical instruments were displayed in glass cases around the walls and on the shelves between the records.

"This is my inner sanctum. In this room is one of the most complete collections of jazz records from eighteen ninety to nineteen seventy."

"You like Jazz then?" Montgomery remarked innocently. The Duke ignored him and remarked proudly, "that cabinet contains Bix Beiderbecke's cornet." Montgomery looked at, what to him, was a battered dirty old trumpet. The Duke then pointed towards the piano. "That was owned by Scott Joplin, he allegedly composed '*Maple Leaf Rag*' on it."

Montgomery didn't like Jazz. He couldn't get the point of it. Old men in smoky cellars drinking heavily while the band played random notes with their eyes closed. That was his impression anyway, and nothing was going to change his mind.

"And this, is Louis Armstrong's trumpet," the Duke continued, reaching up, taking the brass instrument down and offering it reverently to the detective.

Montgomery accepted it awkwardly, not being sure how to react. "It's all tarnished, it could do with a good polish," he said, rubbing it with his sleeve.

The Duke quickly grabbed it back. "Have you no soul? This is patina from years of play in the hazy, intoxicating bars of New Orleans. This was the music of the gods. Not some tin pot amateur brass band that polish their instruments just to see their faces in them."

"Sorry, it's just not my thing. I prefer the Carpenters."

"A few years ago, I was leading a consortium that was going to open a series of restaurants called '*Soft Jazz Café*' but my partners got cold feet and changed it to rock music," the Duke continued scathingly. "Bloody awful row. I pulled out. They did OK though, it went global. I should have left my money in and become a sleeping partner. Still, you win some, you lose some," he shrugged his shoulders.

"Why is this guitar all burnt? Have you had an accident in here?" Montgomery asked noticing the damaged instrument behind the piano.

"That's Jimi Hendrix's Fender Stratocaster. He set fire to it on stage at a festival here in sixty-eight. We saved it from the skip when the site was being cleaned up. I didn't have the heart to chuck it out. I found it in the attic a few years ago and brought it down to add to my collection. He could have been a great Jazz guitarist if he'd put his mind to it, sadly he died before he was old enough to appreciate proper music."

Montgomery picked it up and a shiver went down his spine. This he could relate to, he was holding a piece of rock history, he could still smell the scorched wood after all these years. He pulled himself together. "So, you're saying you were here all night?"

"There's no law against listening to Jazz, young man."

"Can anyone confirm you were here?"

"You mean, do I have an alibi." The Duke slumped down in the chair still holding the trumpet. "James brought me some ice for my whisky at around ten…there's no law against putting ice in whisky, is there?"

"No sir, although some say it bruises the grain, but that's your choice."

"Good, at least you can't arrest me for that," he scowled.

"By any chance did you hear the gunfire?"

"No, I didn't, have you seen the size of these headphones. Anyway, gunfire is not unusual in the countryside, officer. In the country we shoot vermin and game, in the city they tend to shoot each other, although some lowlifes are possibly little more than rats," the Duke said with some venom.

"Thank you, I think that will be all sir, I will leave this time." Montgomery gently replaced the guitar against the wall.

"By the way, the mechanic tells me your car is repaired, you'll need to contact Jules about collecting it," the Duke said, not rising from his chair.

"Thank you sir, I'll call him." Montgomery replied, not turning round but holding his hand up in a lazy backward wave as he walked to the door.

17

What Next?

Wednesday 14ᵗʰ August. Afternoon

The Duke returned to the library and was impressed by the number of volumes Molly had opened for reference. "Getting along alright?" he asked."

"Yes, thank you sir, I'm just compiling notes at the moment. It looks like I need to rewrite the whole thing. Some of the early history doesn't reflect the information within the record books. I don't mean to be rude, but it looks like some of it has been made up."

"You've certainly been busy." He could see some of the books had come from the highest shelves that even he hadn't opened recently, if ever. "How did you get those down? They're awfully heavy and so high up."

"I used your ladder, it was easy," Molly replied while glancing at the impossibly high shelves.

Wilf smiled from the sofa and put both thumbs up in triumph.

"Well, you go careful, we have staff to do the heavy lifting. I don't want you going back to London with a hernia."

Molly laughed, "Don't worry sir, I won't struggle. James said he would help if I needed to get to the high shelves." He hadn't actually said that, but she was sure he would help if asked.

The doors to the room flew open and Jules entered in a flurry, "Father you're never going..." He stopped mid-sentence after catching a glimpse of Molly out of the corner of his eye. "Hello, sorry I forgot you were working in here," he said, changing his tone. "While I think of it, if you're available tomorrow afternoon, I'll be free to finish showing you round the park and introduce you to the lions. We should be given the go ahead to reopen the enclosure by then. You can come and help, if you like."

"That would be lovely, if it's no trouble. I'll let you deal with the lions though, I'm keeping well away." Molly looked at the Duke for approval to leave her work. He nodded.

"Father, can we talk confidentially in the boardroom, I don't want to distract our author." Molly grinned as she carried on her research, she hadn't thought about becoming a published author.

The Duke and Jules moved to the boardroom followed again by George leaving Wilf to assist Molly.

Jules talked as they walked along the corridor, "I've just had Sergeant Dexter with me in my office. He said it was to update me on the investigation, but it felt like an interrogation. You do know it's now a murder enquiry? From the way he was talking, we're prime suspects."

"It's been the same here, Montgomery has been interrogating me as well."

"They're being crafty talking to us separately but we've nothing to hide...have we?" he added, looking closely at his father.

"No, of course not!"

"That's all right then."

"I showed him the music room, he wasn't impressed by the jazz. He's got no soul, that one."

"You never show anyone your inner sanctum, what prompted that?"

"He wanted to know where I was on Friday night, so I showed him... as you say we've nothing to hide. I also told him his car's ready. That is right, isn't it?"

"Yeah, Nick and Carl have done an amazing job on it. I'm thinking of asking him to leave it here for display at the car show over the bank holiday. But never mind that, what do you think he's up to?"

"Apparently, they followed a suspect back to London during the Sci-Fi festival. Good news about getting the enclosure back though, we will be ready for a bumper bank holiday with a bit of luck," the Duke replied, changing the subject.

"I'm not so sure, there's been a lot of adverse publicity since the murder." Jules paused thoughtfully. "Even saying the word murder sends a shiver down my spine."

"Don't worry, the public are inquisitive, they'll be here in their droves to see the scene of the crime."

"That's sick."

"Just look at the takings in sixty-eight, after that suicide, they shot up."

"I don't think shot is the right term to use at the moment. Did Montgomery tell you what they found?"

"Yes… bullet holes. That sounds very disturbing, if it's true."

"Who knows? Anyway, I've got work to do, I have to contact Exford Car Club about the weekend. They've got the marquees arriving this afternoon, also the green keepers are coming down from the golf club to cut the grass. The car club will have to get one of their organisers here to coordinate everything. By the way, did you see the paper this morning? There's going to be another '*Galactic Jump*' feature film. John Pearce called me this morning. They want to make the festival an annual event. I've just seen the receipts from the last one. We made a clear eighty grand profit over the weekend, not including the extra gate revenue."

"Good news, at last," the Duke managed a smile, "don't forget we have the TV Company here next Wednesday to film '*Haunted House.*'"

Jules made a face, "Why did you agree to that? That's all we need. A group of phoney ghost hunters spending the night stalking round the house. Have you ever watched the programme?"

"No, but that's not the point. They're paying us a thousand pounds and think of the publicity."

"It's a cheap, tacky show, father. They just go round with night vision cameras and pretend to be scared while they play spooky incidental music to ramp up the atmosphere. I've only ever seen a trailer but it's the lowest of low television."

"It's an easy thousand pounds and we can't depend on having big festivals every weekend, despite your news. Take this confounded car show for instance, we make nothing! It's all going to local charities, which is very worthy, and it makes us look good, but the way we're going we may soon be one of the charities they have to support."

18
The Picnic

Thursday 15th August. Afternoon

After a busy morning in the library, Molly packed away her notebook, stacked the reference material neatly on the desk, checked her makeup in her compact mirror and waited. At two thirty, Jules arrived, casually dressed in trainers, jeans, a white tee shirt and buff coloured linen jacket. Molly stood up, she was wearing pink trainers, a knee length floral patterned cotton summer dress, with wide belt accentuating her slim figure. She sported an Alice band to keep the hair out of her eyes. After all, they would be outside, and the wind would play havoc with her locks.

"Right, are you ready?" Jules said joyfully. He had been looking forward to an afternoon away from the office, out in the sunshine, something he seemed to do less and less as the responsibility of the estate demanded so much of his time.

"I'm ready, lead the way." Molly grabbed her small green handbag from the back of the chair, slung it over her shoulder and followed Jules down the back stair to the car park. They headed towards the Range Rover, but Jules went beyond it.

"This way," he instructed.

Molly was slightly disappointed that they were apparently not going out in his car. She had fallen in love with the comfortable high seats enabling views over the hedges. Jules stopped, and in front of them was parked an electric golf buggy. Her heart dropped. The open sided plastic body had a roof, of sorts, flat windscreen and bench seat for two people. The fact that it was painted in black and white zebra stripes, like the safari vehicles and had the estate logo emblazoned on the bonnet did nothing to improve its appeal. Jules climbed into the left-hand side and grabbed the steering wheel. "Hop on," he said, "it's left-hand drive but you soon adapt."

Molly studied the vehicle further, assessing the safety of a car with no doors, seat belts or in fact any visible safety features. "Is it safe?"

"Yeah, it's fine, we use them all the time to get around the park. There's a fleet of them up at the golf club, that's where they maintain them. Come on, hop in."

Molly gripped the side of the windscreen and a handle, conveniently positioned by the side of the seat and swung round onto the bench seat. The cart felt even more flimsy than it had looked. She placed her handbag on the shelf in front and tucked her dress under her legs to protect her modesty.

"This is cool," she said politely, the white of her knuckles showing as she gripped the seat tightly for fear of falling out.

"I'm glad you like it, they're great fun… hold on tight." Molly needed no prompting to do that.

Jules turned the key on the dashboard, pressed down on the accelerator and the brake automatically disengaged with a mechanical clunk. The electric motor softly whined, and they pulled away sedately. Now it was moving Molly somehow felt safer. It travelled gently over the ground, its big soft tyres treading lightly over the gravel.

"This reminds me of my dad's milk float," she said with a big smile, remembering the happy mornings she had spent with him in the school holidays riding shot gun in 'Trigger,' delivering the milk to the doorsteps of Holeford.

"Mechanically, it's the same principle as a milk float but without the milk," Jules said laughing. "Right, here's the plan. A spin round the lake visiting the engine shed at Lakeside station, then a cup of tea over at the viewpoint, followed by a trip round the gardens. If you want to stop and look closely at anything just let me know. We're in no rush."

Molly sat back on the vinyl seat and relaxed. "That sounds lovely. May I call you Jules please? I don't much like 'VJ', it sounds a bit medical."

Jules laughed out loud. "That's the first time anyone's said that. Of course, you can, I think this is going to be a fun afternoon."

He drove along the path between the lake shore and the railway line stopping to allow pedestrians to pass safely. Some realising it was the viscount did a stumbling curtsey or nodded their heads, others just said, "Thank you."

Jules was happy to play the host, "Are you having a lovely day? Isn't the weather nice? Enjoy your visit etc." The visitors lapped it up, they would never forget the day they met the viscount. It was priceless.

Molly was amused by the public's reaction and joined in the greetings like an old hand. As the train went by, she waved at the passengers. Parents and children joyfully waved back to them. However, the driver of the steam engine, a large rotund woman, stared straight ahead impassively.

"The train driver looks a bit miserable," Molly commented.

"That's Edith, it's just her way. Very focussed, you might say. She's a very good driver and engineer. She maintains the trains and rolling stock with her apprentice. The rolling stock always looks immaculate. She doesn't suffer fools but she's OK when you get to know her. She's as tough as old boots, a couple of years ago, the train derailed going over the points by the engine shed. She levered it back on the track single handed using a tree trunk."

"Point duly noted," Molly said. Jules continued with a running commentary as they travelled past the back of the steam fair. They could hear the pipe organ playing over the cacophony of joyous shrieks and laughter coming from the rides.

He parked at Lakeside Station. "Right, first stop. I'll show you the station, then we'll walk up to the engine sheds."

As they got out, they heard the steamboat approaching the jetty opposite the station, it's bell clanging to announce its arrival. It was a magical sight. The sunlight danced on the ripples of the water like a million diamonds, as the large wooden vessel paddled towards them. Beyond the island and far shore, the fertile meadows looked like a pile of cushions as the landscape swept up to lush woodland, it was an idyllic scene. Molly waved enthusiastically to the passengers. On the top deck by the wheelhouse, Finn, recognising her, removed his cap and waved it wildly to attract her attention. She smiled radiantly and waved back eagerly.

"I think you're enjoying yourself," Jules said. Spurred on by her enthusiasm, he too then joined in the greeting of the boat.

"It's so beautiful, it must be just like being on the banks of the Mississippi."

"Grandad rescued it from New Orleans and had it restored here. They replaced the steam engine with a British one, the original American one blew up. That's why it was abandoned."

"It's got a Fosters locomotive engine now, hasn't it?" Molly asked.

"Yes, very good, how do you know that?" Jules was impressed.

"Oh… It was in the guidebook," Molly replied, smiling to herself.

"Of course, it was, I sometimes forget why you're here."

They walked up to the engine shed and looked at the work being done to restore the second steam engine. Edith came in for a drink while the passengers disembarked. "Hi VJ," she said wiping her hands on an oily rag, "who's this then?"

"Hello Edith, this is Molly Goodall. She's with us to write a new guide-book."

"Hi Molly, pleased to meet you. It's about time that guide was looked at. If you need to know anything, just come and see me, I'll tell you the real history not the rubbish in that old book."

"Thank you, I may take you up on that," Molly said.

"Now it's time for our tea, come on Molly, back to our chariot," Jules instructed.

They drove around the lakeside path until they were overlooking the house. Jules instructed Molly to hold on tight as he turned left across the grass, climbing bumpily up the hill, pulling up at a park bench placed on a level paved area. "Take a seat," he instructed. Molly looked at the back rail and read its brass memorial plaque before sitting to enjoy the view. '*In memory of Arthur Jones. Miss you always, his loving family.*'

Jules retrieved his two-way radio from the car, "VJ to James…Come in James…over," he said, releasing the button.

There was a static crackle, then, "James receiving…over."

"We're at Arthur's seat now…over."

"Roger…copy that sir, I'm on my way…out."

Jules then joined Molly on the bench.

"What was that about?"

"Just organising our tea, it's on its way."

"Lovely, who was Arthur?"

"He was the head gardener here for years, after he died we placed the seat here in his memory. It was his favourite view of the park."

"It is beautiful." They watched the tractor mowers steadily driving up and down the large field near the Palladian bridge at the end of the lake. The aromatic smell of the grass wafted across the grounds. "I love the smell of freshly cut grass, it reminds me of school playing fields in the summer," Molly said.

"They're preparing for the classic car show over the bank holiday. All the money goes to local charities. It attracts thousands of people."

"Is that the Holeford Car Club show? I remember seeing the posters, but I've never been."

"That's the one. It gets bigger and bigger every year. Look, you can see the marquees arriving now, he pointed to a box van surrounded by volunteers off-loading equipment. As they watched another electric buggy headed across the bridge with a small flatbed where the golf clubs would have been stored. It headed across the field towards them. James pulled up in front of them, removed a square table from the back and laid it with tablecloth, crockery and silver cutlery. Molly looked on in disbelief as he then placed plates of sandwiches and cakes alongside a large thermos of steaming hot tea. "Will that be all sir?"

"Thank you, James, this is fine." James drove off back towards the house. Molly held her hand to her mouth but couldn't stifle her laughter.

"This is so surreal, Jules. Do you live like this all the time?"

"Not exactly, I have to admit it's a bit of a show for your benefit. Shall I serve? One lump or two?"

"You didn't need to do this. A Tupperware box with cheese and ham sandwiches would have been OK."

"I know, but it's a bit of a treat for both of us and an apology for the way I spoke to you on our first meeting. That was inexcusable." They tucked into the picnic, drank the tea and sat back.

"We did have sea lions in the lake when I was small, but father re-homed them. They would swim after the steamboat while the captain threw fish for them."

"Did they go because your mother ran off with the keeper?"

Jules was again surprised by her knowledge, "Yes that's right, but how could you know that?"

"It's my job, don't forget why I'm here."

"That's not in the guidebook… it's not is it?" he asked uncomfortably.

"No, not yet," she teased.

"I think we need to look closely at your manuscript before printing the new one. Some things are better left in the past." They sat quietly looking across the valley lost in their thoughts for a minute.

"Don't worry, I'll be careful," Molly finally said, breaking the silence, "Do you miss your mother?"

"Every day," Jules reflected. "Funny isn't it... she's not been there for most of my life and yet I miss her. Father was devastated, but pretended not to show it, *'life must go on'* he used to say. I know he was no saint, but it left a deep scar."

Molly felt sadness for both of them, "I don't want to upset anyone with the new book, words can injure as readily as a knife, that's not the purpose of this historical document. I'll leave that to the dramatists," she said.

Jules was still in a reflective mood, "This is called *'Sled Hill'*, or at least it is to my sister and me. Up behind us there was a Swiss chalet," he pointed to a small clearing in front of the trees, "in the winter we would come over here and play for hours in the snow while mum and dad made hot chocolate on the little pot boiler stove, and we cooked baked potatoes in the fire... It's all gone now." Molly detected a lump in his throat.

Jules changed the subject. "Speaking of drama, did you know they're going to make another *Galactic Jump* film? But Clive Monkton's being replaced by David Hasselhoff."

"I'm not keen on Science Fiction. You had a festival here just before I arrived, how did that go?"

Jules explained all about the weekend and its overlap with the police investigation. James then returned and gathered up the picnic things, loaded the cart and drove back to the house.

"We also have a TV company here next Wednesday. They're filming *'Haunted House'*, have you heard of it?"

"Yes, I love it! And they're coming here? How exciting! Can I meet them?"

"If you like, it's not my cup of tea. I'm surprised you're so keen on it. You don't look like someone who'd believe in ghosts."

Molly laughed, "You have no idea, Jules," she quickly moved the topic on, "it's presented by Justine Song." She looked at Jules expectantly but he remained impassive. "Come on, you must have heard of her... She was big in children's television in the seventies. She presented the science programme *'What'* with Dicky Dunnage, it was brilliant. She wore the most outrageous clothes, she was a fashion icon, especially in the teen mags. That was until 1978 when she turned up in bovver boots, black leather trousers held together with safety pins and wearing a Sex Pistols Tee shirt with no bra. She then sprayed '*Anarchy*' in red paint all over the set," Molly laughed, "it was a step too far though. The show was axed, and the director ended up on Saturday afternoon wrestling as the '*masked ninja*' so no one would recognise him. As far as I know, she just settled down and had a family. But now she's back presenting the early evening show on ITV '*Justine Song at Twilight*' she dresses more sensibly now." Jules looked at her blankly. "This all means nothing to you, does it?" Molly said, shaking her head.

"Sorry, I seemed to have missed out on that gem," Jules said laughing, "Tell me more."

"Well, she set up her own production company and started making ghost hunter programmes for Channel 4. It's been very successful. Are you sure you've never watched it?"

"I've seen a trailer, but it looks like utter nonsense," Jules pulled a face.

"Don't knock it, it's very popular and the exposure won't do your visitor numbers any harm."

"That's what Father said, it was his idea."

"He's right. I'd love to meet Justine."

"Your wish is my command. I'll introduce you next week."

"So, what about your sister, where is she now?" Molly asked.

"She's in South Africa, we have vineyards there which she manages for the estate. Father gave her the job to get her away from Woodford, she was upsetting too many people. You see, she's rather forthright. Which is a polite way of saying rude, but it works for her out there. It seems to suit the temperament of the staff, they love her. She was never afraid to get her hands dirty and I think they respect her for that."

"So, what happens here, who will ultimately inherit the estate?"

"That's very probing, is this for the guide?"

"No, I'm just interested. Is there no significant other to produce an heir?"

"Even more probing!" Jules studied her, trying to work out the angle of her questions. "No, no one, Father keeps trying to pair me off, but it's not working."

"That's a shame, it must be difficult though."

"His latest introduction was Lavinia Trout," Jules said with a grin.

"Trout, that's an awful name... was she nice?" Molly laughed, "Sorry that's disrespectful."

"Yes, she was very nice actually. She's one of the Sussex Trout's, big landowners on the South Downs. Father introduced us at a charity ball in London. She was good fun, intelligent, well spoken, nice figure, long auburn hair and dressed well. Trouble was her eyes pointed in different directions, I couldn't get past that," he burst out laughing.

"That's not nice, she sounds lovely."

Jules looked into her eyes, "I know, I'm sorry but look at your eyes."

"What's wrong with my eyes?"

"Nothing, that's the point. When you look at the house across the lake, you look at the house. When Lavinia did it, one eye was on the house the other was looking at the road up to the main gate."

"Goodness, she must live her life in permanent panorama vision." They both laughed this time.

"Funny you should say that, she now works for a film company in Italy, so she can wear sunglasses all the time. I hope she gets on well there, she's a lovely girl. Right, it's my turn now. What about you, is there someone?"

"That's a fair question. No, I did have a boyfriend in Oxford, but it didn't last, we wanted different things and I was too wrapped up in my studies for a serious relationship." She paused, she hadn't talked to anyone about Robert before, they shared some happy times, but it wasn't to be.

Jules looked at his watch, "Sorry Molly, the afternoon's flown by, perhaps we can go and see the lions another time when they're finally released back into their enclosure.

"I'd like that."

"Let's have a quick spin round the gardens and then call it a day."

They drove down the hill past the now half-erected marquees and over the bridge. Underneath, water spilled down the weir maintaining the level of the lake, creating a mist over the river just visible between the stone columns. They visited the kitchen garden and orangery where

Molly was delighted to see the colourful citrus fruit hanging from the trees. Finally they parked by the house and crossing the garden, arrived at the ballroom lobby. Jules held the door open for her as they entered the long gallery and followed her in. Molly hadn't studied the paintings closely during her whistle-stop tour with James and now took time to admire them.

"You've got a wonderful collection here."

"Thank you, Father looks after them, they're part of the house's collection gathered by generations of our family. They're rather beautiful. Some go out on loan for special exhibitions, but mostly they stay here to be viewed by visitors," Jules explained.

"It's quite an eclectic mix," Molly commented, "Rembrandt next to a Hockney then Caravaggio with Andy Warhol." With no barriers up, she was able to look closely at the details of colour and application. "They're all in beautiful condition."

"A company of specialist restorers have been here for over a year cleaning them. It cost a small a fortune."

"I don't believe it…" Molly looked closely at a portrait of a moustachioed man with long hair, wearing a silk robe, pointing at a large flower.

"That's a Van Dyck, '*Self-portrait with a Wisteria*,' I think it's called," Jules informed her, rather pleased with himself for remembering.

"I've seen a recent memo about this," Molly said, studying it closely, her nose practically touching the canvas, "... it can't be."

"Can't be what?" Jules said stepping close to try and see what she was looking at, their heads practically touching.

"Have you got a magnifying glass?" Molly whispered.

"Not here, but I can soon go and get one. What is it?"

"It may be nothing, please hurry," Jules ran to his office, grabbed the glass from his desk, ran back and handed it to her.

"Thank you."

She held the glass to the signature and studied it closely.

"Look at this signature very carefully."

"What of it?" he said, not seeing anything special.

"It reads Dan Vyck not Van Dyck… it's spelt wrong. This is a forgery, a brilliant one, but a forgery none the less. What a careless mistake."

"It can't be. It's just been valued by a highly respected auction house before the restoration."

Jules moved away and sat on a large velvet covered bench placed in the middle of the room for visitors to rest and study the artworks in detail.

Molly placed the magnifying glass on the seat next to him, "I'm sorry but it is… there have been several incidents recently of forgeries entering the market with subtle mistakes. A memo's gone round at work to make us all aware. You need to consult an expert and tell the police urgently."

"My God, this is all we need," Jules buried his head in his hands. Molly sat next to him and held his arm to try and comfort him.

"I might be wrong," she said softly, trying to console him, "but you do need to contact the authorities."

19

Moving Out

Friday 16th August. Morning

"Good morning, sir," Inspector Montgomery said, as he entered Jules's office.

"Good morning detective, did you find out any more about the painting?"

"The investigation is proceeding as expected sir. I contacted the fraud squad and they're sending an agent to join our team. There's been a surge of forged paintings on the black market recently, and they believe this may be the work of the same operator. They want you to carry on opening the park and house as normal. If it follows the pattern of other offences, there could be more movement on the scam, but this time we'll be ready. Now, I think you've got something for me."

"Yes, I have. I'm looking forward to seeing your reaction. Did you get a lift to the house?"

"Dexter dropped me off on the way to the compound. He's overseeing the clearing of the incident room this morning and we should be relocated to Holeford Station by the afternoon. We'll finally be out from under your feet."

"That's good news, it'll be good to have the mess room back as well. The lions will be thrilled to get back to their drive-through enclosure. They're getting 'stir crazy' in the paddock. It feels like we're returning to normal... in the park at least," Jules added, now having the additional worry of a forged painting, "Come on, let me drive you to the workshop."

At the vehicle workshop, Nick and Carl were waiting in anticipation of their arrival. Montgomery's car was draped with a large dust sheet and concealed behind the garage door. Jules stopped Montgomery at the door and Nick raised the roller shutter to reveal the protected car.

"Would you like to do the honours?" Jules asked Montgomery.

The detective was apprehensive, '*What have they done to my car? I hope they haven't ruined it. No, they can't have, it was just the ignition that needed attention,*' he thought.

"Well, go on then, pull off the cover," Jules encouraged, lifting the corner of the sheet and handing it to him.

He gripped the sheet and pulled it gently. It slid almost frictionless over the clean bodywork and fell to the floor at their feet.

The car was finally revealed, Montgomery was speechless at first. The copper brown paintwork glinted in the sunlight, the chrome shone like freshly minted silver and all the rust around the seams of the panels had gone, while the door mirror once again sat proud and firm on the driver's door. He welled up, pulled a handkerchief from his pocket and pretended to blow his nose whilst trying to regain control of his emotions. "Sorry, I suffer from hay fever," he said. The others weren't fooled by his actions and were rather touched.

Carl opened the driver's door, it didn't squeak, it just opened smoothly without drama. "Take a seat and I'll run through what we've done."

Montgomery took his place behind the wheel. "It's beautiful... really beautiful. It even smells like new."

"I'm so pleased you like it. It goes as well as it looks," Carl continued, "We've cleaned it up a bit. The upholstery has been completely replaced with a refurbished set from a donor car. The old ones were in a terrible state when we removed them, there was river weed all under the springs and it smelt like a mermaid's armpit, but that's all gone now after we steam cleaned it. The bodywork has been repaired, but we held back on a full respray, we didn't want to take away the patina."

"You've done a fantastic job, it feels like a different car," Montgomery said, lovingly stroking the upholstery.

"You'll find it goes better too. Release the hood, have a look." The eager detective pulled the lever in the foot well and the bonnet popped open. He climbed out as Nick unclipped and lifted the bonnet. The V-six engine, with all its cables and pipes gleamed like new. "We've solved the ignition problem by fitting a BOSCH electronic system from a later model," Carl continued, "while we were at it, we took the block apart, upgraded the valves, re-bored the cylinders, refurbished the carburettors and gave it a thoroughly good clean. When new it had one hundred and thirty-six horsepower. We put it on the rolling road yesterday and you now have one hundred and eighty."

Montgomery's hay fever returned, he blew his nose and wiped his eyes. "It's wonderful, I don't know how to thank you. I will, of course, pay you for your work," he said, looking at Jules.

"I appreciate that officer, after all, we don't want it to look like a bribe," Jules said, only half-jokingly.

"One more thing," Carl said, "we upgraded the ride quality. The donor car we stripped for the seats had adjustable rally suspension, so we fitted that as well. It doesn't wallow round the corners like the old dampers. You'll notice a harder ride, but it holds the road like it's on rails. Fancy a go?" he asked encouragingly.

"Yes, please," said Montgomery like an excited child on Christmas morning.

"Then hop in the passenger seat and I'll take you to a quiet road on the estate where we can really put it through its paces."

They drove out of the workshop, the engine purring like a kitten. When they were clear of the animal park, Carl pressed down on the accelerator and the car leapt forward like a scalded cat. "I forgot to say we upgraded the exhaust. Oh, and watch this." He pushed a new red button on the dash. The sound was deafening as the siren burst into life and the wet road in front of them reflected the flashing blue light. "The lights are hidden behind the front grille," Carl said excitedly, "Exford Constabulary Vehicle Works kindly provided the kit for us when I told them what we were doing and who for." He held back on what the police mechanics had scathingly said about Montgomery's choice of vehicle.

They swapped places and Montgomery took the wheel.

He was in seventh heaven. When they finally returned to the compound, he couldn't wipe the grin of his face. "This is amazing. Thank you all for your work. Don't forget to send me the bill," he said addressing the team in the workshop.

"There is one favour," Jules said, "we have the Holeford Car Club show over the bank holiday weekend. Would you allow us to display it in the 'Cars of the Stars' collection? It will be in good company with 'The Saint's' Volvo, Bessie from 'Dr Who', the Ford Capri from 'Minder', something from 'The Avengers', I can't remember the others."

"That's no problem, sir, it will be my pleasure."

Montgomery's heart skipped, he couldn't wait to show off his wonderful car and the display would be the ideal place. He was like a proud father. "If you'll excuse me, I must check on the clearing of the incident room and the enclosure with the head keeper before we can officially hand the areas back to you." He walked away looking back proudly at his car.

Jules drove back to the house and found Molly in the library, deep in thought. Books and papers were spread all over the desk and more volumes lay open on the coffee table. Molly had a dishevelled appearance, with her hair tied back but odd strands hanging loose. The sleeves of her shirt were rolled up and stained with dust from the old records. Wilf sat on the sofa watching her work, assisting with the selection and delivery of volumes from the higher shelves. The years he had spent in Price Low supermarket helping with the shelf stacking and honing his levitation skills were paying dividends.

"Hi Molly, have you seen father?" Jules asked, as he entered the room.

"Not since about ten, he was having a heated discussion on the phone and left in a hurry."

"He's constantly getting into arguments with the estate manager, I expect he's gone up to his office. Not to worry, I'll catch up with him later. How are you getting on with the guide?"

"It's coming together, or at least the outline of the manuscript is getting there, but I have some big gaps in the early history. I'm finding little gems in the old volumes, some of it is fascinating, but I need more. I think I'm going to be here at least another two weeks, but then I must get back to London, I can't afford to neglect my work there completely."

"In which case I have an idea," Jules sat on the sofa opposite her, "blimey it's cold in here," he exclaimed. Molly smiled as Wilf moved to one side, he didn't much appreciate being sat on!

"It's just the draught from the open fireplace I expect," Molly said smiling.

"You're still staying at the pub, aren't you?"

"At the moment, but I'm going to mum and dads for the weekend."

"That'll be nice for you. The thing is, we have two holiday lodges by the West Gate, one will be vacated on Saturday and if you like, when you return, you can have the use of it for as long as you want, the holiday season's drawing to a close and it's vacant for a while."

"That would be amazing, if I'm not putting you to too much trouble. I can work from there while I complete the information for the first draft. I'll be able to cook for myself as well, you can only eat so much pub grub, you know. I'm putting on weight!" She tapped her tummy.

"Please don't think I'm trying to push you out of the library. This room is still at your disposal."

"No, I don't think that at all, I'll need to be here daily for research but to sit quietly in a lodge would work well."

"Good, that's sorted then. I'll ask housekeeping to service it and stock the fridge with essentials to get you started on Monday."

"Thank you ever so much, I'll do some grocery shopping over the weekend."

"I'll also arrange a golf buggy for you to get round the estate."

Molly clapped her hand, "Can you do that? I'd love it."

"It'll be waiting for you on Monday. Oh! I nearly forgot I've got these for you. He pulled two tickets from the inside pocket of his jacket. "They're VIP tickets for the car show for your mum and dad if they'd like to come along. You don't need one with your access pass, it gets you in automatically."

Molly took the tickets and studied them, "They'll love that. You're being so kind. Thank you."

"No problem, now if you'll excuse me, I must try and track father down before he sacks anyone. You never know what he'll do if he's in one of his tempers."

He left via the secret door and Molly got back to work with renewed vigour.

Montgomery burst into the temporary incident room. The officers, coordinated by Sergeant Dexter, were busy clearing the filing cabinets and desks, placing the paperwork and objects in carefully marked archive boxes ready for return to the police station. Montgomery clapped his hands to gain attention and walked to the blackboard which displayed names linked to the case and a selection of photographs held in place with Sellotape, but now curling at the edges.

"Right ladies and gents, let's just have a little review before the van gets here and we ship everything out."

"This is just like on TV," Tom said excitedly to Alice as they both watched from the back of the room. Dexter and the constables stopped what they were doing, gathered round and looked expectantly at DI Montgomery.

"The facts," Montgomery began, relishing his position as leader, "our victim, one Thomas Carmichael." He pointed to the picture of a smiling student stood at the gates of the arts college.

"Nice picture," Alice said, "you look very happy."

"Thanks," Tom said mournfully, "I was."

"Thomas was working at the market on the Friday of the festival, but he never returned to his digs after storing the stock in the loft of the stables for safe keeping overnight. This was at around eight o'clock. We believe he was then forced into the lion enclosure by a gunman with a side arm. We have hard evidence and reports that confirm it was fired at least twice. The warden's log confirmed the enclosure gate was locked at six pm. The gate must have been unlocked for Thomas to access but was found locked again in the morning. That gate is only ever used for special escorted visits and not by the general public. Therefore, it did not raise any alarm during the Saturday opening of the park." Montgomery stopped and studied the photograph of the locked gate.

"Dexter, was this taken before the gate was opened during the investigation?"

"Yes sir, nothing was disturbed until your say-so."

"And no one has noticed this?" The group moved close to the picture and studied it, looking confused, it was just a padlock looped through a bolt. So what? Alice and Tom moved to the front, they too couldn't see anything suspicious.

"I know he locked it, I heard the key turn in the lock and then he lit a cigarette," Tom said.

"Dexter, pop next door and borrow a padlock and key please." Dexter went into the warden's office and returned with a padlock identical to the one in the picture. "Good, now lock it, remove the key and place it on the table." Dexter held the padlock, turned the key and placed it on the table as instructed. "Thank you. Now you all saw that," he said addressing the room of confused faces.

"Now, I'll do the same," he picked up the lock and key, opened it, turned the key again and placed the secured lock on the table, "now do you see any difference?" There were a few confused mumbles. "I can't hear you. Can you see anything?" The hand of a junior constable was raised at the back of the room. "Yes, constable?"

"You put it down the other way around," said a nervous voice.

"What's your name?" Montgomery questioned.

"Constable Davie, sir."

"All the experience in this room and it takes a junior to see the obvious, well done, Davie."

The Constable smiled and sat taller in her seat. The rest of the team still looked confused.

"Would you do the honour and explain it to the room please, Davie?"

"Because you're left-handed, sir."

"Exactly, now look at the photograph... the lock is also this way round on the gate... our killer is left-handed."

"So that reduces the suspect list to about six million people now, sir," Dexter said sarcastically. Montgomery gave him a hard stare.

"The killer knew exactly what he was doing, he had to be the one that unlocked the gate earlier and then locked it again after cornering Thomas and then he left the scene... But why Thomas? We need a motive. What was the problem with Thomas? Was he a physical threat? I doubt that, he was an art student. Did he know something about the killer that posed a risk? Maybe. Something so damning, he had to be silenced... It must have been serious to commit murder. Or was Thomas just in the wrong place at the wrong time? Those are the questions you need to take back to Holeford with you." He paused to let his audience absorb those thoughts.

"Are you alright Tom?" Alice asked. Tom had become quiet and reflective.

"I don't understand this, I'm standing here while the police try to fathom out who killed me and why. It's like a bad dream. Even I don't know who did it and I was there. How are they ever likely to find out?"

"The left-handed thing does seem a bit tentative," Alice admitted.

Montgomery continued, "Now an update on the robbery. The fraud squad are sending a consultant to work with us on the investigation. We believe the swap took place during the restoration of the art collection here at the abbey, which was completed only two weeks ago. This, ladies and gentlemen could also be linked to the murder of Thomas. We know that during the science fiction festival an operator from a criminal organisation was here talking to one of the suspects while disguised in a *'Galactic Jump'* costume. We lost the trail of the aforementioned alien." He looked over at P.C Singleton who looked suitably embarrassed. "But we did manage to follow a known suspect back to the city. Special Branch are keeping an eye on him for now. Right, that's it, carry on. Dexter come with me, we'll do a final check of the enclosure then I'll go and see the Duke."

As they stepped out into the compound, the police van arrived to collect the boxes of files and incident board. Alice and Tom headed back to the house to report to the others.

"Come on Dexter, we'll go in my car," Dexter's shoulders dropped, much to the amusement of Montgomery, "you're in for a surprise." They walked to the workshop where Dexter saw the restored Ford Consul.

"Is that the same car, sir? Your car?"

"It sure is, get in." Dexter was immediately struck by the way the passenger door opened smoothly and closed with a solid clunk. The interior had lost its contaminated river odour and looked like new. Montgomery turned the key and the engine burst into life after one turn, the six cylinders ticking over assuredly. They pulled out of the garage, John Hammond was waiting to escort them in his Land Rover. They both headed into the enclosure.

The ride in the Ford felt firm and assured. "Are you sure this is the same car, sir?" Dexter questioned.

"They've worked wonders, I've now got one hundred and eighty horses under the bonnet and it's as smooth as silk," Montgomery said proudly. *'Regan would have been jealous'* he thought. "By the way, I've posted two undercover officers at the house for the foreseeable future but only you and I need to know that. We need to find out what's really going on." They drove round the enclosure for one final time taking a close look to ensure it was clear of police presence. Dexter was then dropped off at the compound and Montgomery drove to the house to report to the Duke and return the duplicate keys.

20

Shipmates

Monday 19ᵗʰ of August. Morning

Molly arrived at Woodford Abbey at nine o'clock and parked in the staff car park. Alice and Wilf were waiting to greet her. The back seat of her car was folded down to accommodate bags of shopping and suitcases.

"Did you have a nice weekend?" Alice asked.

"Yes thanks, I went to see Carolyn. It's hard to believe, but little George is four years old, he's grown up so fast. Did you know Carolyn's been promoted to Deputy Head at Holeford Modern? They're all going to be at the car show. The school has a fund-raising stand so she's reviving '*Gypsy Carolyn*,' her fortune telling alter ego, to raise money for the new sports hall. I expect you already know Jack's regional manager for Price Low now?"

"No, we didn't know that."

"Then you probably don't know that his son, Joe is manager of the new out of town store and your old friend Charlie has been promoted to manager of Price Local opposite the museum. Not bad for someone who tried to burgle the place."

"He served his apprenticeship with us well," said Wilf proudly, "I knew he'd go far."

"Oh, Mum sends her regards. She and dad are coming to the car show using their VIP tickets, so it's going to be like a reunion. I couldn't have timed my visit here any better. All of us back together again."

"That's wonderful. Are you moving into the lodge today?" Alice asked excitedly, seeing the car full of shopping.

"Yes, that's the plan, I do hope it's ready. I've already cancelled the room at the Inn. How was your weekend?"

"It was back to normal after the excitement of the festival, so we just did a bit of casual haunting to help the atmosphere of the house. Wilf and George took Tom for a round of golf on Saturday evening."

"Not just any round," Wilf said proudly. "It was the first round of a double header against Holeford Golf Club. They're coming here for the return match over the bank holiday weekend and then we're putting on a show for them in the ballroom after."

"I didn't know you played golf, Wilf. You said it was a stupid game."

"I may have said that, but I have no recollection," Wilf said loftily. "George took me to the Abbey course one evening and I sort of got hooked."

"Well, it's nice to know George has a friend to play with. Now I must get on." She opened the boot, pulled out her briefcase and two large, leather- bound volumes. "Don't try and help with these out here. I think someone might suspect if they see books floating up the stairs! I'll need all your help with some investigation though. Can you meet me by the tree at lunchtime?" They nodded in agreement.

"That sounds interesting," Alice said, "It'll be just like old times."

"Don't get too excited, you don't know what I'm going to ask you, now I must go." Molly laid the books on the top of her case and carried the load in her arms. "I don't suppose it would hurt if you opened the door for me though," she cheekily asked Wilf, with a smile.

At one o'clock Molly sat under the tree by the café savouring a warm shot of caffeine and a piece of cake. From the rendezvous point close to the lion enclosure, she could hear the roars of delight from the big cats as they prowled round their territory once again, after their time confined to the paddock. The keepers had been busy preparing for the lion's return over the weekend. After the police handed back the enclosure, they took the opportunity to clear some of the overgrown bushes, overhaul the shelter and build a new log stack, recycling some of the trees that had been cleared from Woodford forest. The lions love to climb and laze around on the pile of tree trunks. The keepers also hide their food amongst the branches to stimulate the cats hunting instincts.

"That looks nice," Alice said, as the ghosts suddenly appeared from behind the tree.

"Ooh! You made me jump," Molly said, spitting crumbs over her lap.

"Sorry," Alice apologised.

Molly dusted off her dress. "Mum made the cake for me to take to the lodge this afternoon, but I couldn't resist a small taste. It's my favourite, coffee and walnut. I've got to watch my figure though, with all her home cooked food. I'm glad you're all here, I have a little investigation work for you." They all gathered around. Molly went silent. A young couple had glanced over wondering why the woman under the tree was talking to herself. They then continued on their way, proudly pushing a shiny new pram containing a sleeping baby.

"I took some very old volumes home with me to read at the weekend, but I have a mystery. There are some ledgers and diaries missing, which relate to the time before the abbey was surrendered to Henry the Eighth's commissioner." She paused, having noticed their blank expressions. "I know what you're thinking, how are we expected to find five-hundred-year-old documents."

"I think you've nailed it there," George said, with a hint of sarcasm.

Molly ignored him, "I've got a friend who works at the British Library, she investigated it for me this morning. If the missing documents exist, she would know where to find reference to them in the record's, but there was nothing… no mention at all."

The four ghosts looked confused. *'What were they expected to do?'*

"We can do a lot of things, but we can't go back in time, Molly," Wilf said sarcastically. "If we could, we wouldn't be dead now."

"You haven't let me finish," Molly answered reproachfully. I have a hunch that a scribe left a hidden message in one of the documents we do have. Here's a photocopy of a map from the commissioner's report to the King."

"I didn't know they had photocopiers in Tudor times."

"There's no need for flippancy, Tom," rebuked Alice, intrigued to hear Molly's theory.

"Sorry, I'm just struggling with all this," he said.

"You see, here it shows a mausoleum in the grounds by the river." They all studied the map while Molly finished off her cake, washing it down with the now lukewarm coffee.

"I recognise that, it's on the island, they must have dug the lake around it, it's hidden behind the undergrowth, you can't see it from the shore," Wilf said.

"The commissioner's report says, '*it contains the remains of abbots and is of no financial interest*,' so it was never investigated."

"Are you suggesting we go raiding tombs," Alice said, turning her nose up, quite disgusted at the thought.

"It's a bit more academic than that. I've got another friend at Oxford, Lorna Crofton, she's an archaeologist. Her parents are very wealthy, so she spends most of her time in South America looking for lost civilisations and burial sites. She gave me some ideas about where to look, so I studied the ledgers for clues."

"What did you discover?" Alice asked with interest.

"According to the report, one of the Abbots interned there is a Father *Tabulis Rediit*. A funny name, yes, but it's not unusual for the monks to use Latin names when they take Holy Orders, however if you translate it to English, it means ledger. I can't find any other reference to *Tabulis* anywhere, before or after this date. He's an anomaly. I think the missing information may be in that vault."

Alice clapped her hands, "and you want us to go and look for it, how exciting."

"You're bonkers," Wilf said, adding a not so subtle word of common-sense. Tom listened, totally bewildered.

"You're able to enter the mausoleum and have a look for me without having to break anything. Floating through walls is a skill made for this job," Molly pointed out.

George was slightly more encouraging, "Well, it's an evening out. It's not like we have to disturb anything and if it helps, why not?"

Before Wilf could argue, Alice spoke, "Right, you're on Molly. We're all in, we'll go tonight."

"How do we get to an island at night?" Tom said, "Can we float across water?"

"You can, but it needs practice, but I have a better way," George said mysteriously.

"Thank you all so much. It may be nothing, but if you do discover something I can go over there with confidence and retrieve the documents. You'll be like an advanced party searching for treasure in a long-lost tomb," Molly commented encouragingly.

"This would make a good film," Alice said excitedly, "I could be the fearless female archaeologist and the rest of you my trusty team."

"Wonderful," exclaimed Wilf, sarcastically, "I wonder which one of us three would get killed off first?"

Alice poked her tongue out at him.

"I'm moving into the lodge this afternoon, so from now on it's going to be easier to contact each other. Jules is lending me a golf buggy to get around the estate, which is really cool. Now, I must get back." Molly waved goodbye and left the four ghosts in a huddle planning their evening's work. Alice was picturing herself in pith helmet and calf length culottes.

On her desk in the library, Jules had deposited an envelope containing keys and instructions for the lodge. He also added a handwritten note on the front, saying he would pop over at four o'clock to make sure everything was OK.

Molly smiled and got down to work on the manuscript. The layout was beginning to take shape with all the chapter headings sorted, along with bullet points for the contents. However, concentration this afternoon was difficult. Butterflies flitted around in her stomach excitedly, at the prospect of moving into the lodge, coupled with what might be found on the island that evening. The envelope in her eye line was too tempting. At three o'clock she could resist no longer, packed up and headed to her car. She drove round to the front of the house, past the main car park, turning onto the gravel path sign-posted 'residents only'. She drove parallel to the tiger enclosure, towards the west gate holiday cottages. Through the bushes she could see visitor's cars slowly traversing the inner road with faces excitedly pushed up to the windows on the look-out for big cats. Her view then opened out into the deer park where the field was sprinkled with mature trees. She then joined a tarmac road heading due west away from the house. 'This must be the original entrance road' she thought, then caught sight of the huge black wrought iron gates. They were locked and cordoned off by long timber troughs overflowing with colourful shrubs. To the left and right of the gates were romantic looking Victorian lodges. Historically these were the home of the gate keeper, but were now converted into fairy tale holiday cottages. The larger, to the left, had a gleaming, freshly painted zebra striped golf buggy parked outside.

Her heart did a skip, *'that must be my transport'* she thought, pulling up alongside it, grinning from ear to ear. *'And this must be my lodge.'*

She got out and walked up to the front door. This alone was a work of art. The frame was set in a stone surround with the vertical planks of the gothic arched door painted in estate green and enriched by heavy ornate black iron strap hinges. She turned the key, lifted the heavy latch and pushed the door. It opened into a living room with two pastel striped Laura Ashley sofas facing a log burner sitting in the stone fireplace, it seemed to smile at her in welcome. Between the sofas, on the low coffee table, an information folder sat alongside a copy of *'Country Life.'* To the left was a small kitchen, its small leaded window looking back down the road towards the house. On the worktop was a basket containing fresh bread, fruit, pasta, rice and a pot of strawberry jam. The fridge hummed in the corner, inviting her to open it. Inside was milk, cheese and yogurt, all produce from the estate farms along with an inviting bottle of Prosecco. Impressed by the quality of the lodge's furnishings and decoration, she climbed the narrow stairs.

It felt like she was walking through a house that might feature in the magazine lying on the table. Off the landing was the bathroom containing a gleaming white bath with clawed feet, separate shower, wash hand basin and toilet, all in the Victorian style, with floral tiling to the walls. On the right, the main bedroom contained a double bed, wardrobe and dressing table. The windows were framed by flower-patterned curtains, the whole space an explosion of elegant Laura Ashley design. She loved it. It was feminine with a contemporary twist. She returned to the landing and visited the second bedroom. The bed here had been removed and replaced with a desk containing a brand-new Brother electric typewriter and a telephone placed alongside. An office chair and filing cabinet completed the temporary office. The window looked out across the deer park and had a venetian blind in place of curtains. *'A perfect little workplace, they'd thought of everything.'*

Molly returned to the car and brought in the bags of groceries and cases, piling everything up in the living room. She set to work, filling the cupboards in the kitchen and then in the bedroom, hung her clothes in the wardrobe placing her neatly folded underwear in the drawers of the dressing table.

At four o'clock there was a knock at the door. She came down the stairs and opened it.

Jules stood on the doorstep holding a large bunch of flowers. "Hi, you found it alright then?" he said, peeping around the blooms. "The house-keeper forgot to put these in the vase for you. We always have fresh flowers for our guests, they make the place more welcoming."

"It's all lovely, thank you so much for this. There's even a desk set up in the bedroom with a brand-new typewriter. It's perfect for my work... Sorry, please come in, it's a bit of a mess, I'm still unpacking." Jules entered and took the flowers into the kitchen placing them in the sink.

"Actually, the typewriter is a bit of an indulgence for me. I took advantage of your stay to order a new one, which I'll have in my office when you've finished with it. Mine's getting a bit past it and this one has a memory function, so you can check the text before it's typed. It's very clever, I don't know what they'll think of next. I asked estates to prep a room for you as a temporary office so I'm glad you like it."

"It's perfect, and all the food too. I brought so much with me as well, I've got enough for a month."

"Well, you're welcome to stay as long as you like, you're working for the estate, after all."

"Don't tempt me, it's idyllic here but I'll have to go back soon. I have work in the museum to continue and a dissertation for my PhD to complete."

"The cottage isn't booked out again till next spring. You'll have neighbours off and on though. The lodge opposite is still being let for a couple of weeks."

"Sorry, very rude of me. Would you like a coffee?" Molly asked belatedly.

"Yes please," Jules said, looking round the house with interest, "it all looks nice and clean. I haven't visited the lodges recently, they were completely refurbished for this season... looks good." He nodded in approval.

Molly filled the kettle, flicked the switch on and took two mugs off the mug tree. "Sugar?" she asked.

"Not for me thanks. By the way, when you run out of milk or butter just ask in the Café and they'll give you more. Did you see the golf buggy?"

"I couldn't miss it, it looks brand new."

"Not quite but I asked them to give you a nice one. They've installed the charger outside for you. I'll show you how it works later and give you a driving lesson."

"Here you are," Molly came into the living room carrying two cups of steaming coffee. They sat on the sofa and she updated him on her work with the manuscript.

They finished their drink then went outside where Jules demonstrated how to plug the buggy into the big green box mounted on the wall. They then climbed in with Molly in the driving seat. Jules familiarised her with the controls and then she drove off for a spin round the estate. She drove them past the showground where marquees were now fully erected, the parade ring fenced off and areas marked out ready for the trade stalls. Then returned to the lodge by driving across the deer park. The eager little car cruised effortlessly over the grass, its motors whining as its soft tyres swallowed up the bumps.

"I want one of these," Molly said, thoroughly enjoying the go any-where freedom.

"They're not much good on the open road," Jules said, amused at Molly's enthusiastic driving. Returning to the lodge, she applied the parking brake with her foot. "Well done madam, I'm pleased to inform you you've passed your test with flying colours. Welcome to Woodford Abbey Miss Goodall, we're very happy to have you here. Now one more thing, if you need anything just press number 'one' on the telephone and it connects directly to my office. I'll leave you to settle in, I expect I'll catch up with you in the library tomorrow. Unless there is anything else I can do for you now?"

"No, you've been very kind. I've taken up enough of your time."

"My pleasure. Just call if you think of anything," Jules stepped out of the buggy, climbed into his Range Rover and drove off with a wave.

Monday evening.

In the attic the intrepid explorers prepared for their nights mission.

"What do you think?" Alice asked the team, as she twirled round in her walking boots, green socks up to her knees, khaki shorts and white shirt. Her hair was gathered up under a sun-bleached green pith helmet.

"Well, you certainly look the part," George said, "what about me?"

He was wearing leather sandals with grey socks, crumpled cotton trousers, a green fly-fishing shirt full of pockets and a brown Snap Brim Fedora hat.

Wilf watched the proceedings dressed in his beloved pirate uniform. "You all look ridiculous, I don't think you're taking this seriously."

"Have you seen yourself, that's not exactly tomb raider attire... Now what about you Tom? I've got here a nice long leather coat and Tilley hat, try them on. You've got to join in," George said earnestly, handing him the clothes.

Tom looked confused. "Are you really dressing up for this? Is this what it's really like being a ghost?" He reluctantly took the jacket and hat.

"We're born performers, we can't help it, our audience expects us to put on a show," Wilf explained.

"And it's fun, "George added, "if you dress appropriately, you feel like you can do anything. You don't see bank managers dressed like blacksmiths, it wouldn't work. Everyone wears clothes appropriate to their role. I bet you dress up to be an artist, don't you?"

"Well, I wear an apron to catch the splashes of paint," Tom admitted.

"Exactly, and I bet you can't paint properly without it," Tom nodded in agreement.

"There you are then," George said smugly, "you're no different than us. Now pop these on, we need to get going, our transport awaits."

"Don't worry, we'll look after you," Alice assured him. "Just enjoy yourself."

The four of them floated down through the building and out into the cool night air. They could see the silhouette of the island across the lake, framed by the waxing moon, it's light dancing on the surface of the water. The reeds on the bank whispered gently as a light breeze caught the heavy sward. All colour seemed to be absorbed, taking on a sepia monotone but details were still clearly visible. A patrol van drove past them, its bright headlights temporarily illuminating the path ahead. Wilf held out his thumb for a lift, the driver continued on, oblivious to the four unusually dressed adventurers.

"Come on, this is perfect timing, we have to get round to the Lakeside station, he won't be back round the lake for two hours," George said.

"But they can't see us," Tom argued.

"Ah! But we have a little surprise for you," Wilf said mysteriously.

They moved around the water's edge following the path between the shore and the railway line, soon arriving at the station platform.

"Are we catching a train?" Tom asked, now totally confused. '*How would it get across the water?*'

"No, we can't get to the island on a train, but we can on that," George said smugly pointing to the Mississippi steamboat moored nearby.

"Ooh! That's so cool," exclaimed Alice, "But how?" Her question was immediately answered.

"Howdy, come aboard," Finn shouted from the boiler deck.

The hull rested gently against the wooden jetty which moved in rhythm with the moored vessel. They all moved on board via the forward deck.

"Come on up to the saloon deck," Finn said, waving them towards the ornately crafted stairs rising from the lower deck. Seeing Alice, Finn removed his hat and greeted her. "Ma'am, it's a pleasure to have you aboard." The others followed. "Welcome to the good ship '*Louisiana*,' make yourselves at home, we'll be underway shortly." Finn was amused by the strange mix of clothes they were wearing but was far too polite to say anything, after all the English always were eccentric. He was just overjoyed having their company for the evening.

They passed through the pair of glazed doors etched with images of the steamer travelling along the Mississippi. The saloon was large and open, with deep red mahogany furniture upholstered in red velvet. It had windows all round, enabling panoramic views, port and starboard. The far end wall was panelled with a shuttered section in the middle concealing the bar.

"This is just beautiful, Finn," Alice said, looking around in awe. She could just picture ladies in full gowns and the elegantly dressed gentlemen playing poker for high stakes while the '*Louisiana*' sailed down the river.

"Thank you, ma'am, our passengers love sitting in here with a drink while we cruise around the lake. The Duke has applied for a licence to do weddings on board. I hope he's successful, that would be great fun. Now settle down and I'll get us underway. Wilf, will you do the honours and cast off?"

"Aye-aye captain," the pirate said saluting and headed down to the Main deck.

"Can I come with you and see how it all works?" George asked eagerly.

"Yes sir-ee," Finn said, "Let's go." They floated up through the Hurricane deck, an open sided area with timber benches and then up again to the top deck with the Pilot house sat in the middle.

George looked in awe at the highly polished controls and brass inlaid ship's wheel. "This is very smart Finn, I wish we'd done this before. To think this was here all the time and we've never actually been aboard."

"They keep it well, never seen it so good," Finn said in his southern drawl. He moved to the railings and shouted down. "Cast off, if you please, Master Shipman Wilf."

Wilf stared at the rope and concentrated hard. It unravelled from the bollard and slithered onto the ship like a snake coiling up into a neat spiral on the teak deck. Wilf was thrilled.

In the pilot house Finn rang the bell once and moved the brass lever on the binnacle to 'Ahead Slow,' the ship then silently crept forward. He turned the wheel clockwise and they sailed out across the lake, towards the island.

"What y'all up to George? No one goes to the island even in daylight, it's all overgrown. The captain sometimes moors up there out of season but only to shelter the boat from strong winds. He then rows back ashore, never goes onto the island itself."

"We're on a mission for Molly, she wants us to look for something in the mausoleum."

"Rather you than me. At least that explains why you're all dressed up that way. Molly a friend of yours then?" he asked bluntly, "It's not normal, mixing with mortals."

George explained their unusual relationship and the events in Holeford that saved their old home from demolition. Down in the saloon, Wilf joined Alice and Tom as they relaxed and contemplated the job ahead.

"How is this moving?" Tom asked, observing the bow wave and gentle lapping against the hull as it cut through the water, "there's no engine running, the paddle looks like it's just being pushed round by the forward movement." He looked totally confused. Would he ever get used to this strange new existence?

"It's all done by psychic-kinetic power, it's much easier for Finn with all of us here. He can use our energy to boost the force." Tom looked confused. "You know how a poltergeist can move objects?"

"That's just in horror films," Tom said scathingly.

"Not so young man, it's a real thing and you're riding along in an example of it. Isn't it better than just floating over the lake?"

"I love it Wilf," Alice said, looking out of the window, seeing the island getting closer and wishing the cruise could go on much longer. She could already make out the wooden pier. It looked like a tongue poking out from the undergrowth into the water. After only ten minutes, the bell mounted at the front of the upper deck rang twice.

"Nearly there," Wilf said, "I'm going back down to tie us up." He headed down through the floor to bow deck and waited for the signal.

The boat nestled against the rickety wooden jetty. Wilf concentrated, willing the mooring rope into a snake like action, it slipped effortlessly off the deck and wrapped itself securely around a thick supporting post driven deep into the bed of the lake.

"All ashore, you have one hour, then we have to sail back before the patrol comes round again," Finn cautioned.

They all gathered on the lower deck ready to disembark.

"Do you mind if I stay here with Finn, I'd like to see round the ship?" Tom asked. He didn't really want to enter a dirty old tomb, and this gave him a great excuse to avoid it. He found his new existence bewildering.

"If you like, we're not going to be too long, hopefully," George said, "is that OK, Finn?"

"Sure is guys, be glad of the company." Finn was secretly thrilled. He loved showing off his home.

"Right, let's go team," Wilf ordered. The three of them stood on the pier facing towards the interior of the island. Their mission suddenly felt very real. The path leading off was overgrown, with just a narrow opening visible, rarely used in recent years.

They heard something rustle by the shore. "What was that?" Alice cried out, tensing her body, her senses cranked up to eleven. George and Wilf detected her fear and stood silently, listening intently.

"Quack." cried a mallard duck, swimming out from under the pier. This in turn prompted a response from the frogs resting in the weed by the bank, whose croaking then formed the soundtrack for the evening.

They all sighed with relief.

"Come on, nothing can hurt us, the place is deserted," Wilf said rather unconvincingly. They moved off along the just visible path using the moonlight to assist their spectral gift for night vision. To the right they could make out a dilapidated brick building overgrown with ivy.

"What's that?" Wilf said moving closer, "Looks like a small bungalow. You can't see it from the shore."

"That's the old boathouse," Alice said, pointing it out to Wilf, "it's on the estate map in the library but I didn't know it was still here. Don't you remember reading about it in the briefing notes we had before coming here?"

"I've got better things to do than read all that stuff, there were files full of information. I just read the job description and went from there."

"Shush, you two, come on, we've got a job to do," George ordered, hurrying them on. They continued along the path and the island opened out into a clearing interlaced with more narrow paths. The tall grass softly swayed in the gentle breeze.

"This place is huge," Alice said, "Much bigger than it looks from the shore. Will we have time to do this?"

"It's about the size of two football pitches. I read about it in one of the books Molly was researching," George said, "from the shore, it looks like dense woodland but it's only the shoreline that's overgrown. The family used to come over here in the summer for picnics and mess about in the water. That's why the boat house is over here. It all neglected now. They lost heart when the Duke's wife left him."

They could now just make out the outline of the mausoleum at the far side of the clearing and ignoring the paths in the grass, started moving directly towards it.

Finn and Tom waved off the intrepid explorers. "So, I guess you're the one all the fuss is about over in the park. Nice to meet you, at last. Welcome to my steamboat."

"Thank you... you're right, the police are all over the place trying to track down the gunman."

"What really happened?" Finn asked.

"I wish I understood it myself. I volunteered to pack the stuff away in the stables after the market closed. Then a man came out of the shadows and pointed a gun at me. I managed to get away from him but then he chased me into the lion enclosure. I fell over, banged my head and the next thing, Eric is saying 'Hello, you're a ghost'. Then he left me with Wilf, George and Alice and pushed off to finish his holiday. They've been lovely trying to teach me about being a spirit, but I'm just not sure what happens next. I'm still waiting for Eric to come back with the paperwork... Paperwork, can you believe that? I'm dead, but there's still bureaucracy... unbelievable!"

"I know, I couldn't believe it either, it was the same for me. I was stowing away just over there behind the barrels. Not those ones, they're just empty props to make it look authentic. But there I was keeping my head down when suddenly, BOOM! the boiler blew up and my mortal life was over. It was a risk with steam engines in those days and normally the boat went up in flames as a result. Anyway, I digress... The boat was close to shore and settled in the mud. They managed to put the fire out, but the hull was breached so that was that."

"Did Eric come to you as well?"

"No, it was 'Blanche'. She was the reaper in Louisiana, a bit like Eric but she was better prepared, turned up with all the paperwork and options on what I could do as it was an accidental death. She told me to hang on and look after the vessel and it would work out well in the long run. I stayed on board spooking undesirables, scaring them off. Then the current Duke's grandfather turns up one day and offers to buy the wreck. It was too good to be true, Blanche was right. The Duke had it dismantled, shipped over the best of the components and reassembled them here on a new steel hull, replacing the rotten and damaged parts. He fitted a refurbished steam engine. Now it runs like a dream, looks better than ever and I feel right at home. No more hiding behind the barrels for me."

"It does look good, it's so authentic," Tom said admiring the craftsmanship.

"Come on, I'll show you the engine room. We're on the main deck at the moment but that is where the magic happens." Finn led Tom along the wide deck, then around fake barrels and wooden boxes and finally through a narrow door into the engine room. The boiler was still warm from its day's work. Polished copper and brass pipes ran in neat lines along and over the narrow walkway to the side of the huge dark green boiler. The mixed aroma of coal, oil and hot metal was intoxicating to anyone who loved engineering.

Tom looked on amazed, "Wow! This is like something from a *Jules Verne*, book, it's so clean."

He could make out the base of two smokestacks curving into the back of the boiler and the brass plaque reading '*Swindon works, England*.'

"It's still cooling, "Finn explained, "It won't actually get cold in here till they clean the pipes in the boiler at the end of the season when they do a full service." He then told him the names of the large cast iron and steel components dominating the rear of the cabin. "This is the piston that drives the crank and flywheel." A rod as thick as his arm passed through a slot in the end wall. "That goes out to the paddle wheel and turns it. It's simple really!"

"I can't get over the beauty of the engineering. It must be amazing when it's running."

"Why don't you come out with us some time? You can spend the day here if you like, I'd be glad of the company."

"I'd like that."

"Now let's go up to the pilot house and I'll show how that works." They floated up through the decks with lounges and open seating, to the top deck. "This is called the hurricane deck, just because it can get windy up here, not so much in England though but 'the mild breeze deck' doesn't sound as romantic. Believe me, it did get pretty draughty up here when it was on the Mississippi." They moved into the pilot house.

"It's like being in a garden shed with loads of windows." Tom said. Then he saw the ship's wheel, "It's huge!" The teak wheel, passed through a slot in the floor enabling the captain to turn it comfortably. To the right stood a brass column with round top and handle. Through its glass sides he could read, '*Ahead, Astern, Full, Half, Slow*' on the neatly written dial. The room smelt of wax polish and Brasso. The white, painted walls were clean, with a framed map of the lake showing the depths contoured in blue. To the right were other framed documents full of small print too complicated to understand.

"This is the 'Engine Order Telegraph.' The captain signals the boiler room with it. It's like the accelerator and gearbox all in one."

"It's a work of art," Tom said.

"It's the original one, it took a lot of cleaning up. They stripped it down and rebuilt it, but it still works perfectly after all these years."

Finn looked up at the clock mounted high up above the front facing windows. "They'll have to get a move on, we've got to cast off in half an hour."

"Wow, the time's flying by, I hope they find what Molly wants," Tom said, looking down towards the overgrown interior of the island. He wondered what they had encountered.

Wilf, George and Alice continued on their mission through the tall grassland towards the tomb. The grasshoppers chirped loudly as they brushed the top of the grasses. It felt more like a jungle adventure. '*Who would believe it was like this out here,*' thought George.

"Stop!" Alice cried, pointing towards the trees away to the left, "Something moved." She tensed. They all watched the undergrowth intently. A low-lying branch quivered. "There, did you see it? There's something looking at us, I can feel it." It moved again. "That's it, I'm going back, this is too much. I could die of a heart attack out here."

"Bit late for that, dear," Wilf whispered sarcastically. They stood in a circle, they weren't sure why, but they do it in the films so it seemed like a good idea. They then heard the crack of breaking twigs.

From the animal park, the wolves started howling, their high pitched wails cutting through the air like a knife. The three of them huddled closer. "Oh! God, we're under attack…they're going to eat us!"

"Shush, don't be silly," Wilf cautioned, "don't move, I can hear something coming." They tensed for impact, then several deer gambolled across their path, moving effortlessly in near silence, swishing through the tall grass. The three ghosts sighed with relief.

"How the hell did they get here?" George pondered.

"Probably caught the ferry," Wilf joked, trying to calm their nerves.

"I think they can swim," Alice said with relief, "Now come on, let's get this over with."

They moved cautiously again towards their goal and the mausoleum finally came into view. The tomb was in the Greek style with columns and panels carved into the stone walls. It had settled into the clay rich ground and now sat at an angle. The stone blocks were de-bonded and large cracks had opened between them. The roof, also made from stone slabs appeared to be intact but leant to one side like the top of an opened chocolate box that hadn't been put back on properly.

To the end of the structure, the projecting gable was supported by four stone columns. Overgrown steps led down to a rusty iron door three feet lower than ground level.

"That must be the entrance," Wilf deduced.

"Well spotted, Sherlock," George said sarcastically.

"Argh, get them off," shouted Alice, waving her arms above her head while spinning round erratically. They could hear ticking noises as a cloud of bats flew out from a gap under the roof. "They'll get tangled in my hair…get them off…get them off," she screamed.

"Alice, pull yourself together, it's just bats. That's an old wife's tale about getting caught in your hair and anyway, you're a ghost they'll fly straight through you!" Alice was now sat on the top of the steps with her arms over her head for protection. "I thought you were the great adventurer?" Wilf said trying to pacify her.

"I'm seriously going to re-evaluate that, after this," she muttered.

"Stop mucking about you two," George said, "let's get this over with."

They passed through a rusty iron gate protecting the heavy gauge iron door, which was locked and bolted. "We need to tell Molly about that," Wilf noted. They passed through the door into a narrow corridor with niches to both sides, their openings sealed with stone. They could just make out what appeared to be carved lettering on the seals, names of the deceased.

"What do we do now? This is impossible. It's so damp and mouldy I can't make out the carving," George complained.

"Think logically," Alice replied. She looked closely at the stones and was able to levitate a small piece of rock from the floor to wipe over the surface, revealing more of the lettering.

Wilf had a different idea, he randomly put his head through a stone capping and looked inside, quickly withdrawing. "Yuck, it's full of old bones,"

"What did you expect, tins of beans," George said.

"Ha flipping ha," Wilf said not sharing the joke, "I'm going to ruin my clothes."

"Oh! don't be such a big girl's blouse! I told you not to wear your pirate outfit," George said unsympathetically.

"That's easy coming from you in your scruffy getup."

"Boys…boys, stop messing around. We're doing this for Molly and don't forget the boat goes back soon, with or without us," Alice reminded them. "Wait… look here, this could be it," she continued, frantically wiping the face of a stone revealing clear lettering. "Look it says '*Father… Tabulis… Rediit*' this is it. Who's going to look?" She asked reluctantly.

Wilf bravely moved forward, "I'll do it, my tunic's ruined anyway." He stuck his head through the stone slab. It was thinner than the others. No bones this time but a lead box only half the size of a normal coffin, sealed all round and welded shut. He pulled himself back out again. "I think this is it, there's a metal box in there and its welded shut."

"Have another look, what's in the box?" George said impatiently. Alice too urged him on.

"OK, here I go." Wilf stuck his head back in, this time passing through the lead casing and returned to the room.

"There are no bones, just books in there," he said excitedly, "Molly was right, they really exist. They're wrapped in some sort of cloth, but they seem OK, the box must have been sealed well."

"That's brilliant," Alice said excitedly, "Now can we go home please? This place is scary."

They quickly made their way back. Wilf untied the mooring rope and Finn expertly steered them away from the island. They all joined him in the pilot house to describe what they had found in the tomb, with a few additional dramatic exaggerations.

"I can't wait to tell Molly," Alice said.

"Well, there's nothing stopping us visiting the lodge as soon as we land," Wilf pointed out.

"I'll do it," Alice said, "It's late and a lady's bedroom at night is no place for old men." Wilf and George pulled a face. But they got the message.

21
The Island

Tuesday 20th August. Morning

Molly didn't sleep well after Alice's late-night visit. Her mind turning over and over, wondering what information was actually concealed in the mausoleum. Firstly, she was thrilled by the news that her research had been correct, but this soon changed to concern about what the documents would reveal, assuming that they hadn't just decayed into dust. But Alice said not, apparently Wilf had seen something wrapped in cloth, could they really still be legible? She had to find out. She made a decision.

After a light breakfast she grabbed the phone and pressed the direct line to Jules's office. It rang four times before the answerphone clicked on. She heard Jules's voice requesting the caller to leave a message and then a bleep. "Jules, hi, it's Molly, I need to ask you a favour. Would it be possible for me to go to the island? I could use your help, so would you be able to come too? I need to search for something. I can't tell you over the phone. I'll be in the library from nine o'clock... Oh! Thank you." She hated leaving messages, it always sounded so disjointed. Also, her West Country dialect seemed magnified by the tape recording. She didn't think she had an accent until a recording was played back to her during a lecture, when she nearly died of embarrassment. She heard the voice of a milk maid from a narration of a Thomas Hardy novel. *'That wasn't me... was it?'* She wasn't ashamed of her accent, it was a wonderfully rich soft burr. But some people assumed she must therefore be uneducated and naïve, that really annoyed her. No one had commented during her time at Oxford University, after all the students came from every corner of the UK and some from overseas, it was a melting pot of backgrounds and cultures, everyone was different, which somehow made them all the same.

Molly picked up her briefcase, locked the door, placed it on the seat of the buggy and drove across the estate to the staff car park. As fortune would have it, as she stepped out of the cart, Jules pulled up in his Range Rover.

He wound down his window, "Good morning, how was your first night in the lodge?"

"Oh, fine thank you." Molly's mind was distracted, "I just left a message on your phone, I can tell you myself now. So you don't need to listen to it. I sound awful on those things." Jules smiled, he was intrigued and would definitely play it now. "I need your help," Molly continued. She explained about the information she had uncovered over the weekend, pretending she had no idea if it was true or not. She stood by the driver's door, looking up at Jules and adopting her '*I can't manage without you*' expression. It usually worked on impressionable young men, but she wasn't sure if it would work on a sophisticated aristocrat.

"That can be arranged. What about this afternoon? We can use father's boat, it'll do it good to blow out the cobwebs."

"We'll need to go into the mausoleum, it'll be pretty mucky, I expect," Molly said, thrilled that her cajoling had worked. Or maybe he was just naturally helpful.

"I'll see if we have any keys in the safe. Pop in the workshop and see Nick, he can lend you some tools to open the door, just in case. The locks are probably rusted, no one's been in there for years."

"Thank you so much, I'll swing by the compound when I go back to the lodge to change into some old clothes."

"OK, I'll see you in my office at two o'clock, sounds like it's going to be a bit of fun... I've got to go to a meeting now, but I promise I'll delete the message." Molly wasn't convinced that he wouldn't play it at least once now she had mentioned it. '*How embarrassing.*'

"Great, see you at two," she confirmed, grabbed her briefcase and headed for the library.

At two o'clock Molly arrived at Jules office, dressed in a faded Duran Duran tee-shirt, dungarees and Doctor Martin boots. She had her hair in a bun pushed under an old baseball cap for good measure. Jules was also prepared, wearing old jeans and a paint splattered polo shirt. As they passed Molly's golf buggy, on the way to the boat house, Jules lifted a canvas tool bag out of the foot well. "Blimey, what've you got in here? It weighs a ton," he asked.

"Nick lent me a crowbar, a big hammer, some screwdrivers and some masonry chisels."

"Well, you certainly mean business, I just hope these old things I found in the safe are the right ones," Jules held up a bunch of large rusty keys.

"I do hope so," Molly said, nodding in approval.

They headed across the car park to the Victorian boathouse positioned adjacent to the steamboat quay, where visitors queued behind a white picket fence for the next sailing of '*The Louisiana.*'

The boathouse was brick built with a low slate roof, small stone mullioned windows and a narrow gothic arched door. The ornate carved stone façade of the wide opening to the lake was only visible from the water and opposite bank. Jules unlocked the wooden door, and they entered the room, illuminated only by light from the small windows and gaps around the two large doors opening onto the lake. From a narrow stone landing, they stood at the top of four stone steps giving access to the dock side, which wrapped around three sides of the interior.

"Go careful, these steps are wet and slippery," Jules cautioned, as he placed the heavy tool bag on the landing. Molly held the iron handrail to steady her descent whilst her eyes adjusted to the gloom. "Wait here a minute," Jules said, moving along the path to open one of the wooden doors to the lake, securing it open with a thick rusty bolt that dropped into a hole in the floor. The outside light flooded in, illuminating the bare brick walls. Old wooden boxes and coils of rope were piled against the walls from which rusty odd shaped items hung on hooks. Molly assumed these were spares that had seen better days. Sitting on the water was the unmistakable shape of a boat bobbing ever so slightly, covered by a pale green tarpaulin. The hull was secured at the bow and stern by thin ropes around iron bollards. Jules walked to the opposite side and opened the second door, revealing the full view out onto the water. "Right, I need a hand now, if you grab this end," he handed Molly the corner of the boat cover near the open door. "I'll go to the other side and when I say 'go', we'll both pull it back together towards the rear of the boathouse and pile it up on the landing." Jules moved to the opposite side, knelt down and reached over to the corner of the sheet resting on the top of the securing rope. Molly shadowed his movements. They were both now clutching the corners of the tarpaulin.

"Ready?"

Molly nodded.

"OK, now!"

They both pulled at the same time and the sheet slid effortlessly off the boat. They stuffed it as neatly as they could against the far wall and turned to look at the vessel.

Molly's jaw dropped. "Oh my God, it's beautiful," she said, admiring the open topped, highly polished wooden motor launch. With sweeping wraparound windshield, gleaming chrome fittings and white leather seats, it radiated a timeless elegance.

Jules beamed, "Lovely isn't she, its Father's pride and joy, a Riva Aquarama."

Molly studied the stylish rake of the stern and noted the name written in gold on the varnished teak. "*Eleanor*, that's your mother's name. How lovely, that's a beautiful gesture."

Jules went quiet at the mention of the name. It conjured up the carefree time of his childhood when, as a family they would go off for picnics in the boat. He would lie on the cushioned sundeck alongside his sister with mother in the passenger seat as the Duke opened up the engines and they skimmed the surface of the lake without a care in the world. What he would give to have that time back again.

"Sorry, have I said something wrong?" Molly asked noticing the change of mood.

"No... not at all," Jules blinked away the moisture in his eyes, "Now come on, we've got work to do." He stepped aboard and laid out a blanket on the sundeck then he carefully lifted the heavy tool bag onto it, being careful not to scratch the hull. He held out a hand, beckoning Molly to the passenger side and assisted her to board.

"I thought your car was posh, but this is simply stunning!" she said settling into the soft wide seating. She couldn't resist running her hands over the polished wood and leather. "Beautiful," she said softly.

Jules smiled. "Right, let's get her going." Quickly he leant over the curved windscreen and cast off the rope. The wide dashboard looked just like that of a car. Dials and switches neatly arranged, with an oversized steering wheel taking centre stage. Jules settled into the driver's seat and turned the ignition.

Lights glowed and needles on the dials sprang into action. "Are you ready?" He was keen to get underway and re-acquaint himself with '*Eleanor*.'

"Yes, but I do feel a bit underdressed. I should be Audrey Hepburn, but I look more Felicity Kendal going to muck out the pigs!"

"You'll do," Jules said. As he pressed a button on the dash a mechanical whirl came from somewhere under the deck behind them, followed by a series of controlled explosions as the exhaust blew out smoke from the twelve-cylinder engine. The boathouse throbbed in rhythm with the intoxicating sound of pure power. It then began to fill with a heady mix of petrol laden fumes on top of the aroma of wood polish and musty building.

"Right, that's number one engine," Jules informed.

"Number one!" Molly exclaimed, "how many are there?"

"Just the two." Jules pressed the second start button and the sound magnified in the closed confines of the boathouse. They both had the widest grins, they couldn't help it, it just made them feel more alive. Jules, of course, knew what to expect but the wonderment never left him. It felt like a living thing, crafted from wood and metal by genius. He revelled in the joy on Molly's face and gently eased the boat out onto the lake. The sunlight hit them. Curious visitors had gathered on the shoreline to see what all the noise was about. Molly waved at them, and Jules also raised a hand in recognition, he then opened up the engines and the world instantly got smaller. The engine sound was now a joyous roar as they sailed away at speed. The far shore was now getting increasingly closer as they skimmed effortlessly over the surface.

"Do you need two engines?" Molly cried out in delight, "How fast does it go?"

"Well, it comes with two, so it seems a shame not to use them." He grinned widely. "Of course, it's really designed for the Italian lakes so we're a bit limited by the size of our lake, but she can do upwards of fifty knots given the space. Do you like it?"

"Like it… I love it! It's gorgeous. Can we go round the island before we land, I just want to savour this moment."

"Very good, madam." And so they did, while envious onlookers on the shore and those riding on the steamboat admired the spectacle of the majestic craft speeding over the water.

"Right, I guess we had better get on with the task in hand," Jules said reluctantly slowing down and making course towards the jetty at the northern end of the island. Molly took a deep breath and gathered her thoughts after the exhilaration of the journey. *'Back to business now, I do hope this isn't a waste of time,'* she thought.

"As I dock, you climb onto the landing stage and I'll throw you the rope," he instructed. He reversed the engines and stopped to lower the fenders over the side to protect the boat from rubbing against the wooden pier, then slowly manoeuvred alongside. Molly climbed out carefully onto the fragile timber jetty and took the rope, tying it onto a post to the best of her ability.

"I think your knot work needs some practice, but that's fine, she's not going anywhere," Jules said as Molly glared back at him.

"I'm doing my best!"

"I know. I'm only kidding, come on let's go." Jules lifted the tool bag onto the planking and climbed out. "While you're here working on the book, I'll give you some lessons and maybe even let you have a go at driving her."

"I'd love that," she beamed and grabbed the crowbar out of the bag to lighten the load for Jules.

"The mausoleum is this way," he said, "I haven't been over here for years, we used to spend summer days here as children and even camped out on occasion."

They passed the ruin of the old boathouse and followed the path which was barely discernible in the tall meadow grass.

"Psst! Over here." Molly heard a familiar voice coming from the bushes. She veered off the path under a tall mature weeping willow. It's green canopy rustling in the breeze as the branches hung in curtains mantling the ground. She passed through the draping leaves to a surprisingly clear area. Serpent like roots radiated from the trunk, interspersed by moss and small leafed plants growing in the dappled light of the microclimate. The far branches reached down into the water like straws in a cocktail glass.

"What are you doing here?" Molly asked.

Jules then appeared through the branches, "Who are you talking to?"

"Quack," a mallard duck who had been resting by the shore inside the canopy looked up crossly at the two intrusive humans.

"Oh, just the duck," Molly quickly improvised.

"How did you get here?" she asked looking at the duck but addressing Wilf who was stood by the tree wearing his pirate garb complete with parrot on his shoulder.

"I expect he swam here…he is a duck after all," Jules commented with a hint of sarcasm.

"I came over on the steamboat, it comes close to the island and then I only had to float a short distance over the water," Wilf explained. "I thought I'd come to show you the way and save you time. The name takes some finding in the tomb."

"Isn't it beautiful under this tree, it's like a different world, so peaceful," Molly commented innocently.

"Yes, it's lovely, but we do have a job to do," Jules reminded her, "I hope you're right about this, I feel like a burglar." He was beginning to feel a little uneasy at what they were doing. It had seemed OK initially, but now they were here it felt like grave robbing.

"Come on then, let's get on with it." Molly signalled to Wilf out of sight of Jules. They headed to the path now lead by Wilf.

"What are all those paths through the grass? I thought you said no one has been here for years," Molly asked.

"That's the deer, they swim over here for the fresh grass. I think some live here permanently. This island is just begging to be used for something," he said, surveying the overgrown meadow of the interior. "It could be another visitor attraction. With a proper pier the steamboat could drop people off. I'll have to mention it at the next estate meeting."

They continued on through the waist high grass. They could just make out the stone building ahead.

"This way," Wilf instructed pointing to the right.

"I think the door is on the right-hand side," Molly said. They continued wading through the grass and stood outside the Greek style tomb.

"It's in a bit of a state Molly. The stone work's full of gaps and that column looks unstable," Jules looked concerned, "maybe we shouldn't do this, what if it collapses while we're inside?"

Molly too felt uneasy. She looked at the wonky steps covered in green slippery moss leading down to the iron-gate protecting the steel door beyond. It looked impregnable. They both stood there considering the next move.

Wilf went down to the entrance, disappeared through the door and stuck his head back out. "Come on, what's the matter with you? What would your friend Lorna Crofton do?" he asked Molly, referring to her archaeologist friend at Oxford.

"You're right, come on Jules," she said determinedly.

"What do you mean, I'm right?" Jules asked.

"Oh nothing, come on, where's your adventurous spirit?"

"I might well be an adventurous spirit, if this all collapses on us, we'll both be real spirits!" He replied sarcastically.

Molly negotiated her way down the slippery steps to the iron-gate, which was made from thick square sections of iron woven together by a skilful blacksmith. It was secured by a padlock. Everything was thick with rust. Molly lifted the padlock which reluctantly shifted in the loop on the gates depositing red dust on her hands and clothes. "Where are your keys?" she asked.

Jules remained at the top of the steps. "I put them in the tool bag."

"Bring them down, let's try them," she ordered impatiently.

He tiptoed cautiously down the steps to join her and took one look at the ball of rust in her hand. "I can't even see the keyhole. Come on Molly this is hopeless, let's go, it isn't going to work."

"You're right," she replied. Jules was surprised that she had given in so easily but was relieved and turned to climb back up. Then he saw Molly reach into the tool bag, take out the crowbar and slide it through the lock to lever it against the frame. "What are you doing?" he asked horrified.

"Breaking in... with your permission, of course," she said pulling down with all her might on the bar. At first it held firm, then the rust started to flake off the lock and rain down on the ground. The bar was flexing under the strain. "Come on, grab it and pull with me, it's working!" Jules reluctantly stepped back down, gripped the bar and pulled with her. The lock snapped and fell in two pieces. They fell backwards in a heap landing on the filthy steps. "Sorry, you'll need to buy a new lock," Molly said as she wiped the sweat from her brow with the back of her hand.

"You don't say, now can you get up please so I can move?" Jules replied, aghast at what they had just done.

"Come on, that was just the first hurdle," Molly said, clambering back to her feet, "We have to finish it now." She laughed, brushing the rust off her tee shirt.

"OK, let's do this," Jules said, resigned to finishing what had been started. He stood, grabbed the rail of the gate and pulled hard, it moved an inch and jammed.

"There's oil in the tool bag," Molly said, retrieving a tin of WD40. She liberally sprayed the hinges. Clouds of vaporised oil caught their breath and they both coughed. "Give it a minute to work."

"How do you know so much about this oil?"

"I used to help dad service the milk float, this stuff is brilliant." She wiped the oil and rust mixture off her hands onto her tee shirt.

They allowed time for the lubricant to penetrate the hinges. Jules wiggled the gate, and it began to move. Molly sprayed the hinges again while Jules tugged at the gate, it reluctantly opened a little more. Mortar dislodged above them and showered them with dust. After five minutes of pushing and pulling it was open enough to squeeze around. They were now faced with a solid steel door, again covered in layers of rust.

"Have you ever been in here?" Molly questioned.

"No, I haven't, it's always been off limits. I can see why now!"

Molly hit the door with the crooked end of the crowbar. The sound reverberated in the tomb beyond. The solid steel door shook in its frame but didn't move. She pushed the chisel end of the bar into the gap next to the barely visible keyhole. "Right, I need your muscle again, grab and pull... after three. One...Two...Three." They both pulled the bar with all their might.

Thunk!

The door gave way and fell into the room. They both fell back against one of the stone columns, still holding onto the bar. Dust billowed out into the cooling afternoon air. They both looked into the depths of the coal black room beyond. They could see nothing. The twisted door lay at their feet, covered in a film of rust and stone debris, while dust continued to fall from the damaged opening.

They both looked at the mess. Molly quickly regained her balance and looked in through the entrance. What had they done? She felt guilty and prayed all this would be worth it to the family. She looked at Jules who was standing in disbelief at the mess. She didn't know what to say to him.

"Hello, you took your time," Wilf complained, emerging from the gloom.

Molly laughed at the obscure sight of a pirate and his parrot.

"Bless you," the bird squawked.

"It talks," she exclaimed and sneezed.

"That's all it ever says. I would prefer 'pieces of eight,' it would be more in keeping but hey, why not?"

"What talks?" Jules asked stepping up to join her on the fallen door.

"I said, pass me the torch please, it's in the tool bag."

He shrugged his shoulders and followed the order.

The beam of light cut through the dusty mirk. Wilf pointed to the alcove she was looking for. Molly cautiously stepped into the room. The floor was uneven with stone slabs laying at awkward angles, she gingerly moved forward.

Jules could see numerous alcoves lining both sides of the chamber "Where do we start for goodness' sake?" he testily asked, "it could be anywhere." He was not feeling very amenable anymore.

"Here," Molly said excitedly, swinging the torch to where Wilf pointed. She brushed her hand over the engraved stone sealing the alcove, and revealed the words '*Father... Tabulis... Rediit*'

"How could you know that... that's not possible... there must be over fifty alcoves in here!" Jules said unbelievingly.

"I'm an historian," Molly said, as if that explained everything.

"What does that mean exactly? No research could tell you precisely where that was. No one's been in here for years."

"Then perhaps I'm a psychic. What does it matter? Hand me the hammer and chisel," she was keen to push on now.

"I'm seeing you in a new light, Molly Goodall. There are hidden depths to you and not all of them honourable."

"I do my best to keep to procedures but sometimes you have to push the boundaries. At least that's what the Prof taught me, now pass me the hammer and chisel please." She was keen to get down to business.

Jules handed her the tools. She held the chisel against the edge of the engraved slab and with the precision of a master mason struck the chisel. Again and again, she repeated the blows, moving it a little each time. Jules held the torch and watched in awe at her dexterity. The stone eventually fell forward, and she carefully lowered it to the floor. "Torch please," she said authoritatively. This was her world, and she was in control now.

He handed it to her reluctantly, worried what they might see, "I don't think we should be doing this."

She peered into the dark chamber. Sure enough there was the lead box, just as Wilf had said. "Well done, Wilf," she whispered, "this is brilliant."

"Who's Wilf?"

Molly was startled at Jules's acute hearing, for a moment she had forgotten he was there, "Oh! He's one of my colleagues, he's been helping with the research."

"You've never mentioned him before. I'd like to meet him."

"Maybe you will one day but not for a while, he's a bit of a recluse," she laughed as Wilf pulled a face.

"Bless you!" the parrot squawked.

"Come on Jules, I know you've got your reservations, but I'll need some help with this." and she winked at Wilf. Jules came forward and looked in the vault seeing the small casket. His initial feeling was one of relief. It was not what he had dreaded they might see.

"You get one side and I'll get the other." They did so and the lead box slid out easily as if pushed from behind. "Now we need to get this back and examine it further."

Jules studied the lead box. It was too small for a coffin and seemed on first inspection to be welded shut. It felt remarkably light for a lead box, the two of them easily carried it. Jules was unaware of Wilf's levitating skills taking the brunt of the weight. They pushed the gate closed and secured it as best they could. Resting the tool bag on the box they carried it all back to the boat.

"You're one hell of an historian, I'll say that for you, but how do you know what's inside?" Jules asked.

"I don't exactly, but I have a hunch." '*Too late now though*' she thought. Molly's conviction was too compelling for them to stop now.

They placed the box carefully on an old blanket on the sun deck of the boat, then draped more blankets over the seats to protect the leather from their filthy clothes. This time Wilf joined them in the back for the ride home.

"This is a fine schooner, Miss Molly and no mistake," Wilf said in his best pirate accent. Molly turned and gave him the sweetest smile.

"Bless you," the parrot said.

"I second that," Wilf agreed, and they sat back to enjoy the ride.

They soon returned to the boathouse. The visiting public watched them motor along close to the shore, wondering who would drive a beautiful vessel like that dressed in such scruffy clothes. Jules expertly turned the boat and slowed the engines to tick over. He lowered the fenders over the side and with the stern facing towards the opening, he engaged reverse and expertly inched the speedboat back into its mooring. Molly sat on the sundeck alongside the mysterious metal box whilst using a boat hook to ensure that the hull didn't rub against the wooden posts of the landing.

She sensed a presence before seeing the Duke standing in the gloom at the back of the boat house.

Jules was totally unaware of him as he concentrated on the delicate manoeuvre. "Right, engines off, hop out and I'll tie her up."

The thrum of the twenty-four cylinders subsided and all that could be heard was the lapping of the water against the hull.

"What the hell do you think you're doing?" The red-faced Duke spluttered, simmering on the landing, "This is no time to go showing off… did I say you could take '*Eleanor*' out?"

"No but…" began Jules, shaken by the unexpected appearance of his father. He knew he should have asked his permission.

"Our whole existence is in jeopardy, we have police all over the estate, a dead body and now a fake painting."

He paused for breath and held onto the iron railing alongside the step. Molly reeled at the sight of the Duke's anger.

"And you go off playing at sailors… I'm sorry Molly, this is not of your doing, it's just my mad impetuous son wanting to impress you." He then noticed the state of their clothes, Jules's paint splattered Polo shirt, now with added green and brown from the moss and lichen in the mausoleum, his jeans covered in mud.

Molly was no better, the straps of her dungarees now tied around her waist and Simon Le Bonn partially hidden by the stains on her tee shirt. Strands of hair now hung down in matted tresses from under her baseball cap while her face was streaked with a mixture of rust and oil. The Duke's imagination went into overdrive. "My god, you've got a nerve Jules. This lovely young lady comes here to help us and…"

"It's not what you think Father…look," Jules said quickly. He removed the blanket from the filthy lead box sat on the sundeck.

"What on earth is that? Get it off the boat now, you'll ruin the upholstery," he screamed.

"It's on a blanket and we covered the seats before sailing back."

The Duke was now incandescent with rage, he sat down on the steps, his legs becoming too weak to hold him up.

"It's all down to me sir, it's my entire fault," Molly said, "Jules was helping me retrieve a casket of historic documents hidden in the vault on the island. He was only trying to help me. I'm so sorry, truly." She was so ashamed of the outcome of her impulsiveness. She hadn't meant to get Jules into trouble.

"Don't try to protect him, Melinda," said the Duke. He then looked at the box in more detail. "What exactly is it then?" he said, the ire in his blood subsiding.

"I believe it may hold information from the monastery which could tell us what happened to the abbey's valuables when it was dissolved."

"Why should you know about this and after all this time, surely minds greater than yours would have discovered this before?"

"No offence taken," Molly said cocking her head to one side, slightly offended, despite her words. She had his interest though and hopefully that would continue to offset his anger.

"Sorry for my bluntness, but I don't understand. Why you… now?"

"During my research for the book I found a clue in an ancient journal. That made me curious. That, and the fact I have some very clever colleagues to call on."

"She does father, she knew exactly where to go, how to open the vault and went straight to the alcove containing this box. I don't know how she did it, but we need to open it and see if she's onto something."

"Get it off my boat, clean yourselves up and then I need to see YOU in my office in half an hour," he pointed his shaking hand at Jules, "you've not heard the last of this, my boy."

He turned and climbed the steps. "As for you Molly... I thought better of you, I suggest you settle down to your job and keep well away from my son."

Molly knew not to argue with an angry employer. It was better to agree and leave him to cool down. "Very good, sir. Jules, can you give me a hand to put it on the golf cart and I'll take it to the workshop? Carl will have the tools to open it, I'm sure."

Wilf had watched all this undetected until called upon to help levitate the heavy box.

"I still can't work out why a lead box should feel so light," Jules said.

"It must be some sort of alloy," Molly replied, winking at Wilf who returned a smile. They lifted the box into the foot-well of the golf-cart. As Wilf relaxed his levitation the suspension groaned under the full weight of the cargo. Molly put the tools in the back and climbed aboard.

"Thank you, Jules, let's hope it was worth it… I'm so sorry if my actions have put you in an awkward position with your father, I'm too impulsive sometimes. He hasn't even seen the damage to the vault yet, are you in serious trouble?" She was feeling really guilty and hoped it hadn't caused a rift between them.

"He'll calm down, he's very stressed at the moment, I guess we all are… It was rather fun though, now get going. I want a full report as soon as it's open. Wish me luck," he said turning and heading towards the house to face the further wrath of his father.

Molly drove off very slowly, worried that any big bump or pothole could be the final straw for the buggy's suspension.

After a shower, Jules put on clean clothes and reluctantly went to the library for the dressing down from his father. He took a deep breath, stood up straight and entered the room via the back stair. It was like being summoned to the headmaster's room at his old boarding school but worse. The Duke was sitting at his desk. He looked solemnly at Jules over the top of his reading glasses.

"What's going to become of this place Jules? If you don't settle down soon, your sister's going to be back over here staking a claim. Much as I love her, she'd have this place emptied and sold to a hotel chain in no time and then bugger off back to South Africa, all those years of our history gone. Don't dismiss this, Jules. She's been putting out feelers to a company already. At the club, Harry was telling me about her clandestine approach. He's the owner of the company she's talked to. What was the matter with Lavinia Trout? She was from good stock. Her father owns half of Surrey for goodness' sake," he sighed wistfully, "we would have been safe for at least another generation."

Jules was not expecting this change of tack, the boat incident seemed to be completely forgotten. "Come on Father… you've seen her. It's those eyes, they just follow you around the room without having to move. It was too unnerving."

"That's unkind Jules, she's just visually challenged. If you ignore her face, she had a lot going for her."

"Oh, come on dad, give me a break," Jules said, exasperated.

"Well, what about Gabriella Loveday, then?"

"I grant you she appeared to be very nice, if a bit obsessed by her horses. But the biting incident at the horse trials last year was just too much."

"She happens to be a very good horsewoman, I thought you'd like that. She's also not a bad looker."

"That's true, as long as she keeps her mouth shut. It was one thing when she lost the trial and blamed the horse, but to bite it on the neck for letting her down… that was too much. There should have been a steward's enquiry. Anyway, she could give a beaver a run for its money in a tree felling competition with those teeth… she drew blood you know. They were worried it would become infectious and the poor thing would have to be put down. The horse I mean."

"You seem to be spending a lot of time with Miss Goodall."

"I've only shown her round the estate, as you requested, and now helped her with some research. Anyway, the boat was due for a run round the lake."

"You've also put her up in a holiday lodge, I hear."

"That just makes more sense than a room in the pub. It's the end of the season, it's not booked out and anyway it's only for a couple of weeks."

"Be careful Jules, goodwill is never misplaced but sometimes it can be misunderstood. I'd hate to think she's getting the wrong idea."

"Come off it Father... and anyway you haven't been completely truthful with me. You said a new guidebook but she's writing the whole history of the estate."

"Guidebook, history book what's the difference?"

"Well, several thousand pounds I expect." It was Jules' turn to be on the offensive.

"We could ask her to distil the contents for another smaller glossy booklet to sell to visitors with the entrance tickets," the Duke suggested.

"That's not the point Father and you know it."

"What was in the box?" The Duke asked, catching Jules off guard, yet again. He could be crafty with his interrogations.

"No idea yet, but I'm sure we'll find out very soon. Molly's totally convinced there are documents inside it. I've no reason to doubt her, she seems to have second sight, she knew exactly where to find it in the tomb. How could she know?"

"She's an historian, that's her job."

"That's what she said. Even so, you weren't there, there's something extraordinary about her and the way she found the box."

"Tread carefully Jules, that's all I'm saying. Now tell me, how's '*Eleanor*' running?" he asked excitedly.

"Like a dream, why don't you take her out for a spin sometime? Carl's done a fantastic job tuning the engines, they purr like a kitten... well more like a lion." Jules beamed. "When you open her up, you're soon reminded our lake isn't big enough to do her justice." Jules looked at his watch. "You'll have to excuse me father. I need to sort out some repairs to the gate on the mausoleum. We made a bit of a mess in our enthusiasm. Mind you, I had an idea while we were over there. We need to think of ways to open the island to the public, it could be a good money spinner and needn't cost a fortune. It's got an unusual atmosphere, sort of otherworldly. I think people would love it. Especially at Halloween."

"Whatever you think, come up with some ideas. I've got things to do, now go away, you're dismissed."

Jules, relieved that he had got off so lightly, stood up and quickly headed for the door.

After leaving the box at the garage Molly drove back to the lodge for surgical gloves, disposable overalls and her camera. Each stage of the opening had to be recorded meticulously.

She didn't change out of her dirty clothes just yet, after all, the next process would be just as messy but with the added risk of damaging the contents. '*Who knows what condition the books are in? There could be toxic residue in the box*' she thought, and dug out a face mask from her kit bag before driving back to the workshop.

On her return to the compound, Carl was able to cut round the top of the casket without the use of heat or sparks, using tools normally reserved for cutting metal roofing sheets.

Molly slipped on the disposable overalls and handed her camera to Carl's colleague Nick, who now became the official photographer. The lead box on the workbench had attracted an audience of staff who happened to be working in the compound. They stepped to one side as Molly studied it carefully while Nick took pictures from all angles under her direction.

They all heard the crunch of the gravel from a vehicle and then the burble of the V8 engine as Jules arrived in his Range Rover. He entered the workshop to witness the tableau of Molly dressed like a surgeon leaning over the casket surrounded by a rag tag of mechanics and staff.

"What on earth are you dressed like?" he asked her, laughing.

"I can't afford to contaminate the contents and you never know what nasties may be lurking in the box. You can't be too careful. You haven't missed anything yet. Is the Duke alright now?"

"He's calmed down, thank goodness, but never mind that, let's see what's in there."

Molly addressed the onlookers, "Right, everyone, please stand back, we need some space. I expect the air in the box will be pretty foul. OK Carl, when I say, lift the top gently and place it on the bench behind. Not you Nick, I want shots of the inside as we lift the top off." Nick and Carl were now wearing dust masks normally used when grinding metal. The tension was palpable, the dark recesses of the workshop were full of shadows in the late afternoon. They worked by the artificial light coming from the fluorescent tubes' high overhead. The onlookers held their breath adding to the tension as Molly took up her position. Her stomach felt knotted, her muscles were reluctant to move and breathing became shallow. '*What if she was wrong? What if the box contained human remains? She would have desecrated a grave.*

But on the other hand, what if there was nothing? She'd have to live with the consequences of her actions for the rest of her professional life. The risk of failure could cause irreparable damage to her burgeoning career.' She took a deep breath, no turning back now.

"Ok Carl...lift."

They raised the metal top in unison and placed it gently on the empty bench by the wall, Nick fired off several exposures, the strobe from the flashlight blinding the onlookers who quickly looked away. The group then gathered like moths to a flame, gazing into the box, curiosity overwhelming the instruction to keep back. Molly held her breath now, she was terrified to look. But look she must. She moved back to the workbench and cautiously peered in, finally viewing it's contents. Her future as a respected historian was wrapped in dirty, rotting muslin. Molly started carefully pealing back the material with a large pair of tweezers.

Wilf arrived in the attic to find George and Tom pouring over paperwork.

"Oh, the wanderer returns," George said sarcastically.

"Come on George, give me a break, you know where I've been."

"Oh yes, sorry, I'm trying to sort out the pairings for the golf match tonight. It's no fun being Captain. Wolf Gore made it look so easy when I was playing with him at Holeford Golf Club."

"Well, he's been doing it for a hundred years longer than you, so that's no surprise. Aren't you going to ask me how I got on?" Wilf asked, slightly put out at their lack of interest.

Alice got up from the sofa and drifted over to them, "Yes, come on Wilf tell us all about it, this golf stuff is boring." She stroked 'Flint' who was sitting on Wilf's shoulder.

"Bless you," it squawked and flew off through the wall.

"Off he goes again. We probably won't see him for days now," Alice commented.

"Never mind the parrot, are you going to listen or not?" Wilf asked impatiently.

The group silently moved away from the pile of paper and sat on the sofas, offering Wilf the floor. "Good, now I finally have your attention, I shall begin."

He told them every detail of Molly and Jules' trip to the island and the return on the speedboat where they were confronted by the Duke in a foul mood.

"Is Molly in trouble?" Alice asked.

"I don't think so, but Jules is in for a rough time, the Duke was furious. What a boat though, you should see it."

"Stuff the boat! What was in the box?" George asked impatiently.

"Exactly what was in it when we looked, I expect," Wilf said with a hint of sarcasm.

"Wilf you are useless. Why didn't you follow them back to the workshop?" Alice folded her arms and gave him a hard stare.

"Don't look at me like that, we'll find out soon enough. It's going to take ages for Molly to examine the contents. Anyway, I've done enough damage this afternoon, I think Jules suspects something, he overheard Molly talking to me. She pretended she was talking to a duck, but I'm not sure he was convinced. Also, he was amazed how quickly she found the right alcove, we need to tread carefully, we don't want to make things awkward for her."

"Everyone talks to ducks, that's not unusual," Alice said. The other three looked at her strangely.

"Even so, you didn't see his expression."

"Fair enough," George said, weighing up Wilf from the comfort of the sofa, "how do you fancy playing with Ferret Blood in the four ball?"

"Must I? He's an awful bore, and if we're teamed against Wolf Gore, I won't get a word in. Those Iron Age chieftains are as thick as thieves… Anyway, I didn't think he was playing."

"We're picking him up on the way, you'll be fine, you're not playing with Wolf Gore anyway, I have to do that, it's part of the golf etiquette, the captains have to play against each other. Tom's going to caddy for you. It'll be a good introduction to his new afterlife." Tom smiled at Wilf but inside was totally confused. He had often wondered about 'life after death'. He was prepared for playing a harp, whilst floating around on a cloud, although his musical ability was limited to 'Chopsticks' on the piano. He wasn't sure if you could play 'Chopsticks' on a harp, but he was happy to give it a go. However, nothing had prepared him for golf competitions, nowhere in his wildest dreams were they included.

'If only people knew'.

George continued, "The bus is picking us up at eleven o'clock, then up to the clubhouse to pick up the rest of the team, then on to Holeford for round one of the Bank Holiday double header. We tee off at midnight. That reminds me, we need to get in some rehearsal time for the after-match show on Monday." Tom looked even more confused.

In the workshop, Molly's worries about the contents had been unfounded. She lifted out four muslin wrapped volumes. Carefully unwrapping the first to reveal a large leather-bound book. The condition of the cover was remarkably good considering its age. The once red leather with gold illumination was now a dirty brown colour with some of the muslin now bonded to its surface. The cover was dry and cracked where it folded around the spine, which lifted her heart. '*If the cover was dry the contents should have survived,*' she thought. With her audience watching closely, with gloved hands, she lifted the cover gently, just enough to look at the first page. To her relief it was legible. Being written on vellum it had survived incarceration well, but the language was, as she had suspected, unintelligible to her. The crowd looked confused and a little disappointed at not seeing some treasure, at least.

"Sorry guys, it's not that interesting for you. It's as I expected though. It's written in Medieval Latin. All Monastic records were, not that there are many surviving in this condition." Disappointed, her spectators sighed in unison and started to drift away. She closed the cover and Carl helped her to re-wrap the contents in polythene to protect them from exposure to the elements.

Jules moved over to her, studying it all. "I have to hand it to you, you were right but what are you going to do with them now?"

"I need to get them into a controlled environment and then translate them. There's only one man I know who can do that and fortunately he's in Holeford. I need to make some phone calls. Then I need to tell the Duke what we've found."

Jules was confused, "What exactly have we found?"

"I can't tell for certain yet, we need to decipher them. It may answer questions about the missing wealth of the monastery. Or it could just be agricultural records. Whatever it is, it will be valuable information academically, if not financially," she shrugged her shoulders, "they must have been hidden for a very good reason though, exciting, isn't it?"

"Yes very," Jules replied, baffled, "you go and make the calls and I'll tell father what you found, although I think he'll be underwhelmed. Let me know if you need anything."

"Thanks, Jules," Molly gently tapped the back of his hand, "I'll put these books somewhere safe."

"Carl, I need your help to repair the door and gate to the mausoleum, we made a bit of a mess over there," Jules said.

"Ok VJ, I'll go over there in the morning and see what needs doing."

Molly handled the books carefully, loading them into the golf cart and drove sedately back to the lodge. Carl reunited the lead box with its top, wrapped it in a tarpaulin and stored it safely at the back of the workshop whilst muttering to himself about having yet more work to do on the island, repairing their damage, '*All this trouble just for some old, musty books.*'

22
The Professor

Wednesday 21ˢᵗ August. Very Early Morning

Assisted by Alice, Molly worked till the early hours attempting to decipher the ancient text, but her limited knowledge of the subject and the 'O level' Latin dictionary were not up to the task. She managed small passages about crop productivity which confused her even more. '*Why go to so much trouble to hide a book about farming? No, there has to be more significant information hidden in there somewhere.*'

"Don't you know any spirits from that period? There must be some still around here." Molly was sure monks must be haunting the house or grounds somewhere.

Alice pulled a sad face, "They're not here, or at least I've never met one. They weren't mentioned in the briefing notes we got from Eric. The thing is, they were all deeply religious, so they went straight upstairs… They must have been relieved when they found out their beliefs were correct."

"I'm pleased for them but that doesn't help us. I'm going to contact the Prof. in the morning, he'll be able to help, I'm sure. He's bound to have books in the museum library that can help us."

"Ooh! Can we come," Alice pleaded, she hadn't been back to Holeford for ages.

"No reason why not, but you'll have to keep a low profile, you know how nervous Wilf gets about being around during the day. Where are they all anyway?"

"They're playing in a golf tournament. They've gone to Holeford Golf Club for round one, then the Holeford team comes here over the Bank holiday for the return match. They're obsessed with that game, after all George and Wilf said about it being a stupid waste of time. Now they've dragged Tom in as a caddy." Alice shrugged her shoulders.

"I'm going to get some sleep," Molly said. "I've got a busy day tomorrow or rather today."

"See you later," Alice said chirpily and floated off though the wall back to the house.

Molly had a restless sleep as she turned ideas over in her head about how to proceed with the investigation. She rose at seven, made some notes and began to execute her plan. After a light breakfast and two strong coffees, she loaded the books into her car, made a phone call to the museum and arranged with the manager of the supermarket opposite, to reserve a parking space for her. She was conscious that she owed the Duke an explanation and would need his permission before discussing estate business with the professor.

It was a cool morning as she drove slowly along the estate road towards the house. She heard the distinct roar of a tiger as she passed near to the enclosure, '*It must be feeding time*' she thought. As the summer began to fade into autumn, the sun was more reluctant to rise. The leaves on the trees had also lost their enthusiasm, edges curling and losing their vibrancy. Morning dew turned the grass to silver as the low sunlight shone across it, highlighting millions of gossamer threads from the microscopic spiders who weave their satin sheen. Several deer stood in the shadow on the edge of the far-off woodland, which marked the estate border and shielded the main road beyond. They lifted their heads and watched the small red Renault pass. The crows, high up in the branches called out as if to say, 'good morning'. Molly wound down the window to allow the fresh aroma of nature to engulf her. '*It is a truly beautiful place*' she thought, as the car engine gently purred, the wheels crunching the gravel like a thousand sweet wrappers in a busy theatre just before the curtain goes up.

She drove to the staff car park and pulled up overlooking the lake. There was no sign of Jules' Range Rover. '*Good, I have the Duke to myself.*' Molly had prepared for the meeting and didn't want any distraction. She had to explain her actions of the previous day, feeling guilty that she hadn't sought his approval before embarking on the exploration and subsequent damage to the mausoleum.

Molly took a deep breath and stepped out of the car, hardly daring to imagine how she would be received in the library. The sunlight twisted and turned on the ripples of the water as the light breeze ruffled the reeds at the edge of the lake. The scene mellowed her apprehension a little.

She took one volume wrapped in its polythene protection from the boot of the car. It didn't seem right for her to use the rear stairs and enter through the bookcase, so she walked through the kitchen garden and entered the house via the lobby to the ballroom. Walking down the long gallery she met James, carefully wrapping China ornaments in tissue and loading them into a cardboard box.

"Good morning, Miss Molly," he said warmly, in his usual clipped tones.

"Morning James, are you preparing to move house?"

"No, nothing as dramatic I'm pleased to say. The film company are here tonight and the Duke wants me to lock the more fragile items away, in case any get disturbed while they film in the dark." He saw the package in her arms. "Is that one of the books you found in the mausoleum?"

"Yes, but how did you know about that?"

"You can't keep a secret round here miss, everyone below stairs is talking about it."

Molly laughed, it sounded like a TV drama. "Below stairs!" she repeated.

"Yes, you've become quite a topic of conversation," he said, missing her point entirely.

"Oh dear, James, that wasn't my intention."

"I shouldn't worry Miss Molly, they'll soon get bored, something else will crop up to gossip about. I expect the arrival of the film crew will soon distract their attention."

"I hope so." Molly then continued along the gallery to the hall and on up the stairs to the library. She paused and tapped on the heavy wooden door.

"Enter," said a distant voice from within, but unmistakably that of the Duke. She tried to determine his mood from that one word, but she didn't know him well enough for that. Taking a deep breath, she pushed the door open and walked nervously to the far end. The Duke was sat at his desk, a mug of coffee in one hand and a sheaves of papers in the other, reading glasses perched on the end of his nose.

"Good morning young lady, you're being very formal this morning by entering from the hall. Did you have a productive day yesterday?" he peered over his spectacles at the ancient book in her hands.

Molly relaxed, whatever happened in the boat shed yesterday, he appeared to have put behind him. The Duke's mood was warm and welcoming.

"Well yes I did, thanks to Jules's help." She dropped his name into the conversation deliberately to prompt a response. *'Just as well get this over with'* she thought.

"Ah! Yes, good old Jules. You seem to be spending a lot of time with him."

"He's been very helpful, I hope he's not in trouble for borrowing your wonderful boat. That's the last thing I wanted to happen."

"Let's just say, I was not happy about him taking it without asking… we'll get over it. You need to tread carefully around him Molly, he's easily influenced. You're a very attractive young lady and he is a very impressionable young man."

Molly laughed out loud, "Jules, and me? Is that what you think? He's been very kind but… really. Honestly, is that what you think?" Molly sat down opposite the Duke and looked him directly in the eyes.

"Do you think I'm the sort of girl to throw myself at the first viscount I bump into? I'm disappointed in you. I have a lot of ground to cover in my career before I would even think of a serious relationship, with anyone." She held his gaze. The Duke blinked first.

"Well, it did enter my mind and now you're making me feel terrible. I entirely misread the situation… I feel rather foolish. I'm truly sorry, please forgive me." His expression was full of remorse.

Molly took pity on him. "Would you like to see what we found?" She asked changing the subject.

The Duke was reassured that there wouldn't be any permanent damage to their working relationship. "Yes please." He cleared a space on his desk, reached forward and took the book. Molly moved to his side of the desk, slipped on a pair of protective gloves and un-wrapped the polythene protection.

"I wanted to show you this and ask your permission to take it to a specialist to be translated. I should have asked your permission yesterday before I impulsively entered the mausoleum and started ripping the doors off. I am very sorry about that. It was wrong."

"Apology accepted, now what do we have here" the Duke said looking at the ancient tome.

"I have only limited Latin knowledge, and this is written in a medieval monastic style. I can only work out basic details of crop rotation but there must be more. Why would they go to such lengths to hide an agricultural record?"

He studied the ornate writing while being careful not to touch the pages. "This is beyond me," he said.

"And me," she reassured him, "But I know a man more able than us, at Holeford Museum. With your approval, I'd like to take it to him. I believe you know him."

"You mean Dom?"

"If you mean Professor Dominic Halford then yes, that's him."

The Duke's face lit up, "Wonderful, give him my regards, I haven't seen him for ages. Is the silly old fool still there, it's about time he retired." The Duke picked up a photo frame from his desk and pointed at the black and white picture of two men in shorts and pith helmets stood by an ancient ruin alongside camels and local Bedouin tribesmen. "We had some wonderful escapades when we were your age. I funded several of his excavations and joined him when I could. Never found anything, but what adventures we shared."

"He has a copy of that same picture on the wall of his office. You really should go and see him, I'm sure he'd be delighted to see you. I'd like to include a chapter in the book about your adventures, if you would both give me permission."

"A wonderful idea, are you going to see him this morning?"

"Yes, right now, if that's OK?"

"Of course, but wait a minute." The Duke grabbed a notelet from the letter holder on his desk and quickly scribbled a message, sealed it in an envelope and handed it to Molly.

"Give him this. I'm sorry I jumped to conclusions. Is there anything I can do to make amends?"

"As far as I'm concerned it's all forgotten, but please don't be unkind to Jules, he was only trying to help."

"Message received."

"How's the police investigation going? I haven't heard any news for a while?" Molly enquired.

"They're being very secretive, I know the fraud squad are now involved and there are undercover officers mixing with the visitors, but you can't tell who they are. I suppose that's the point. Well, apart from PC Single-ton, who seems to spend most of his time in the kitchens chatting up the cook and eating cake."

They both laughed, but Molly could see from his expression that he was worried. She re-wrapped the book, picked it up and held it close to her body like a new-born baby.

"I'll let you know how I get on."

"Don't forget the note." The Duke turned back to his paperwork and Molly left the room via the bookcase doorway.

In the car park she returned the package to the boot alongside the other volumes.

"Come on, where have you been, we're all waiting," George admon-ished from the passenger seat. Wilf, Alice and Tom were sat on the back seat, arms folded looking impatient. Their bodies merged together slightly to fit into a space designed for two people. It was rather unnerv-ing.

"What on earth… I wasn't expecting all of you."

"We didn't want to miss out on a trip to our old haunting ground. We want to show young Tom where we lived in the supermarket. Now come on let's get going," Wilf said impatiently.

Molly shrugged her shoulders, shut the boot and sighed, "Ok, but don't forget we need to be back to meet Justine Song this afternoon."

"We can't wait either, we've never been on the telly," Alice said excit-edly.

"No and you're not going to be this time, I don't want you causing any trouble."

"As if we would," Wilf said. All four of them had their fingers crossed. This was their chance for stardom. Of a sort.

On the way Molly told them about her conversation with the Duke. They'd seen several individuals wandering round the grounds, mingling with the visitors but reluctant to leave. That explained it. The police pres-ence means they must be expecting another incident. They debated the possible scenarios and agreed to be more vigilant. But perhaps not when the TV crew were there, that was too exciting to miss.

Wilf and George gave a blow-by-blow account of the evening's golf tournament. Alice and Molly feigned yawns but that didn't stop them.

Apparently, they had won by two points but the return match was still to come on home soil. They hoped to go on and win, but it was going to be a tight match, they said excitedly.

"I'm pleased for you," Molly said. Time flew by as they talked of the events at the park and reminisced about how they used to meet up in the storeroom of the supermarket while Molly did her homework as she waited for her mum to finish work and walk home together.

At 'Price Less,' their old friend Charlie was waiting in the car park, he'd vacated his parking space for Molly's use and directed her in. The supermarket was built on the site of the Opera House where in 1955, Wilf, George and Alice were killed in a devastating fire. Charlie was so excited to see them all. He was a gifted psychic and thanks to his friendship with the ghosts he had secured a job at the store. This, despite the fact he and his brother Brian had tried to rob it weeks before! But that was all in the past and with hard work and enthusiasm he had progressed from shelf stacking to manager in only ten years. Brian was now working for a locksmith where he could legally break into safes.

"Thank you for this parking space, Charlie, it's so convenient, the books I have are really heavy," Molly said getting out of the car.

"No problem, I'm glad I could help." He found himself surrounded by the ghosts.

"Hi guys, I wasn't expecting to see you as well, this is a pleasant surprise," he said, addressing all of them while glancing at the newcomer with interest.

"This is Tom," Alice said, "he's just joined us at the Abbey."

"Pleased to meet you," Charlie said, still looking confused.

"But what about you and how's Charmaine?" Molly asked, "it's not long now, is it?"

"No, it should be very soon, she's just started her maternity leave." Alice clapped her hands in excitement.

While they chatted, Molly started to retrieve the books from the boot of her car.

"Would you like a hand with those?" Charlie asked, noticing the large packages.

"Yes please, the Prof is expecting me, if you could carry these, that would be very helpful." She split the pile in two and handed one over. They stood by the back of the car with the boot wide open, hands full of documents. "Would you do the honours please, Wilf?"

Wilf stared at the boot and magically it closed itself and locked.

"Wow, that's a neat trick, I wish my car could do that," Charlie exclaimed.

"Maybe it will, one day," Wilf said.

It was market day, and the town was exceptionally busy. The group moved over the road and quickly entered the museum. The ghosts bade farewell and headed to the basement where they could access the tunnels leading to their social club and catch up with old friends. Tom had heard stories of this mysterious social club where spirits from all periods of history met to share stories and entertain themselves. He met some of them at last night's golf match and was looking forward to seeing where they hung out.

"Don't be late back. We're leaving by two thirty," Molly warned.

"Who's leaving? You've only just got here." The familiar voice of the Professor came from the back office hidden from view behind the reception desk.

"Morning Prof," Molly said ignoring the question.

Charlie placed his books on the desk, "I must be getting back, good luck." He turned and headed for the door.

"Thank you, Charlie," Molly called after him. He waved and ran back over the road dodging quickly between the busy traffic.

"So, this is what all the fuss is about," the Professor said, as he studied the covers of the books through the polythene and lifted one to feel its density. "Mmm... Nice weight," he said, "And you found these lying around in a mausoleum? Nice work, you have learnt well. Let's get them to the research centre for a proper look." They headed down the stairs into the vaulted brick lined basement where a new state of the art laboratory had been installed behind a glass wall.

"This is very impressive," Molly said, as they passed from the basement through the automatic sliding door into the richly illuminated room. On either side were sliding racks maximising storage for the museum's many artefacts. Against the wall opposite, stood a long workbench with clean white drawers and cupboards.

There was a deep sink with huge taps looking down into the bowl and glass cabinets with extract systems for the delicate cleaning of objects. Everything was gleaming white and dust free. "This looks like a science lab at the British Museum, how long has it been here? It's amazing."

"'It's just been installed. We received funding from an anonymous donor and along with the profits from our exhibitions we were able to join the twentieth century. Makes a change from cleaning and preparing exhibits in the kitchen amongst the dirty plates and coffee cups, doesn't it?"

"Don't remind me," Molly said, thinking back to her days volunteering under his guidance. Somehow though, despite being less sophisticated it had been good fun and she had learnt a lot.

"Right, let's have a look." He slid open the drawer under the worktop and pulled out two pairs of cotton gloves, handing one pair to Molly. He then unwrapped the first book and gently opened it on the bench. Molly explained about the discovery and her theory on why the monks had been so secretive about their existence.

"Mmm…," the Professor rubbed his chin and studied the text through his wire framed spectacles, "well, definitely medieval monastic Latin. This is quite a find Molly. Not much of this material has survived. I've seen some examples but never one as fine as this. This is going to take some time. Did you say you have to be back by three thirty?"

"Yes, I do unfortunately. Oh! I have this for you." She reached into her pocket and retrieved the letter from the Duke.

He opened it and read the scrawly handwriting. "Dear Boy!… His handwriting's no better… how lovely to hear from him. I must go and see him, he's right, it has been too long." He placed the letter to one side and returned to the documents. With Molly's help, they unwrapped each one of the four books and carefully opened the front covers spreading them along the bench. He looked closely for any evidence of dates, then began to delve deeper.

"Mmm… I see," he muttered turning page after page, "Ahh!… Well, just you look at that."

Molly stood by his side entranced by the way his fingers lovingly ran over the lettering, his eyes dancing back and forth. The vellum was in remarkable condition considering its age and the means of storage, the calligraphy was beautiful.

At the beginning of some pages there were small, coloured embellishments. The books emitted a strong musty odour like a second-hand bookshop but ten times more powerful. The Prof' reached up and pulled a switch cord hanging above their heads. "That's better, we have a very good ventilation system, so the aroma will soon disperse. We're climate and humidity controlled as well," he said proudly. "I think it would be wise to leave them here while we do the translations. There'll be a lot of scholars interested in the contents, so we need to keep quiet about our findings until we're ready to tell the world."

Molly was becoming impatient. "That's fine Professor, but I can only make out certain words. It just looks like farming records. Do you think there's anything more significant?"

"You're right about the farming records but there is something else too. I can't see it yet, but I can feel it, just like you can. It's an instinct, you can't learn it, you're born with it. Let's keep going."

They continued, stopping only for coffee and a sandwich. The clock on the wall was going too fast for Molly's liking but she wanted to be back to meet her childhood hero. Much as she craved to know everything now, it wasn't going to happen quickly. She had to be patient, as always with archaeology.

"What is so important that you have to be back?" The Prof asked curiously.

"It's silly really but there's a film crew coming to record an episode of Haunted House. Justine Song is going to be there, and I hope to meet her."

"Why?"

"Well, I've been a fan of hers since childhood and I love her ghost programmes."

"No, I mean, 'Why?' Wasn't that the name of that science programme she presented on children's TV? She went a bit crazy and got the sack."

"The programme was called, 'What?' But that's her, fancy you remembering."

"I remember she inspired a lot of children before going off the rails. Such a shame, she was a good broadcaster. You must go and meet her, she may have planted the seed in your brain that led to you being here today."

"I hadn't thought of that, you're right, I'll tell her if I do get to meet her."

"Then go on, leave this with me. I know where to contact you."

"Thank you, Professor." Molly walked to the doors which obediently swished open, and she stepped into the exposed brick basement area. Sat at the bottom of the stairs were the four ghosts.

"Well, is there treasure?" Wilf asked excitedly as they stood up.

Molly put her finger to her mouth and ushered them up into the entrance hall.

Charlie waved them off and they all settled down for the journey home. Wilf and George, expecting instant results were disappointed at Molly's news, or lack of it. She reassured them that the Professor would be in touch as soon as he found anything.

Alice was more realistic. "Rome wasn't built in a day. I'm sure we'll get some news pretty quickly," she said.

"Well Tom, how was your trip to the social Club?"

Tom who sat in the back between George and Alice remained silent. Molly could see his baffled face in the rear-view mirror.

"Tom's confused… poor thing," George said. "I think it was a mistake bringing him along, it's all been a bit overwhelming."

"I don't understand," Tom spluttered. "There was a room with people from all periods of history sat around chatting like nothing had happened to them. It's all so confusing, and I still don't know where I fit in to it all."

"Don't worry dear, just enjoy the ride. I'm sure Eric will be back soon with the paperwork and more news about your future." Wilf tried to reassure him. "In the meantime, we have the return match to look forward to at the golf club and better still, tonight we become TV stars."

"You will not!" Molly exclaimed, "I've told you to behave yourselves. I don't want you attracting unnecessary attention. The Duke and Jules have enough to contend with at the moment without you adding to their problems by attracting all the barmy ghost chasers here."

"Can I just say, if you invite a film crew to look for ghosts in your haunted house, which will be broadcast to the nation, aren't you asking for trouble?" Wilf declared.

"I realise that, but you don't have to overdo it. I know you, once the cameras start rolling, you'll want to perform."

"It's what we do dearest, we can't help it, we're entertainers. That's what we were born to do."

"I know, that's what I'm afraid of. Please, just for me, save your talents for the show after your golf tournament… Just this once…Please." Molly looked around the car at all of them.

"Ok Molly, we promise we won't overdo it," Alice said.

"Thank you, that means a lot to me."

The journey back continued in silence until they passed through the village. They noticed a large white van parked outside the Abbey Inn.

"That must be the film crew," Wilf said excitedly. They all turned to look and became animated with excitement.

Molly gripped the steering wheel tightly. *'This is going to be a long night,'* she thought.

23
Haunted House

Wednesday 21st August. Evening

The phone rang in the office, Jules reluctantly picked it up.

"Hello, sir, the TV people are here," the security guard confirmed excitedly. Jules was expecting the call from the main gate but not relishing the prospect of allowing access to the house for what he considered to be a second-rate television programme. "I'll escort them down to the house and meet you in the ballroom as arranged."

"Thanks Colin, I'll be there in ten minutes," Jules then phoned the library and invited Molly to join them. Molly's heart skipped a beat. She hurried to the ballroom via the main stairs where she could look out of the window towards the main gate. She could see a Jeep escorting a 'Song Thrush Productions' van along with a saloon car following closely behind. '*That must be them!*' She practically skipped down the rest of the stairs.

She entered the ballroom to see Wilf, George, Alice and Tom sat on the edge of the stage expectantly.

"How did you know they were here?" Molly asked.

"We've been watching the gate since we returned, we're not going to miss a second of this," Alice said excitedly.

"OK, but just sit there quietly and try not to distract me, I don't want to look stupid. These people are ghost hunters, and they may be able to detect you so be prepared for a quick exit. Did you hear me, Alice?" Molly asked her sternly.

"Yes, we heard you," Alice replied, looking down at her shoes like a scolded child.

"Now, quiet, I can hear them coming."

Colin entered followed by the film crew including Justine who looked the consummate professional with short cropped blonde hair and large hooped ear rings. She was dressed in a loose-fitting buff coloured cotton suit and white blouse, with vivid blue open toed sandals.

"Hello Molly," Colin said, "glad you could come." He then turned and addressed the crew. "This is Molly Goodall. She's here to write the updated story of the estate, she grew up watching your children's programmes and requested to meet you."

"Good afternoon," Molly said, approaching and shaking hands with them all in turn, "It's lovely to meet you. I am such a fan of your show." Justine was much smaller than she had expected and heavily made up. Molly shook her hand warmly.

"Thank you," Justine said, "We're looking forward to filming here."

The side door opened, Jules entered and joined the group of visitors. The near empty ballroom echoed as the door clicked shut behind him.

Colin approached him, "Sir, I took the liberty of starting the visitor briefing in the car park. Miss Song, would you do the honours please?" He indicated that she had the floor.

"Good afternoon, sir, it's a pleasure to meet you. My name is Justine Song and this is my production crew. Peter Fellows, Co-producer. Alex Tulloch, sound. Dylan Lee, camera, Stephen Henderson, production assistant, Chloe Nolin, programme assistant and Fred Smith who is with us at short notice to assist with the night vision equipment. It's his first time with the show. Our usual operator was sadly involved in a car accident and Fred has kindly stepped in." As they were introduced, Jules moved along the line and shook their hands. "Oh! There will be one other joining us later tonight, Mystic Michael," she announced with a flourish.

Only Molly showed any sign of being impressed by this last remark. Justine was a little disappointed. Michael was one of the main draws of the show, but wasn't always available for filming. They were lucky to have him here. Without fail, they had larger viewing figures when he was known to be appearing.

"Do you watch *'Haunted House'*" Justine asked accusingly, now slightly off guard.

"Yes, I love it," Molly chipped in enthusiastically, while Jules looked stoic.

"No, I'm sorry I haven't had the pleasure, but I hear it's supposed to be entertaining," Jules said politely.

"I would like to thank the Duke personally for allowing us to film here," Justine said hopefully, but her expectant expression fell on stony ground.

"I'm afraid he is otherwise detained but sends his welcome. Now tell me, how do you want to proceed?"

Justine felt slightly snubbed but continued undeterred. "We'd like a tour of the house this afternoon to select possible camera positions and potential sites of interest. We'll then go and get something to eat at the pub and return at eight to set up. Michael will join us later. Filming usually starts at around eleven o'clock and we'll be all done by 4 am. As agreed, we'll be long gone before you open to the public."

"Very good. Colin, have you arranged the security cover?"

"No problem VJ, all sorted."

"Excellent," Jules turned to Justine, "security will shadow you during the evening. We have to consider the health and safety implications for everyone. Also, our insurers will not allow strangers to wander around the house unattended. I trust that will be acceptable?"

"No fear of that," Wilf said, "we're going to be with them every minute."

"This is so exciting," Alice chirped.

George was more sceptical, "I suppose it might be fun," he said.

Tom watched on in total fascination, "Mystic Michael's really funny. He hears things and goes into trances. Without him the show's not worth watching. It'll be interesting to see it being filmed."

"Before we start the tour, can you tell me about any sightings you or your staff may have experienced that could assist us?" Justine asked.

Jules got the feeling that she was just going through one of the shows standard procedures. She lifted her clip board ready to take notes.

"I have to tell you, I am very sceptical about the presence of ghosts," he said.

Wilf, George and Alice stood on the stage and did a little jig. "Sceptical indeed, the very thought of it," Wilf shouted loudly. Molly frowned at them. Wilf got the message and they all dutifully sat down again.

"I'm sorry to hear that, sir," Justine said.

"On saying that, I am not unaware of the fact that members of our staff have supposedly experienced strange occurrences. There have been reports of a monk wandering around the long gallery and things have been heard moving around in the attic."

"That must be us, I've told you both to be careful," George said to the others accusingly.

"The housekeeper has allegedly seen a Victorian girl walk through the wall in the Ladies Bedchamber," Jules continued.

"Ooh! That's me, I wonder who saw me," Alice said excitedly.

"And a pirate of all things has been seen on the main staircase," Jules added.

"Hooray, fame at last," cried out a jubilant Wilf, punching his fist into the air. Flint let out a squawk of excitement.

"But I believe all these things could be rationally explained, or are figments of overactive imaginations," Jules concluded.

"That's such a shame. Don't you believe in magic?" Molly asked disappointedly.

"Magic, in my view, is just an illusion used for light entertainment and I believe this television programme is no different…I'm sorry but there you are."

"Molly, you really need to educate this man," George called out from the stage.

"Thank you for your time sir. I appreciate it must be very difficult at the moment with the murder case on the estate and now the discovery of the fake painting. There's been a lot of adverse coverage in the press. You must be worried for your future," Justine stated sympathetically.

Jules was taken aback by this sudden change of tack. "Well, yes we are, it's all been very traumatic for the family and all of our staff."

"How do you see the future for your animal park? Could you be forced to close?"

Jules was silent, his mind a whirl of confusion. Molly stepped over to him and took him by the arm.

"Can I have a word in private, Jules?" She led him away from the TV crew to a safe distance by the stage. She spoke quietly, "You see that camera on the tripod? It has a red light on, they're filming you. I think Justine is trying to get an exclusive interview. Much as I like her programmes, she's a journalist at heart and they can be unscrupulous. I've seen reporters do it before, at the museum. They twist things to get a new story and then it's on the evening news. Don't answer her, just make your excuses and leave."

"Thanks, Molly. I wondered why she was being so nice, that's very sneaky. I'm so naïve."

On the stage, the ghosts listened intently to the whispers. "The camera's running," Wilf whispered. George and Alice stood up and started doing their sand dance routine.

"Stop messing about," Wilf said sternly, still trying to listen to Molly.

"But what about what's already recorded, could they use any of that?" Jules asked anxiously.

"I don't think so, but I have a plan, you just go."

"Thanks, Molly," Jules said and went back to Justine and her crew. Dylan subtly turned the camera towards them both. Jules was now wise to him. "I'm sorry Justine, something has just come up and I need to get back to the office, I'll leave you with Colin."

While Jules was occupied, Molly quickly briefed Colin on Justine's attempts to get a scoop from Jules. Molly then turned to the stage and whispered to Wilf out of earshot of the others.

"Would it be possible for us to start the tour?" Justine asked. Her attempt to catch him off-guard had failed. He obviously had reservations about the show but the information he gave on sightings would give her material to work with. She also had some footage of him she could edit and use, or hopefully sell to a newsroom.

"Very good," Jules said, "Colin will take you around. If you need any help or assistance he knows where to find me. I hope you have a successful evening. I'll be in the office if you need me. Are you going straight back to the Library Molly?"

"Yes, it's been lovely to meet you, Justine. Would you be kind enough to sign this?" She held up her copy of her 1975 'What?' annual.

"It'll be my pleasure. I haven't seen one of these for years. I looked a lot younger then," she grinned, while signing below a large picture of her on the inside cover.

'To Molly, with love Justine Song x'

"Thank you so much, I used to run home from school in time to watch your show, it inspired me to study hard and learn as much as I could. Luckily I had some wonderful teachers to help me."

"I'm glad it reached out to you, we had great fun making the show," she said, handing the book back.

Jules, watched on, mystified by Molly's hero worship. "Right, I really am going back to my office," he said, and strolled quickly away.

"Yes, and I must get back to my work," Molly said clutching the album.

As they moved away, Colin started formally briefing the crew before the tour could begin in earnest.

The long gallery was thankfully empty as Molly left the ballroom. Alice, George and Tom followed and were soon joined by Wilf.

"Now you lot, much as I love you, you must promise me again that you'll behave yourself tonight."

"No problem," Wilf said. Flint squawked in agreement.

"Thanks, Wilf." Molly said.

"Not even a little mischief?" Alice said disappointedly, "After all, it's what the show is about. It'll be boring for the viewers if nothing happens."

"We'll be on our best behaviour, you can rely on us," George promised, discreetly winking at the others.

"Good, as long as we've got that straight, I don't want you to let Jules or the Duke down." A door banged and they could hear the film crew being led by Colin, crossing the lobby heading their way.

Dylan was gesticulating wildly and shrugging his shoulders.

"What, nothing at all?" Justine asked sharply.

Dylan held up a fridge magnet that had attached itself to the side of the camera. "It's scrambled the magnetic tape. I've got no playback… nothing."

"How on earth did that get there?"

"I've no idea."

Molly knew. "Is everything all right?" she asked innocently.

"Yes, fine thank you," Justine lied.

"Good luck with the filming," Molly then walked back to the library. Wilf and George followed to help with book selection, while Alice and Tom waited to follow the film crew and find out what their plans were in preparation for the evening's events. "Good work Wilf," Molly said, grinning, "That saved Jules's embarrassment."

At eight o'clock with the shadow of night beginning to fall, the park was now empty of visitors and the TV crew returned to set up. Justine was joined by cameraman Dylan, Soundman Alex and Chloe to film the introduction piece to camera. While Chloe did the make up for Justine, Dylan and Alex went ahead and sorted out the camera angles on the carousel in the steam fair looking towards the house and lake. The ride operator met Dylan and turned on the canopy lights.

The strings of yellowing bulbs radiated from the centre giving a background glow to the intricately decorated horses and ostriches frozen in mid canter. The up-lighting that illuminated the house, some distance away, accentuated the architectural detail of the stone work, all adding to the ambience in the half light.

Justine and Chloe soon joined them.

"I've set up on the carousel, I can get a good view of the house and who doesn't like the look of a deserted fairground?" Dylan asked.

"Very Scooby Doo," Justine said approvingly, climbing onto the ride. "Right, let's get this over with. Chloe, you're on lighting but be sure to shine onto the left, it's my best side."

Chloe positioned herself at the centre of the ride and opened a white reflective umbrella which bounced the light from the lamp towards Justine. She then fixed it on a tall frame and held it steady on the uneven floorboards of the ride. The camera was mounted on its tripod with the steel points of the legs jammed between the boarding for stability. Justine climbed onto a beautifully painted horse near the outside of the ride and Alex held the microphone out of shot on a long boom.

"Is this OK?" Justine asked, shuffling on the saddle to get comfortable. "I hope the camera works this time, Dylan," she said with just a hint of sarcasm. He ignored the remark.

Alex did his sound check, and they were ready for the take.

"Isn't this exciting?" Alice couldn't contain the thrill of filming, "I could have been a big film star if the theatre hadn't burnt down."

"In your dreams," George said crushingly, "look at it, it's all so false. There's no glamour in this, it's just a process to them. There's no artistry involved. Now when I was in film, it was a different story. That's when there were real film stars, they were worshipped like royalty." They were both sat side by side in an oddly shaped but no less elaborately painted boat near the centre of the ride.

"Shush, they're starting," Alice ordered.

"Take one, action!" said Alex sharply.

Justine shuffled and looked into the camera. "You join us this evening at Woodford Abbey. Once a great monastic site in the County of Exford until Henry the Eighth dissolved the monasteries and declared himself head of the English church. He stripped its wealth, exiled the resident monks, stole the lead off the roof and destroyed the buildings. The estate is now owned by the fifth Duke of Exford, his forefather was keeper of the keys for Henry and was given the remains of the estate in perpetuity for his loyal support. The current house was built from the ruins in 1585 and with its long history, including partial destruction by the parliamentarians during the civil war and use as a hospital during the First World War, has an abundant spirit energy. Only today a maid has told me of sightings of an ugly Victorian girl and a strange man in uniform stalking the corridors."

"I object to stalking, that makes me sound like some sort of predator. Flipping cheek," George complained.

"Never mind that, she called me ugly!" Alice exclaimed, "How dare she, she can talk with all that make up on."

"Cut," Dylan cried out.

"What?" Justine said, "I was in full flow."

"Sorry, but the carousel moved." He turned and stared at the operator sat on his stool in the centre of the ride, he held his hands up innocently and shrugged his shoulders. "Nothing to do with me mate, it's all off, apart from the lights, must have been the wind... how much longer you goanna be, I've got a pint waiting for me down the pub," he complained.

Dylan ignored him, "It's OK now. Go from stalking the corridor."

He paused for Justine to clear her throat and then shouted, "Rolling!"

She resumed, "Stalking the corridor. With the animal park opening in the sixties the estate has not been untouched by violent death and only recently for the second time in its history, a victim has been killed by a lion. Perhaps we will meet those tragic souls tonight."

"What is she saying? She's making the place sound like a war zone. I've gone right off her. That's it, the gloves are off now," Alice said, rolling up her sleeves.

Justine continued. "Tonight, I am pleased to confirm, we'll be joined by Mystic Michael, and we hope to contact the spirits doomed to walk these halls for eternity. Come with me now as we enter the haunted house," Justine dramatically concluded, continuing to look into the camera.

"OK, that's a wrap," Dylan said, "thank you all, let's go and have a cup of tea. Michael should have arrived by now, we can give him a briefing before the evening starts."

Dylan thanked the fairground operator and gave him a fiver for his trouble. They quickly packed up the equipment and moved off towards the house.

Alice was intrigued by the filming procedure. "Tom was talking about Mystic Michael, he sounds like an interesting character. He pretends to be possessed by spirits and prances around gesticulating and doing funny accents, apparently the viewers love him."

"We promised to behave ourselves," George reminded her, as they floated down off the ride and followed the crew back to the house.

"Yes, but accidents happen," Alice said, innocently shrugging her shoulders.

George did a wry grin, "Yes, I suppose they do."

Back in the ballroom the filming equipment was laid out on the dance floor. The co-producer, Peter Fellows, was unpacking the night vision equipment from a steel case when Justine entered with Dylan, Chloe and Alex.

"What on earth is that?" Justine asked looking at the heavy battery box and large camera with shoulder mounting linked by a thick cable. All painted in camouflage colours of green and brown.

"It's our new night vision equipment," Peter informed her, struggling to lift the heavy camera onto his shoulder to demonstrate.

"It looks like military kit, what happened to the usual gear?" Alex asked.

"Another crew rented it from the studio, so I went out and bought my own. It's Ex-Russian army stock, apparently very reliable but…Ooh! It is heavy." Peter grunted as he held the camera steady on his shoulder.

"You'd better only use it on ground level, you'll get a hernia trying to lift that thing upstairs with its power supply."

"You're not joking, you try and lift the battery pack," Peter challenged.

Alex grabbed the webbing handle on the top and just managed to get it off the ground using both hands and all his weight as a counterbalance, before dropping it down again with a thump. The empty Ballroom echoed to his efforts. "Blimey they saw you coming, who sold it to you?"

"It was one of Fred's mates," Peter said pointing at Fred Smith, "he's standing in for Dave, who was injured in a car crash on Monday."

Alex looked at the sallow looking stranger with suspicion. "We appreciate you stepping in at short notice, Fred." Alex eyed him cautiously, he didn't trust strangers and why hadn't he heard about the car accident until tonight?

"That's OK gov," Fred said.

Justine could detect an uneasy atmosphere between the two men. She made a mental note to keep them apart, this was going to be a long night. "Right, let's do the walk through of the house as a group, filming the areas we're going to use later when it's dark. I'll do some pieces to camera in the rooms and introduce the crew at the same time for the benefit of the viewers."

The door by the stage slammed shut and a man in a black cape and fedora hat walked towards them.

"Evening Mike, good of you to join us, I was getting worried." Justine was relieved to see Mystic Michael.

"Hello darlings, sorry I'm late, got held up by fans in the lounge bar at the Inn."

Peter shook his sweaty hand while trying to ignore the smell of alcohol on his breath. "Glad you could join us tonight, this is going to be a popular episode, what with all the recent publicity at the park due to the suicide, and the fake painting."

"Wouldn't miss it for the world, old boy," Michael said with about as much sincerity as a politician.

Wilf and Tom watched proceedings from the edge of the stage and were soon joined by Alice and George.

"How did the filming go on the roundabout?" Wilf asked.

"I hate them!" Alice said with some venom.

"Justine reckons there's an ugly Victorian girl and a man in uniform stalking the corridors," George explained.

"Where on earth did she get idea that from?" Wilf asked.

"I reckon it's that bumptious tour guide, Barbara Greenacre. I saw Justine talking to her this afternoon."

Wilf grinned, "Well, here's something to cheer you up. Have a look at Mystic Michael. Do you recognise him… bear in mind it was ten years ago."

Alice and George moved closer to the crew, grouped in the middle of the room.

"No, it can't be!" exclaimed Alice.

"Arthur Ray, as I don't live or breathe," George exclaimed in disbelief. "He just can't leave the psychic stuff alone."

Tom looked confused. "Arthur's an actor and conman of dubious talent who impersonated a priest and tried to carry out an exorcism on us at the supermarket," Wilf explained. "We sent him packing then, but here he is again. He keeps turning up like a bad penny."

"I think he's going to get another surprise, horrible little man," Alice said, her eyes piercing into the phony psychic. She was in the mood to terrorise them all tonight. They want psychic happenings, then they're going to get them.

"Don't forget our promise to Molly," Wilf reminded everyone.

"Accidents happen!" George repeated, as the corners of his mouth curled up to form a mischievous grin.

In the middle of the ballroom Justine was briefing the crew on the security arrangements and schedule for the evening's filming.

"Right, it's now nine o'clock, let's get underway. For the benefit of Michael, I was just saying we'll do the room shots then go for the lights out material at around ten thirty. Are you all ok with that?" They all nodded in agreement. Peter placed the night vision camera on the floor and they headed off to the main stairs. Dylan filmed and Alex operated the sound equipment as Justine explained the history of the house and started the introductions in well-rehearsed short sequences. They then moved to the library, then the Italian Room, Justine continuing to build up the picture for the audience. Finally, they returned to the Long Gallery to conclude this part of the show's opening sequence.

"Nice pictures ere!" Fred commented, unclipping a barrier and touching a small portrait mounted in an elaborate gold frame.

"I didn't know you were an aficionado," Alex said.

"I'm not, I'm a Scorpio. I don't see what difference that makes," Fred said, scowling as he fingered the gold frame lovingly.

"Keep away from the paintings." To the surprise of everyone a security guard stepped forward out of the shadows.

"Sorry sir, it won't happen again," Justine apologised, she grabbed Fred's arm and pulled him back into the centre of the room. "Don't touch anything, this is not 'The Antiques Roadshow'. You heard what I said in the briefing, we are under strict instructions from security. They'll be monitoring all our movements, it's a condition of the insurance."

Fred didn't say anything he just glared at her. Justine felt uneasy at his cold challenging gaze. There was something unnerving about him. *Who was he exactly?*

The ghosts watched with amusement at the proceedings.

"It's a well-rehearsed format. They've obviously done this hundreds of times, I guess all the programmes are more or less the same," Wilf said.

"It's a load of old bunkum," George was more concise. He then noticed Tom wasn't joining in but was studying every move of the chap called Fred. "What's up Tom, you look worried?"

"It can't be… but you see Fred Smith? He's limping and he's the same build as the gunman who locked me in the lion enclosure."

"You're getting paranoid," George scoffed.

"I'm not. You look. He's wearing his watch on his right hand and…" As they all studied the crewman, he reached out and grabbed the rope barrier clipping it back onto its post with his left hand. "There you are! Left-handed, DI Montgomery said he was left handed. It's him… I'm sure of it."

"Wow! This is brilliant," Alice said, shaking with excitement, "we've solved it, we've found the murderer."

"OK, let's take this one step at a time," Wilf said, trying to contain his excitement, "let's assume Tom is correct. Why would he return to the scene of the crime? How did he get involved with the film crew? Who is he? Fred Smith does sound like an alias."

"It has to be made up, that's such a common surname… it's just like an Agatha Christie story, the baddies always call themselves Smith, it's much more difficult for the police to trace a common name," Alice said confidently.

"Let's not jump to conclusions. We need to follow them round tonight and see what he's up to, then tell Molly if we discover anything. She'll know what to do next," George said wisely.

"Always the voice of reason," Alice said disappointedly.

"We have to be sure, or we'll make Molly's position here untenable. What would the Duke think if she tells the police and we're wrong? We need real evidence," George stated firmly.

The film crew headed back upstairs to the library. Justine and Peter returned to the Ballroom to pick up some props and then joined them. The ghosts followed.

The group gathered round the desk Molly had been using earlier in the day. James had locked away all the valuables and placed some old vases and ornaments of no great value in the rooms, in case the film crew had an accident whilst recording. Justine produced a candlestick holder from the box she had carried from the ballroom, placed it on the table and lit the candles. With camera set up and sound levels checked they began the recording.

"Here we go!" Alice said excitedly.

Justine cleared her throat and the group gathered closely together. "You join us now in the library where, according to legend, the spirit of a monk is seen to walk across the room and through the panelling at the far side."

"What rot," George said scathingly. "We've never seen a monk any-where."

"Shush," Wilf admonished.

The group moved slowly towards the candles, ensuring that their faces were above the flames to give them an eerie glow. "The monk is believed to have been killed under orders from Henry the Eighth's Commissioner, his spirit doomed to walk the corridors for eternity." Peter held forward a handheld electrical device the size of a portable radio. It had a small, illuminated screen with numbers written in a semicircle radiating from green to red. He adjusted the dial and lifted it in view of the camera.

"I'm not getting any reading from the EMF," he said.

"What's that thing?" Wilf asked.

"It's an Electro-Magnetic Field detector." Tom said. "I've seen them use it before, it's supposed to detect changes in the atmosphere. A ghost detector, if you like." He shrugged his shoulders, "Obviously it isn't working."

Suddenly Mystic Michael started shaking. Dylan quickly turned the camera on him as he lifted his arms and started groaning.

"What is it Michael?" Justine whispered, grabbing Peter's arm for dramatic effect and acting like she'd seen a ghost herself.

"Leave this place...you are not welcome here!" Michael ranted in a deep Yorkshire accent, his body contorting as if racked with pain. "Go now...you blasphemers...Go." Justine and Chloe screamed and moved back. Michael relaxed his expression and returned to normal. "Did you get that, he's not happy about our presence. He feels we have come to take him from this place."

"I had a reading on the EMF, did you get it Dylan?" Peter fibbed.

"No, I was focusing on Michael."

"He didn't see it because nothing happened and, what was all that garbage Arthur was spouting? There are no monks here, they've all gone to Heaven, idiot. Who's he trying to fool?" George ranted.

Wilf floated over to the group and touched the EMF device. The needle swung violently over to the red numbers and let out a high-pitched squeal. Peter cried out, nearly dropping the machine in surprise. "Wooah! It's never done that before and now it's suddenly gone very cold." The others looked on wide-eyed, glued to the spot, watching the needle's reaction. The temperature had certainly dropped.

"Well, it works," Wilf said with satisfaction.

"Fascinating," George added, enthusiastically waving his hand towards the bookcase door which obediently popped open with a creak.

Justine screamed and they all freaked out. Chloe ran for the hallway door. Michael, Fred and Alex cowered down behind the sofa and Peter dived under the table.

Justine and Dylan however held their ground. "Is there someone who wants to make contact with us? Are you making contact with us now?" Justine said, her voice trembling despite her best efforts.

"This isn't in the script," Peter whispered to the others behind the sofa, while he remained below the table, curled up in a ball.

"Can you do it again?" Justine was shaky but managed to stay professional, this was gold dust for the show.

Wilf moved away from the EMF machine and it stopped wailing as the needle slowly drifted back to green. The only sound was the heavy breathing of the disorientated crew.

"I think it's gone. Well viewers, we've just witnessed an astounding phenomenon and the night has only just begun." Her hands shaking, she held tight to the table top to maintain her balance.

"I'm not coming back in there," Chloe cried, from the safety of the hallway.

It took ten minutes for the crew to calm down, collect up their equipment and gather in the hall outside the library.

"Right, are we ready to move on to the Italian room?" Justine was all too aware of the limited filming time agreed with the Duke.

"I need to go to the toilet," Chloe whined.

"So do I," said Dylan.

"And me," added Fred.

Justine sighed and became agitated, "Oh! For goodness' sake...right, let's have a comfort break. I need you all in the Italian room in ten minutes. Those who don't feel nature's urge can come with me now and we'll start setting up. Be careful there are no spooks in the toilet," she warned sarcastically.

In the Italian room, Justine again relit the candles and turned out the lights. Eventually everyone returned and gathered around the dining table. The silver cutlery sparkled in the flickering light from the candles. For visitors touring the house, the setting represented the farewell banquet in 1915 before several members of the family went off to war, sadly only one of them returned. Edward, the son of the fourth Duke, never fully recovered from the trauma of the First World War. He offered the house as a hospital to help those recovering from injuries and shell shock, which The Ministry willingly accepted. However, he always carried the guilt of surviving whilst so many of his comrades perished needlessly.

The room had an atmosphere of melancholy which Justine wanted to somehow convey on camera. "If anyone is here, give us a sign… is there someone here who wishes to contact us?" The room was silent.

"Give her credit, she is trying," Alice said, feeling some sympathy for Justine.

"Edward, you are here, aren't you Edward? You love this house, don't you? You can contact us, we are listening, please give us a sign," Justine continued.

"I'm feeling nothing," Michael said, "There's no one here."

"Cooee," Alice said waving her hand whilst sat in the carver at the head of the table.

"Don't Alice," Wilf scolded, "remember our promise." Tom and George watched the proceedings with amusement from the comfort of the sofa in the corner.

"Right, let's blow out the candles and go over to special night vision," Justine instructed.

"But the camera is downstairs," Fred commented.

"Sorry, I forgot you've not been with us before. It's all smoke and mirrors Fred. Dylan and Chloe will do the honours."

And so, they did. Chloe put green cellophane over the lighting and Dylan added a green filter to the lens of the camera. Justine blew out the candles and they were bathed in an olive-green glow.

"This is rubbish," Wilf said. "They're conning the viewers into thinking they can't see." True enough, the crew moved around the room looking in different directions, bumping into the furniture and yelping at every opportunity.

"I can smell damp cloth," Michael said, "no wait, it's more like fire. I can feel residual activity…someone in torment… a soul not being able to forgive."

"Is that you Edward?" Justine whispered, "We mean you no harm... Please contact us." There was no sound as they all stood perfectly still and listened intently.

"Can I please?" George pleaded with the others, "just one little bump...please?"

"No, not yet, we've already overstepped the mark," Wilf reminded him.

Justine shrugged her shoulders. "Please Edward, we know it's you... Can you make a noise...Please." They continued for another fifteen minutes. Fed up, Justine did a piece to camera and then packed up the candelabra.

"That's a wrap here, let's go down to the long gallery with the proper night vision and see what we get. I'm disappointed in you Michael, I was expecting more content."

"Sorry, I just wasn't getting the feeling," he said.

"I don't care about 'the feeling,' I need footage for the show. It started so well in the library. Come on, let's have a cup of tea in the ballroom first." Disgruntled, she led the team downstairs.

There was a sudden movement in the corner of the empty room. Alice jumped. "Ooh! That was scary I never noticed him." The other ghosts laughed.

The security officer positioned behind the curtain, stepped out and tidied the furniture before following the film crew downstairs.

After a short break, the team returned to the Long Gallery with the cumbersome night vision camera. They gathered around a circular table placed in the centre of the gallery.

"Right, we'll do a bit of the, 'is there anybody there stuff,' to camera, then get out the Ouija board. Are you ready with the night vision?"

"Ready," Peter signalled to Fred. Fred reached down to the large metal box containing the power pack while Peter heaved the deadweight of the camera onto his shoulder.

"Ok Fred, turn it on." The box began to hum and a small red lamp in the viewfinder indicated there was power. The hum got louder and louder.

Justine had to raise her voice to be heard over the drone of the camera. "Is anybody there?...we mean you no harm..." She paused, "What on earth is that sound. We can't use it if it's going to make that racket!"

"Never mind the noise," Peter shouted. "It's getting flipping hot." The battery box was now beginning to quake causing the furniture in the room to move around on the tremoring floor. Smoke then began to pour from the body of the camera. It was the best paranormal action so far.

"Get it out of here...Now!" Justine howled over the din. A security guard came from the shadows, pushed open the fire doors and with the help of Alex and Michael, grabbed the equipment and ran out into the night throwing it all onto the gravel path where it promptly burst into flames.

Justine stood in the doorway, the inferno illuminating her rage.

The guard ran out with a fire extinguisher and sprayed foam all over the kit. The sound from the battery pack subsided, it did one last little burp, and all was silent.

"Did you get that Dylan?" Justine fumed, turning to the cameraman. Dylan nodded.

"You mercenary, cow! I could have been severely injured," Peter yelled, looking daggers at the presenter stood in the doorway.

Justine smiled. "I hope you've got a guarantee for that thing. Now wipe that foam off your trousers and let's get this finished... I assume that is foam," she added sarcastically.

"You really don't care, do you?" Peter said, frantically wiping away the extinguishers pungent spray, "If I wasn't married to you, I'd be phoning my lawyer." He then started to laugh, "We'll need to add some good narration to this when we get back to the editing suite." He turned to the guard. "Thanks for your help. Don't worry, we'll clean this up afterwards," he reassured him.

It took half an hour to reset the room. Justine got the Ouija board out, placed it on the table and they all sat around. With everyone distracted Fred was again moving around the room looking closely at the pictures.

"Move away from the paintings sir... I won't tell you again," the guard instructed as he returned to the room.

"Come and sit here," Peter said. Fred moved back across the room showing no remorse for his interest in the paintings. "What's the matter with your leg? I saw you limping earlier."

"Gout," Fred said as he sat down, "comes and goes."

"Why are you so interested in the paintings?"

"No reason," Fred replied and turned to look at the set up on the table, indicating that the conversation was over.

"He's at it again," Wilf observed. "There's more to our Fred than meets the eye. Let's see what we can find out."

"It's Showtime," George announced with glee. All four of them gathered closely round the table. The lights were dimmed and Dylan stood behind the seated team with the camera looking down into the circle, with Justine centre stage.

"Ok, place your finger on the upturned glass," she instructed. They all obeyed.

Wilf placed a hand on Michael's shoulder.

"I can feel a presence," Michael said with a noticeable tremble in his voice.

Alice repeated the move on Justine. A shiver went down her spine causing her to shuffle uncomfortably in her chair.

"I feel it too," she whispered, "If you can hear my voice, make a noise." She paused. They all listened intently. The atmosphere was electric, all were on tenterhooks.

George disturbed a chair at the other end of the room. The scrape on the floor caused them all to quickly look in its direction.

"I know you are here. Who are you? We mean you no harm. Will you communicate with us? We have a medium with us, try to channel him and talk to us."

Michael was feeling uneasy, this was too real, and he was certainly not comfortable in the role of a conduit to the other side. He held his breath.

The glass started moving. The crew watched in disbelief as it slid across the table. H…E…L…L…O it spelt. The temperature in the room plummeted, as did their bravado but their fingers remained anchored to the glass.

"Hello," Justine said shakily, quickly glancing up to make certain Dylan was filming. "Who are you... do you want to communicate with us?"

The glass moved rapidly now, taking them all by surprise. A...R...T... H...U...R, it spelt in quick succession.

Michael felt sick to the pit of his stomach. "No, it can't be," he cried out. The others assumed he had been possessed by a spirit, such was his sudden change of humour.

The glass continued spelling, R...A...Y.

Michael was visibly shaking now. He quickly withdrew his finger from the glass as if electrocuted. "No not here, is it you again?" he questioned, looking erratically around the room.

The others, unaware of his real name, watched the man crumble in his chair. To them he was Mystic Michael, Spiritualist to the stars.

But the glass wasn't finished with him, it kept sliding around the table without his touch. R...E...M...E...M...B...E...R, it continued. Michael nodded subordinately at the glass, his breathing now laboured and body shaking. P...R...I...C...E...L...O...W. The glass then slid back to the centre of the table.

"Yes...Yes I remember," Michael broke down in tears, "I'm sorry... please forgive me...I meant you no harm."

The others watched on in disbelief. Their mystic friend appeared to be having a nervous breakdown before their very eyes.

Alice felt sorry for him now, and guilty that he was being traumatised by their actions, whilst Dylan was getting good footage for their show. "Stop it, George. He's had enough." Tears were beginning to well up in her eyes.

"Yes, that's enough George," Wilf agreed.

Justine was thrilled at the action being recorded. This could be their first BAFTA nomination. "Who's Arthur?" she asked staring up at the ceiling as if talking to the spirit in the room.

"It's me!" Arthur said through his sniffling.

"No, you're Michael, you're communicating with the spirit world," she corrected him, "you're doing really well," she added.

He shakily stood up, "I'm not. I can't communicate and I am Arthur Ray. The spirits are right I'm a charlatan. I've been lying and cheating my way through life all this time. I'm just a washed-up actor. Well, no more. I've had enough of this. Lying and cheating has brought me nothing but years of misery. I was the face of 'Crunocks' biscuits in the sixties until the devastating 'Hob Nob' takeover. There must be other jobs in television. I've still got time to start again. I'll get a decent agent and go for legitimate acting jobs."

Wilf stood back. Arthur felt the spirit's touch leave him and he felt relieved. He looked round at the gathered crew, drying his eyes with his handkerchief.

"I'm going to leave now." His voice had a controlled soft tone. "Don't follow me, I'm going to be all right. There's nothing to worry about." With that he walked to the fire exit, pushed the door open and disappeared into the night.

"And that my friends, is the best performance he's ever given," Wilf said.

The crew around the table just stared at each other in disbelief. "W... What just happened?" Justine stuttered.

"I think Mystic Michael just retired," Peter said.

"But he just admitted he was communicating with spirits in the room. He called out to them! You all heard it. What are we going to do now? That's our big draw for the show gone!" Justine said anxiously.

"We just have to carry on, we'll have to find another medium and in the meantime, we have all this in the can. That's worth a Christmas special on its own," Peter said.

The guard closed the fire doors and watched as Arthur drove off along the drive towards the main gate. Justine tidied the chairs around the table and took charge, "OK, let's just finish this off, everyone, back round the table for one more session then we'll wind up. I'll do the closing piece with Dylan and Chloe while you all pack the equipment back into the van." They all agreed, the sooner they could leave the better.

"Make sure you're in the same seat for continuity."

They all resumed their positions, and the lights were dimmed by the guard who was now beginning to enjoy himself. This wasn't the boring evening he had been expecting.

"Fingers on the glass then, are the light levels OK Dylan?" Dylan nodded.

The ghosts, stood back this time, deciding not to interfere further. They'd done enough for one evening.

Justine looked up into the room. "Great spirit, if you are still here, please make your presence felt," she paused, "We mean you no harm... if you wish to contact us, we are listening."

The glass moved.

"Is that you George? Stop it!" Wilf instructed.

"No, it's not me."

"Nor us," Alice said, including Tom for good measure.

"Fair enough, I think Justine is up to something."

The glass moved to the letter F and stopped. "If you want to say something please continue...we are all friends here." The glass moved again, quicker this time R...E...D.

"Fred," she said, "What about Fred?" The others looked curiously at him. The blood was draining from his face and beads of sweat were forming on his forehead.

The glass moved again, quickly spelling, W...H...O...A...R...E...Y... O...U. The crew had also been considering that question all day.

Fred stood abruptly, his chair falling over behind him. "That's enough! I don't know which one of you is doing this but stop it now, I'm warning you. Give me the tape in the camera." He turned to face Dylan and held out his hand authoritatively.

"You've got to be kidding, this is gold dust." Dylan stood his ground.

"I won't ask again," Fred stated menacingly.

"I'm not giving you the tape."

Fred reached into his pocket and pulled out a handgun, pointing it at Dylan. The crew round the table jumped up fearfully.

"Sit down," Fred shouted turning the gun towards them. They obeyed as one, their eyes not leaving the firearm.

"I told you, it's him. That's the guy in the stables. It has to be. Can't you do something?" Tom said angrily.

"Stay calm," George said coolly, "no one needs to get hurt, don't move anything, he's too volatile, someone could get seriously injured."

Dylan slowly lifted the camera off his shoulder. "OK Fred, I'm going to place the camera on the table now and give you the tape."

Fred said nothing but held his hand out.

Unnoticed in the gloom on the far side of the room, the security guard silently pulled a gun from his concealed shoulder holster.

Fred kept his eyes on Dylan's actions but said over his shoulder, "Put that gun down on the floor and step away from it."

The guard was stunned. '*How had he detected him? This was no chancer. He had to be a professional.*' He obeyed, slowly placing the gun on the floor.

"Kick it over here," Fred instructed.

Paralysed with fear, the others watched his movements, dumbfounded by the situation.

Dylan removed the tape from the camera and nervously placed it in Fred's hand.

He slid it into his pocket and backed away, picking up the guard's gun from the floor whilst watching their every move and continuing to pan his gun slowly around the room. "Stay here all of you, don't move and no one need get hurt. I'm going now, don't try to follow. I'm not afraid to use this."

They needed no convincing. Fred backed to the fire exit and pushed the bar on the door. It swung open and he backed out. "Don't follow," he repeated and disappeared into the dark. They could hear his laboured run down the gravel drive, hampered by his limp.

The guard lifted his two-way radio, "Gallery to base... Gallery to base."

"Go ahead Gallery."

"Suspect has left with tape recording. He is armed, do not apprehend. Repeat, do not apprehend."

The film crew were in shock. Peter wrapped his arms around Justine as she burst into tears. Chloe dropped into a chair and began sobbing. The others gathered by the table in stunned silence.

"Bloody hell, what was all that about?" Alex finally said.

"I didn't like the look of him from the beginning," Dylan replied.

The guard came over to them, "You're all safe now, he's gone. The Ouija board spooked him. That's some special talent you've got."

Through her tears Justine mumbled. "It was me...I pushed the glass round the table, I just wanted to know who he was."

"I told you it was one of them moving the glass," Wilf said smugly.

They all heard the roar of an engine as an Audi Quattro whizzed past the smouldering night vision camera, spraying gravel against the windows as it passed the gallery. They rushed to see what was causing the noise.

"Hey, that's my car!" Dylan cried out. The car progressed at speed, smoothly negotiating up the twisting drive, its tyres gripping the tarmac, squealing with complaint but never losing grip.

The guard lifted his radio. "All units… all units. Suspect is driving a white Audi Quattro towards the south gate registration Delta, Yankee, Lima, Alpha, November, One, do not apprehend, open the gates and let him pass."

"No, don't let him pass. He's got my car, stop him!" Dylan shouted frantically to the guard. "I only picked it up yesterday, it's brand new."

"I think we pay you too much, personalised plates as well!" Peter observed.

"Not from working for you, I've got other clients you know!" Dylan stated, looking daggers at him. "Why don't you stop him?" he pleaded to the guard.

"We want to know where he's going," the security guard calmly explained, "he can certainly handle a car." He reached into his pocket, withdrew his warrant card and flipped it open.

"Sod his driving skills," Dylan exclaimed grumpily.

Alex looked closely at the badge the guard was holding out for inspection, did a double take at the Woodford Abbey uniform and read out. "Metropolitan Police, Firearms Unit …You're not one of the estate guards at all!"

"Don't worry, we have a tail on him, he's got a few questions to answer but not just yet. He's only a monkey, we want the organ grinder."

"Just make sure he doesn't hurt my car. Anyway, Justine, if you want some good news, the tape I gave him only has two minutes of recording on it, I changed it after Michael's breakdown. The tapes with all tonight's footage are in the ballroom," Dylan said smugly.

"Brilliant, this is going to be our best show ever," Justine said, recovering surprisingly quickly from the evening's events.

"I'll need those for evidence sir," the officer said coldly.

Justine's heart dropped. All the evening's revelations were going to be taken away. Her hopes of receiving her first Television Award were evaporating, like a ghost vanishing into thin air.

The ghosts watched on thoroughly enjoying the spectacle.

"Well, that was even more exciting than we were expecting," Wilf said with a satisfied grin.

24
Washed Up

Thursday 22nd August. Morning

Sergeant Dexter called Jules at eight o'clock requesting that he and the Duke attend a meeting in the security office at 9am.

The police had given little information to Jules about the evening's events. The burnt debris of the night vision camera was now cordoned off and watched over by a police officer. Even the estate security were under strict instructions not to disclose any information until this morning's meeting.

At the lodge, Alice had been less security conscious. She told Molly everything they had witnessed. Molly could hardly believe that not only had the scoundrel Arthur Ray resurfaced again after all these years, but Tom's mysterious gunman was also there and escaped arrest by stealing the cameraman's car. It was all just too exciting.

"If I included this in the new book no one would believe it," she mused.

"Never mind a guidebook. It would make a great novel," Alice said excitedly. "It was an incredible evening. We didn't expect anything like that, not in our wildest dreams. George did behave himself, sort of. But with Arthur Ray turning up again... well, he had to be taught another lesson."

"I've watched the programme many times, but I had no idea it was Arthur," Molly said.

"He does look different, probably aided by the dark lighting and make up. But there was no question when we saw him in the flesh. And then when the Ouija board spelt his name. Well, you'd have really thought he'd seen a ghost!"

"But what's going to happen now? Who's this Fred Smith then?"

"We don't know. He was a late replacement for someone who'd been hurt in a car crash. The others are watching the movements at the house. The police are everywhere."

Suddenly Wilf appeared through the wall causing Molly and Alice to jump.

"Don't do that, Wilf!" Alice cried.

"Sorry but… Oh! Good morning Molly, pardon my sudden intrusion."

"Good morning Wilf, any more news?"

"All I know is that the Duke and Jules have been called to a meeting with the police at the gate house. George and Tom are already on the way up there."

"OK Wilf, I'm coming with you. Sorry, I have to go, Molly," Alice said quickly, and without another word she and Wilf passed through the side wall and headed to the South Gate.

Jules drove from the car park, pausing to look at the burnt out molten mess of the camera, fenced off by blue and white 'police incident' tape which flapped gently in the breeze. He collected the Duke from the front steps and headed to the 'Estate Office'. Neither knew exactly what had gone on overnight but were aware it must have been serious.

"James tells me the gunman returned last night," the Duke said, his brow so furrowed you could plant potatoes in it.

"We don't know that officially, father. Hopefully we'll learn more very soon. We've been instructed not to open the house to the public this morning. The police have closed off all the rooms and they're not even letting housekeeping in. I told you not to let them film that third rate nonsense here. I knew nothing good would come of it."

"I wish I'd listened to you now, but you can't predict things like this. I hope they still pay us," the Duke mused.

"Are you telling me they haven't paid yet? You let them do this before we got their money… unbelievable!" His father looked somewhat shame-faced.

The south entrance gateway was soon in sight and Jules swung the Range Rover off the road pulling up in his space by the front door of the Victorian lodge. The car park had several other estate vehicles, and three police cars lined up against the low black chain fence.

The Duke said nothing as they entered the hallway through the black painted door. The upper panel contained a stained glass representation of the Woodford Abbey logo. The entrance hall was expansive, the smell of furniture polish hung in the air and their footsteps echoed in the cavernous space.

The tiles on the floor showing depictions of flora and Christian symbols had been reclaimed from the ruins of the abbey. To the left was a side table containing the visitor's book and to the right, a pitch pine stairway of rich patina rose to the upper floors. Its heavily turned newel posts and balustrade giving a feeling of timeless permanence.

Sybil, the estate manager's secretary greeted them. "This way please, everyone's gathering in the meeting room. They're waiting for the arrival of DI Montgomery. Would you like tea or coffee?"

Colin and Bob from Estate security, John Hammond, Sergeant Dexter and PC Singleton were sat in silence, sipping their coffees. The oak table was of similar design to the one in the conference room at the house, oval in shape with the family crest inlaid in the centre, surrounded by twelve modernist style chairs produced from oak trees that were unfortunate victims of devastating storms in 1975.

"Good morning gentlemen," Jules said.

"Where's that confounded Montgomery then?" the Duke blasted, as he sat down on the throne-like carver at the head of the table.

"He'll be here shortly, sir," Dexter assured him. The staff now chatted quietly amongst themselves as Sybil served drinks to the new arrivals. The two policemen sat in silence observing the group. Dexter constantly checked his watch. It was now five past nine.

"Biscuits," Sybil announced with a pleasant trill, placing a plate of 'Woodford Abbey originals' on the centre of the table.

"While we're waiting Sergeant, can you just tell us what happened last night?" Jules enquired, impatiently.

"Sorry sir, we need to hear that from the Inspector himself. He shouldn't be long."

"He needs to get a move on. We can't wait here all day," the Duke complained impatiently.

Hung on the wall, adjacent to the doorway was a faded map of the estate, set in a heavy wooden frame. Next to it was a more recent Ordnance Survey map of the area and a smaller detailed map of the safari park, house and gardens. On an easel in the corner was a flip chart, which contained a detailed plan of the showground indicating the layout for the weekend's car show.

Seeing the drawing, Jules turned to Colin. "How are the preparations for the car show going?"

"All going well sir, fortunately we don't get involved in the actual running of the event, Holeford Car Club take control of all that. You'll have seen all the marquees in place. They're setting up the arena today, while they wait for the funfair to arrive. It seems to get bigger every year."

They all heard the unmistakable burble of a six-cylinder engine and crunch of gravel. Inspector Montgomery had arrived. The car door banged shut and Sybil opened the front door. The expectant group around the table were relieved and greeted the inspector warmly as he entered the room.

"Black coffee, no sugar, thank you. Good morning gentlemen, thank you all for coming." Sybil handed him his drink, topped up the others from the coffee pot and left the room, closing the door softly.

"Right," said Montgomery, taking his seat, "I'm going to keep this brief. Following last night's incident I want to share with you certain developments with our investigation. What I'm about to reveal is frankly, against police procedure. However, it's also against the norm to be operating on the estate of a Duke and viscount, so to that end, I believe it is prudent to keep you informed. Please be aware that what I am about to tell you is in the strictest confidence, not a word of it must be discussed outside this room." He paused, looking at each of them in turn. He shivered and looked round for the cause of the sudden drop in temperature. *Had the door opened again? Was a window open?*

"What's he stopped for?" Wilf asked, as he passed through the window with Alice to join George and Tom.

"Don't know," George said, "You haven't missed anything though, Montgomery's only just arrived."

Satisfied that no one was eaves dropping on them, Montgomery continued by explaining details of the recent events.

"We know all that, when's he going to get to the juicy stuff?" George said impatiently.

"Dexter and Singleton aren't even watching Montgomery, they're looking at the others. I think they already know what he's going to say. Look, Singleton's doodling, he's not even listening," Alice observed.

Tom moved round behind PC Singleton. "He's making notes, I can't make out what he's writing, it's just illegible scribble."

The group listened in disbelief at the blow-by-blow account of the night's proceedings. "Now, I get to the confidential part of this briefing. The production assistant from the television company, who should have been with them, was involved in a car crash, but it was no accident. He was deliberately run off the road sustaining serious but not life-threatening injuries. An Audi Quattro stolen last night following the incident in the gallery was tailed back to London where it was abandoned and is now subject to a detailed forensic examination.

The thief, a gentleman calling himself Fred Smith, is known to the police… his real name is Alexi Banjetski. Don't be fooled by the name. Although linked to the Russian Mafia he is actually from Peckham. He's nevertheless very dangerous but is only a pawn in a bigger game linked to art theft. This brings us back to the fake painting spotted by Miss Goodall. The original Van Dyck is still missing and our sources in the fraud squad believe that it has not yet been received by its client. Therefore, it's logical to assume one of the gang is still holding it."

"Why don't you just arrest this Banjetski chap and put the thumbscrews on him," the Duke asked, shifting uncomfortably in his seat.

"Be assured sir, we are watching his movements. In fishing terms, we are giving him some line, before reeling him in. We need to know who he's associating with. All will become clear in good time. The net is closing in."

"That's all very well but why are you breaking protocol and telling us this?" Jules queried.

"That's a fair question. I want you to know who we are dealing with. We believe, that is, the fraud squad and I believe, that despite the heightened security there may be another attempt made on your gallery."

"What rot! You know who it is," the Duke accused. "Just get on and arrest him and put an end to all this."

"I appreciate your feelings sir, but we have the opportunity to break a fraud ring that goes back many years. We'll be maintaining the joint surveillance with the estate security and hope to close the case very soon. Now, I've taken up enough of your time this morning and assure you I'll keep you updated on developments… in confidence of course," and he again glanced seriously around the table.

The meeting was clearly over. They all rose and went their separate ways. The Duke and Jules drove back to the house.

Jules dropped the Duke at the front door and headed to his office where he reluctantly had to deal with a pile of neglected paperwork.

Montgomery received a phone call and within minutes, Carl arrived from the workshops to pick up his car for storage before going on show at the weekend.

The policemen remained in the meeting room with DI Montgomery to debrief on the meeting. Dexter and Singleton had been tasked with watching the reactions of the Woodford Abbey members whilst Montgomery had shared the information. He wanted to know what they had observed.

Alice and Wilf returned to the lodge to tell Molly all about the informative meeting. They then returned to the house, leaving her to work on the manuscript.

Jules was also relishing some peace to catch up with his paperwork, a bit of normality after the drama. At mid-day he had an idea. He lifted the receiver of the phone, noticing that the light linking to the Music room phone was glowing red. This was unusual, his father normally used the phone in the library. He liked to keep the music room for relaxation only. Thinking no more about it he called the lodge.

Molly picked up. "Hi Molly, do you have any plans this evening?"

"Not particularly, why?"

"Would you like to come over here for dinner? It would be nice to have some company and we have lots to talk about."

"I've a better idea, you come here, and I'll cook you my speciality."

"Ok, deal. How about six o'clock? I'll bring the wine."

In the attic, Alice flipped through the stack of canvases and framed paintings leaning against the wall while Tom looked them over.

"So, what do you think Tom, any masterpieces amongst them?" Wilf asked.

"No, I'm afraid not, not so far anyway. Even so, there are some well painted landscapes of the estate. I'm surprised they're not on show in the house."

"I like the modern ones," Alice said. " You know, the pop art stuff, they're so vibrant. Like that one in the gallery of the swimming pool and palm tree, that's lovely."

Tom was not so impressed, "No, that's not my cup of tea, I like the old masters. I'm studying them for my art degree, the level of skill is outstanding. They even had to make their own paint you know. You couldn't go to an art shop and buy it in tubes, they had to grind up minerals and mix them with linseed oil etc.… genius," he reflected. "Now take your popular modern painters. They started on the traditional path and produced some exciting work, then people with money took an interest and it got all commercial. Take Picasso for instance, he started off producing some lovely portraits… I mean real quality work, then he started drawing cubes and just a few squiggles, gave them a silly title and handed them to the galleries. They then wrote a load of guff about how wonderful they were, stuck a high price tag on them and idiots with too much money were queuing up. Matisse was even craftier, he just stuck on coloured paper cuttings and charged a fortune. Emperor's new clothes if you ask me. That tack didn't always work though. Take Constable's purple cubist departure. He wasn't avant-garde enough. He went back to painting fields and carts stuck in a river."

"I've never heard of Constable's Purple cube paintings," George said.

"Exactly, they were brushed under the carpet. I expect they're locked in a vault at The Royal Academy or better still got painted over. No, give me an old master any day."

"I think the car show's going to be great fun," Alice said changing the subject, art wasn't her thing. "You know Carolyn's going to be there doing her fortune telling to raise money for the school?"

"That'll be nice, perhaps she'll need some help," Wilf said excitedly. "Did you see Carl collect Montgomery's car after the meeting, it's going to be on show with some other TV cars."

"That'll boost his ego even more," George said cynically.

"Look guys, I'm having a lovely time here, but I don't understand why we haven't seen Eric yet. It's nothing personal, but I feel like I've been overlooked," Tom said. "You all had a career. I didn't get to be anything and I don't know what's going to happen to me now, it's all out of my control."

"Don't worry, he'll be here soon enough. Let's face it, you have an eternity, so a few more days won't hurt," Wilf pointed out, "We all enjoy your company, and don't you want to know how all this crime stuff ends?"

"You never know, you may be able to stay here with us," Alice tried to reassure him.

"That's a good point," Tom reflected. "Why isn't an historic house like this overrun with ghosts? There must have been numerous deaths over the last thousand years."

"Not many stay around, they move on to other venues or jobs upstairs, the admin department is huge with the country's population increasing all the time," Wilf explained.

"Can you picture it if they all stayed, it would be ridiculous? Can you imagine all those ghosts from different periods existing together? All squeezed into one building, it would descend into absurdity like a cheap TV comedy. It just wouldn't work. Don't worry, Eric will be back soon enough. He knows what he's doing. He's been at it a long time. Now, who fancies a trip down to the showground to see how they're getting on?" George asked.

"Good idea," Alice replied. "We need to find out where Carolyn's gypsy tent will be located. Did you hear Montgomery this morning? He thinks there may be more trouble, we need to make plans on how we can help him."

They all agreed and went down to the ground floor and off across the lawn towards the marquees.

Meanwhile, in the study of her little cottage the day was dragging for Molly as she reviewed her notes. The book was beginning to take shape, much to her relief. A few more days at the abbey and she could return to London to finish the text and sort through the pictures while spending more time on her PhD work. Much as she was enjoying her time nearer home and living on the park, she was missing her friends and colleagues at the museum, along with the excitement of the big city.

Jules spent the day in his office. The reality of running the estate was a heavy burden. Despite the management team keeping the park running like a well-oiled machine, at the end of the day, the buck stopped with him. He had to be aware of all the decisions involved in the day-to-day operations and importantly, be thinking ahead and guiding his team leaders. He was beginning to understand why the Duke had aged so quickly and why he'd had limited time to spend with him and his sister when they were children.

He vowed that he would never neglect his own children in the same way, if he was to have any at all. The thought of his sister returning to help, filled him with dread. Much as he loved her, she would undermine all that he was working for and ultimately suck the estate dry. No, it was much better that she remained in her role in South Africa where her fierce management skill was necessary and appreciated. The wine they produced wasn't bad either, perhaps he should take a bottle along this evening.

At the lodge, Molly stopped working on the book at five o'clock and drove over to the restaurant to collect some last-minute provisions. She returned, showered and then started preparations for the evening meal. At six fifteen, she could hear the whine of a golf buggy and crunch of the gravel on the path outside. She quickly wiped her hands, turned down the gas on the stove and walked to the front door just as Jules knocked.

"Hello, sorry I'm late," he said awkwardly, holding a small bunch of flowers he'd picked from the kitchen garden, together with a bottle of wine.

"That's very thoughtful, thank you. Come on in. You look like you need a drink." She took the flowers, turned towards the kitchen and placed them with the bottle on the worktop. "Will you do the honours?" she said handing Jules a corkscrew as he followed her in.

"Something smells nice."

"Why thank you, it was a present from Mum last Christmas, 'Seaspray' by Boots. I think it's about five pounds a pint." she joked.

Jules laughed, "No, I mean whatever's cooking on the hob... Sorry, I'm sure the 'Seaspray' is very nice too." Jules opened the bottle and poured two glasses which he carried through to the lounge.

"Don't get too excited, it's just my student standby Spaghetti Bolognese served with breadsticks from the restaurant with Tutti Frutti for dessert."

Jules was unfortunately sipping his wine as she said 'Tutti Frutti'. He nearly choked and had to spit the wine back into the glass.

"Are you alright?" Molly asked with concern, handing him a paper napkin from the table. He took it and wiped his mouth, laughing.

"Yes fine, it was nothing, it just went the wrong way." There was no way he was going to tell her the details about his father and the girl from Zambelli ice cream.

"So, has it been a particularly bad day? You look worried. Mind you with all that's going on, you must be stressed."

"Promise me we're not going to talk about work this evening. It's such a pleasure to get away from the house for a few hours."

"But it's a huge house, it must be amazing to have so much space."

"You might think so, but believe it or not, it can be very claustrophobic, not to say lonely. Father spends most of his time in his apartments or in his music room and I seem to be working or sleeping. The staff are very supportive and unendingly loyal to us both, but they are always a presence. It's very difficult to be yourself, to be private. Sometimes I feel like one of the creatures in the animal park. I know I sound pathetic really, I'm grateful for my privileged position but just sometimes it would be nice to be ordinary."

"Being ordinary isn't always fun either."

"I'm sorry, I sound like a spoilt brat. There just seems to be so much going on that's beyond my control at the moment."

"The death in the lion enclosure was terrible, poor Tom and what about his family they must be... well I can't imagine what they're going through."

"There's more now though. Before I left the house, DI Montgomery phoned. That's why I was late by the way, sorry about that."

"Don't keep apologising, its only 'Spag Bol' I can make it with my eyes closed. Go on."

"I don't know how much you know about the 'Haunted House' filming and I'm not supposed to discuss it. We had a meeting with the police this morning and it's all a bit hush hush."

"I know that Mystic Michael turned out to be a fraud, they cheated with the night vision filming by using a green filter and Fred Smith pulled a gun, is there more?"

Jules put his glass down on the coffee table. "How on earth could you know all that? I only learnt it this morning from the police and they said it was not common knowledge."

"I have my sources," Molly said mysteriously.

"Yes, but unless you were there you couldn't possibly…"

There was a knock at the door.

"I'll tell you more over dinner, excuse me. I wonder who that can be!" Molly got up and opened the door.

"Prof! How lovely, this is an unexpected surprise."

"Hello Molly, I hope I'm not disturbing you."

"Not at all, come in, I think you know Jules."

Jules stood up and stepped towards Professor Halford. "Hello Uncle, this is a pleasant surprise," he said shaking his hand warmly.

"My boy… I didn't expect… well, I am disturbing you. Please forgive me," the professor said, looking back and forth at Jules and Molly.

"Now don't you start jumping to conclusions, I've already had that trouble with father, we're just friends."

"Yes, just friends." Molly confirmed.

"Even so, I am disturbing your evening. Is that your wonderful 'Spag Bol I can smell?"

"I don't know about wonderful."

"Jules…you're in for a treat tonight, no one makes a Bolognese sauce like Molly. I'll get to the point. I've really come to see your father after getting his note. I spoke to him on the phone, and I think he could do with some company… anyway, it's about time we got together. Also, I wanted to see you Molly, with an update on the ledgers."

"Come through, would you like a glass of wine?" she asked.

"Just a little one, thank you. I won't keep you long."

Jules went into the kitchen to get the wine. He glanced with interest at the saucepan containing the meat and tomatoes concoction simmering gently on the hob and returned to the lounge, handing the drink to the Professor.

"Thank you, my boy… So Molly, you need to come to the museum, I need to share with you the cryptic writing in the ledger. It was hidden in the third volume and it may be that your hunch was right. The religious artefact from the monastery could still be here, hidden for all these years."

"What did it say?" Molly asked excitedly, perching on the arm of the sofa.

"It's difficult to explain you must come and see for yourself… please say you'll come tomorrow?"

"Yes, just try and stop me. This is so exciting."

"There's something else I wanted to ask you. As you know I'm not getting any younger and next year I'll be retiring."

"You're not that old and anyway what about the museum…it needs you," Molly said sincerely.

"It needs new blood my dear. Which prompts me to ask you if you would consider taking over my position as curator?"

Molly slumped onto the sofa. "Oh! Professor, I…"

"You don't have to say anything now, just think about it, we can discuss it more tomorrow." He sipped the last of his wine and placed the glass on the table. "Enough…I will leave you to those thoughts. I hope it hasn't spoilt your evening, which certainly wasn't my intention."

"Not at all Prof you have just… well I wasn't expecting that at all."

"Do you seriously think the valuables are still here?" Jules questioned.

"I'm very serious and I'm also serious about Molly taking my place. Now I must be going, your father will be waiting for me. He moved to the door and headed out into the cool of the evening. "Shall we say ten o'clock? See you in the morning. Goodnight."

Molly closed the door and briefly leant against it deep in thought. Jules looked at her, trying to read her thoughts.

"Well, that was certainly a surprise," Molly said.

"Is that all you can say?" Jules said, aghast at the cool way she responded.

Molly was determined to stay calm. Inside she wanted to jump up and down and scream at the top of her voice. "We need to investigate further before getting our hopes up. Wouldn't we look fools if it's all some medieval hoax? My profession is strewn with failed historians and archaeologists who jumped to incorrect conclusions. I don't intend to be one of them."

"You've got steel running through you Molly Goodall, I admire that."

"Right, you can do the spaghetti and I'll complete the sauce, come on." They returned to the kitchen.

"It's funny, hearing you call him uncle."

"He's always been a close friend of father, I can't remember a time when he wasn't in our lives," Jules mused.

"Here you are, boil the water in the pan and put this in, twelve minutes should do." She handed him a bunch of spaghetti as if they were going to start a game of 'pick up sticks.' "Do you like Kate Bush, Dire Straits or Phil Collins?"

"I don't mind any of them, why?"

"Because that's the only tapes I've got here, most of my music collection is at the flat in Eltham."

Molly served up the meal on hot plates from the oven and they sat around the small dining table in the corner of the living room with Phil Collins quietly playing in the background on her portable tape player.

"Uncle's right, this tastes amazing. Where did you learn to cook like this?"

"Oh, it's nothing. I got the recipe for the pesto from an Italian friend of mine, Max. He's in the Italian army." What she failed to say was Maximus Gurillus was one of the leaders of the second Augusta Legion that had stormed Monkton Hillfort near Holeford in AD 43. He played golf with George in the Holeford Ethereal Golf Society before they moved to Woodford Abbey. That would be just too much information.

"Well, it's delicious, I'd love him to teach our chef recipes like this."

"That could be difficult."

"What a shame. So, you live in Eltham but work in Kensington. That must be a drag having to travel right across central London."

"It's not the best but that's all I can afford. I share with another girl from the museum, it's OK and it's not for ever." Molly shrugged her shoulders and took a sip from her glass. "This is a very nice wine."

"Thank you, it's a Merlot from our estate in South Africa. Sis calls it '*a cheeky little number*,' I prefer to call it a full-bodied red with blackberry and coal undertones. But then she's the expert."

"I just don't get all these descriptions of wine flavours, to me it's either nice or vinegar."

"It can all get a bit pretentious, but the wine lovers can't get enough of it. Some sommeliers make a career out of spouting nonsense about taste and aroma. She's doing a good job. You're going to see a lot more New World wines on the supermarket shelves in coming years."

"Well, if they're as good as this one, bring them on." Molly said lifting the glass and admiring it's contents. "I'm going to miss this place Jules but I'm going to have to return to London soon. I can complete the first draft at the museum."

"I'm going to miss your company. It's certainly been an adventure since you arrived."

"It sure has. Who would have thought it, still I'm here another week then I must get back to my PhD. I promised originally I'd only be here a week so I'm pushing my luck with the curator. At least I'm not going to miss the car show at the weekend. Mum and Dad are really looking forward to it, some of my old school friends will be there as well, it's going to be fun."

"I look forward to meeting your parents," Jules said with genuine feeling.

He was enjoying himself. It was nice having time away from the house and it's worries for a few hours. For Molly too, it was a chance to relax and find out more about Jules and his family, which would no doubt filter into the pages of her work. Both were intrigued by the news from the Professor and Jules agreed to drive them both to the museum in the morning. At ten thirty he helped with the washing up and drove back to the house while Molly dried the dishes, put them away and arranged the flowers in a vase. A good night's sleep was in order, for tomorrow who knows what was waiting to be discovered in the pages of the ledgers.

25
Holeford Museum

Friday 23rd August. Morning

The supermarket manager had reserved a parking space for Molly and waited excitedly for her arrival. His jaw nearly hit the floor when a huge Range Rover turned in off the High Street driven by the Viscount of Exford and headed towards him. The window slid silently down and he then saw Molly waving frantically from the passenger seat.

"Hi Charlie, thank you for this, I hope we're not putting you to too much trouble."

"No problem," Charlie said, his eyes looking past Molly towards Jules who also smiled and waved. He wasn't sure whether he should salute or bow to the viscount, who was smaller in real life than he imagined from the pictures he'd seen. He moved the bollard, allowing Jules to park, then opened the door for Molly, while Jules climbed out of the driver side. Charlie took the opportunity to admire the lavish interior, he had never seen such luxury on four wheels.

Jules joined them. "Good morning. You must be Charlie," he said, holding out his hand.

Charlie bowed his head and shook his hand. "It's an honour to meet you, sir."

"Molly's told me all about you on the way down here. Congratulations on your promotion."

"Thank you, sir."

"Charlie's an electrician as well," Molly chipped in.

Charlie looked at Jules, trying to read from his expression how much he knew about his past.

"That must come in very handy," Jules said. "Do you know anything about air conditioning?" He unexpectedly asked him, "Mine seems to be on the blink. It was stuck on freezing all the way down here this morning."

Charlie then noticed four figures move through the back door out into the car park and he understood the problem.

"I'm no expert but I think you'll find it's a content problem." Charlie sounded very convincing as Molly looked away to hide her grin as the ghosts joined them. "In my experience you'll find the system will reset later today. Probably once you return to the abbey."

"Well, I hope you're right, thank you for your advice. Come on Molly, uncle will be waiting for us." They crossed the road towards the museum, "What a nice lad, I've never heard of content problems before, he obviously knows his stuff."

"Yes, he certainly knows his stuff," Molly replied, then laughed out loud. Just down the road Wilf, George, Alice and Tom were stood on the pedestrian crossing in a neat line emulating the cover of The Beatles '*Abbey Road*' album. Wilf looked back at Molly with a wide grin.

"What's funny?" Jules asked.

"It's nothing," Molly said.

They entered the museum and went immediately downstairs to the basement where they'd arranged to meet the professor. Jules was fascinated to see the modern facility built into the brick vaulted space. It had certainly changed since his last visit. Molly approached the automatic doors, which obediently opened with a hiss and they both entered the laboratory.

"Hello, you two," the professor said, looking up from a large microscope.

"This is like something from a science fiction film." Jules said looking around, impressed by the modern storage facility and expensive looking equipment on the work benches. In the middle of the room stood a metal table on which the books from the tomb were laid out. One of them was open to view.

The professor slipped down off of his stool. "I'm glad you like it. It was kindly funded by an anonymous benefactor to whom the museum will be forever grateful."

"You mean you don't know who paid for it, that's amazing."

"I have a few ideas, but that person won't own up," the professor said, while studying Jules's face for any reaction. Nothing was forthcoming. "Right, let me show you what I've found. Firstly, there's this. It's of no real consequence but it is amusing." He pointed at a section of Latin wording. "Roughly translated this passage mentions Brother Augustine who owned a parrot called 'Bishop.' The monk worked on one of the farms and sang in the choir but wherever he went the parrot followed."

Molly's eyes lit up. "Bishop... his name's Bishop," she mused.

"Yes, I know. Isn't it fun? Even the Benedictines had a sense of humour."

Molly was thinking of Wilf's parrot, 'Flint.' *'Could they be one and the same? How exciting'* she thought.

"Now, let's look at the second volume. Again, apart from the rarity of the text, it's all about farm yields and crop rotation. There was nothing unusual until I found this illumination around the beginning of this particular passage. Firstly, why illuminate any entries to a farming record? And let's be fair, they haven't held back. There are many examples of decoration throughout but this one has a twist." He held a large magnifying glass to the illustrated border of the text.

"It looks like something from '*The Lord of the Rings*,'" Jules said in fascination, he loved that book. All three of them leant in close, trying to work out the wording.

Molly took hold of the glass and studied the text closely while the other two stepped back out of her light.

"You have a rare and precious object here Jules, it needs to be well cared for," the professor whispered as they both watched Molly studying the text intently.

"I've become very aware of that," Jules replied.

"It might be rare and precious, but can I try something?" Molly asked interrupting their conversation. "Jules, can you pass me my handbag?"

He collected her bag from a chair by the door and handed it to her. She unzipped it and fumbled around inside. "I know it's in here somewhere...trouble with this bag is, it has so many compartments," she continued, using both hands to pull apart and unzip pockets. "Ah! There you are." She pulled out a small mirror from a pouch that both men assumed was some sort of make-up bag. "Right, I wonder if this will work?" She held the mirror at right angles to the illuminated text. "Prof, look at this."

The professor lowered his reading glasses perched on his forehead, bent down and looked into the mirror. Jules watched on bemused by the two academics. From the basement beyond the glass doors the ghosts watched with interest.

"My goodness Molly, you're right. It's mirror writing. Jules, grab a pen and paper from the desk and get ready to write this down."

Jules joined them at the bench, pen ready in hand.

"Now hold the mirror steady Molly."

"I'm trying," she said, her hands trembling with excitement.

The Professor slowly read out the text revealed in the mirror, letter by letter, "REX MAGNAILA DEI, QUAE OPINIONEM NOSTRAM SUS-TINENT, NUNQUAM OBTIEBIT. Are you getting all this Jules?"

"Yes…Yes go on. What does it mean?"

Molly moved the mirror around the artwork. "I'm not sure but there's more."

The Professor continued reading out what seemed to be random letters. "OCCULTA ERUNT DONEC REVERTAMUR AD OPUS SUUM IN AETERNA GLORIA RESUSCITATUM." Molly put the mirror down and they all gathered around Jules' notes.

"It's just a series of indiscriminate letters," Jules said, disappointed. The professor wasn't listening. He ran his fingers along the writing mumbling to himself.

"Not so, young Jules, this is a clue." The room suddenly cooled, as the four ghosts moved in for a closer look. Molly discreetly held up a finger to tame their excitement.

"The king will never obtain… the wonders of God… that sustain our belief… They shall be hidden until we return, resurrected in… everlasting glory to continue his work." They all stood silently as they digested the implications of the words.

Jules trembled, "Wow! that sends a shiver down my spine. Does that mean the monks concealed the treasures of the monastery?"

"It would appear so. If the king's commissioner had found this, they would have lost their heads as well as their pensions."

"So, my hunch was right," Molly said with great relief.

The Professor smiled at her and continued, "I can only assume there's more information hidden in these pages indicating where they concealed it. It could be a long job. But we get first go. The British Library already have scholars queuing up to see these documents. You can't keep a secret these days. I need to keep going on this. You must go back to the abbey and don't tell anyone what we've found for the time being."

"But prof," Molly appealed.

"You are better carrying on with your work at the house. If you're seen spending too much time here, someone may become suspicious. We need to buy some time so that I can examine them carefully before we're under pressure to release them to the national archive."

Molly looked crest fallen, "OK, I understand, but please promise me you'll call me as soon as you find anything else."

"Don't worry, you'll be the first to know. This is a once in a lifetime discovery, you've done exceptionally well."

Molly placed the mirror back in her bag and took one last look at the documents before turning to the door, "Come on Jules, the prof has work to do." Jules could sense her disappointment at having to leave further investigation to someone else.

"Ooh! One more thing before you go. Have you thought any more about my suggestion last night?" the professor asked, holding his hands out to indicate all the facilities that would be at her disposal if she became the new curator.

"I've thought of little else. I don't know the best way to say this." She paused trying to recall the words she had rehearsed in the early hours of the morning. "I'm flattered that you asked me and maybe in the future I'll regret saying this, but I still have so much to learn. London is where I can expand my horizons, there are so many opportunities available there. It's an exciting place to be and with my PhD hopefully in my hand next year and all the contacts I've made... well, I hope you understand." She looked anxiously at him.

"I understand perfectly Molly, you have a wonderful career ahead of you. Never forget, we are all here for you and we are all incredibly proud of you."

"Thank you for understanding, I'm eternally grateful for your support and encouragement."

The topic of conversation on the way home was dominated by what other information might be contained in the books.

"I'm sorry you're not staying to help uncle Dom… Look, I can turn round and take you back to Holeford, our book can wait a few days."

"No, much as I'd like to, the prof is right, I mustn't draw too much outside attention. Anyway, I have to complete my research for your book. I only have a few days left and then I must get back to London. I can finish it off there between my own studies."

"Fancy a monk having a parrot. You don't think of them having pets."

"They were only human, Jules. They had hopes and fears just the same as we do today. I'm sure they had fun as well. Why not? It must have been a novelty though. I can imagine a dog or a cat, but that was rather exotic, I wonder where it came from? Fancy calling it *Bishop*," she added, dropping hints to the ghosts in the back of the car.

"Do you think 'Bishop' is your 'Flint'?" Alice asked Wilf.

"I doubt it. That was nearly five hundred years ago. I assume Flint fell off his perch in the aviary a lot more recently."

"Even so, you could ask him."

"Don't be ridiculous. You can't have a conversation with a parrot, this isn't some Disney movie. All he ever says is 'bless you.'"

"There you are! That's just what a bishop would say… I rest my case." Alice said, smugly folding her arms.

"Anyway, he's not 'my Flint.' You know full well, he comes and goes, sometimes for weeks at a time."

"Probably goes off to visit his flock," George commented sarcastically.

As they approached the estate there were a noticeable number of veteran and trade vehicles on the same route.

"I thought the show didn't start 'till tomorrow?" Molly questioned.

"It doesn't, but the stands will begin to fill up this afternoon and into the evening in preparation for the morning. The club organise a pre-show party in the beer tent tonight for the volunteers and traders camping overnight. Last year they even had a band playing. They certainly know how to enjoy themselves."

Jules steered the Range Rover off the main road and through the South Gate entrance. The barrier lifted automatically, and they headed down the long winding drive towards the house. They were taken aback by the flash of colour and activity on the show field.

"Blimey, they've been busy," Jules said. Flags were flying and cars of all eras were moving into position on their club stands. Stall holders were busy setting up their pitches and more tents had appeared. The food marquee was surrounded by vehicles as traders beavered away carting their goods inside. Caravans and tents had started to populate the camping area high up by the trees. Officials in hi-vis vests were busy waving and pointing as they orchestrated the arrivals. The rides in the travelling funfair were spinning and whirring as the engineers carried out their safety checks.

Blips and squeaks could be heard as the PA sound system was being checked. A short, fat man in an orange coat was walking round the arena with a radio mic, "One… Two… One… Two… Icicles…Bicycles… Testing… Testing."

The sound reverberated off of the house and echoed through the trees of the distant forest.

"Gracious, I think the giraffes will be able to hear that and they're two miles away," Jules laughed.

The sound man raised the mic to his mouth again, indicating with his left hand towards the commentary booth to reduce the volume. He repeated the test. His voice was still clearly audible but now at a volume that didn't blow the spectators hats off.

"That's better, he was very loud. There are a lot of people over there already," Molly observed.

"That's nothing, you wait till you see it in the morning. Tell your mum and dad to get here early to avoid the traffic queues. They've got the VIP parking pass, so once they're in they won't have far to walk. I'm looking forward to meeting them."

"My old history teacher's coming as well. She's doing her fortune telling to raise money for the school."

"That's unusual, is she any good?"

"Yes, she's ever so good at it. I hope she's bringing her young son with her, I haven't seen him for a while."

"Maybe I should consult her, she may be able to predict the future of the estate and perhaps even solve the murder?"

"Perhaps," Molly said. She was absolutely certain Carolyn could help but unfortunately the sceptics in this world may not be so convinced. As deputy head she could lose her credibility if she went too far. The board of governors simply wouldn't understand. Sadly, she could only use her skills as an entertainment.

"Father's on the board of governors for the school," Jules added.

Molly grinned, for the moment, she had forgotten the company she was keeping.

"I didn't know that, your family seem to be involved in everything."

"It comes with the territory I'm afraid, we don't just inherit the estate we also inherit a bucket load of responsibilities far beyond our land and buildings."

Molly looked across at Jules. "I don't envy you all of that."

"Hey, you needn't feel sorry for me, it's not all bad, we work hard but then so do a lot of people. I don't envy the dairy farmer who gets up at unearthly hours to milk and tend his cows 365 days a year. Look where we get to live, it's pretty special."

Molly looked at the vista unfolding in front of her through the windscreen. Panning from left to right, she could see the chimney of her little gatehouse cottage poking out from the trees, the safari park, the house and gardens and the show field with its road stretching away through the trees towards the east. "It is lovely here and so beautifully kept."

"I can't take credit for that, we have some brilliant ground staff."

"Even so, they only do what you tell them. Don't be so modest, you and your father are the driving force behind all this. Without you this place would be nothing."

"Maybe, but we're only custodians for the next generation. Who knows what the future will bring? Perhaps I do need to see your fortune teller friend after all," he grinned.

The car rumbled over the cattle grid at the end of the drive.

"Can you drop me at the front door please? I need to tell the Duke what happened and pick up some books from the library," Molly said, gathering up her handbag from the foot well.

Jules swung the car around the gravel turning circle and stopped at the front of the house. James appeared, walking down the steps to greet the arrivals and opened the passenger door for Molly.

"Thank you for coming with me this morning, I'll keep you posted on any progress." She slid out of the seat and stood by the door, smiling at James. "Thank you," she said, trying to hide a grin. She would never get used to the treatment she received from the staff, it was all too surreal, like being in a TV drama. The ghosts slid out through the back door and waited.

Jules remained in the driver's seat, fiddling with the heating controls on the central consul. "OK, I'll catch up with you at the car show tomorrow. Your friend Charlie was right about the climate control in here, it seems to be working fine now. Just as I pulled up it corrected itself," he shrugged.

"There you are then, see you tomorrow, thanks again for the lift." She closed the door and waved as he drove off.

Molly turned to the ghosts and out of sight of James, raised an eyebrow.

"Don't look at us like that. We can't help it, being cold goes with the job," Wilf said, shrugging his shoulders.

She turned and ran up the steps into the cavernous hall as James calmly closed the door behind her.

"The Duke is waiting for you in the library, Miss."

"Thank you," she called back.

Molly arrived at the library doors, knocked gently and entered. The Duke was sitting behind his desk at the far end surrounded by paperwork. He looked up over his reading glasses. "So, tell me how did you get on?"

She joined the Duke and sat in the green leather high backed chair opposite and told him all that had they had discovered that morning. The Duke's eyes lit up. It sparked long forgotten memories of when he himself had spent time with Dominic on their archaeological adventures. He remembered the thrill from the smallest of discoveries magnified by the effort needed to find it.

"How does it feel, Molly? Tell me. It must be thrilling to find out your hunch was right."

"It's exhilarating, sir. I guess it's what we all work towards in our profession, but it never ceases to be a wonder when the hours of investigation bring such rewards."

"Do you really think there are any of the monastery's valuables still on the estate?"

"To be honest, it's very unlikely. It was nearly five hundred years ago. The chances are, even if they did hide anything, someone will have stolen it during or not long after the disillusionment. Just like the grave robbers in Egypt. Those who buried it also knew where to find it, but I'm only guessing. There may be yet more clues in the documents." Molly shrugged her shoulders wishing she was at the museum, ploughing through the volumes, looking for any hints.

"Be sure to keep me informed when Dominic finds anything."

"Don't worry, you'll be the first to know."

"A little bird tells me you're heading back to London soon."

"Yes, my research here is nearly complete, so I can finish off the manuscript there. I have deadlines on my PhD work which has been a little neglected and I need to do some catching up."

"I hope we haven't been too much of a distraction for you. That wasn't the intention."

"Not at all, I've been able to prepare some work at the lodge, so it won't be too onerous and I wouldn't have missed this opportunity for the world. I'm so glad that you asked me."

"The feeling is mutual. I look forward to reading the first draft. I also heard that you share a flat in Eltham. That's a long way from the British Museum," he commented.

"You're well informed, Sir." '*The little bird had to be Jules,*' she thought.

"My father was good friends with the Courtauld's. They lived in Eltham Palace. Is that near your flat?"

"It's just round the corner. It's a beautiful house. I love the Art Deco architecture and walking round the gardens. English Heritage look after it now and I have a pass, so I spend some of my free time there enjoying the grounds well away from the madness of the city. I guess, despite enjoying lots of the benefits of London, I'm still a country girl at heart."

"Even so it must be a hideous journey from there to the V&A."

"It's not the easiest trip on the underground, fortunately my work is quite flexible, so I try to avoid the rush hours."

"Then I have a proposition for you." Molly sat upright in her seat looking a little perplexed. "I think this may help you. We have a house in Kensington that's been divided into three apartments. Jules has the top floor and I have the first floor. Not that we have much time to use it currently. This is where you fit in, the ground floor flat is unoccupied at the moment so you're welcome to use it while you're working at the museums. The V&A is only a short walk from there."

"What me… live in Kensington? I can't afford to stay there, that's very generous of you, but I simply don't have the funds."

"What if we call it payment in kind for your work?"

"No, I couldn't, that's too much. Thank you, but really, that's far too generous."

The Duke looked down at the paperwork on his desk rubbing his stubbly chin as he considered her situation. "What rent do you pay at present, if you don't mind me asking?"

"Not at all, two hundred pounds a month, I share with another girl who, coincidentally works at Eltham Palace."

"So, how about if you pay the estate two hundred pounds a month. You get to stay near your office, and you'd also be on hand while working on the book for us. I appreciate you won't necessarily work at the museum after your studies are complete, but I think it would be helpful to you in the short term."

"Can I go and see it before agreeing," Molly asked with caution. Inside, her mind was saying '*Yes, Yes, Yes, what are you are waiting for?*'

"Of course you can." The Duke smiled warmly. "Let me know when you're able to visit and I'll tell the housekeeper to expect you. She'll be pleased to have some company. She lives in the basement flat and keeps everything spick and span for us."

Molly tempered her enthusiasm. "Then I think that would be very acceptable." '*No more long journeys on crowded public transport, easy access to central London, walks in Kensington Gardens and a classy apartment,*' her mind was a whirl of excitement. "This is very generous of you, I don't know what to say."

"I think the arrangement would work well for us all. Now, I must get on with this correspondence and I'm sure you have work to do," he said dismissively.

"Thank you, yes I do." She rose and walked to her desk at the opposite end of the room, picked up several files, put them in her briefcase and walked to the door. As she opened it she turned to face the Duke. "Thank you again."

The Duke raised a hand and waved absently, his mind absorbed by the document on his desk.

26
Showtime

Saturday 24th August. Morning

At ten o'clock, Molly locked the door to the lodge, boarded her golf buggy and headed to the car show. The excitement at the showground was already tangible. She couldn't help noticing the build-up of traffic on the road outside the estate and the increased movement in the safari park. The sound from the main road was different this morning, it was more than just the weight of traffic, unusual engine sounds and snorting exhausts passed by as exhibitors continued to arrive. She couldn't see clearly through the trees and shrubs forming the boundary of her little garden but there were definitely a lot more sounds. She drove the buggy along the path towards the house. In the distance, she could see the kaleidoscope of colour covering the showground. The spectator's cars poured from the east gate coming into view through the woods. Their vehicles moved into the temporary car parks high on the hill. Marshals in their brightly coloured tabards buzzed around like little insects, directing the drivers into neat rows.

Molly drove past the front of the house and over the Palladian bridge, towards the VIP parking area. She stopped after crossing the bridge to fully take in the spectacle. She had been surprised by the activity in the field yesterday, but this was on another scale. The show field stretched from the railway station at the north end of the lake, over the east gate road and off to the far side of the estate in the south. The stands were now full of cars of all makes and colours. Crowds gathered around them like ants to an accidentally dropped ice lolly. The aisles were fluid with visitors moving in orderly lines, while flags and banners fluttered like a thousand butterflies. The heady sound of all the activities were being blended together and carried off on the westerly breeze, adding to the atmosphere.

Molly drove on again entering the VIP parking area. She looked around in the hope of seeing her father's blue Austin Ambassador but without success. Still, not to worry, she'd arranged to meet them by the big wheel at eleven.

An area by the entrance gate was reserved for staff vehicles, she couldn't help the satisfied grin as she pulled up. She was going to miss some of the perks that came with her temporary position. Wearing her estate pass on the lanyard around her neck, she walked the few steps to the security entrance. Colin was on duty and waved her past with a warm greeting.

She now entered the main throng and was immediately approached by a programme salesman. "No, thank you," she politely said.

Not to be deterred, he again offered the programme, "You're staff," he said pointing at the lanyard, "You get a free copy."

"Well, thank you then." She took the booklet and placed it in her shoulder bag. Her mum and dad would like it.

Now she was inside the park barriers, her senses went into overload. Thousands of people already occupied the field and with them came thousands of voices. Not one conversation was discernible amongst the burble of chatter. Then the smells hit her. Bacon and burgers mixed with candyfloss, ice-cream and doughnuts played havoc with her tastebuds, all culminating in an unexpected yearning for food. Her mouth began to water with the sudden impulse to eat. *'Don't be ridiculous, you've just had your breakfast,'* she thought, moving slowly with the flow. As she headed deeper into the site her hearing was assaulted by a mixture of musical styles all playing at the same time. Steam organs and the PA system competed with the fairground for attention as the children screamed with joy as they spun, whizzed, slid and whirled on the rides. Passing the crowded activity in the huge white canvas food tent, she headed towards the 'Holeford Modern School' flag flying at the end of the trader's aisle. She passed the beer tent with its makeshift garden of straw bales, now beginning to populate, as a four-piece folk band burst into song. She had fifteen minutes to kill before meeting her mum and dad and was thrilled to see Carolyn, with her son George talking to passers-by.

"Hi, how lovely to see you," Carolyn called out, frantically waving Molly over to join her. They hugged affectionately while Jack gave her a warm smile as he polished his convertible car.

"Hello, this is great, you look amazing." Carolyn was dressed in full gypsy outfit for her fortune telling act. "And look at you George," Molly said, admiring their young son who was also dressed for the part in dungarees over a white shirt and bandana. "I can't believe your four, you're so grown up."

"He's becoming quite a handful," Carolyn said warmly.

"I thought you might have been busy with your fortune telling by now," Molly observed.

"I'm just having a break, I started at nine thirty, it's been frantic. Fortunately, I do have some help this year." Molly looked towards the colourful red and white striped tent as Wilf, George and Alice all waved, before passing back through the canvas wall to the interior. "They're trying to keep a low profile, you know what they're like with big crowds in the daytime. Tom's there as well, poor thing. He seems a nice lad but what a sad story. Still, he's in good hands." Jack quickly put the cleaning materials in the boot of his beloved Triumph Spitfire and joined them. "Hello Molly, you look wonderful."

"So do you and young George has grown so," she said, thinking how much he was beginning to look like his father. "Your car's looking lovelier than ever."

"Thanks, I do my best. We thought we might see you. After all, you are a resident here, at least for a while."

"I wasn't going to miss this. I'm only staying on the estate for a few more days, then I must get back to London."

Carolyn clapped her hands together. "I forgot, you're a high-flyer. It only seems like yesterday you were in my history class, now look at you, I'm so proud of you."

Molly smiled, "I've got you and the ghosts to thank for that. After all, it was you that introduced me to the professor."

"And the rest is history... history, get it?" Jack said, pausing for a laugh, but receiving only groans.

"You're not going to believe who came to have his fortune told this morning." Carolyn said excitedly, "The viscount himself, he made the security man wait in his buggy while he came into my tent and had his palm read."

"Jules joked that he was going to try and see you, I didn't think he'd actually come."

Carolyn's eyes opened wide, "Jules... you're on first name terms with him?"

"Yes, he's been helping with the research."

"Oh! I see." Carolyn said, wondering about their relationship.

"Sorry, I can't stop just now, I'm in a bit of a hurry. I have to meet mum and dad over by the big wheel, but we'll all come back and see you later for a cup of tea and a catch up. Maybe I can take George to the fairground, I'd enjoy that." She headed off towards the rendezvous point, following the aisle past the stationary engine display. The heavy machines were thumping rhythmically, spitting water and exhaust fumes up into the air. Men in overalls were fiddling with other machines, attempting to bring them to life, while behind them their families sat contentedly outside their caravans and tents chatting, with coffees in hand. Molly was amused as a hose pipe pulsed a jet of water into a tin bath from a pump that was connected to a Lister engine by a leather belt. In the bath, a disgruntled-looking plastic duck spun round in the whirlpool, its eyes pleading for rescue from its spinning hell. All the while, its proud owner wiped over the freshly painted green engine block with a damp cloth. The smell of the hot oil and steel, even the noxious exhaust fumes, added to the ambience. As she closed in on her target, she passed between two showman's engines in full steam. Again, her senses were overwhelmed by the smell of coal, smoke and oil. Their polished brass and candy twist columns rising up, supporting roofs over their glossy painted iron bodies, was striking.

The heat from the boilers along with the gentle rhythm of the giant mechanical beast's pistons ticking over, evoked an earlier time.

The house and gardens were also getting increasingly busy as the visitors drove out of the safari park and parked in the overflow area to continue their visit before heading over to the showground. Amongst them and unknown to the general staff, were specifically deployed plain clothed police officers. Montgomery was convinced something was likely to occur using the cover of the Car show. After all, the Sci-Fi festival had been used to hide criminal activity only a short time ago. He was convinced that their business hadn't been concluded. Leads from that event were still being followed up in London, but he was certain the painting forgery was linked to the murder. Pieces of the jigsaw were starting to fall into place. He had ideas, but that was not good enough, he had a feeling, a coppers intuition, that another attempt would be made, probably in the gallery itself. To that end, he had detectives disguised as estate security monitoring the house.

On the surface no more patrolling was visible than on a normal day, he didn't want to raise any suspicions. But with all due respect to the estate guards, his men were trained professionals and better able to deal with serious crime.

In the house all was quiet. In the Long Gallery, guards sat at either end watching the visitor movement closely. Their demeanour was jovial and warm as families and couples drifted along admiring the paintings and antiques. Small, escorted groups regularly passed through with their guide, Barbara Greenacre, pausing at prominent pieces to give detailed information. Her audience nodded and mumbled as they navigated together down the corridor of art, eventually passing through the door into the lobby to use the public toilets and exit the building. At eleven o'clock, Barbara had finished her tour and returned to the gallery with a tray full of drinks from the coffee machine set up in the corner of the ballroom for staff use. She handed them out to the guards and rested on the chair by the door, passing time with them before the next tour, at twelve thirty.

In the travelling fair, Molly was thrilled to find Peter and Joan waiting by the ticket booth under the big wheel. "Are you going to have a go?" she asked as she hugged them both.

"No, I don't think so dear, not with Peter's vertigo."

"Not with my vertigo," he repeated, as he looked up high into the workings of the machine, his fears confirmed by the screaming and giggling of the riders as they spun around sedately above them.

"Have you been here long, dear?" Joan asked.

"No, I just had time to see Jack and Carolyn and then come over here. It's a huge event. Do you remember when it all started as a small car display at the school fete? Now look at it, there must be thousands of people here."

"Did you know the food tent is the longest temporary food hall in the South West? I read that in the Exford Chronicle, so it must be true," Peter said confidently.

"It certainly looks big. I'm parched, do you fancy a drink? We can go to the member's tent using your VIP passes. It's all included, and you get a good view of the arena without the crush of people," Molly said.

"I'm not sure dear, this is very generous of your employer, but I don't feel right about it," Joan said, feeling nervous at the thought of mixing with fully paid members and those who she perceived to be of a higher class.

Molly detected her reticence, "Come on mum, you don't get this chance very often. It's mostly car club people in there, Jack and Carolyn might well turn up. If not, I'll take you to their stand later."

"Alright then, dear," Joan agreed, nervously.

Negotiating the crowds of people, the three of them set off towards the member's tent.

"Hey look! There's Regan's car from '*The Sweeney*' parked next to '*The Saints*' Volvo," Peter said, veering off to the 'cars of the stars' exhibition. Molly and Joan reluctantly followed.

"You remember Sergeant Montgomery, from the supermarket robbery... well, the Sweeney car is his. He's here investigating the safari park death and the fake painting. He's a Detective Inspector now."

"You're joking... he was hopeless at arresting those burglars," Peter exclaimed.

"Not so hopeless now. He's been with the Metropolitan police for years. He still appears to be useless, but I think it's a bit of an act now, don't underestimate him."

Montgomery and Sergeant Dexter mingled with the masses around the arena while viewing the parade of post-war cars. However, their attention was concentrated on the people rather than the vehicles. All the police and security staff were on red alert, ready to pounce at a moment's notice.

"Look gov, there's Miss Goodall with her parents heading towards the arena. They've stopped to look at your car."

"They've got good taste, Dexter." Montgomery grinned, he was proud of his car and thrilled to be showing it off after all the mockery he had received from his fellow officers.

Their earpieces crackled. With two-way radios hidden inside their casual clothes to avoid detection, the undercover officers were contacted by the control room every thirty minutes to ensure all was in order.

Montgomery leaned into his collar "Bug eye one, affirmative," he whispered.

"Bug eye two, confirmed," Dexter said, also leaning into his collar.

They continued to watch the event as an 'Austin Seven' spluttered by with the mayor in the passenger seat waving enthusiastically to the crowd. He was followed by a stream of pre-war Austin's circling in the arena before lining up in the middle. Along the aisle behind the policemen, a string of cars from the 1960's moved slowly along, escorted by marshals in 'hi-vis' vests keeping the public a safe distance from the moving vehicles. At the back of the line was a black, *Mk II* Jaguar, its 3.8 litre engine hardly audible as it idled with enough torque to travel at walking speed. As the parade turned towards the entrance to the arena, the car broke rank and carried on towards the exit to the VIP parking area, the driver paused to talk to the guard then passed through the gate and over the bridge towards the house.

Molly and her family arrived at the VIP tent to be greeted by security. "Hello again Colin, you get everywhere," Molly said. Peter and Joan were impressed as they passed through without question, not even having to show their passes. They were greeted by a waitress and shown to a table right by the window overlooking the arena.

"I could get used to this," Peter said. "Is it always like this for you now?"

"I wish," Molly said.

A group of well-dressed visitors stood in a circle near the bar drinking champagne. They were talking loudly, laughing heartily as they boasted about their cars, holidays and life in general, each one determined to outdo the other. The man at the centre of attention politely made his excuses, broke away from them and headed to their table.

"Hello Molly, how lovely. I wondered if I might see you in here. And this must be your mum and dad."

They all stood up, but Peter's chin was still on the floor. "Hello Jules, please let me introduce you to Joan and Peter. This is Viscount Exford."

"Delighted, please call me Jules." They shook hands. "Have you got a drink?"

"Not yet, we've only just arrived," Molly said, sitting down next to him at the table while Peter and Joan sat opposite, both stunned into silence.

"Molly's told me so much about you, you must be so proud of her."

"Y…yes we are very proud… lovely place you have here," Peter said, feeling embarrassed at this ridiculous comment.

"Thanks, yes, it is a lovely place to live. Have you visited before?"

"We visited with Molly to see the animals when she was younger. She loved the petting zoo."

"Dad, shut up, you're embarrassing me," Molly said, looking a little flushed. Jules grinned as he saw her unease.

He requested champagne from the waiter while they chatted warmly. Peter and Joan soon relaxed in his company aided by the sparkling wine. The group that Jules had left were all taking furtive glimpses towards them and whispering. Outside, the announcer was addressing the crowd through the PA system, reeling off a stream of information on the cars and further attractions coming to the arena. The crowds were getting bigger and more animated, but in the members tent all was calm. The gentle burble of voices, clink of glasses and clash of cutlery created a relaxing atmosphere.

Peter was becoming even more relaxed as the drink flowed. He talked of how he met Joan whilst working in the theatre. Then of the milk float he had seen on the Holeford car stand and told of the days when he himself delivered milk with Molly joining him during the school holidays. He was tempted to show off his magician skills, if only he had a pack of cards. Joan squeezed his knee hard under the table. He got the message and stopped talking, giving the others a chance to join in the conversation.

The ghosts progressed cautiously around the showground, quickly moving between stands and sitting in empty cars to watch the day unfold.

"I don't understand this cloak and dagger stuff," Tom said. "Why can't we just wander around and look at everything nicely."

"Not that easy old boy!" George said. "You forget that amongst all these people there will be a small percentage of psychics and we don't want to cause a scene."

"And dogs," Wilf chipped in. "Don't forget dogs."

"Yeah, dogs are the worst, they don't miss a trick. You need to be careful around dogs, they're hypersensitive." Alice added.

All four of the ghosts were squeezed in the back of the *Mk I* Jaguar leading the 'big cat' parade towards the arena.

The chairman of the Jaguar Owners Club, a middle-aged man dressed in a tweed suit wearing his club tie, topped off with flat cap and buff coloured driving gloves, was totally unaware of their presence. With his arm resting on the window sill, left hand on the wheel, he was soaking up the adulation from the passers-by.

"That's odd, where's he going?" Wilf said, noticing a black Jaguar at the rear of the parade turn off towards the VIP entrance, "Excuse me everyone." He quickly went out through the side door, floated up above the crowds, caught up with the rogue Jaguar and dropped down through the roof, expertly landing on the back seat.

"That was impulsive, even for Wilf," George commented.

The men in the front of Wilf's car were silent, the passenger constantly looking at his watch. They pulled up at the gate and the driver wound down his window.

"Going somewhere, sir?" the guard asked politely.

"We're picking up a VIP, at the house," the driver explained and wound the window back up.

"Very good sir," the guard waved them through and radioed the control room.

The car continued slowly around the front of the house turning right along the side towards the petting zoo. The driver turned the car round outside the stable yard and pulled up by the gallery entrance facing towards the south gate over a mile away. The passenger checked his watch again.

Wilf was confused, who were they going to pick up? Jules was at the show, so that only left the Duke, but he never attended these functions. It then dawned on him, he felt a heavy sensation in the pit of his stomach, '*Something was very wrong here.*'

The engine ticked over as the visitors to the house poured out of the lobby into the daylight. They slowed to look at the gleaming black Jaguar which they assumed was placed there to advertise the car show.

The long gallery closed at twelve to allow housekeeping time to spruce it up for the afternoon visits. The car remained parked, the driver impatiently tapping the steering wheel while his passenger watched the exit door. Wilf looked around but everything seemed perfectly normal from his position in the back seat of the car.

At ten past twelve, a well-built man in black jeans, black collarless shirt and a baseball cap pulled down over his eyes, came out of the lobby. He was carrying something wrapped in a sheet, he opened the boot dropped it in, closed it with a thump and got in the back seat alongside Wilf.

"All good," he announced, and rubbed his hands together, "Bloody cold in here," he complained.

"Air con," the driver replied, as he released the handbrake and slowly pulled away, allowing the pedestrians to part and give him clear sight of the road ahead.

"Hello, Fred Smith I believe, I see the gout's cleared up," Wilf said sarcastically, "Been shopping, have we?"

Fred didn't answer.

Montgomery and Dexter watched the parade of Jaguars enter the ring and circle the perimeter. Their radios crackled and burst into life.

"What do you mean asleep?" Montgomery whispered into his collar as Dexter listened intently. "How can they be asleep on duty?... and the tour guide?" He was now becoming more animated. "Coffee?... the coffee was drugged?" The Inspector was now trembling with anticipation. "Please repeat... I'm sorry, did you say a painting is missing... when was this discovered?... The black Jag, yes, I saw... It's leaving from outside the gallery, were on it... call all units." He let go of the collar mic. "Come on Dexter, let's grab my car." They both ducked under the rope and sprinted across the arena towards the 'Cars of the Stars' stand.

"We seem to have a pitch invasion," the commentator announced sarcastically over the PA.

In the member's tent, the announcement had alerted the guests to the antics, they all moved to the windows for a better view.

"Isn't that Montgomery and Dexter?" Molly observed trying to focus through the soft plastic windows of the tent.

"Certainly looks like it. If you'll excuse me, I need to find out what's going on," Jules said, rising to leave the table. He looked at Molly's parents, "It's been a pleasure meeting you both, I hope you enjoy the rest of your day." He then moved quickly through the tent to his buggy and grabbed his two-way radio.

Montgomery and Dexter arrived puffing at the stand, caught their breath and jumped in his Ford. Montgomery started the engine and gingerly moved off through the crowds of people.

They attracted additional interest at the sound of the engine firing up. The public politely moved out of the way, but even so, they made slow progress towards the gate.

"There he is gov!" Dexter pointed excitedly at the black car far in the distance, crossing the cattle grid onto the road winding towards the south gate. They were limited to a walking pace and very aware that their prey was getting away. Dexter had time to admire the refurbished Ford, "Nice car gov. they did a great job."

Montgomery grinned, "It was built for this moment, Dexter. Once we get through the gate, I'll show you what it can do." Dexter looked worried.

PC Singleton, casually dressed in jeans, tee shirt and a denim jacket emblazoned with a '*Motorhead*' logo, ran to the 'Holeford Car Club' stand. He had spotted the old Morris Minor earlier, painted in full police panda car livery of pale blue and white including a blue flashing light mounted on the roof. It looked as if it had just left the set of a sixties TV show. He shrugged his shoulders, '*Beggars can't be choosers*' he thought and jumped into the driver's seat. Behind the car, the owner's family were sat in their folding chairs around the open boot enjoying a well-prepared picnic. They had just taken a bite of the beef paste sandwiches when they saw the car shudder. The owner rose and observed a figure in the driver's seat. Singleton quickly reviewed the simple controls and was pleased to see the keys in the ignition. He turned them and the engine fired readily, blasting the picnickers with a cloud of oil laden fumes. They quickly moved away, coughing and upsetting their chairs with *vol-au-vents* flying in all directions, much to the interest of the dogs parading in the show ring, only a few paces away. The stout lady judge in her tweed suit, who was carefully examining an old English sheep dog, was unceremoniously knocked off her feet, as the canine entrants made a beeline for the discarded picnic, much to the disgust of the owners and amusement of the spectators.

The car owner, choking, angrily pulled open the driver's door. "What the hell do you think you're doing?" he shouted, reaching in to grab the coat of the hijacker.

"I am requisitioning this vehicle in the name of Her Majesty the Queen," the policeman solemnly said, holding his warrant card in the face of the man who looked ready to punch him.

"No, you're bloody not!" the red-faced owner bellowed. Singleton now waved the card to further attract his attention. The man squinted at the warrant card.

"Police? You don't look like the police," he said, accusingly.

"Well, I can assure you I am, sir. Now if you wouldn't mind closing the boot and moving out of the way, I have a villain to catch."

"Where are you taking Monica?"

"Don't worry, I'll be gentle with her," Singleton lied.

He pulled away into the aisle and joined the pursuit at walking pace, the small engine ticking over like a sewing machine while the interior smelt of old car, stale and musty. "In pursuit," he confirmed into his collar mic. He grinned, '*some pursuit*' he thought as he crawled along followed by two dogs, ever hopeful for more sandwiches. He could see Montgomery's car ahead just reaching the gate, having created a pathway through the crowds, this gave him a chance to gain ground.

Montgomery looked in the rear-view mirror and caught a glimpse of the veteran panda car. "What the hell's he driving?"

Dexter looked over his shoulder and laughed. "Well, I suppose it is fitting."

"I'll give him fitting. Of all the cars to commandeer, he picked an old moggy... idiot!" Montgomery exclaimed, as they reached the gate. Security had quickly cleared the public and waved him through, then continued to hold the crowd back while the little panda car caught up.

George, Alice and Tom watched the action from the arena and on seeing the little Morris following Montgomery, quickly joined PC Singleton in the car.

Montgomery now drove cautiously, not trying to attract the attention of the escaping Jaguar until he was ready. '*Not yet*' he thought, '*be patient.*'

He manoeuvred in front of the house so that he could see a direct line from the cattle grid to the south gate. The Jaguar was now nearing the top of the winding road, slowing at each hairpin, the soft suspension causing the heavy vehicle to wallow and oversteer.

"Grab onto something," Montgomery instructed, pushing a red button on the dash. The wail of a thousand banshees erupted from the siren and the ground in front of the car flashed blue, reflecting back the lights mounted behind the grill.

He pushed the accelerator to the floor, gripping the steering wheel tight. *'This was it, time for the chase.'* The rapid acceleration pressed them back into their seats, Dexter grabbing the armrest with his right hand, his eyes wide open with terror.

The Ford leapt forward, wheels spinning, tyres desperately clawing at the ground for grip.

The driver of the Jaguar heard the commotion behind him and saw the flashing light in his mirror. He accelerated hard, the car lurching from side to side as he fought the controls, frantically steering towards the red and white security barrier below the stone archway of the south gate. His passengers gritted their teeth.

Behind them, the Ford passed over the cattle grid at speed.

"Corner gov!… corner ahead!" Dexter screamed.

"We're not doing corners today," Montgomery announced over the roar of the engine, "Hold on tight."

They left the road and hit the adjoining field at force, mud and grass flying past the windows.

"Rally suspension," Montgomery shouted, gleefully maintaining a direct line towards the gate.

Tyres fought for traction on the turf, before the car accelerated across the road, then grass, road and even more grass until finally leaping over the kerb towards the gate, their prey now only yards ahead. Montgomery grinned, his eyes wide open, hands firmly on the wheel, leaning forward, relishing every second of the pursuit. He was Jack Regan, and this was no TV show.

PC Singleton had now joined the chase, he could see the tramline trail through the grass left by the Ford but wasn't brave enough to follow, sticking to the winding single track tarmac road instead. *'More haste less speed,*' he reminded himself. Not that he had a lot of choice about the speed.

The Jaguar continued towards the barrier. Two guards stood in the road holding up their hands. The driver scowled and accelerated.

The guards dived out of the way as the car hit the barrier shattering it into a thousand pieces, showering them with the splinters.

"He's going to kill someone," Dexter screamed, his fingers digging into the arm rest.

Montgomery studied the route ahead. The busy main road was very close, his mind computing the various scenarios in a split second. His high-speed pursuit training now showing its worth.

The Jaguar swung violently, out onto the main road. Paying no attention to traffic, its tail slid into a passing Volvo which in turn spun into the path of an approaching Mercedes.

Montgomery changed down a gear and with expert use of the hand brake swung his car onto the road whilst avoiding the carnage. Dexter's eyes were wide open at the scene of devastation outside. Siren wailing and lights flashing, the traffic ahead, had at least some warning and took evasive action, swerving into the overgrown verges to make way.

PC Singleton exited the estate onto the main road and followed as fast as he could. He had time to see the faces of the drivers in the crash. They were both moving, so he assumed they were not too badly injured. They looked in bewilderment at the panda car taking up the rear of the chase, its little blue light flashing apologetically on the roof.

"That's a 3.8 *Mk II* Jag ahead, it's got the same engine as the E Type," Montgomery explained.

Dexter didn't really care. His teeth were gritted, expecting impact at any time. How they'd turned onto the road and remained in one piece had defied the law of physics. He wanted to close his eyes, but they were out on stalks, meanwhile his heart was trying to beat its way out of his chest.

"The Rembrandt's gone." A voice from the control room said over the radio.

"Message received," Montgomery replied, weaving violently between the stationary cars stopped at awkward angles either side of the road. The

Jaguar see-sawed from side to side, suspension springs fighting to keep it level as it also laced its way through the obstacles.

"Got more power than us but we have the chassis of a rally car... this thing can handle anything," Montgomery shouted over the roar of the engine.

The road was becoming less congested with show traffic as they headed towards the junction to the village. Smoke poured from the Jaguar's tyres, as the driver fought the controls.

Montgomery's car was engulfed in the cloud of burnt rubber, as the Jaguar turned violently towards the village.

"Left... Left!" Dexter instructed, coughing on the fumes.

Montgomery grabbed the handbrake, executing another controlled slide, with the tyres squealing, the smell of their burnt rubber now filling the car as he swung it through ninety degrees. He hit the accelerator to the floor, now closing in on the Jag again, smoke still poured from its tyres or was it from the twin exhaust?

"He's burning oil, valves are going," Montgomery said smugly.

"Oh, goody, he might break down before we all die," Dexter barked back sarcastically.

Both cars unashamedly passed the villages thirty mile an hour sign at well over seventy on the narrowing road. The houses were now in sight but to enter the hamlet, they first had to negotiate a charming historic medieval humpback bridge.

The Jaguar again braked hard, this time shredding rubber from the tyres. The front wheels rammed into the hump and the suspension pushed up into the chassis. Momentum carried the vehicle over, nose diving down the other side as the rear lifted off the ground, wheels spinning wildly in the air, then it smacked down on the apex of the bridge, gained purchase and miraculously the car accelerated forward. The driver fought the steering to gain control of the heavy car which weaved and finally straightened as it tore past the Abbey Inn. It had taken Wilf some considerable concentration to stay in the car, his head and shoulders now popping up through the roof as they landed.

"He's still going gov," Dexter said, expecting any minute to see the car plunge through the side of a cottage.

"Hold on!"

Montgomery took his foot off the accelerator, gripped the wheel and pushed himself back into the seat. The car took off over the hump and the world appeared to go into slow motion. Momentarily weightless, Dexter was lifted off his seat. Sweets and cassettes that had fallen onto the floor from the open glove compartment took on a life of their own flying into the air.

The Ford landed on all fours twenty feet past the bridge, all the airborne debris hit the floor and Dexter thumped back into his seat as gravity returned to normal.

"What a car!" Montgomery said admiringly, as it assuredly gripped the road and sped on like a young gazelle.

Beyond the village, the narrow road followed the perimeter of the fields. The two cars hurtled past a barn at the entrance to a farm.

In the back seat, Fred pulled a gun from his shoulder holster, wound down the window and leaned out, taking pot shots at the Ford now closing in on them.

"They're shooting at us!" screamed Montgomery unbelievingly. Dexter sunk down as low as he could, pushing his lower half into the foot well.

"They couldn't hit a barn door travelling at that speed," Montgomery shouted confidently as a bullet ripped through his door mirror.

"Wow! That was close," screamed Dexter, not convinced.

Montgomery's grin became wider and his determination to nail these criminals greater.

The road was patchy with mud from tractor movements but caused no significant problems while they headed in a straight line. Montgomery knew the road well, and realising his chance was coming up, he kept the pressure on the car in front.

It was too late for its unsuspecting driver. With a farm gate directly ahead confusing his judgement, the road took a sharp turn to the left. He gripped the wheel and pressed hard on the brakes, but they were frazzled and had little effect. The brakes glowed red and squealed in protest as the bare metal of the pads pressed against the discs.

The gate gave no resistance, disintegrating on touch, as three tons of Jaguar hit it at sixty miles an hour. One of the wooden rails bounced off the windscreen, smashing the glass into thousands of pieces. The wheels then hit the deep ruts of the freshly ploughed field. The already stressed suspension compressed, pushing the shock absorbers through the body-work into the engine bay. They continued on, bumping violently over the surface, skimming uncontrollably like a stone over ripples in the sea, with no sign of slowing. The men inside bounced around like dried peas in a jam-jar.

It was a large flat field, being prepared for its next crop, surrounded by hedges with a copse running along the right-hand side. A lonely oak tree stood in their path. It had been there for over 400 years, long before the field was created, it had watched the farm develop and survived the clearing of the land to become a trusted and well-loved landmark and home for all manner of wildlife.

The Jaguar struck the tree head on, its bonnet flipping up as the radiator wrapped itself around the trunk. The engine was torn from its mount-ing and pushed into the cabin. The shock wave distorted all the body panels, the front wheels broke free on impact and with their retained momentum, bounced off across the field. The three men were conscious, if somewhat bruised and disorientated by the sudden stop.

The pursuing Ford slowed as it entered the field, it's rally-prepared sus-pension absorbing the ruts, Montgomery slid to a halt alongside. He and Dexter leapt out of the car.

Dexter headed to the passenger side and Montgomery to the driver, both ripping open the crumpled doors and simultaneously pulling the men free of the car. With no concern for their state of health, both crim-inals were cuffed before they knew what was happening.

"You're nicked," Montgomery shouted in the driver's ear, his whole body tingling with excitement as the adrenalin peaked.

The gunman in the back was sprawled across the bench seat, his gun lost when the car hit the gate. He could see his comrades being held by policemen. He kicked what remained of the rear door open and slid out, remarkably he was able to get to his feet and started running towards the gate, just in time to see the Morris Minor tip toe into the field.

"What is this, a bloody time warp," he shouted, as Singleton moved into his path. Dodging to the left he tried to run past the advancing vehi-cle.

Singleton spun in his seat, released the catch and using his right leg violently pushed the driver's door open. The door struck the gunman like a flipper in a pinball machine, knocking him to the ground. In one seamless balletic move, Singleton left the car, landed on the back of the thug, pulled his arms behind his back, cuffed him and remained kneeling on him for good measure.

"You're not stopping me, copper," shouted Fred. His face full of dirt, he tried to wriggle free.

Singleton subtly pushed his arm up his back. He screamed in agony.

"I rather think I am," Singleton said. Fred tried the same move again and Singleton tweaked his arm again. Once again Fred screamed with pain. "Now this is hurting you a lot more than it's hurting me, so be a good boy and lie still," Singleton advised. This time Fred did as he was told, swearing and spitting soil from his mouth as he lay in the muddy furrows.

"Now, while we wait for your transport, let's see if I can remember the procedure," Singleton announced calmly, "Fred Smith or is it Alexi Banjetski? Anyway, I am arresting you on suspicion of murder and attempted robbery. That'll do for starters. You do not have to say anything but anything..." he continued the statement of arrest.

"Good work, Singleton," Montgomery shouted across, as he and Dexter pulled their captives over to his Ford and pushed them face down on the bonnet, spreading their legs apart for good measure. They could hear the sound of approaching sirens and shortly, a white Transit van, followed by three police cars and an ambulance arrived at the field. Uniformed police joined them and took control of the three captives escorting them to a purpose-built cage, welded inside the unmarked van.

"The painting!" Dexter suddenly remembered and ran towards the remains of the Jaguar. The boot was closed, trapped between the twisted rear wings. Smoke, rising from the inside of the cabin, began to billow out of the open doors and flames were now visible, licking at the upholstery.

Montgomery saw Dexter move towards the vehicle. "Get back, Dexter," he shouted urgently, "Leave it, it's got two fuel tanks."

A ball of flame erupted from the boot and the lid flew up in the air. Dexter hit the ground covering his head with his arms. Then Whoomp! The sound of the explosion could be heard back at the showground. Dexter, bruised and frustrated looked out from under his arms at the burning shell. The painting was lost to the fire.

From the back of the Morris Minor, Alice, George and Tom watched in horror. "Wilf was in there… Oh my God! Even he wouldn't be able to survive that explosion!" Alice cried out.

"Talking about me?" Wilf said, materialising by their car.

"Wilf…thank God! Are you alright?" George asked anxiously.

"I'm fine… a little shaken maybe, but fine."

"How could you survive the explosion?" They couldn't believe it.

"Easy… I wasn't in it. When the car hit the tree the momentum kept me going forward I passed through the front of the car and the tree and ended up in the field. Is there any chance of a lift home?"

"I could hug you," Alice said, wiping a tear from her eye. "I thought you were a goner."

Montgomery, Dexter and Singleton stood together in stunned silence looking at the burning wreckage, as the fire engine from the showground arrived to extinguish the flames. They watched the firemen stem the heat, the smoke now turning to steam rising up through the charred branches of the shaken but still proud oak tree.

"We need to debrief," Montgomery said, breaking the silence. "I'll get the first round in. Let's go to the pub in the village." They all nodded in agreement.

"You've got some explaining to do," Dexter said, as they looked at the badly dented driver's door on the Morris Minor.

"Still shuts though, look." Singleton demonstrated. The door swung limply on its hinges, "Well sort of," he shrugged.

They returned to their cars reversed out of the field and drove in convoy to the Abbey Inn, leaving the uniformed officers and fire brigade to secure the field for forensic investigation.

27
And Back Again...

Tuesday 27th August. Morning

Molly finished her breakfast and prepared to visit the house to return some research documents and gather more information. She took the books out to the golf buggy and returned for her briefcase. After all the excitement of the weekend, the park was noticeably quiet. As she re-entered the lodge, the phone rang. Her heart skipped a beat. She was on tenterhooks waiting for any news from the museum. She picked up the receiver. "Hi prof, I've been worried, it's been ages, please tell me you've found something," She could instinctively tell by the tone of his voice it was not good news. "What, nothing more... Nothing?"

Professor Halford had spent all his working hours on the documents. The mirror writing was still the only evidence that the monastery's treasures were not taken by the Kings Commissioner. The ledgers were however of great historical value, and he was now under increasing pressure to hand them to the British Library.

"That's so disappointing," Molly said bitterly. "So, you have to give them over or they could take out an injunction? That's a bit strong. Though I suppose there's the chance they may find something we missed." As he continued to explain the procedures that they could take to secure the ledgers, an idea came to her. "Sorry to interrupt you, but why don't I take them to the British Library myself? It's no trouble. I've got to go to London anyway to check on a new flat and visit my mentor in the British Museum before I return full time, that's where the library is, so it couldn't be easier. She's not without some influence, so hopefully, she can introduce me to those requesting access. That way, I can keep an eye on their research." Professor Halford reluctantly agreed. "That's settled then, tomorrow it is." Molly replaced the receiver, her mind a whirl of emotions.

Disappointment about the ledgers, excitement at seeing the flat offered by the Duke and a route of access into the British Library, the one institution on her list she had yet to fully infiltrate.

She drove to the house to break the news to Jules and the Duke. Following the recent theft of the Rembrandt, the house was closed to the public to enable the police to carry out their investigation. All entrances were locked, and all staff were instructed to only use the front door. She rang the bell, and it was opened, not by James, but by a policeman. Molly showed her pass and was given access to the lobby but had to sign a visitor's book before being able to proceed further. It was eerily quiet as she went up the main stairs towards the library. As she walked along the landing, she could hear muffled voices behind the closed door of the conference room.

"Morning Wilf," she whispered, as she entered the cavernous library. He was resting on the sofa in front of the fire, awaiting her arrival.

"Hi Molly, any news?"

"Sorry, nothing new, I'm afraid. Can you give me a hand with these books? What's going on in the conference room, I could hear raised voices?"

"There's a meeting with the insurance company, George is in there monitoring. He'll let us know if it gets exciting."

With Wilf's assistance, she returned documents to the high shelves. Then pointed out two other volumes she needed from the very top. The books were floating down as the door flew open and Jules entered. He was in a foul mood and fortunately for her, didn't notice the books gently landing on her desk.

His mind was distracted, having just walked out of the meeting. He slumped down on a sofa, wishing the cushions would swallow him up, his face worn with worry.

"Jules, what's wrong? You look terrible," Molly said, moving to sit opposite him. "Is it more bad news? I perfectly understand if you can't tell me but if I can help in any way."

"There's nothing you can do, but thanks for the offer. I'm sorry... it's just so frustrating. Have you ever had to deal with insurance companies? They're just so difficult. Quite happy to take the premiums but when it comes to claims, they throw every obstacle in your way. Sergeant Dexter is in there with father and Colin from security. The insurance men are pulling apart our procedures, saying they were not adequate. One painting stolen, one destroyed by fire and a death in the animal park, all happening within a few days. I have to admit, put like that, it doesn't sound good."

"That's not normal though. Surely they can see that you've just had a run of bad luck…That's putting it mildly I know, but you know what I mean." Molly struggled to think of comparisons in her own life to normalise the events, but she couldn't.

"I shouldn't tell you this, but the consortium that have been seeking to buy the house and turn it into a hotel have now thrown their hat back into the ring but with a much reduced offer, they're just vultures," Jules spat out angrily.

"Sell the house? But it's your home… surely the estate income is able to support your home?"

"I wish it was that simple. The paintings are a hugely valuable asset, we use them at times to prop up the cash flow. They support the house, park and gardens in lean times. If the insurance company don't pay up, which is looking more and more unlikely, we'll have no choice but to sell the house to protect the rest of the estate."

Molly moved across and sat by him struggling to think what to say. "Something will come up, Jules," she said, reaching for his hand. She had no adequate words of comfort so opted for physical contact.

Jules sat in silence pondering his position, "Do you believe in fate?" he reflected, her warm touch calming him.

"I know you talked to 'Gypsy Carolyn' what did she say?"

Jules eyes brightened and his mouth turned up at the corners. "It was just nonsense, horoscope stuff really, totally non-descript. I can't remember the exact words. But I will say she was very convincing. Do you have any confidence in her predictions then?"

"I do believe we have a destined path. It's better not to know what that path is but to enjoy the ride and make the most of opportunities as they appear, the trick is to spot the signs," she calmly said.

"You're so lucky, Molly. You know where you're going. You have a bright future ahead."

"I don't know about my destiny, I'm just following the path of the moment. Anyway, you know your destiny, it's here all around you."

Jules stared into space, his mind still in a whirl. "Do you believe in ghosts?" he said unexpectedly.

Molly stiffened slightly, looking across at Wilf who folded his arms and settled into the sofa, '*This is going to be interesting*', he thought.

"Why do you ask?" she said warily.

"I guess living in an old building makes you wonder. Surely all that history must seep into the fabric of the house. Maybe there's something in it. If so, I wonder what my ancestors will make of all this. Justine Song made me think about it, I suppose. Her show's just fabricated nonsense but… I don't know. Sorry, I'm just being silly."

"I believe in them as a force for good. There's one sat opposite us now." Molly winked at Wilf.

"Now you're just humouring me. If that is the case, I hope they're not everywhere, imagine if one ended up haunting a toilet." He laughed, but he detected a truthful candour to her expression.

"That's better, you're smiling again." Molly let go of his hand. "I heard from your uncle this morning… not good I'm afraid, he couldn't find out anymore, and now I have to take the ledgers to the British Library before the scholars take action to claim them."

"Is that it then, all that effort for nothing?"

"Maybe not, I'm delivering them tomorrow and I'll make sure I get in on their research. My contact at the museum will be able to keep me updated."

"That's good, there's always hope, I suppose."

"Yes, there is," Molly said positively. "While I'm there, I'm going to check out the flat your father's offered to rent to me. I'll have to go back full-time next week so I hope it's OK."

"I think you'll love it. I do hope so. It'll be so handy for your work, with most of the museums on your doorstep, and it'll be nice for Mavis to have someone coming and going."

"Mavis?" Molly said frowning.

"Mavis is our housekeeper. She keeps the house lovely, but we've seldom been there in recent months, this place seems to take up all our time."

"Then I look forward to meeting her."

He stood up. "Sorry, but I need to get back to the conference room, they think I've just popped to the toilet. Thanks Molly, you've been a great help."

"I'm not sure what I've done, but you're welcome."

In the attic, Alice and Tom sat around reliving the excitement of the car show. Wilf rose up through the floor to join them. He told them about the conversation Jules had with Molly.

"And she actually told him you were sat there?" Alice asked in disbelief.

"Yes, I didn't believe it either. Fortunately, neither did he. She changed the subject very quickly."

"Just as well. With all his problems, that might have been enough to tip him over the edge," Alice added.

Tom looked thoughtful as he reclined on the chaise lounge. "Why can't we just follow the parrot? If he really is 'Bishop' he may lead us to the gold."

"One small problem there, he's not here. And we don't know when he'll show up." Wilf said, "Anyway, he flits around very quickly, I've never been able to catch him... Is there any news from George?"

"Not yet," Alice said.

A Holeford police car headed down the drive, crunched over the gravel and pulled up outside the front of the house. The driver retrieved a parcel from the boot, walked up the steps and rang the bell. He was greeted by the officer on duty, after a short conversation, the visitor signed in and climbed the stairs to the conference room.

Sergeant Dexter sat at the head of the table by the two pale faced insurance men. They were dressed in identical tailored black suits with matching green and black striped old school ties. At the other end of the table, the Duke sat in his large carver chair with Jules sitting alongside. Opposite the insurance men, a red-faced Colin and his secretary from the security department sat fidgeting uneasily. Colin was not used to being on the back foot. After the judgement from the two men opposite, it felt like a court room, with them in the dock.

There was a gentle knock at the door. Sarah, the Duke's secretary, got up, opened it gingerly and slipped out. After a short conversation with the visitor, she returned to the room.

"Sergeant, there's a constable here who would like a private word."

"Please excuse me gentlemen," Dexter got up from the table. Everyone stopped talking and looked towards the door.

"This had better be good, constable," Dexter warned as he slid out through the half open door.

Five minutes later he returned holding a long cardboard tube, his expression giving nothing away to those gathered at the table.

"Gentlemen, there has been a significant development." He paused for dramatic effect and having gained their attention, he continued. "A young boy, named Nigel, had a surprise present from his family yesterday. The father, one Mr Graeme Shaw, attended the 'Galactic Jump' festival with his younger son Anthony, who purchased a poster for his brother Nigel's upcoming birthday. Yesterday, Nigel duly opened his present with great excitement only to find this inside."

Dexter cleared the centre of the table and slowly removed the content of the tube. It looked like a simple roll of glossy white paper. The assembled onlookers looked unimpressed. All they could discern was the 'Galactic Jump' logo, they looked up at Dexter questioningly. He carefully continued to roll out the picture, a torn piece of material appeared. When it was completely unrolled, they could see a second picture of different material carefully wrapped inside the poster. They all gasped in disbelief.

"But it can't be!" The Duke uttered, rising abruptly from his chair.

Jules moved in closer and studied the picture and the signature in the bottom right-hand corner. He found it hard to believe what he was seeing.

"The Van Dyck... this is the stolen Van Dyck... but how?" He shook his head bewildered. "I can't believe its back."

The two insurance agents produced magnifying glasses from their briefcases and leant in close to scrutinise the painting, their noses nearly touching the canvas. As one, they stood up, looked at everyone and addressed the room, "We need verification, of course, but, on first examination this appears to be the original Van Dyck."

Dexter smiled smugly, straightened his back and stood tall. He wished Montgomery could be here to share this moment, but he was still in London working with the fraud squad to round up members of the forgery gang.

The Duke stuttered something incomprehensible then sat back down.

"How the hell did that get there?" he asked, regaining some composure.

"Must've been hidden there by the thief, I suppose," surmised Jules.

"Exactly," agreed Dexter, "Placed there to be collected later by a courier, I would imagine."

George rose up through the upper floor to the attic so quickly, he misjudged and passed halfway through the roof and had to come back down again.

"What on earth!" exclaimed Wilf as they watched his sudden appearance, disappearance and more controlled reappearance into the room.

"Have you quite finished George? Or are you on a bungee?" Wilf laughed.

"Come with me now…all of you, now! Quickly, you're not going to believe this." And he shot back down through the floor again.

The others looked at one another and quickly followed him down to the conference room where the assembled men were all gathered around the table staring at a painting. All that is, apart from the Duke who was still sitting bemused. His face ashen, his knuckles white, as his hands tightly gripped the arms of the chair.

"Is that the missing painting?" asked Alice, "But how?"

"I don't believe it," Tom declared. He saw the poster and its discarded cardboard wrapping now on the floor. "It was there all the time, in the loft room." He sat down in one of the vacated chairs. If he had only found it, he could have given it to the gunman and would be back at Art College now. He put his head in his hands.

As they all continued gazing dumbly at the painting, Sarah moved to close the window. "It's getting a bit chilly in here," she observed.

"So, this means we can cancel the claim for the missing *Van Dyck*," Jules said. The words of Molly echoed in his head '*something will come up*.' She was right! Something had certainly come up. A little of the weight on his shoulders lifted as he turned to look at the Duke. "Father, this is wonderful… Father, are you alright?"

"No, I need a whisky," he stood up and unsteadily moved to the music room door, fumbled for the door knob and headed in, closing it softly behind him.

The insurance agents quickly pulled the forms out of their brief case and started writing. "This still leaves the Rembrandt claim and any claim against the estate from the deceased person's family," the older agent said coldly, his face a picture of indifference.

Alice was taken aback by his attitude. "Cold fish," she stated, looking daggers at the insurance men. "Let's go back upstairs, we need to talk about this. I don't think our presence here is helping the atmosphere in the room. Did you see the Duke's expression?" she asked. "He didn't look very relieved." They all nodded and rose back up through the ceiling.

In the attic the ghosts were full of delight and disbelief.

"I reckon that's why you were bumped off. You disturbed the courier collecting the painting and then he had to get rid of the witness." Wilf had opted for a Sherlock Holmes stance by pacing up and down the rug in front of the chimney stack addressing the room while pretending to hold a large pipe to his mouth. "I deduce that the fiend, who we now know as Alexi Banjetski, returned the following day disguised as an alien to try and recover the goods. However, it had already been sold to this unsuspecting fan and has only come to light following the birthday party."

"It all fits," George agreed.

Tom slowly nodded in agreement. "But why didn't he just go back that evening?" he said.

"I reckon he made too much noise and was afraid the security patrol might investigate," Alice said logically. "Someone might have heard the gunshots, so he did a runner."

Wilf moved across to the wardrobe to retrieve his frock coat, deer stalker hat and fancy pipe. If he was going to take the part of detective, it was time to dress correctly. As he opened the wardrobe door, Flint flew out into the room and settled on the back of the sofa.

"So, that's where he's been," said Alice.

"Never mind the painting, we have to follow this little chap," Wilf whispered, slowly closing the wardrobe door, not wishing to frighten the bird.

"Hello Flint," Alice said to the parrot, sitting to her left on the back of the sofa. "Or should I call you 'Bishop'?"

"Bless you," it squawked.

"There... I'm sure it's him," Alice trilled satisfactorily.

"He always says 'bless you,' that's not much evidence." Wilf said scathingly, hovering close to the sofa. "Bishop," he repeated firmly looking directly at the bird.

"Bless you," it said again.

"Mmm, more convincing," he admitted, beckoning the others to follow him to the other side of the room. They gathered in a huddle. Wilf then whispered to ensure the bird couldn't hear. "I want you all to disperse around the house. George, you go outside, Alice on the stairs and Tom to the gallery. Then I'll try to scare him into flying off, hopefully he'll fly to wherever he normally hides and one of us will see him. It's worth a try. If you do see him, try to follow, then we'll meet back here in fifteen minutes to report."

"You're clutching at straws, Wilf." George whispered.

"Got a better idea?" Wilf asked challengingly.

"No... let's try it then, what have we got to lose?" George replied begrudgingly.

"Good. OK everyone, I'll count to one hundred to give you time to get in place. One... Two... Three..."

The other three ghosts dispersed as instructed, slowly counting in their heads so they would roughly know when Flint might emerge from the attic.

"...Ninety-nine... one hundred!" Wilf finished dramatically to the empty room. He suddenly banged the door of the wardrobe and quickly rushed towards Flint. The startled bird flew up into the air and quickly dived down through the floor. Wilf speedily followed him straight through the conference room where the meeting was still in progress. They both passed into the drawing room and through the stone floor into the kitchen where Flint took up position on the mantelpiece above the fireplace. Wilf gently slowed down and stopped at the opposite end of the large kitchen, by the dresser containing shiny, polished copper pots and pans. Flint seemed to be gathering himself together after the exertion of the chase and slowly regained his composure. He then saw Wilf, and immediately straightened up eying him suspiciously.

It was a face off.

They both gazed at each other warily watching for the merest hint of movement.

Wilf levitated a particularly large copper pot from the sideboard while holding his fixed stare. Flint immediately saw the pot and eyed it malevolently, taking his gaze off Wilf.

This was what Wilf had been waiting for and he quickly dropped the suspended pan. It hit the floor with a satisfyingly loud and reverberating clang.

Flint immediately shot back up into the air, flew to the centre of the room and dived through the table and flag stone floor below. Wilf was surprised at this but quickly followed.

He unexpectedly found himself in a crypt. He'd never been here before. Stone columns rose from a dirt floor supporting bulky stone arches. It was a long cloister-like space, similar in length to the art gallery but dark and cold. He could just make out the shape of openings at high level that must have once been narrow windows to provide illumination. Flint sat on a stone in the middle of the space eying Wilf suspiciously.

"Where are we then Flint?" Wilf whispered. "I haven't been here before… but I think you have. Is this where you hide?" He looked around the arcade of columns and the penny dropped. "So, this is part of the ancient abbey isn't it Flint, or should I say… Bishop!" He said the name loudly in a staccato voice that echoed round the stone vaults, surprising the bird.

Bishop flew up in the air then further down the cellar turning right past the next column and through the stone wall. Wilf moved down to the position where it had disappeared. There was no discernible opening or even signs of a blocked-up doorway. He tentatively pushed his head through the wall, expecting to find solid matter. But no, it opened into a narrow stone corridor, perhaps an underground tunnel. He wasn't sure. Cautiously he entered the space. It was long, probably linking a building that formed part of the old priory. There was no record that he could recall in the plans of the old buildings and lord knows he'd spent hours studying them whilst in the library as Molly worked on her manuscript. "Flint… where are you?" he asked urgently.

"Go back, heathen. You are not welcome here," an unexpected voice boomed from the depths of the dark corridor, surprising Wilf, who looked around anxiously for the speaker. Then a dark figure slowly emerged from a side passage. It was a monk, wearing a rusty breast plate on which were painted three heraldic lions.

Also, he wore a helmet resembling a steel bucket with a slit enabling him to see out. The armour was worn over a heavy woven cassock, making much movement difficult. In his right hand he held a sword, rusty and misshapen by time, which he held aloft in a threatening manner. "Go forth, before I bring the wrath of God himself upon you," he boomed threateningly from inside the bucket.

Wilf was taken aback by the presence of another, previously unknown, ghost of such presence and age, but held his nerve and asked innocently. "Have you by any chance seen a parrot anywhere?"

"I repeat, go hence from here or you will feel my anger!" the monk continued, ignoring the question completely.

Wilf continued unabashed, "A green parrot, answers to the name of 'Bishop'?"

It was only at that moment he became aware of the significance of the parrot's name. *'You're getting a bit slow in your old age,'* he thought to himself.

"Bless you," the parrot suddenly squawked benevolently, although he couldn't be seen anywhere by the two men facing each other in the confines of the dark tunnel.

"That's him," Wilf announced happily, looking about him for the bird.

"I'm sorry but I did warn you," announced the armoured monk who suddenly thrust the sword into Wilf.

"Oi! What are you doing?" asked Wilf angrily.

Realising he hadn't slain his enemy, the monk repeated the attack three more times and for good measure tried to cut Wilf's head off. In the confines of the narrow tunnel, the blade of the rusty sword swung into the right-hand wall, then through Wilf's neck and continued into the left-hand wall. Wilf looked on totally unhurt but with an annoyed expression on his face. The Monk studied his sword with total disbelief.

"Will you stop doing that?" ordered Wilf angrily. He was, by now, totally irritated by the monk trying to kill him and interrupting his search. "Will you take that tin can off your head so we can talk properly?"

"What is that strange armour you wear?" enquired the monk looking at Wilf with new respect and awe. "It must be truly powerful to survive the sword of destiny."

Wilf glanced down at his clothes. He'd forgotten he was wearing the Sherlock Holmes costume. "I'm a ghost, you stupid monk. And so are you, for that matter. Exactly how long have you been down here?"

"Since the year of our lord 1566, and I am no ghost sir, I am the protector of the faith. I vowed to safeguard the possessions of the abbey from the tyrant king. Did he send you? Are there others?" he enquired, looking around anxiously.

"No, of course not, you idiot," replied Wilf. "I've got news for you. You're the dead protector of the faith. Now, let's get down to business. Where are the treasures of the abbey hidden?"

"By all the powers invested in me… I shall never tell," the monk stated bravely, waving his sword once again in front of Wilf. Although confused, he was however, determined to stick to his duty and hold his ground.

Whilst sympathetic to the bewildered and yet brave monk, Wilf was tiring of his antics and was equally determined to get on with his own quest. "Right, I guess they're in here, then," he said, noticing a narrow opening to his right. He ignored the monk completely and moved towards the new tunnel.

"Bishop," he shouted, the name echoed through the tunnels.

"Bless you," the bird replied.

Wilf, smiling smugly, slipped through the narrow passage and passed through a steel door similar to the one in the mausoleum on the island.

The room contained several large wooden chests designed for the storage of vestments. They were long and low to allow the ceremonial robes to lay flat. The decomposing timber cases were held together by corroded wrought iron straps with heavy hinges. The monk had cautiously followed him and now sat on one of the boxes and removed his helmet. He had had enough.

"I'm not a proper monk," he admitted wearily. "I'm a Lay Brother, they wouldn't let me become a monk. They said I was too volatile and lacked the necessary determination and intelligence. That was their opinion of me. But when they needed protection, who did they turn to? I wasn't stupid and up to now I've guarded nobly and well. You're the first person I've seen since they shut me in here."

Wilf was horrified. "You mean they shut you in, blocked up the opening and left you to die alone, that's cruel."

"I have 'Bishop' for company," the pitiful monk replied.

"What's your name?"

"Brother Leopold."

"Well, Brother Leopold, I think it's time you left here and took your place in the daylight. You deserve it. But first, I've got a job to finish." He held his hands out towards one of the boxes and using his powers of levitation, the lid awkwardly creaked open. Inside he could see the glint of gold. He gasped and leant forward. He could make out the shapes of ornate crosses, goblets, a chalice and candlesticks amongst the many items poking out of their decaying canvas wrappings. He couldn't wait to show Molly and the others. "Come with me Leopold, I have some people you may like to meet. I think all this is safe enough here for a while longer."

Brother Leopold got to his feet and reluctantly leant the ancient sword against the stone wall. "That might be nice, I don't get out much," he said, smiling.

"Not since 1566 anyway," Wilf replied with a wink. "Brace yourself, you're in for a shock!"

28
London

Wednesday 28th August. Morning

After a light breakfast, Molly drove to London. She had arranged to join her mentor, Dr Julia Griffin in the British Museum at mid-day, where they would meet with the library manager. Conveniently, the British Library was located in the same building, another of her friends from Oxford, also shared the same office. The network of contacts from the university proved very useful for her studies and career prospects. Her headquarters at the museum meant she could use the staff car park. It was conveniently close to the door to the administration centre, making it easy to drop off the ledgers. After going through her thesis with Julia, they had lunch and afterwards, with her help, retrieved the ledgers, placed them on a trolley and wheeled them to the library office where they were officially handed over.

In the afternoon, Molly drove to the Victoria and Albert Museum, her current base, again using the staff car park. She popped into her office to meet colleagues and get up to speed on the gossip, before her full return in a few days. She then walked towards Kensington Gardens, passing the Royal Albert Hall and along Kensington Road towards the Duke's house. The opposite side of the road was lined with trees, with glimpses of the parkland beyond. It was a different world to that of her little Eltham flat where she overlooked the town centre's tired sixties architecture. There was wealth here, it oozed from every brick. The pavements were clean, wide and surprisingly quiet. Behind black decorative railings, the five-story, white terraced houses stood like giant wedding cakes topped with mansard roofs. Their decoration was of the highest quality with exquisitely carved masonry. The entrance doors were framed by stone columned porches, supporting railing-edged balconies with windows as tall as houses, looking out towards the park and Kensington Palace beyond. Molly continued along the row studying the doors until she found number twelve. Her heart skipped a beat, Could this be it? Could this possibly be her new home, here, close to work with the park on her doorstep?

She pinched herself, "Ouch!" No not a dream then. She climbed the steps to the front door, and it opened as if by magic.

"My dear, I was getting worried." A smartly dressed middle aged lady held the door open and waved her in. "You must be Molly."

"And you must be Mavis." Molly held out her hand, which was politely shaken.

"Now come in my dear, the kettle's on. We've got lots to talk about and then I'll show you around."

Molly felt immediately at home. But what a home! The cavernous entrance hall was big enough to park a bus in. The floor was tiled in a medieval pattern similar to that of Woodford Abbey. Gold framed paintings hung along the walls. The figures seemingly looked out approvingly at the possible new tenant. Mavis wafted down the hall ahead of Molly, past the antique furniture and turned left through an open door into a lounge.

"Come on in my dear," she invited. The room was large and square with high ceilings. The huge Carrera marble fireplace was surrounded by a 'horseshoe' arrangement of large, soft, welcoming sofas on a thick rug with a coffee table in the middle. The grate was hidden by a screen and fresh flowers arranged in a vase added a splash of colour to the white stone of the mantelpiece. The flowers matched the colours on the furniture and carpet. Molly wondered if this was a happy coincidence, but her instinct told her not. She was immediately drawn to the bay window and moved to look across the road into Kensington gardens.

"You can just about make out Kensington Palace over on the left, of course it's much clearer when the trees are bereft of their leaves," Mavis said.

"It's lovely, I can't believe I'm still in London. It feels just like Woodford Abbey, minus the sound of the animals, of course!" She watched the people carrying their files and brief cases busily striding along the numerous weaving paths, one man even aptly wearing a dark suit, bowler hat and carrying a black umbrella. She reflected on the pace of life in the city after the more pedestrian speed in her home town and her few days at the estate. She had felt at home in the little lodge surrounded by the flora and fauna of the parkland. *Would she feel so here?*

"Tea or coffee?" Mavis asked.

"Oh! Tea please," Molly said, reluctantly turning away from the window. Mavis soon reappeared with a silver tea tray containing tea pot, bone china cups, milk jug and sugar bowl with silver sugar tongs along with a plate of biscuits.

"It's lovely to finally meet you. His grace speaks highly of you, you must have a made a good impression. He's not one to suffer fools."

"I had no idea he'd told you much about me, he always seems to be so busy with his paperwork in the library. It must be difficult for him to relinquish the running of the estate to Jules, but he still has the house to look after."

"Between you and me, I think he's finding it hard to do even that," Mavis said, leaning forward in a conspiratorial whisper. "He's not a young man anymore. Now, milk and sugar?" she asked.

"Just milk please," Molly replied, settling comfortably amongst the voluminous sofa cushions. She took a refreshing sip of the hot, nut-brown liquid and told Mavis all about her work on the updated guidebook which had quickly expanded into a full-blown history of the family and estate. She also chatted about her own childhood in Holeford, life in Oxford and her recent work with the London museums. Mavis listened, and asked intelligent questions to find out more and more about the girl on the sofa. Molly realised this was turning into an interview of some sort, but she didn't mind. It was fun to share her story, although she left out ghosts and grave robbery, which was a bit too much for a first meeting.

"I do hope you'll stay, Molly. We're going to have so much fun. Will you be having any parties?"

Molly was surprised at the question. She had obviously passed the test. She smiled. "I wouldn't be so presumptuous as to abuse the Duke's kindness."

"I do hope you'll arrange some. His Grace has hosted some wonderful parties. We've had them all here, popstars, actors, politicians and royalty. Some of them were really naughty, but it was all in good spirits... I do miss those days," Mavis reflected.

"This has been lovely," Molly said, deflecting the question, "but I'm afraid I have limited time today. Would it be possible to see the little flat that has been set aside for me?"

"Oh! my dear I'm so sorry, yes of course. I do chatter on a bit... Well, this is your lounge."

Molly gulped, "What'... this is part of it?"

"Yes. Now let me show you the rest. Follow me."

They stood up, Molly looking around in disbelief. "My flat in Eltham would fit in this one room!" she stated.

Mavis grinned, she loved showing off the house she had cared for over so many years. "This way." She unfastened the double doors at the back of the lounge which opened into a dining room, revealing an eight-seater mahogany table, décor of equal quality to the lounge and a large painting of the Duke over another marble fireplace. Mavis continued through a large door to the left, "And this is the kitchen... fully equipped of course." Molly followed, awed by its space and style. It was elegantly decorated and filled with all the latest appliances. Why it even had a sandwich toaster! "Through here, we have two bedrooms," Mavis continued, as she went down a corridor at the back of the kitchen, Molly in tow, now in a complete daze. "Oh, I nearly forgot, His grace said you'd need a study, so the third bedroom has been re-furnished for you." She opened a door off the corridor into a smaller room equipped with an oak desk. A large window overlooked the small, well-manicured rear garden, while shelves lined two sides, partly filled with books. On the large desk was an electric typewriter identical to the one in the lodge.

"This is amazing, Mavis... I may call you Mavis?" Molly asked. "It's too much. I can't possibly stay here."

"I know it's only for a short term," Mavis said in response to Molly's protest, "but his grace would be so upset if you didn't take up the offer. He said you've been working so hard on the book for little reward, and this would be so convenient for you." The tour continued, visiting the other bedrooms, both with en-suite bathrooms, another family bathroom and dressing room with a balcony overlooking the rear garden.

Molly felt out of place in it's grandeur. It was one thing using the Lodge and visiting the house, but this was way beyond anything she was used to.

"Please say yes," encouraged Mavis. "It would be so lovely to have you here. You're more than welcome to invite guests to sleep over. His Grace and VJ stay here occasionally in their apartments but they've both been so busy that they seem to have less and less time to visit. I keep it all ready for them though, you never know when they'll find time to come to town."

Molly was deep in thought, a little uncomfortable with the luxury she was being offered.

"Do you like swimming?" Mavis asked suddenly.

"Sorry?"

"There's a pool in the basement with doors opening onto the garden. I use it myself sometimes… it's a shame not to," she confided.

Molly laughed. "I'm sorry, I didn't expect you to say that… but of course there had to be a swimming pool."

"Then you'll stay?" Mavis pleaded. Molly lifted her eyebrows and smiled. Mavis clapped her hands together. "Wonderful." It was decided.

"I need to give notice on the flat and move my things over."

"Yes, of course you do… I can arrange the transport for you. The delivery man at Harrods is very helpful. He'll collect your things for you I'm sure, he's so obliging."

Molly resigned herself to the offer *'Harrods… who else?'* "That would be lovely, thank you. Now, I'm sorry, but I must be going."

They exchanged details for the move and she headed back to the car, her mind a whirl of excitement. She couldn't wait to tell her mum and dad and have them to stay with her. It all felt so surreal.

At Woodford Abbey, the police investigation was complete. The Van Dyck was in its original position on the wall of the gallery and alongside was the faded shadow of the vacant Rembrandt, sadly lost in the fire of the bungled theft. The housekeeping team passed from room to room, cleaning and preparing the house for its reopening to the public. Outside, the gardeners were making extra special efforts to tidy the ornamental gardens, mow the lawns and edge the paths. The staff felt unsettled after the events of the last few days and all were attempting to physically wash away the disturbing memories.

In the library the Duke finished a telephone conversation and replaced the receiver. Jules sat in the chair opposite. "That was Mavis."

"I guessed it was."

"Molly's just left, she's going to take the flat," he said with some relief, and drank the last of his afternoon tea.

"That's good, it'll be much more convenient for her. Also, It'll give me an excuse to go into town and see how she's settling in. I haven't been to the flat for ages. I don't think she's far off completing the first draft of the manuscript. I bet she'll be glad to see the back of it and get on with her own work."

There was a tap at the door and James entered. "Pardon me, your grace, but Detective Inspector Montgomery is here to see you."

"Thank you James, let him in," the Duke said, as he carefully screwed the top back on his Mont Blanc fountain pen and placed it neatly on the writing desk companion. Montgomery entered the room, flanked by two uniformed officers. The Duke slowly shuffled his papers and placed them all in a neat pile. Montgomery walked the length of the library to join them while the two policemen waited by the door.

Jules stood and shook his hand. He detected coolness in the handshake which unnerved him slightly. This looked official. "Hello Detective, I assume this isn't a social call. Have you got some news for us?"

"Yes sir." He paused awkwardly and coughed into his hand to clear his throat. "Following our investigations in London, there has been another significant development."

The Duke sat back in his chair and calmly folded his arms. "Come on then, out with it man," he said anxiously.

The two constables moved slowly into the room and stood either side of Jules.

"I'm sorry there's no easy way of doing this, your grace, however it is my duty." Montgomery paused and cleared his throat again. "Aloysius William Henry D'Macey, Duke of Exford, I am arresting you for attempting to defraud the Lloyds insurance company of London and as an accessory to the manslaughter of Mr Thomas Carmichael. You do not have to say anything but…" The detective continued his mantra.

The blood drained from Jules, he felt faint and clutched the back of his chair for support. "Don't be stupid. There must be some mistake!" he protested. He looked across at his father who remained sitting rather impassively in his chair. "Tell him father, this is wrong… this is a mistake. Tell him," he insisted.

The Duke cocked his head to one side and shrugged his shoulders. "I'm sorry Jules, it all got out of hand. I thought I could raise funds by selling the original painting on the black-market, no one should have been hurt. The chap collecting the canvas was a loose cannon, even his boss admitted that latterly, but it was too late, I couldn't stop the deal. The people I thought I could trust were ruthless, and started to threaten me when the original wasn't found at the pick-up point. Then the forged painting was spotted by Molly and the whole plan began to unravel. The Rembrandt was stolen as compensation by the 'organisation'. It's a mess Jules... I'm sorry... I was just trying to raise money for the house restoration... it's all rather backfired," he finished, looking somewhat bemused.

The two officers shuffled round the desk and repositioned themselves by the Duke. Jules watched on in silence as the dreamlike pageant unfolded in front of him. He had no words, it was unreal. His eyes were wide open, and a bead of sweat ran down his temple as he tried desperately to understand it all. One of the policemen unclipped handcuffs from his belt.

"That won't be necessary," Montgomery said gently. "His grace will come quietly."

The Duke nodded and slowly rose from his chair and the four of them walked to the door. He shook hands with Montgomery, "Good work officer." The Duke was relaxed and in a way relieved, the weight of the events now lifting from his shoulders. He looked sadly back at Jules still standing by the chair. "Can I have a moment with my son, please?"

"Certainly, your grace." Montgomery said.

"I am truly sorry, Jules. I really thought it would solve everything. In hindsight I know it was stupid, but I was desperate to protect the house. It seemed like a good idea at the time. I hope I haven't made it all worse for you."

"Father, I don't believe all this. Don't worry, I'll contact the family lawyer at once, you'll be home later." He felt nauseous, his whole world was collapsing around him, and he didn't know what to do.

"Thank you Jules, I'll need to speak to him. You'll be all right son, you're a good man. Take care of the place and especially take care of the treasure you have in London," the Duke said enigmatically.

"But I can't do it on my own, I need you! I've always needed you. We're a team."

"Well, if you have any questions, you'll know where to find me," the Duke said, with a hint of a smile. "I'll see you soon, but you'll manage fine. I have complete confidence in you and you have a good team here at the estate. I'm very proud of you, I always have been. I'm sorry I messed up."

As he was led through the door the Duke glanced back into the library and disappeared from Jules's sight. The policeman closed the door, and the only sound now was of their footsteps moving away, until all was silent. Jules sank down and held his head in his hands. Minutes ticked away and then there was a gentle tap on the door. James entered the room, turning to face Jules while closing the door quietly behind him. "What do you want me to tell the staff sir?" he asked gently.

"Just say the Duke's helping the police with their enquires. Thank you James."

"Very good, sir," James left the room, his eyes misting up.

With the echo of the heavy door closing in its frame, the library felt large and empty. Jules tried to contemplate what had just happened. He felt so alone.

29
Time To Go

Saturday 31ˢᵗ August. Evening

The ghosts were preparing for their evening duties which involved dressing up in period clothes and circulating through the rooms on a well-rehearsed route. While they waited for the clock to strike midnight, they sat around the attic discussing the day's activities. They were now joined by Brother Leopold who sat on the sofa stroking the feathers of Bishop as the bird perched happily on his outstretched arm.

"What do you think is going to happen to the estate?" Wilf pondered.

"I assume Jules will just keep it going exactly the same, he has a good team behind him," George said.

"I would have thought the Duke would be released on bail. He's no threat compared to those in the organisation he got mixed up with," Tom said.

"Well, I think Molly should come and live here permanently, he needs a steadying hand," Alice stated.

"You're just thinking of yourself," Wilf said, "I know you'd like that, but her place is in London doing her doctorate not here at Woodford."

"Perhaps I could go and stay with her in Kensington… or at least visit," Alice suggested. "Molly said the house is amazing… like a palace, she can't believe her luck. I could visit all the sights while I'm there. I'd love to go to Buckingham Palace or the Tower of London. You could all come. Just think of all the famous ghosts we'd meet." She came back down to earth and continued, "She thinks the Duke will be alright. According to Sergeant Dexter, they're using his information to close down a European fraud ring. At least that's what she heard…or something like that."

As she spoke, a pool of smoke began to gather in the middle of the rug. Tom and Leopold sank back in their chairs, watching with trepidation as the mist thickened into a swirling cloud across the floor.

"What alchemy is this?" cried Leopold, fearfully.

"Nothing to worry about old chap, it's about time he returned," Wilf said knowingly. "I wonder what trick he's got up his sleeve this time."

They began to hear the mechanical whine of an electric motor and muffled sound of a violin.

"Curious," George said, "It can only be Eric."

Then smoke began to rise and then cascade from the top of a large metal box that emerged slowly through the floor. It finally stopped and sat in the pool of mist. The music could be heard coming from inside what now appeared to be a lift carriage. It's bare metal panels riveted together through raised seams with steel cables wound around large pulleys going back down though the floor.

'Ping.'

The door's slid open as a ladies voice politely announced, "Attic room." The music became louder and Eric appeared holding his bony hands to the side of his hood to protect his ears from the noise. The words 'Swindlers Lifts' were engraved into the metal threshold.

"Sorry about the music," Eric said, stepping into the room and looking slightly embarrassed.

"Is that supposed to be '*The girl from Ipanema*'?" Wilf asked, trying to recognise the squeals and groans of what sounded like a badly tuned violin being played by an orangutan.

"It's bloody awful," Eric stated as the door slowly closed, thankfully muffling the sound. "Old Nick went to America looking for souls and wagered a gold violin that he could play better than a young fiddler. Silly fool lost the gold violin and he's been practicing ever since. Even recorded an album… that's what you can hear…believe me it gets no better. Anyway, what do you think?"

Eric tapped the side of the box, "It's a new innovation. Trouble is for any newly departed, it only goes down. I'm only allowed as far as reception you understand and that's warm enough for me!"

He pressed the button on a panel and the doors slid open. He reached in and retrieved a briefcase. The doors automatically closed, once again dampening the offensive melody.

"It's quite a thing," Wilf said, admiring the monstrosity in the room.

"Made by some clever engineers at purgatory level, probably trying to earn a reprieve," Eric informed them, admiringly.

"But why are you using it today?" Alice asked, looking a little worried.

"All will become clear." Eric then noticed Brother Leopold cowering behind the sofa. "Hello, who are you? You're not on my list."

The monk lifted his head cautiously above the cushions, "B...Brother L...Leopold, guardian of the riches. Are you the Grim Reaper?"

"Yes, that's me, not keen on the grim bit but the title comes with the job, although I do feel it's disparaging to my true, cheerful nature. Well Brother, it seems you've managed to slip through the net. That doesn't happen very often." Eric placed his briefcase on the coffee table and checked through a moth-eaten book using his boney finger to scroll down the list of names. "No, not in here, you're going to have to stay while I delve further in the archives."

"I'm not in a hurry to go anywhere... I've only just emerged from the secret hiding place."

"Good, as long as you're comfortable, it may take a while to locate your records. Now, let me see," reaching once again into the briefcase he retrieved some official looking forms. "Now Tom, let's get you sorted out."

Tom stepped forward, anxiously glancing at the lift. "Are they my forms?" he asked timidly.

"They are. To save time I've taken the liberty of filling out most of the details using your records. Please check through them and then sign here." Eric pointed to a dotted line at the bottom of the three-page parchment.

While Tom read the documents, Wilf and George looked around the outside of the 'Swindler Lift' in wonder.

"Heatproof steel, well insulated with NASA-developed shielding, same as they use on the space shuttle," Eric boasted, tapping the side with his boney hand.

"Only goes down though?" George questioned.

"Well, it comes up, obviously, but only to the surface. Old Nick won't share his technology with those upstairs. Not that they need it anyway... they've got wings!" He laughed.

"But why are you using it? I didn't think you dealt with... 'down there'?" Wilf whispered, after inwardly debating what to call the underworld.

Tom interrupted, "OK, it's seems about right." He placed the documents on the table and looked anxiously at Eric.

Eric pointed at a dotted line at the bottom of a form. "Now, if you would kindly print and sign your name here, we can get going."

Tom took the offered quill and scratched his name slowly on the bottom line. Eric lifted it and studied the signature carefully.

"What do you mean 'get going'?" Alice asked, her eyes flitting nervously between Eric and the lift. "Surely he can stay with us?"

"Not possible Alice. You see Tom has not been totally honest with you all, witness his signature." Eric turned the form for them all to see. Tom looked shameful and moved slowly away towards the attic door as they studied the writing.

Chomas Tarmichel was inscribed on the dotted line in a nervous scrawl. Wilf took hold of it as Alice and George gathered around to look even closer. Confused, all three glanced at Tom then back at Eric.

Eric took back the document. "You see, Tom is a brilliant artist, could have been a master in his own right but he was led astray for the easy money option... forgery."

Then the penny dropped, "Good grief, you're dyslexic!" Alice exclaimed.

They all turned to face Tom, who was now backed up to the attic door trying to push his body through but without success. He tried again but he was trapped.

"That explains the Dan Vyck painting," George exclaimed, "You messed up the spelling... rookie mistake," he tutted, shaking his head.

Tom turned once more and tried to physically push the door open, but it wouldn't budge. "I would have gotten away with it if it wasn't for that meddling historian," he said bitterly.

"How dare you say that about our friend," Alice was trembling with anger. "We all liked you and went out of our way to help you settle into your new after-life and all this time you were lying to us. You're despicable," feeling betrayed she turned away, unable to look at him.

Eric retrieved the forms from Wilf and watched Tom, trying to push himself through the door. "You can't get out. The lift emits a force field to stop you escaping. Now, Thomas, are you going to do this the easy way or the hard way?"

"What's the hard way?" George asked excitedly.

"It's not very nice, it involves a lot of prodding with red hot pokers. Still, if that's what you want, I'll have to go back down and get security to collect you." He pressed the button and the lift doors slid open, again the room filled with the sound of the screeching violin.

"No, it's OK," Tom said quickly. "I'm sorry everyone. It wasn't meant to be like this. Just one job they said. It was enough money to get me through university." The doors slid shut again and he looked at them sadly.

"You messed up big time," Eric said. "The good news is, you have a chance to redeem yourself, you're not going to hell and damnation, just as far as purgatory reception."

"Sounds bad enough," Tom said, his head bowed in remorse.

"Your reputation goes before you young man, His nibs wants the reception hall decorated like the Sistine Chapel with added suffering. Do a good job and you stand a chance of redemption."

"I studied that ceiling for my entrance exam, that's not so bad, I could probably knock that out in a couple of years." Tom perked up.

"It's not that easy. Think of Kings Cross station and you get an idea of the scale," Eric informed him.

"That'll take forever!" Tom exclaimed.

"Well, you've got an eternity, so the sooner you start…" Eric held out an arm and gestured towards the lift.

Tom shuffled towards it. "I am truly sorry," he said looking towards Alice, "you've all been so kind to me."

Alice pursed her lips and crossed her arms in disgust. She couldn't find the words to express her feeling of disappointment and refused to say goodbye to him.

"Don't worry, Brother, I'll find your records and get you on your way soon. Now come on Tom." Eric pressed the button, once again the doors opened. This time the strangled notes of '*My Way*' filled the room. They both stepped in.

Just as the doors began to close Tom leaned forward and quickly shouted, "I can spell 'Rembrandt,' it's behind the Hockney." The door clicked shut with a metallic thud and he disappeared from sight. Mist appeared around the base and it lowered through the floor leaving a cloud which spiraled after it, like water down a plug hole.

"That's one hell of a machine," Wilf said, admiringly.

"Literally," George added. "Personally, I never want to see it again."

Alice was deep in thought. "Tom came good in the end," she said sadly. "Don't you all see? If the painting destroyed in the fire was a forgery and the original is hidden behind the Hockney, everything is going to be alright." She clapped her hands excitedly.

"I have to go and tell Molly immediately." She rapidly floated down through the floor and was gone.

Wilf took off his deerstalker and stuffed it along with the cape back into the wardrobe. "Well, that just about wraps it all up. We can tell Molly about the treasure another day. That piece of good news will keep. Don't want all your Christmas presents in one go, do you? But it will certainly be a welcome boost for Jules."

"I could do with a rest," George said, slumping into the deep cushions of the sofa. "There's been too much excitement around here lately. I don't know about the rest of you but let's get back to some simple haunting and the odd round of golf," he said closing his eyes.

"Bless you," said Bishop.

Epilogue
Three Years Later

Kensington.

Molly brushed her hair, checked her make up in the mirror and headed to the kitchen. Mavis was busy placing the finger food on plates ready for the party. Neatly cut sandwiches (no crusts), quiches, pizza slices and crisps placed in bowls. A silver tray held champagne flutes, all standing to attention in regimented rows waiting to receive the sparkling wine currently chilling in the fridge. On the worktop, cocktail sausages and vol-au-vents sat neatly on baking trays ready to go in the oven. In the centre of the table sat a 'hedgehog' made from half a melon with cheese and pineapple on sticks forming the spines. It looked vacantly through its black, pitted olive eyes at Molly as she entered the room. She checked the time on the wall clock.

"This looks lovely, we've got fifteen minutes 'till they arrive, do you need me to do anything."

"No Ma'am, it's all in hand, go through and rest before they arrive, you've had a busy day," Mavis turned to Molly who was wearing a red velvet cocktail dress and high heels. It was a complete transformation from an hour before, when she'd rushed in from the studio wearing trainers, jeans and a sweatshirt. "You look lovely, I thought this was just a casual evening."

"They've never been here before, so I felt I needed to make an effort. A friend told me, if you dress for the occasion, it gives you confidence. They were right, but I must admit I'm still very nervous."

"There's no need, you've been working towards this for months, it's so exciting."

"I know but tonight it all becomes…well public I suppose." Molly looked at the clock again, "Where's Jules? he should be here by now."

"He won't be far away, he called to say he was leaving two hours ago. I expect he's held up in traffic. Now go and relax."

Molly walked through into the drawing room. The sofas and chairs were arranged in a circle facing the extra-large television brought in especially for this evening. The grandfather clock in the hall chimed a quarter to seven. Her thoughts went to her mum and dad gathered with friends at her childhood home having their own party in anticipation of the show.

In the long gallery at Woodford Abbey the party had already started, the staff were tucking into the buffet generously supplied by the production company. As the wine and beer flowed, the volume rose with chatter and laughter, it was a rare occasion for all the different departments to be together. At the end of the gallery, nearest to the hall entrance, a television had been mounted on a high stand. It was turned on but with the sound turned down. The door from the hall opened and James entered, followed by the Duke. Someone tapped a glass with a spoon for silence and the gathering turned and looked to the end of the room. On seeing the Duke, they all burst into spontaneous applause. The Duke looked embarrassed at the welcome. Since returning from Her Majesty's pleasure, he had kept a low profile, residing in the dower house on the perimeter of the estate and seldom venturing into the park, too ashamed to show his face.

James stood proudly by his side, "You see, I told you sir, everyone wants you back where you belong."

The Duke looked down the length of the room and felt a weight lift from his shoulders. He had been dreading returning to the estate after his behaviour. James raised a hand for silence. It didn't come. Instead, there was a spontaneous chant of "Speech…Speech…Speech," from the assembled staff. The Duke was overcome with emotion, his eyes glazed and lips trembled as silence fell.

"Friends, I thank you for your warm welcome." He paused briefly.

"Your reception overwhelms me, for I did you all a great wrong and brought the house into disgrace, casting a shadow over you and all your wonderful work. I've learnt a valuable lesson in who to trust in the world, I was led astray by greed. The easy buck, which I mistakenly thought would help us all without hurting anyone. I was wrong… it hurt you all and all I can do is apologise from the bottom of my heart." The room burst into applause again.

"I think you're forgiven, sir," James whispered, smiling.

The Duke nodded penitently. "You're all too kind, I know I have a long way to go to regain your trust but tonight is a starting point. As you know, Colin has moved from security to become events manager. He has proved a great asset to Jules and is working tirelessly to build on recent successes. Sadly, Colin can't be with us tonight as he is on another of those confounded management training courses, but their worth is now being felt by us all. Molly's writing success has led to new opportunities which we will witness very soon. Sadly, she can't be with us tonight either as she's in London working with the production team finishing the recording of the television series. Jules has driven over to be with her and in their absence please raise your glasses to them both."

Glasses were duly raised, and a cry of "Jules and Molly" reverberated around the room.

Molly relaxed in the chair, reflecting on the events of the past two years. Her life had changed so rapidly and unexpectedly, writing the 'History of Woodford Abbey' and its subsequent success had opened new doors, her marriage to Jules was a joy and now…

The doorbell rang. She jumped up.

Mavis hurried to open the front door. In the drawing room, Molly could hear the muffled voices of her guests, she opened the door into the hall.

"Welcome, come on in, this is so exciting," she said warmly. Mavis took their coats and hung them in the cloakroom.

They embraced Molly, kissing her on both cheeks as they entered the lounge, all looking admiringly at the beautiful room.

"Sorry we're late," Justine said, handing her a bottle of champagne. "The underground was so busy, but here we are." She was joined by her husband Peter and Alex Tulloch from 'Song Thrush Productions'. "The others are on their way," Justine confirmed.

"Please make yourself comfortable, would you like a drink?" On cue, Mavis entered with a silver tray containing a choice of red and white wine. "We'll save the champagne for later," and she handed the bottle to Mavis to put in the fridge. "Jules is on his way from the Abbey, but he must be held up in traffic."

"I'm not surprised," Peter said, "There's something on at Wembley tonight, the streets are heaving."

They heard the front door open, and Jules entered the room, quickly discarding his coat on the back of a sofa. Mavis pursed her lips, picked it up, shook it, folded it over her arm and took it away. Jules gave a wry smile.

"Sorry I'm late, the roads are so busy." He held Molly by both hands and kissed her warmly. "I hope I haven't missed anything," he added, looking to see if the television was on.

"No, you're fine, our guests have only just started to arrive." He greeted them individually as Mavis brought in plates of food and placed them on the sideboard.

Jules addressed the gathering. "Is everyone ready? I left all the staff so excited as they started to assemble in the long gallery to watch it. It's turning into a bit of a party there, James is going to make sure father's there as well, he's reluctant to show his face but fingers crossed, he'll be persuaded." He looked directly at Molly, "And how are you, I hope you're not overdoing it."

"Stop fussing, I'm fine… a bit nervous, but I've kept busy."

"She's been in the studio all day recording the 'voice-overs' for the final episode. I told her to come back early, but you know what she's like," Justine said, looking affectionately at her prodigy and friend.

"You must take it easy, darling, you'll wear yourself out."

"I will, we've nearly finished the last programme."

The doorbell rang again. Mavis answered it and escorted the remainder of the production crew, Chloe Nolin, Dylan Lee and Stephen Henderson into the drawing room.

"Wow, what a place you have here," Chloe said, trying to take in the sumptuous surroundings. She then saw Jules, "Oh, sorry your grace, I didn't see you there."

Jules laughed, "Please call me Jules. Its lovely that you've all been able to join us tonight, please help yourselves to a drink and some nibbles."

Just before eight o'clock, Jules turned on the TV and they all sat down to watch.

"And now on ITV, we join Justine Song for the first of a new series and there's not a ghost in sight," the announcer said, jokingly referring to 'Haunted House.' The theme tune started to play. The programme opened with sweeping views of Woodford Abbey's parkland as the camera flew from the safari park over the house. This was followed with a montage of other properties to be featured later in the series. Then the house came back into view. The title then appeared across the screen. 'Ancient and Modern' with Justine Song and Dr Melinda Goodall.

Molly went bright red. She'd seen it all before in the production suite, but this felt different. She could imagine the pride of her mum and dad sat at home surrounded by friends and wondered what the estate staff would make of it.

The camera then swooped low, past the house, over the lake, on towards the Mississippi steamboat, where Justine and Molly sat on the top deck. Then, seamlessly, the camera appeared to leave the helicopter and land in front of them, with the house in the background.

"How on earth did you do that?" Jules exclaimed.

"Shush, Jules," Molly said, tapping him on the arm for silence, "we're beginning our opening banter."

"Good evening viewers," Justine announced, "welcome to the first in a new series exploring the stories behind some of Britain's greatest houses. Please welcome Dr Melinda Goodall, who will join me on these adventures, bringing to life the people and historic events of the places we will visit in this series.

"Thank you, Justine, good evening. I'm excited to be with you for these adventures and it's a pleasure to begin the series at Woodford Abbey. This is rather self-indulgent of me, as it is not only a wonderfully historic house, it also happens to be my home."

The camera then cut away to a recorded section with Molly on the island standing adjacent to the mausoleum. "The story for us begins here, by the only building remaining from the original abbey complex…"

In the Long Gallery, Wilf and George were jumping up and down with excitement, "This is it, watch closely, we're going to come out through the wall behind Molly," Wilf said excitedly. They all watched intently.

"No, nothing," Alice said. "Serves you both right! I told you not to interfere, the cameras can't pick you up, you twits!"

Wilf looked dejected, "I suppose you're right. We just wanted to be TV stars."

"Never mind that, doesn't Molly look great, she's so professional. Our performance training has paid dividends," Alice said proudly.

The Duke, along with the staff watched in admiration as Molly took the viewers on a journey through the story of the house showing off its extraordinary history.

Molly was able to promote the new exhibition of artefacts discovered in the buried cloister, much to the pleasure of Brother Leopold who had assisted her with the curation of the now nationally acclaimed collection. Her presentation was humorous whilst being factual and entertaining.

Aimed at a family audience, both of them wore historic costumes representing characters from the past and acted out scenes which guided viewers through the stories of the people who had once lived there. Their enthusiasm radiated off the screen.

The show concluded back on board the steamboat. Justine did the final address to the camera. "Thank you all for watching, we hope you enjoyed our first trip through the ancient and modern history of Woodford Abbey. Next week, we will be in South London visiting Eltham Palace. I do hope you will join us."

"See you next week," Molly said with a big grin, as they both waved. The camera swooped away from them looking back at the lake and house then off across the fields. The credits rolled.

'Ancient and Modern'

Written and presented by Dr Melinda Goodall

(Viscountess of Exford)

Additional material by Justine Song.

Produced by Peter Fellows.

A Song Thrush Production.

The book accompanying the series is available now.

The cheers from the gallery could be heard all over the estate. The house looked amazing, as did Molly singing its virtues. The Duke had the biggest grin, he hadn't felt this happy for years. He rose and quietly exited through a side door leaving the staff to party on through the evening.

In Kensington, Jules popped open the champagne to a big cheer. "Well, that went well. Your filming was cinematic Dylan, how on earth did you get those sweeping views?" Jules asked.

"You'd better ask Molly, she arranged that with a little help from some friends."

Jules looked intently at her, "You didn't use Wilf, did you?" he whispered knowingly.

"Well, he did offer, it was rude not to!"

"You're incorrigible," and they both grinned.

"I know." Molly sat back in the chair looking proudly around the room at her friends and colleagues, resting her hands on the bump which was now beginning to show under her dress.

They heard a strange burble coming from behind the sofa. Justine rushed to her bag and retrieved a large Nokia mobile phone.

"Excuse me," she said, and with some urgency pressed a button on the illuminated keyboard and held the phone to her ear. "Hello, Justine speaking, Is that you, Maurice?" They could hear a man's voice on the other end but couldn't make out what he was saying. Justine was wide eyed with excitement, "Seriously? They liked it... thank you, we've all been watching it together, I'll talk to them now and get back to you tomorrow to arrange a meeting... Thanks again...speak soon, bye."

The group all looked on, captivated by the mobile phone and intrigued by the conversation.

"Sorry, new toy," Justine awkwardly waved the handset in the air, "I hope they'll be able to make them smaller one day. It fills my bag up and it weighs a ton."

"Never mind that now," Peter said impatiently, "what did he say?"

"Sorry everyone, that was the head of light entertainment," she said, prudently placing the phone back in her handbag, she'd been expecting a call from the studio following the broadcast. "They had an audience panel reviewing the show last week and with the feedback tonight from the programme controller they want to commission another series... what do you think?"

"I think that's marvellous, but I'm going to be a bit preoccupied for a few months," Molly said.

"No problem, we can build that into the negotiations. It'll take a couple of years for us to research, write the scripts and supporting book, if we can agree terms."

"What do you think, Jules?" Molly said, holding his hand.

"Sounds like a good plan," he said, looking distracted. "Now, can I see that phone please? We've got to get one of those!" Jules said, searching for it behind the sofa.

"Now, who's being incorrigible?" Molly asked, laughing.

In the gallery, the ghosts stood at the end of the room watching the revelries. The sound on the TV was turned down as it broadcast the 'News at Ten.' No one was taking any notice of it anyway.

To their surprise, Eric entered the room through the outside wall carrying his backpack.

"We weren't expecting you, how lovely," Alice said, looking inquisitively at the bag.

"Has it started yet?" Eric asked eagerly.

"Too late sunshine, it's just finished," Wilf stated bluntly, pointing at the telly.

"Damn it. It's no fun being an Angel of Death, I'm always late for everything. I brought this to celebrate your friend's new show." He reached into the bag and pulled out a glowing bottle of distilled ambrosia, a drink of the Gods. Brother Leopold looked in awe at the cloudy amber liquid swirling in the bottle.

George reached into the bag and pulled out five glasses, "Shame to waste it," he said, placing the glasses in a row on the sideboard. The bottle duly opened itself and filled the glasses one by one. "Cheers everyone, here's to our future."

They each raised a glass and swallowed, glowing softly as the satisfying liquid slid down. They all felt warm and content, excited about what new adventures awaited them.

Acting on Impulse

Written, produced and directed by.... Andrew Trim

Editor / additional material............. Shareen Trim

Artistic Director........................... Sam Zambelli (That's Rich Artwork)

Book design and typesetting............ Chella Adgopul (Honeybee Books)

Also in the series:

Acting Strangely

Teacher Carolyn Jenner develops a gift for fortune telling but wants to know the extent of her skills.

Actors Wilf, George and Alice haunt the remains of a burnt out theatre now built over by a Price Low supermarket.

The owner however has plans for expansion, which could mean the destruction of their home.

With the assistance of schoolgirl Molly Goodall, they set off a chain of events that will impact the town and its residents.

Can the past return to save the future?

ISBN code 978-1-913675-08-0

Praise for '*Acting Strangely*'

"*Very funny, some hidden and not so hidden 1970's / Dorchester references...Loved it...excellent character work.*"
Ian Barnett

"*I really enjoyed it... I was unable to put it down...
can't wait for the next instalment.*"
Kevin Singleton

"*An amazing story with humour, ghosts, Dorset history & references, a love side-story, a fortune teller and a happy ending.
I've read it three times now.*"
Sam Zambelli

"Fantastic read… I totally adored it. Finished it in four days, I couldn't put it down."
Sarah Williams

"Wonderfully entertaining"
Barry Archerson

"Absolutely brilliant. Very imaginative. Once I started reading I couldn't put it down and at the end wanted more. Really enjoyed it and can't wait for another. Brilliant read for all ages."
Jackie Williams

For enquiries contact Andrew Trim:

actingstrangely@gmail.com

BV - #0052 - 131123 - C0 - 228/152/18 - PB - 9781913675387 - Gloss Lamination